St. Martin's Paperbacks Titles By

LORIE O'CLARE

Tall, Dark and Deadly

Long, Lean and Lethal

Strong, Sleek and Sinful

Play Dirty

Get Lucky

Stay Hungry

Anthologies

The Bodyguard

Men of Danger

Stay Hungry

Lorie O'Clare

St. Martin's Paperbacks

This is a work of fiction. All of the characters, organizations, and events portrayed in this novel are either products of the author's imagination or are used fictitiously.

STAY HUNGRY

Copyright © 2011 by Lorie O'Clare.
Excerpt from *Go Wild* copyright © 2011 by Lorie O'Clare.

For information address St. Martin's Press, 175 Fifth Avenue, New York, NY 10010.

ISBN: 978-0-312-37218-7

Printed in the United States of America

St. Martin's Paperbacks edition / October 2011

St. Martin's Paperbacks are published by St. Martin's Press, 175 Fifth Avenue, New York, NY 10010.

10 9 8 7 6 5 4 3 2 1

Stay Hungry

Prologue

Marianna Torres swore every vein in her body was on fire. The burning sensation would have been enough to make her scream if it weren't for how messed up her head was.

She'd tried drugs before—the light stuff. During high school she'd smoked pot a few times and she had drunk alcohol sometimes at parties. Marianna had never had much of an interest in the harder drugs. The thought of something else controlling her thoughts and actions didn't appeal to her at all. She couldn't imagine anyone voluntarily giving up control of their own actions.

Which was why she was now slowly going insane.

Marianna had been excited to come to the states, yet the moment she'd set foot on U.S. soil she'd been abducted. It had shocked the hell out of her when a strange man had slipped his arm around her neck, pulled her back against him, and hugged her tight enough so that anyone around them would believe they were just two people excited to see each other.

As she'd been escorted out of the airport, panic had grown, fermented, and spread like a debilitating fever.

There had been a sharp pinprick, she thought. But by the time they were outside the airport, it became frighteningly clear that she had no control over her own actions. The man had released her almost immediately, then told her to walk alongside him, so she had. He had told her to watch her step at escalators, so she'd looked down. He mentioned amiably that she watch her head when climbing in the backseat of his car, and she'd done just that.

He had drugged her. Marianna hadn't realized at first how incredibly terrible the drug was she'd been given. She was taken to a hotel, had slept on the floor and eaten when food was given to her. The strange man had told her his name was Mario. He had continued drugging her, injecting something into her vein while she watched, holding her arm out obediently and not moving as a drug flowed into her bloodstream through a tiny needle. Her will was no longer her own. No matter how many times Marianna told herself to fight him, to run the moment Mario's back was turned, she never did. The drug made her mind her worst enemy.

"We're going to have some fun tonight, my sweet pets." Mario smiled as he held the car door for her. "This is the perfect town to test your skills. Don't you agree?" Mario's laughter was demonic. "Of course you agree," he said, still chuckling.

Mario's mean laughter chilled Marianna to the bone. That was a good sign, right? Maybe once he parked she could escape. If he would just go long enough without telling her what to do. All he needed to do was walk away and forget to tell her to stay. He'd done that once already and Marianna had walked across the hotel room suite of her own accord. Mario's phone had rung and he'd come out of the bathroom, distracted, and hadn't noticed she'd moved.

She'd sat motionless, not moving as Mario often instructed when he was busy doing whatever it was he did. Marianna hadn't figured that out. But during those motionless times she'd analyzed the effects of the drug. While under the influence, which was always, her body did whatever she was instructed to do. Her brain was helpless in preventing her from complying.

"All you do is agree with me. Tonight will finish your training. Except for you, my adorable *puttana*." He glanced over his shoulder, flashing white teeth as he grinned at her.

Marianna stared at him, grateful at least for her thoughts. She was far from a slut, but Mario owned her body. She was terrified what he might do with it.

"You've got a lot of training ahead of you. And I do believe you'll absolutely love it. You were a *puttana* before the slave juice, though, weren't you?"

How many days ago was that? Her mother, and probably her sister by now, would believe Marianna simply had vanished off the face of the earth. There were times when she was pretty sure she had.

Fortunately, Mario didn't expect her to answer. Which was a good thing, since it was getting harder for her to differentiate her past from the present. Whatever this drug called slave juice was that he kept injecting in her, she prayed it didn't have residual effects. Sooner or later this insane captivity had to end. God, it really needed to be sooner.

Marianna wanted to walk away, refuse to acknowledge his commands, let alone carry them out. She hadn't decided yet if it would have been better if the drug stole her memory, instead of allowing her to retain every vivid detail of the many atrocities she'd endured in the hotel room. She'd been forced to watch other women under the influence of the drug being sexually abused. How many men had fucked them while she and Mario sat and watched? Each time Marianna was scared to death she would be next. She wasn't a virgin, but her sexual experiences had been few and limited to college boys as inexperienced as she was. These men knew positions Marianna had never dreamed of. She remembered every degrading sexual act inflicted on the women. The women would probably never forget the atrocities; Marianna knew she wouldn't.

One thing she'd begun to accept: the only way this would end was if she put an end to it. No one would rescue her if they didn't know she needed to be rescued. Mario had kept the TV news on. Marianna had never heard mention of any woman disappearing at the airport. In fact, there weren't any mentions of missing persons at all. And she wasn't the only abducted person. There were the two men with her, and at least two other women.

If she was going to end this nightmare, she needed to keep her brain alive and active. Somehow she needed to overpower the slave juice, which was trying to turn her into a zombie. So far all she'd managed was making herself move her head or lift her hand and place it on her lap. It was a start but a far cry from ordering herself to open the car door and jump out and run. As simple as the instructions seemed to be, making her body pull off all those actions seemed a bit too overwhelming.

"Everyone out." Mario turned off the motor after parking and opened his car door.

Marianna unbuckled her seat belt and opened her passenger door, seeing the simple command through without giving it a thought. She stood in the perfect night air, breathing in the sweetness of some flower growing nearby.

She was a slave inside her own body. Marianna hadn't figured out how to do it yet, but somehow she had to get her body back under her own control.

"Walk alongside me, say nothing, and don't run into anyone," Mario instructed the two men, who got out on the other side of the SUV.

Marianna didn't know their names. Mario used derogatory adjectives to address all of them. That didn't matter as much as not knowing what town they were in. When they'd left the hotel parking garage, Mario had instructed all of them to relax their heads in their hands and stare at the floor of the SUV. She wasn't able to look out the window. Although, not knowing a thing about America, Marianna doubted she'd have recognized the city by any of its landmarks. She'd seen the Statue of Liberty on TV, knew there was an arch in St. Louis, and possibly could identify the Golden Gate Bridge if she saw it. Otherwise, she'd never given much thought to learning about America.

Mario came up alongside her, resting his hand at the small of her back. Marianna looked into his cold, sinister eyes. Her expression wouldn't give away her thoughts. After all, he hadn't told her to smile, frown, or scowl. She simply stared at him.

"Let's go have some fun, shall we, slut?" He frowned. "Look at me and smile," he instructed, whispering.

Marianna stared into his black eyes, her mouth moving and forming a smile. She didn't want to smile at him. She wanted to kick him in the balls. Maybe if she got angry, seriously pissed and filled with rage, she'd conquer the drug searing her veins with continual heat one day after the next.

Or was it weeks?

"Now look ahead of you, hold your head high, and let everyone see what a gorgeous slut I have on my arm," he said, no longer looking at her but glancing around them as he started across the parking lot.

At least staring straight ahead, Marianna focused on everyone who passed by. She told herself to shift her attention to the buildings across the street. There were people everywhere, most of them laughing and hurrying, some running and some walking fast, all anxious to get where they were going. They were all dressed as if they were out for the night: bright colors, short skirts, flashy ties.

They were in L.A., which was nowhere near Chicago, where her half sister, Angela Huxtable, lived. Marianna prayed her half sister would find her. They hadn't seen each other in years, but Angela was a detective. She found people all the time. Marianna's mother, Mona Torres, also Angela's mother, bragged about Angela all the time.

Although Marianna had been eleven when her older half sister had left their home and gone to live with her father in America, Marianna remembered Angela and her mother fighting more times than not but didn't remind her mother of that part of their lives. If Marianna's mother wanted to remember only the good times with her older daughter, Marianna wouldn't deprive Mona of being proud of Angela.

Marianna knew her mom was proud of her, too. She had finished her first year of college and instead of summer school had decided to come to the states to spend time with Angela. Marianna and Angela had exchanged e-mails, chatted on Facebook, and both agreed getting to know each other again would be better in person than through the Internet. It had sounded like the perfect escape from books and exams for a couple months. The last thing Marianna had thought would ever happen was something like this.

Marianna was ashamed of being dressed the way she was. It wasn't hard for everyone to notice the slut on Mario's arm. Marianna wore a dress that might as well be a few straps of material wrapped around her body. It wasn't cold out, actually far from it, but nonetheless she was aware of her nipples hardening against the thin silky fabric barely covering her breasts. Not wearing underwear in public was the ultimate humiliation, especially when her dress barely covered her ass.

Mario's hand slid lower until he cupped her ass, moving the material out of his way and exposing her rear end to whoever might be behind her.

"We want everyone to know you're a good *puttana*, right?" Mario lowered his head, nipping at her neck.

Marianna continued focusing on each person who passed them, making eye contact with some, while others moved by too quickly or with their heads down and prevented her from seeing their faces. She didn't pay attention to Mario, what he said, or how he groped her. Instead she stared hard at each person they passed, who watched with either disgust or lustful curiosity.

They were out in public. People were everywhere. All she had to do was start screaming and police would probably show up. Mario would be arrested. Her nightmare would end.

She needed to give herself an order. She'd ordered herself to turn her head, and it had worked. Maybe if she started simple.

She instructed herself to open her mouth. When her lips parted, the two men passing by, who each gave her a hungry look, both settled their attention on her mouth. The fire in her veins intensified, the drugs' way of keeping her in line.

"I think we're just about where we need to be." Mario slapped her ass, slowing his pace and taking her wrist in his sweaty palm. "This is going to be so much fun," he mumbled under his breath.

She focused in on a couple nearing her. Open her mouth. Speak. Say the word "help." That was all she had to do. The couple neared. Marianna parted her lips. Her brain instructed her to follow the second half of the command and speak.

"Help," she grunted, the one word completely inaudible, even to Mario, whose shoulder brushed against hers.

Either way, the couple looked at her. They didn't say anything. Their expressions didn't change and they kept walking. But they focused on her, albeit just for a moment. She hoped eventually her disappearance would hit the news. If a picture of her was posted, possibly someone would come forward and announce they had seen her in Los Angeles.

"This is a good spot." Mario slowed after they turned a corner, then stopped and instructed the men on the other side of him to stop as well. His hand dug into the side of her waist, pressing her against him, and turned them both to face the dark side of a building.

There weren't as many people walking along this sidewalk, although loud, thumping disco music reverberated off the sides of the buildings on either side of the street. It came from a nightclub at the end of the street. Different-colored lights flashed off the building, creating somewhat of a surreal atmosphere, even this far down the street. She quit trying to give herself orders and instead fought to keep her equilibrium. All those bright lights were making her dizzy.

"Okay, you two thugs, let's see." Mario tapped his finger against his lips and glanced around him. He let go of Marianna and turned his back on her, giving both men his complete attention. "You," he instructed, slapping the back of his hand against the arm of the guy closer to him. "Go start that blue car parked on the street. You're going to hot-wire it. Do you know how to hot-wire a car?"

"Yes."

"What did I just tell you to do?"

"Hot-wire the blue car parked on the street." The man's accent might be American, but if it was, he spoke a dialect Marianna wasn't familiar with. He never looked at her but

stared at Mario, his expression so blank he might as well
have been asleep.

Mario grunted, taking a step backward. "Amazing you
remember that much. I need to make a note you can't control
a brain that isn't there. Avoid the dumb fucks."

The man left them, oblivious to the insult, and sauntered
over to the car, then opened the driver's side door. It wasn't
locked. No one said anything as the guy knelt outside the car
and messed with something until the engine roared to life.

Marianna had never stolen a thing in her life. She waited
for panic to kick in. She was watching a man steal a car.

Although, wait; if they were caught, the police would take
her. Eventually the poison burning her veins would wear off.
She'd finally be free. Instead of panic, a wave of excitement
washed over her. It was strong enough to distract her from
the burning sensation inside her, at least for a few moments.

"Very good," Mario purred under his breath. He slapped
the guy next to him on his arm, then pointed to the car. "Go
get in the car with dumb fuck. You're going to drive," he
said, deciding at the last minute.

Marianna's gut tightened. She waited for someone to say
something. A car was being stolen, a crime committed. People hurried past them. No one stopped. No one said a thing.
What kind of country was this?

"Come on, my sweet *puttana*," Mario purred, insulting her
with his vulgar Italian. "It's time to put you to use, although
trust me, I already know how to best use you." He slapped
her ass and laughed under his breath. Then reaching up, he
tweaked her nipple through her dress, squeezing it hard
enough for her to register the pain.

She should react, slap him, tell him to stop. Marianna
forced her mind to work: *He just insulted and degraded you.
You are not a slut or a whore. You should tell him as much.*
By the time she formed the thought, Mario had already
walked her toward the car where the two men sat inside, the
car idling, neither of them moving until they were instructed
where to go. Are they fighting to tell him to go to hell, too?
If they were, it sure wasn't obvious by their expressions.

"Bend over and lean against the window," Mario said, whispering into her hair. His breath smelled of alcohol and his nauseating cigars.

If she remembered anything from this horrendous experience, Marianna was sure it would be the stench from those grotesque cigars Mario was so damned proud of. No decent Spaniard would strut around with such a thing in his mouth. At least not the Spanish men she'd grown up around. The Torres family didn't associate with *ladrones*.

"Keep your legs straight. I want a really good ass shot," he grumbled, rubbing her ass, which still stung from being slapped.

Look at him. She managed her simple command, turned her head, and stared into his black eyes. Mario would have been an incredibly good-looking man if he weren't so evil. It consumed him, stealing any glow from his eyes and leaving them flat, opaque, with hard lines on either side of his mouth, probably from scowling so much.

Mario wasn't fazed by her turning and staring at him without him instructing her to do so. More than likely he didn't think anything of the act, other than that she was paying attention. It was such a major accomplishment for her, yet the asshole couldn't care less about her movements. He was wound so tight, almost ready to spring with anticipation over putting whatever insane plan he'd conjured into effect, he merely glanced at her before returning his attention to the car.

"You're going to give the men an order, *puttana*," he instructed. "Tell them to drive the car down the road and into the side of the building at the end of the street."

Mario pointed with his hand and Marianna shifted her attention, focusing on the large brick building, lit up with its flashing lights, and the continual thumping of disco music. There were people in the parking lot. Others were entering and leaving the place. It was a very busy nightclub.

"Do you understand, slut?" he demanded, tightening his grip on her arm.

"Yes."

"Are you my good little slut?"

"Yes." The answers slipped out of her mouth without giving them any thought. She continued staring at the building.

"Do it." He again slapped her ass, then backed up until he stood behind her.

Marianna placed her hand on the hood of the car, then bent over, keeping her legs straight, and rested her arm on the open window.

This is wrong, Marianna thought. Her mind rejected her instructions to keep her mouth shut, to not say anything.

"Drive down the street," she said, staring at the side of the man's head.

"Okay," he said, reaching for the gearshift.

"Drive into the building at the end of the street."

"Okay."

Marianna took a step back, straightening when the car pulled away from the curb. She couldn't take her words back. She couldn't make herself yell at them, order them to stop, do anything to prevent the inevitable. The tightening in her gut increased, growing worse, until she had an overwhelming urge to put her hand over her tummy, bend over, and puke. Maybe if she vomited long enough it would cleanse her body of the poison controlling her. Not only could she not successfully put her hand on her tummy and bend over at the same time, but her gaze was stuck on the annoying nightclub and its blaring lights also.

I'm a goddamned zombie! She hated herself, hated this drug, hated Mario with every thread of her existence.

"You're such an incredibly good *puttana*." Mario draped his arm lazily over her shoulder. "Shall we? You deserve to see the fruits of your labor."

He began strolling down the sidewalk. She moved alongside him, once again zoning out on the building ahead of them as her mind contentedly went blank.

"Watch the car," Mario instructed.

They're going to get hurt, Marianna thought. She couldn't take her eyes off the rear end of the car. It ran the stop sign. Two cars coming from either side screeched to a stop, causing pedestrians to jump out of the way and start yelling.

She and Mario were almost to the end of the block. The car continued driving straight into the parking lot, not once swerving or slowing for any other vehicle. The driver of a fancy sports car slammed on its brakes to avoid a collision and another car rear-ended it. People were suddenly hurrying to the parking lot as more cars slowed, cut each other off, did whatever they could to keep from being hit by the runaway car.

Marianna couldn't even manage tears. The car crashed head-on into the side of the building, creating a horrific sound that reverberated off buildings surrounding it and temporarily blocked out the repetitious thumping disco music. People were yelling, screaming, but Marianna just stood there. She didn't jump. She wasn't startled. She knew it would happen because she'd instructed him to do it.

"You're such a *buena chica!*" Mario pulled her into his arms. "Did you see that? You've just committed murder. And look at you, all composed and relaxed, not a care in the world. You truly are perfect," he purred, hugging her as he whispered over her head.

Chapter One

Jake King held his clipboard under his arm and pushed the door open with his shoulder. The blast of air conditioning hitting his body probably felt better than a much-needed fix would to a junkie. Jake almost sagged from the cool air as he traipsed into the office and kicked the door closed with his foot.

"I'm grabbing a beer." He dropped his clipboard on one of two couches in the office and slipped out, heading into the living room before Natasha could respond. More than likely she gave him a scathing look, but he didn't check. He wasn't in the mood to hear how bad her day was. They were all overworked right now. At least she was overworked in air conditioning.

Six years ago his father, Greg King, had retired from the LAPD and opened KFA, King Fugitive Apprehension. Greg's enthusiasm toward his new line of work was contagious and Jake, along with his older brother, Marc, signed on to the business almost immediately. There were no regrets, even on a day as hot as today and with the lowlifes of L.A. seeming to be crawling around worse than cockroaches.

Jake headed to the refrigerator, glancing at the stack of mail on the kitchen table, and pulled out a longneck Budweiser. After popping the cap, he leaned against the counter and let the cold brew slide down his throat. God, it tasted good. He should sort through the mail. His parents were running as hard as he was and no one had time to keep up around the house.

"Nothing better than a cold beer on a hot day," he announced, toasting Natasha when she appeared in the doorway.

"You're not drinking and working and you aren't off the clock." She slipped around him, grabbed a water from the refrigerator, unscrewed the cap, and drank. She slipped her perfectly straight, silky black hair over her shoulder, leaned her head back, and downed a good half of the bottle. "Rita Fulsom is faxing over the details on two females," she said with her head still leaned back and her eyes closed.

Natasha was one hell of a looker, and if she hadn't been raised more as his sister instead of his cousin he saw only once or twice a year he might be able to look at her for the incredibly seductive creature she was. Instead, acknowledging her good looks was about as far as it would ever go. He also saw her as intelligent, sometimes humorous, and lately a pain in his butt. "If I'm going to die in that heat out there at least let me chase some ladies."

"You're such a slut," she muttered, turning her back to him and staring at the 13-inch set Haley King, Jake's mom, kept on the counter so she could watch TV while cooking. "Both women are in their fifties and jumped bail yesterday."

"What are they wanted for?" He didn't really care. Anymore it seemed all the Kings' cases were the same. Idiots skipped out on court dates. Bondsmen called to have them chase down the idiots. Jake or his dad caught them. End of story. Ever since Jake's older brother had left the business to play house with his new girlfriend out in Colorado, Jake had felt the weight of the workload increase. Not that he would ever admit missing his brother. Marc was happy and that mattered, most of the time.

"Shoplifting," Natasha told him, and tapped the Bluetooth in her ear. "KFA," she announced, once again using her cheerful tone that apparently Jake didn't rate receiving.

He slumped into a chair at the table, stared at the newscast on TV, and placed his beer on the table. He was tempted to down it quickly. Natasha was right, though. If he had to go back out today, drinking a beer wasn't a good idea. The damn thing looked really good, though.

He pulled out his cell and glanced at the text messages he hadn't had a chance to respond to and blocked out Natasha as she slid into the chair alongside him and explained to a caller the policy of KFA. They were bounty hunters, not private investigators, although Jake and both his parents had their PI licenses for the state of California. It wasn't the first time Jake had heard Natasha explain to someone that KFA didn't track down cheating spouses. He could easily recite what she would say to the person on the phone but instead began reading the texts he had yet to answer.

His love life was suffering. Jake started answering one text but paused. What was the point? He could use a booty call right now more than anything, and that was exactly what was being offered. God, when was the last time he'd gotten laid?

Jake growled, tossing his phone next to his beer, then stood and stretched. Heading out for a night on the town and a good piece of ass would do him a hell of a lot of good but not when his father and mother were left holding down the fort. They would have his head if he went MIA just to get his dick wet. It was tempting to endure their wrath, though. He glanced back at his phone as Natasha ended the call.

"Hey, what's that about?" She didn't comment on the call but instead pointed at the TV.

"What?"

Natasha grabbed the remote and turned up the volume as a hot news reporter in a snug sleeveless blouse and mini-skirt spoke seriously to the camera. Her light brown hair was cropped short around her cute, innocent-looking face. Jake preferred longer hair on his women, at least enough hair for him to grab and pull to encourage them to arch their back when he slid deep inside them. He quit dwelling on how the reporter looked and started listening to what she was saying when the words "Slave Juice" appeared across the screen.

"According to bar owners Margaret and Steve Young,

who own and manage the popular club Aristotle's, slave juice is quickly becoming the drug of choice amid the night-life of L.A."

Natasha waved her finger at the screen. "Isn't Aristotle's where you hang out?"

He used to hang out there, when he had a life. "It's one of the clubs," he muttered, listening to the reporter.

"Slave juice is proving to be one of the more dangerous drugs to hit the streets. The LAPD states that it isn't obvious when a person is high on this drug since it has no apparent visible side effects," the reporter continued, shifting to look at the club behind her as the camera scanned the scene. The reporter stood just beyond the yellow tape of a crime scene. "But we're seeing now how lethal this supposedly recreational drug can be. Two young men, who allegedly were high on slave juice, drove a stolen car into the side of the popular nightclub less than an hour ago. From what we know at this point, other than the toxic levels of the drug in their system, there is no known reason why the men gave up their lives when they drove into this brick wall."

The reporter at the station broke in and the camera switched to show one of the main newscasters of that channel. Jake would have rather continued staring at the hot young thing in the miniskirt.

"Jane, isn't it true whoever takes this drug will do whatever anyone tells them to do?" the reporter with his way-too-deep voice boomed in a somber tone.

"That's why they call it slave juice, John." The cute young thing appeared again on camera, this time offering a small smile that made her appear even more innocent. It was an odd mix, considering the seriousness of what she talked about. Jane now stood next to two other young women, both shifting nervously as they shot furtive glances at the camera, then the microphone Jane stuck in their faces. "Joan Cash and Linda Sparroway both witnessed the accident." Jane shifted her weight, facing the two women but still able to shoot side-glances at the camera. "Tell us what you saw," she suggested, sticking her microphone in front of the woman closer to her.

"At first I thought the driver couldn't turn his steering wheel," the woman said, chewing her lower lip and focusing on the reporter. She lowered her mouth closer to the microphone as she continued. "I saw him run the stop sign," she said, pointing toward the camera.

The screen shot changed and suddenly Jake was looking at the familiar T intersection next to Aristotle's.

"Cars smashed into each other trying to avoid him. That's when I figured he must be drunk. But he just kept going. He didn't even brake when he hit the wall."

"Yeah, we noticed that right away," the second lady cut in, stepping around her friend to get closer to the microphone. "His brake lights never came on. We told the police that."

"Why would someone choose to do slave juice if it could end their evening, and life, like this?" Jane, the reporter, asked, waving her hand at the building. The camera scanned behind them, showing the smashed car surrounded by emergency vehicles.

"They didn't choose to do anything," the woman next to Jane said, and tugged on her halter top, offering the camera a fairly nice view of her fake boobs. "You take slave juice and you're doing it to impress someone else. You don't feel a thing. It's not a drug that gets you high. The only person it gets off is the person who gave it to you."

"Interesting. Have you two taken slave juice?"

Both women laughed, although their nervousness was apparent by the way they shifted and glanced at each other.

"No. But I know people who have. Girls do it to make their guys happy, but obviously men do it to make their women happy, too." The second woman, who was definitely prettier than the first, leaned into the microphone as she continued explaining. "It's a power trip, you know? And it's a complete submission. Take slave juice and that is exactly what you are, a slave to whoever gave you the stuff. It's not the kind of drug you would take by yourself because all you would do is sit there."

The two women found this rather funny and giggled at the joke.

"So you're telling me slave juice renders you useless until someone tells you to do something?"

"Exactly. Whoever is on it quits thinking for themselves. They'll do whatever someone else tells them to do, no matter how ridiculous or insane the act might be."

Jane looked knowingly at the camera. "Which tells us that these two men were murdered," she stated. "This is Jane Hall with Channel Four news. Back to you, John."

"Crap," Jake grunted, pulling his attention from the TV when it went to a commercial. "Slave juice. Is that what they're calling it now?"

"Do you think it's the same drug Evelyn Van Cooper used to try and help control the captives for the game?" Natasha asked.

Jake didn't like thinking of their time in Arizona, imprisoned underground by a maniac and his wife, Claude and Evelyn Van Cooper. "It sure as hell sounds like it. I can't imagine that bitch is too happy with her perfect drug being turned into a street drug."

"It might not be her doing." Natasha stood, downed more of her water, and walked over to the counter to grab a peach. "The woman was on a power trip, convinced she had created a drug that would make a perfect army."

"She could still be using it for that means. We never found her."

"The only good thing out of that nightmare was Marc finding London." Natasha cursed under her breath when the door to the office opened and a buzzer announced someone had entered the office.

Jake would have to agree with her. Marc had fallen hard and fast for the dark beauty from Colorado, and Jake didn't blame him a bit. London was beyond sexy and head over heels for Marc. They made an awesome couple and last Jake heard were working on opening a private investigation office in Aspen, where they now both lived. Jake was told it got pretty warm in August in Aspen, Colorado, but he would bet good money his brother wasn't sweating his ass off right now like Jake was.

Natasha was already in the office, talking to an older man who had come in to bring information on one of the men wanted by his bonding company. Jake paused in the doorway, not wanting to be cornered into a conversation when he could be missing his only chance for a shower. There were papers resting in the fax machine and he would get stuck working up a profile before he headed back out. It was already after three, but at the rate the bonding companies were faxing over cases to them or walking cases through the door, putting this one off until tomorrow would just make that day as bad as this one.

The phone rang as Pete, who worked for Rita Fulsom, one of the bonding agents KFA worked with, made himself comfortable on the couch in between the long windows that offered a view of the beachside road they lived on. Natasha pulled open the top drawer to the filing cabinet by her desk and glanced over her shoulder, giving Jake an imploring look when the phone rang a second time.

"Get that, please?" she asked, before turning to search through the files.

He was stuck. Jake moved around her desk, sitting in Natasha's expensive office chair his dad had bought her the year before and reaching for the phone.

"KFA," he said, lowering his voice and picking up the pen Natasha had tossed down on her desk earlier.

"I need to speak with Greg King, please." The man's urgent tone wasn't surprising. Everyone called KFA sounding as if they had an emergency, and oftentimes they did.

Jake hadn't bothered asking Natasha where his father was, although last he'd spoken to Greg both he and Haley were on the south side of L.A. tracking an underaged mother who'd kidnapped her children after escaping from the juvenile detention center. KFA was brought into the search when her court date came and went and, since she'd been in lockdown, she was considered a serious flight risk. It wasn't as easy to sneak into Mexico as it once had been, but most of the time when anyone wanted to escape an inevitable sentencing they tried skipping out of the country. The Kings' reputation for finding their man, or woman, was impeccable, although too often they weren't given a case until it was almost cold, because LAPD detectives were too cocky to admit they didn't have the skills Jake's family possessed.

"He's not available." Jake opened and closed the pen he'd picked up off the desk, glancing up when Natasha whispered to Jake that Greg wouldn't be back for at least a few hours.

"It's imperative that I speak with him. He needs to work a case for me. Give me his cell." The man didn't make it a suggestion.

Jake wasn't daunted. He continued pushing the button at the end of the pen to open and close it and turned his attention to the door leading into his house when he thought he heard his cell phone ring. Probably one of his ladies was growing impatient for some of that classic King loving. If he didn't make time for at least a few of them, they would look elsewhere. Jake had an image to uphold.

"You can leave a name and number and I'll give it to him when he comes in," Jake said.

"Is this Greg King?"

"No. Do you want to leave your number?"

"Who is this?"

Jake tried not to sigh too loudly. "This is Jake King."

"How are you related?"

The man didn't know much about KFA if he was asking that question. "I'm his son. What can I do for you?"

"Are you familiar with the game?"

Jake quit clicking the pen. He stared at Natasha's desk but didn't focus on the paperwork scattered across it. The game, which was a very loose title for one of the deadliest war games taking place on this planet, had been responsible for dragging them down to Mexico, where Jake's father had taken a bullet and wound up flat on his back in a hospital for a couple weeks. Eight months later a case took them to Phoenix, where they'd been held captive underground and first learned about the drug that apparently now was being labeled slave juice. Marc had met London while the Kings worked that case.

"Who is this?" Jake asked, feeling his chest tighten, and straightened while a knot formed in his gut. He would kill to bring down the players of the game once and for all. Twice his family had been pulled into the sick, warped world of the too rich and too demonic who believed they could make the planet their game board and whoever lived on it their players. It was a sick form of terror, manipulation, and greed. Worse yet, slave juice was being used to control the players' pieces, or abducted citizens, to make them commit the horrendous crimes needed to advance in the game.

"That's what I thought." The man on the other end of the line paused for only a moment. "I'm already aware of your past involvement with the game and know KFA has tried ending it twice now. That is why I need to hire Greg King. No one else will do."

"Who is this?" Jake demanded.

"I know about your involvement with Marty Byrd in Mexico and I know Greg King is responsible for his death."

Jake didn't see the pen in his hand anymore. Instead he remembered standing in the hot, dry desert for hours and staring at a mansion that had been built out in the middle of nowhere, waiting to learn if his father was alive or dead. They had stuck it out in that desert, parched and melting under a sun too hot to bear, and watched the FBI blow that mansion to smithereens, while Jake's father was in it.

KFA had been responsible for locating Marty Byrd when the FBI couldn't. Jake's father had suffered a gunshot wound and was damn lucky to make it out alive. Byrd wasn't so lucky, which prevented them from learning the truth about the game.

"What is it you want?" Jake asked. "And I didn't catch your name?"

"James Huxtable. I'm flying out to L.A. tomorrow and will discuss the details of the assignment your father will handle for me at that time. Name the location. I will meet you anywhere."

"I don't set up my father's appointments. Leave a number and he'll call you back. But Mr. Huxtable, I can tell you now we don't handle private investigation."

"I don't blame you. Chasing around cheating spouses gets old in a week." Huxtable's laugh had no humor in it. "Evelyn Van Cooper's slave juice has taken the game to a dangerous level, even deadlier than it was before. I can't put off my meeting any longer. I'll be in L.A. tomorrow at two P.M. We'll discuss the details at that time."

"Leave your number," Jake repeated. He wouldn't admit his interest was piqued, but he couldn't plan his father's schedule. At this point, though, Jake would be willing to bet Greg would meet James Huxtable.

Jake wrote the number down and James Huxtable's name above it. He stared at it, unsure whether Huxtable was a good guy or criminal. It sounded like they would find out tomorrow.

"What did he say?" Jake joined his parents on the back porch later that evening, taking his time enjoying the beer he hadn't been able to enjoy earlier. It was after nine and already he felt like crashing. He was too young to be living like this.

"I just got off the phone with Marc." Greg King sat in one of the large wicker chairs surrounding the table on their screened-in back porch. The sound and smells of the ocean drifted toward them, adding to the peaceful setting.

"I thought you were talking to James Huxtable." Jake took the chair next to his mother. In the King family, furniture was large, since none of the men stood under six feet. Haley King, however, was a lot shorter and looked dwarfed in the large high-back chair.

"I did talk to him, but when I hung up I called Marc." Greg nursed his beer, taking a long drink, then staring at the bottle for a moment before lifting his dark gaze to his son. "James Huxtable approached London in Colorado when she first started seeing Marc."

Jake didn't know London very well other than that his

brother was in love with her. He felt a wave of protective energy surge through him, though, as he stared at his father. "Why did he do that?"

"According to Huxtable, he was searching for evidence of who was part of the game."

"He thought London was part of it?" Jake asked.

"No. He thought her parents were."

Jake remembered London's parents. They were criminals, a modern-day Bonnie and Clyde. After the ordeal in Phoenix, London's parents had bowed out of the scene quietly, leaving before Jake ever had a chance to talk to them. More than likely all of the law enforcement people who were present when they were released from their underground prison made them nervous.

"His story checked out. Marc confirmed James Huxtable came around the ski resort, asking London questions about her parents." Greg took a drink of his beer. "London said he made her nervous."

"Why does he want to see you?" Haley asked before Jake could.

"He's flying out here." Greg focused on his wife before shifting his attention to Jake. "He wants to meet in person to discuss the game."

"What does he know about it?" Jake had a weird feeling about this Huxtable guy. That he knew Jake's family had involvement with the game was unnerving enough. But to seek them out, ask to discuss it, didn't sit right with him.

Apparently his thoughts were easier to read than he realized.

"It doesn't sit right with me, either, and I don't know what he knows about the game," Jake's father said. "Yet."

"I'm going with you," Jake decided.

"I'm good with that. We'll figure out what this Huxtable guy is all about."

"So what do you think? Is Huxtable coming here because he wants to play the game, or bring it down?"

Greg King's hand tightened noticeably around his beer. "I don't know yet."

"Either way, if he's coming to talk about the game, it can't be good." Jake met his dad's gaze and knew he agreed. The game brought trouble and death, neither of which Jake had time for in his life.

Jake followed his father through the crowded restaurant. The popular steak and burger place was heavily air-conditioned and felt good with temperatures already hotter than they'd been the day before. Summer couldn't end fast enough for Jake. He was sick of it being so hot.

"I'd say that's him," Greg muttered over his shoulder.

When James Huxtable called after his flight arrived at LAX, he told them he'd meet them at the restaurant and be in the last booth by the windows. Jake wondered how long Huxtable had been sitting here, since he knew an hour ago where he'd be sitting.

The man at the last booth stood when they approached. "Greg King," he offered, extending his hand in greeting and smiling. The arrogant, determined son of a bitch seemed to have transformed into a relaxed, peaceful soul. He nodded to Jake after shaking Greg's hand. "You must be the son. Jake, right? I definitely see the family resemblance.

Greg slid into one side of the booth, making room for Jake when James sat again opposite them. "I haven't ordered yet." James looked past them, searching the restaurant, then holding his hand up and snapping his finger. "But I hear the food is incredible here."

"It is," Greg said, his tone serious as he watched a wait-ress approach. "We have a very busy schedule today," he continued.

James nodded knowingly. "Understand. Shall we do burgers all the way around? My treat, of course."

Jake let his dad take the lead and was surprised when Greg didn't argue over who would pick up the tab. Jake couldn't remember his father ever allowing anyone to treat. The King men always paid their own way. It was best never to be in debt to anyone.

Greg interrupted when James tried ordering for all of them, though: "I'll take my burger plain, well done."

Jake took his cue: "I'll have the same."

When the waitress left with their order, Greg straightened in the booth, clasping his hands on the table, and faced James Huxtable. "What's this all about?" Greg asked, the rough growl in his tone enough to intimidate most men.

James' smile faded. "How much would it take for you to clear your schedule and handle a case for me?"

Greg leaned back. Jake shifted, easing to the corner of the booth, where he leaned, fingering the corner of his paper napkin, which was wrapped around silverware, as he focused on James. The man's brow appeared damp, although his expression was determined.

"I can't think of any case I would clear my schedule for," Greg said without hesitating.

James leaned forward. "What if it were to bring down the game?" he whispered.

"Is this what you've been working on, ending the game?" Greg didn't whisper, but his soft growl didn't carry to the next table. Jake would have a hard time hearing if he weren't paying attention.

"For over a year." James leaned back when the waitress returned with drinks. "My daughter and I run a private investigation firm based out of Chicago," he continued when the waitress had left. He reached inside his tweed jacket, complete with patches on the elbows, which made him look like some kind of absentminded professor. "This is my card."

Greg took the card, glanced at it, and handed it to Jake. The card didn't say much. There was no address, no contact number, nothing more than what James had already told them about himself.

"Since I've instigated this meeting and the two of you need to be sold on my credibility, I'll start with the exchange of knowledge." James looked serious, as if he sincerely believed that if he told them what he knew, Greg and Jake would then spew out what knowledge they possessed. Neither of them stopped him from continuing. "We were very aware of Marty Byrd being a game player. He was too loud about it. I'm sure you would agree. It was the beginning of the end for the acclaimed assassin. We followed him to Mexico, as did you and your family," James said, nodding at Greg. "We didn't guess he would abduct you to be a piece on his board. But then, possibly he wouldn't have if you hadn't gotten too close to learning the truth about his strategies. Don't you think?"

Jake thought James just had insulted his father. He straightened and was acutely aware of the two men ignoring him. Greg stared into James' eyes and the PI returned the hard stare.

"What else do you know about this inscrutable board game?" Greg asked instead of answering James' question.

"My daughter and I discovered the Van Coopers were players of this game shortly after she returned from Mexico."

"How did you find this out?" Jake asked. He was suddenly curious about this daughter James Huxtable kept mentioning. If he had a partner, why wasn't she here with him? If the answer was that James was protective of her, he certainly wouldn't have let her go down to Mexico and become involved in such a deadly investigation.

"You weren't the only one who didn't die when Byrd's hideaway was blown up down in Mexico. A handful of people were hospitalized after the explosion that killed Marty Byrd. My daughter is a master of disguises." When James smiled there was something different in his gaze than when he'd first began their conversation, something almost sad. He shifted his attention from Greg to Jake when he continued explaining. "Angela, that's my daughter, went into the hospital in L.A. where most of the men pulled out of that mansion were taken. She went undercover as a nurse. As I just said, she is the best when it comes to posing as someone she isn't, almost too good. I've never seen anyone like her and I've been in this line of work over half of my life. Angela got a lot of information out of the men recovering after Byrd was killed."

"And that is when the two of you learned about the Van Coopers." Greg didn't make it a question.

"Two of the men hospitalized worked for Marty Byrd, helping gather the people he'd use as his board pieces." James stopped talking and folded his hands in his lap when the waitress returned with their food.

Jake stared at his plate for a moment when it was slid in front of him. The waitress asked the usual questions, making sure they had everything they needed, before leaving them alone again. He didn't pay attention to anything she said. Nor did he have a large appetite for his food. His thoughts raced over what James Huxtable had told them so far. If his daughter had been in Mexico and also in the hospital while Jake's father had recovered there for two weeks, quite possibly Jake had run into her at least once. There had been a couple nurses tending to his father who stuck out in Jake's mind. Both had been rather hot. Had one of them not really been a nurse but James' daughter working undercover and just waiting for Jake's father to be alone so she could pump him for information? The thought made Jake's skin crawl.

"Where is Evelyn Van Cooper now?" Greg asked after taking a bite out of his burger.

"Damn good question." James also bit into his sandwich but put it down on his plate and used his napkin to wipe his lips. He fingered his silverware, straightening the knife and fork on either side of his plate with meticulous care. "We think she's out of the country, but she isn't our primary concern right now."

"Why is that?"

"She's not playing the game."

"You know this for a fact?"

"We're pretty sure her interests have turned elsewhere." James waved his hand in the air. "That isn't what matters right now." Something shifted in his expression. "My daughter is on the inside and needs a good partner. Your reputation precedes you, Mr. King."

James Huxtable picked up a leather case next to him. Glancing around the room as he placed the case on the table next to him, he exhaled slowly as he pushed the snaps on either end to open it.

"You've flown all the way out here to ask us to go to Chicago and work with your daughter?" Greg also tossed his napkin, but he dropped it on his plate, indicating he was done eating. "Mr. Huxtable, I'm sure we were clear on the phone. We're not private investigators. My caseload is so high right now I barely have time to hug my wife. I sure as hell don't have time to go to Chicago."

"Please." James held his hand up to silence Greg.

Jake didn't have to glance at his father to know what look was on his face. Greg King didn't like being silenced by anyone. Jake didn't blame him. The gesture offered little respect, and Jake would tell James Huxtable that much if he cared. The man wasn't presenting his case very well.

"Are you familiar with a man named Mario Mandela?" James pulled a glossy eight-by-ten out of his briefcase and closed the lid. "He's the most recent member to enter the game. The reason I believe Evelyn Van Cooper isn't playing the game is we know she approached him, offering to sell her new drug, the one the media is calling slave juice, to him as an aid in controlling his captives, or board pieces, if you will."

"Did he accept her offer?" Greg asked.

"Yes. We're pretty sure he purchased an incredibly large quantity of the drug, which makes us think he's already kidnapped quite a few people to turn into his army." James sighed, fingering his briefcase. "You've worked the game twice now. You understand how tortured a family is when they don't know if their loved one is dead or alive, or worse," he said, giving Greg a knowing look.

"The game is terrible. The FBI were involved in fighting to end it when we were in Mexico. I'm sure they're still on the case," Greg offered.

James nodded. "They haven't solved it yet."

"The game is global. It will come down, though."

Jake decided to make the best of the lunch break and down his food. Huxtable was a disappointment, thinking he could fly out here and convince them to drop their caseload to go assist him in Chicago. Talk about an arrogant chump.

James slid a glossy eight-by-ten across the table. "This is my daughter."

Jake stared at the woman in the picture. For a moment he didn't hear what either James or his dad said. The young woman laughing at the camera had the most beautiful long black hair Jake had ever seen. Her olive-colored skin implied her mother might not be Caucasian, but in Jake's opinion that added to her sex appeal. It was something in her eyes, though. They were a unique shade of green, and even in the photograph the camera had caught her defiance. It was as if she laughed at the camera with a dare in her eye, something in her gaze saying, *Come find me if you can.*

Jake swore she stared right at him. His insides hardened as he tried processing this new angle. Jake had never thought he'd see her again. He'd already tried to find Angela once, although he hadn't known then she was a private investigator. KFA's case had ended and he'd figured he would never see her again. Now here she was, staring up at him in a glossy eight-by-ten. What were the odds?

"Once we determined Mandela was in Chicago and had set up housekeeping in a rented mansion, Angela started doing some undercover work." James had another picture with him, one Jake hadn't noticed he was holding until now. "She met him for drinks at a country club he belongs to in Chicago. While Angela was entertaining the Italian Mafia lord, I was able to do some snooping around his place. And I have more pictures, along with some recorded conversations. Nothing, though, to warrant taking him down. Not yet."

"If sounds as if the two of you are well on the right track." Greg King didn't praise another person lightly. "If the two of you are this close to nailing a member of the game, why come to us?"

James placed the picture of a dark-haired man on the table next to the picture of his daughter. "Angela is determined to take down Mandela, but she's put herself too close to the monster. The other day I got a phone call." Again something crossed over his expression. It was like a shadow, a shift of sunlight. In the next moment it was gone. "I have a missing-person case I need to give all my attention to but can't leave my daughter without sufficient backup. I don't make a habit of asking for outside help."

"What would her backup do?" Jake asked, once again focusing on the picture of Angela. His father gave him a hard look, but Jake ignored it, not focusing on either one of them but staring at the seductress in the picture. He couldn't help wondering if she'd suggested her father seek them out or if she knew her father was here.

"You're going undercover with my daughter." James leaned back on his side of the booth. "You're a father," he said, sounding imploring. "Angela is my own flesh and blood. She's worked hard to impress me, to show me that she knows the business as well as her old man. You have to know what that feels like."

"I thought you said she's done undercover work before?" Greg asked.

It didn't surprise Jake his dad wouldn't comment on his feelings toward his sons. Greg was proud of his boys and he'd told them so on numerous occasions. It wasn't something he'd brag about to a stranger, though. Jake wouldn't want him to.

"Of course she has," James hissed, coming forward and hitting the table with his fist. He ignored those sitting around them who glanced their way curiously. James did have enough sense to lower his voice: "My daughter is an outstanding detective, as good as me. But she's in over her head without me beside her. I won't have anyone helping her in this case who isn't top-notch, which is why I was willing to fly out here to meet you. My time is limited. We need to return to Chicago."

"If your time is so precious, why did you fly out here when

you knew we don't do cases like this? We're bounty hunters, not undercover cops."

"I've made a mistake coming here," James grunted. "My daughter needs me and she needs serious protection. I was wrong thinking I could find it with you."

James pulled out his wallet and dropped a couple twenties on the table, then grabbed the pictures and his briefcase and slid out of the booth. Greg didn't hesitate but slid out of the booth as well. Jake followed him. He didn't try to chase down James Huxtable but instead smiled when the waitress hurried to them.

"The food was great," he offered gallantly. "Our business meeting is over, though."

Her expression lightened considerably when Greg tossed another ten onto the table. "I understand completely," she said, smiling, and winked at Jake before he left the restaurant.

"What did you think about all of that?" Greg asked, squinting against the afternoon sun as they walked outside.

Jake scanned the parking lot and spotted James Huxtable climbing into a compact car, possibly one he'd rented at the airport since it appeared a rather tight fit for him. "Dad, I know Angela."

His father stopped before reaching their truck and stared at his son. "What? Why the hell didn't you say something? How do you know her?"

"Remember the night Marc and I got thrown in jail when we were in Mexico?"

Greg grunted. "Pissed your mother off to no end."

"There were two ladies in the nightclub. We escorted them to their cars and they offered us some information on finding Marty Byrd. The next thing we know, we're being hauled off to jail and accused of paying the ladies for their time."

"Yup. I remember. Your mom and I didn't buy into that for a minute. Neither of us believed you two would pay for something that is so often offered to you for free."

Now Jake grunted. "Thanks, I think."

Greg opened the driver's side door of his truck but Jake glanced over at James Huxtable once again. On an impulse, Jake walked across the parking lot, grabbing James' attention as he put his car in gear. James watched Jake instead of driving away, his expression masked, before slowly rolling down his window.

"I'll take your case." Jake stopped next to James, feeling the cold blast of AC hit him when he leaned over to better see the man. "Give me a card that actually has your number on it."

Chapter Two

Angela Huxtable, or Angela Torres, the name she was using while undercover, took her time walking across the lobby of the Drake hotel. Her snug-fitting mini-dress, complete with high heels, too much makeup, and bags from some of the most expensive shops in Chicago, would hopefully convince anyone she was loaded, with too much time on her hands.

Angela wasn't trying to convince just anyone, though. Mario Mandela was the deadliest, most heartless son of a bitch she'd ever met. For almost a week, she'd played the part of the rich socialite, presenting herself as the type of lady Mandela liked. All she'd had to do was come across as a wealthy slut and she'd grabbed his attention. Undercover work could seriously suck, especially when a murdering, demonic asshole groped and fondled her all evening. It had paid off, though. Angela had spent the entire day with Mandela, which was a major step forward.

Mandela thought he was buying himself a slut, a young, carefree, and bored rich lady who thought the idea of being seen on the arm of an Italian warlord was a serious turn-on. It unnerved Angela how Mandela made no secret about who he was. If anything, he'd bragged to her how he'd made his millions crushing anyone who wasn't intelligent enough to get out of his way. She'd actually pulled off laughing when he'd said that, fluttered her painted nails in front of his face, and informed him lightly that she loved a dangerous man. The chills rushed over her body when she remembered the sinister smile he'd given her at that comment.

Just be careful, she reminded herself, nearing the elevator and slowing, making sure to keep her feet together and her legs straight, a pose that allowed her to look her best in the getup she had on. God, she couldn't wait to get out of these damn high-heeled shoes. Were there really women out there who wore shoes like this by choice?

Several older ladies stood huddled near the elevators, occasionally glancing up to see which elevator door might open first, as they discussed a meeting on something about insurance. Angela glanced their way, then lowered her head, looking at one hand, then the other, as she gripped the bags in each of them. Mandela had spent a hell of a lot of money on outfits for her. Clothes she would willingly burn the moment this case was solved.

She shifted her weight, having half a mind to slip out of her heels and head up to her room barefoot. The Drake was expensive, elegant, and very classy. For the price she was paying a night for a suite, if she wanted to gallop across the lobby barefoot she should damn well be able to do so.

The thought calmed her nerves a bit and she continued looking down as she smiled. Then relaxing her expression, she glanced up when the elevator doors in front of her dinged. Everyone lingering around her closed in, anxious to be the first ones on when the doors opened. Which was fine with Angela; she hated being crammed in the back of the elevator. If her feet weren't killing her and her room was not on the twelfth floor, she might have taken the stairs.

Angela joined the three older ladies, one man in a suit, and two teenagers. She was the last one on and turned, facing the doors as the gentleman made sure everyone's floor buttons were pushed. She stared at the lobby, waiting for the doors to close. A man across the open space watched her.

Her heart began beating faster as she locked gazes with the incredibly tall, well-built man. Tousled brown hair bordered his attentive face. Even from across the lobby, with people walking between them, Angela swore dark forest green eyes latched onto hers, not only capturing her attention but also sending a silent message only she would understand.

I've found you.

Suddenly her palms were damp. Angela ached to rub them down her sides but instead readjusted the bags she carried and waited for the elevator doors to close. She stared at the man. The doors were taking forever. Either that or possibly time really could stand still when the situation called for it. As much as Angela loved a sensual moment, she was a far cry from what she considered a romantic. But the man she stared at wasn't into romance. He was as hard and ruthless as his body, impermeable, reckless yet filled with a level of honor serious pricks like Mario would never comprehend.

All that honor Jake King possessed probably made it easier for him to strike the pose of royalty. His last name fit him. He stood in the middle of the lobby, not in anyone's way yet not moving for a soul. People eased their way around him as if asking him to shift his weight would be something close to a mortal sin. The way he was poised, relaxed yet ready to spring into action the moment anyone or anything around him was threatened, reminded her of that night a year ago. Angela would never forget what it was like being in his arms.

Men like Jake King didn't ache to protect and care for a lady; they commanded the ability to do so. Not that there could be another man like Jake King. They weren't right for each other, never would be. No one would ever control her. Nonetheless her fingers tingled as she remembered stroking all that hard-as-rock muscle. Jake had been wound tight that night about a year ago. He and Angela had torn up the dance floor, dirty dancing to the hard-pounding sexual music and clutching each other during slow dances. For weeks after parting ways with Jake King she'd regretted the hell out of not sleeping with him.

His hair was still shaggy, thick brown waves that just

touched his collar. And those eyes. They were watching her now just as they had in Mexico, and just as they had in the fantasies she had had of him for weeks after they parted ways.

Damn it! He shouldn't be here. That night in Mexico he looked at her as if he already knew her darkest sexual fantasies. A man like Jake King was nothing but trouble. Angela had come to terms with that. She hardly ever fantasized about him anymore.

Jake continued watching her. He was larger than life, taller than anyone else in the lobby. More than one woman gave him an approving once-over. All those deep, kinky scenarios she'd created about him resurfaced. Angela returned his stare and worried that he'd already guessed where her thoughts were headed. Angela watched as Jake moved his hand, raising it to his forehead, and saluted her right before her view of him was replaced by the closing elevator doors. She stared at her reflection, fighting to regain her breath. Suddenly she felt as if she'd raced across town in her high heels to get here. She closed her eyes, willing herself to calm down and dismiss her emotional and physical reaction to Jake King. The last thing she needed was a distraction so strong she wouldn't be able to focus on her work.

What the hell was he doing here? Angela didn't believe in coincidence any more than she believed in chance. Things happened because people made them happen. People plotted, schemed, and manipulated. Especially men like Jake. He was here for a reason. She'd barely regained control over her breathing and managed to get her heart to quit pounding in her chest when nervous energy damn near sent her to the edge again.

He sure as hell better not be here because I'm here.

Oh, God. Or worse yet, he'd better not be here because her father had arranged it. Just the other morning her dad had told her he would accept only the best running backup for her if he wasn't able to be there himself. Anyone else would be second-best, though. Angela would only be safe if her dad was the one at the helm, watching her back when she went into the lion's den, or with this case it would be more like the devil's pit.

The doors dinged, sliding open, and the three ladies left. The gentleman in the suit got out on the next floor. The teenagers followed suit a few floors up. Angela rode alone to the twelfth floor, trying to organize her thoughts.

Even then, Jake's image remained in her brain. He was well over six feet, with sex appeal that would put a god to shame. As tall and muscular as he was, he didn't stand out as much as one might think such a large man would. It was his casual demeanor. He was dressed well, but not over-dressed, in clean jeans and an untucked T-shirt. The duffel in his hand suggested he might just be arriving at the hotel. He certainly wasn't checking out. Angela had been here for several days and would have noticed him if he'd been in the hotel before.

No one was in the hall during the time it took her to slide her card into the lock and push her hotel room door open. It closed and locked automatically behind her and Angela dumped her bags on the king-size bed, then put her purse next to them.

"There's work to do," she told herself, trying to keep her brain focused. There wasn't any getting Jake's image out of her head, though. His hair seemed a bit longer than she'd remembered it and a shade or two lighter, possibly from all that California sun. She dragged her large suitcase out of the closet and brought it to the middle of the room.

He didn't seem surprised to see me, either. She shook her head as she narrowed down possible reasons for Jake King, son of the great bounty hunter Greg King, being at the same hotel she was, halfway across the country from L.A., where he lived. "He's obviously here on a case."

Was he once again trying to end the game? It was why they'd crossed paths in Mexico, although he hadn't known who she was at that time. Something told her he knew a lot more about her now. The way he looked at her, confident, relaxed, as if he'd expected to see her standing in the elevator. He sure hadn't acted surprised.

Kicking off her shoes and sitting on the floor, Angela reached inside her large suitcase and released the fake bottom. Tools of the trade were neatly nestled away just how she'd left them. If anyone had snooped through her room and discovered what she had hidden there, the contents of her suitcase would have been out of order. She'd made incredible progress today, taken a giant step forward with her undercover work. That was all the more reason to make sure her cover hadn't been blown and that no one had planted any bugs.

Hopefully, the asshole saw her as a rich, bored prima donna, which was necessary to lay her trap.

Angela was damn proud of herself for teasing the prick into a pathetic horny and whining asshole before leaving him. She had the prick's eyes rolling back in his head from his sexual suggestions. Not that he would ever lay a hand on her and live to talk about it. Angela might not be six and a half feet tall with muscle bulging all over the place, but she did know how to take care of herself. Unfortunately, she couldn't kill Mario until she connected him to the game and took him down, along with all the other players.

"I can torture the crap out of him until that precious moment arrives, though," she mumbled under her breath, grinning and feeling rather evil herself, at the moment.

Which was why she needed backup. Her father had tailed her when Angela and Mario spent the day driving around Chicago and shopping. She couldn't imagine any case being so important that he thought someone else should be watching her ass. What she was doing could turn deadly without a moment's notice. The best of investigators wouldn't do what she was doing without top of the line backup, someone with enough skills and training to remain invisible but close enough to have her back if needed. Angela trusted only her father.

She had laid low while he'd been in L.A., a trip he'd been rather vague about. When he'd returned to Chicago, he hadn't said a thing about his trip. Angela had been anxious to talk to him about her case.

"That was because I didn't think he was doing something

sneaky behind my back," she grumbled, keeping her voice quiet and pulling everything out of the bottom of her suitcase.

She spread all of her spy equipment around her on the floor, getting comfortable and sitting cross-legged, still anxious to know what Jake King was doing in Chicago. Now that she had bugs planted, setting up her equipment would help keep her focused and grounded. She loved all this high-tech stuff. When she had it up and running, listening to the bad guys reveal their secrets was the best damn adrenaline rush in the world.

The highly sensitive listening devices she'd planted in the backseat of Mario's limo would, she hoped, bring in enough damaging evidence. She needed to know where he was keeping the people he'd abducted to play the game. And she had to find out where his first attack would be. In the time she'd spent with him today she'd overheard a couple phone calls that suggested he already had his board pieces, or the people he'd abducted and drugged so he could turn them into murderers and terrorists, lined up and ready to go. If she didn't move soon enough, the people Mario had abducted would kill, or be killed. An arrest had to be made before innocent people died.

Angela pushed herself to her feet, picking up a small black box and taking it over to the round table by glass doors that led out to a small terrace overlooking Lake Michigan. Heavy curtains were pulled closed and blocking the view. This wasn't a vacation. Her job had never been more serious.

After placing the box on the table, she grabbed her sweeping device off the floor. A couple times Mario had led her into a shop and walked straight up to a rack, pulling off an outfit and insisting it was perfect for her. He might have made previous arrangements for the clothes he purchased for her to be bugged. Angela knew she had a wild imagination, but she never ruled anything out until proof swayed her one way or another.

Today's listening devices could be so small they were barely detectable with the naked eye. Angela went over every inch of the hotel room, ran the detector over her body and purse, then finally the shoes she'd kicked off. She double-checked her body and clothes just for good measure. Mario's hands had been all over her. There weren't any bugs, which meant Mario didn't suspect her of being anything other than what she had told him she was. "I'm definitely taking a shower," she grumbled, her stomach churning at the thought of how often he'd groped her.

It had been a necessary evil. She'd learned Mario conducted a lot of his business while in his limo. He didn't seem to care if she overheard his conversations when his phone rang. He would interrupt their conversation to talk on the phone. Angela had overheard enough to help convict him, once she had her proof.

She was curious that he spoke so openly in front of her. He possibly thought her an idiot, planned on keeping her around, or viewed her as expendable. None of those options sat well with her.

It made her sick, thinking of the part she had to play in all of this. Granted, it had been her idea after she learned Mario's MO. Angela knew it was the only way to get close to him. What she had to do didn't disgust her half as much as did thinking of all the people he'd kidnapped, taken from their families, and drugged so he could make them blow up buildings and kill people. Mario would use all his kidnapped victims just so he could win a terrorizing board game.

"And do you have a role in this sordid game, Jake King?" she pondered as she put away her bug detector.

Moving to the table, she fumbled with the box, glancing over the directions as to how her new gadget worked " 'Once the bugs are in place, the monitor allows you to listen to live-feed, record, and save important conversations,' " she read, running her finger over the instructions, then comparing the pictures to the box in her hand.

Angela unwrapped the wire headset and adjusted it to her head. Static crackled in her ear and she leaned over, studying the knobs on the box, then adjusting them until the static faded.

"I know damn good and well why he came to Chicago."

Mario's voice came in so loud and clear it sounded as if he sat at the table across from her. "That fucking private investigator went out to California and hired the bastard, thinking he could pull me out of the game."

Angela froze, the instructions sliding out of her fingers and falling onto the table. It was just her luck he would be saying exactly what she needed to hear from him the moment she put the earpiece in her ear. He'd mentioned the game. But what else had he just said? What was this about a private investigator thinking he could pull Mario out of the game? Mario had said "he," right? She leaned over again, running her finger over the few buttons on the box, then set it to record the conversation.

There was a slight pause and she started to bend over again, ready to mess with the controls in case she'd lost reception. She'd barely touched the knob to clear out interference when Mario began talking again. This time, a row of red lights began dancing as they matched the levels of his vocal inflection.

"I know. He should stick to doing what he does best, capturing punks who miss court dates. The only way you get a court date is to get caught, which won't happen to me." Mario had the kind of laugh that sent icy chills down a person's spine. "Why? Because I'm better than those assholes!" he shouted, his accent thickening as he bellowed what appeared to him to be the obvious truth.

"Your persuasive skills are definitely not your best asset, sweetheart. There is one thing you forget. King couldn't destroy the game when he killed your husband. Now the asshole has made the mistake of entering my town and thinking he can learn my operation. He'll be dead before we make our first attack." Mario's laughter in her ear was so wicked and dripping with hatred it made Angela's blood run cold. "Don't worry, my dear. I think I can still cut you in for a piece of the action. You shouldn't believe everything you hear. I'm not completely heartless. In fact, if you want, I'll even allow you to kill King for me. Although my sweet little *puttana* has taken a liking to ending people's lives."

Angela studied the instruction booklet another minute until she figured out how to put the conversation on speaker. Once she was sure it was still recording, she stood, suddenly antsy and impatient. She pulled the curtains back from the sliding glass doors and stared out at Lake Michigan. It was one hell of a breathtaking view but not one she appreciated at the moment. Mario also knew Jake was here. How did he know? Did Mario have eyes in the lobby? It wouldn't surprise her a bit if he did. Was Jake the only one in Chicago, or had his entire family come out here? Either way, there was a mark on his head.

Angela turned away from the panoramic view out her window and stared at the small black box. Mario had said the private investigator went to California and hired King to take him down. Was he talking about her father?

"Dad," she whispered, hurrying to her purse and pulling out her personal cell phone. The track phone she'd bought to use while undercover was next to it in her purse. She checked her personal cell, noting the missed call from her father and that he'd tried calling over an hour ago. Angela had her phone on Silent, which her father knew. They'd also agreed, until the case was over he wouldn't leave voice-mail messages. She cleared the missed call and put in a call to her father.

Staying close to the black box on the table, she studied it as she listened to her father's phone ring. Even though the conversations would be recorded, Angela wanted to know immediately if crucial information was revealed. When the call went to voice mail she hung up and put her phone on her bed next to her purse.

Mario wasn't talking at the moment and Angela rewound the recorded conversation and hit Play.

He did say the private investigator went to California and hired King. Mario hadn't said "a private investigator" but "that fucking private investigator." And he didn't say "Kings," or "the King family." He'd said "King," as in one person.

The image of Jake standing in the lobby, staring at her and offering her a final salute, appeared in her mind again.

Immediately her insides tightened. As much as she was dying to know if her father had hired Jake and brought him out here to help her, at the same time Angela wasn't sure she wanted to talk to her father about Jake. Possibly it was leaving her mom when she was sixteen and moving in with her father, all of her teenage rebellion already focused on her mother, that had allowed Angela to build such a strong friendship and alliance with her dad. For whatever reasons, she and her dad were very close. She couldn't remember him ever yelling at her the way her mother had or treating Angela like a child. The bond she and her father had was based on love, respect, and sheer enjoyment of each other's company.

A year ago Angela hadn't given a thought when she'd shared the events of her evening with Jake with her father. They'd been in the middle of a case, hot on the pursuit of Marty Byrd. When she'd told her dad how she'd shared some crucial information with Jake, her father had immediately accused Angela of being infatuated with the man. Other daughters might have disputed such a charge, but Angela and her father had discussed her feelings, Jake's character, and the kind of man that would make Angela the happiest. The conversation was quickly forgotten the next day when they learned what Jake did with the information Angela gave him.

Jake had messed up her plan for attack a year ago. The second she had let him know where Marty Bird was, Jake and his family had hurried down there and blown up the damn mansion. All chances of learning anything about the game had been shot to hell. Her father knew how Jake screwed everything up for them. Would her dad seek Jake out again, in spite of what Angela had told him, to help Angela and be her backup?

"Damn it," she hissed, and dragged her fingers through her hair, tangling it and encouraging herself to take that shower now.

Mario wasn't talking anymore, but she thought she heard the engine running, which meant he was still in the limo. That or Tomas was driving somewhere without Mario.

Angela looked at the remaining bugs. Two more black

thin pads, no larger than the size of a dime, remained in the box. She pulled them out, keeping them in their wrapping. When she got inside Mario's house tonight, she would bug it, too.

"One for the inside of your house, and one for the outside," she said out loud, holding the small packages up in the air and studying the flat, round disks. Once she peeled off the small paper on the back side of each disk, there was a sticky substance that would allow her to leave it anywhere and keep it secure. "I'm going to know every time you take a shit, motherfucker."

The words were barely out of her mouth when a loud explosion rattled the small speaker on the black box.

"Holy crap!" Another booming sound came through the speaker. Angela swore it shook the box. "Somebody talk! What the hell just happened?"

Angela slid a flash drive into a USB port in the side of the black box where the file would be saved once the conversation ended. She actually loved her new toy. The little box enabled her to listen, record, then would automatically save the conversation and allow her to play it back at her leisure.

"Come on; come on," she muttered. "You don't explode like that without giving me some kind of doable explanation."

It sounded as if a car door opened and closed, then the engine roared, accelerating quickly. Angela wondered if a police scanner might be a good addition to her setup here. If Mario just blew something up, it would be nice to know if someone had witnessed it and if police were on their way. She couldn't set up too permanent a headquarters in her suite. This arrangement was temporary. Not that Mario would ever set foot inside her suite. All he needed to know was she stayed at the Drake hotel because she was a spoiled rich girl who'd rather live on the edge than with her annoying parents.

She forced her thoughts to quit meandering throughout her brain when there was a noticeable rustling sound. Angela leaned forward, resting her elbows on the table, and stared at the black box. Her insides constricted painfully when she heard laughter. The sound was demonic, almost bordering on insane.

"That was quite the show," Mario said, sounding incredibly happy. His voice was as clear as if he stood in the room with her. "It was almost as good as watching my sweet *puttana* tell those two dumb fucks to drive into the side of a building. God, that was classic. The stupid little bitch never batted an eye. No remorse or fear or concern. Nothing."

"You're so easily entertained," a woman said, laughing along with him. "Did you expect anything other than perfection out of my drug?"

"Your slave juice?"

" 'Juice' is such an inaccurate term, but it will work for the nonscientific brain," she said, sounding rather full of herself. "Get your board pieces warmed up on the stuff and, darling, they'll do absolutely anything you want them to do."

"Just like you?" Mario asked, his baritone a soft growl. "Or do I need to give you the drug, too?"

"You know, if you're very good I might show you how to make your army respond to your command with a remote control. You won't need to be anywhere near them."

Angela forced herself to breathe, realizing just then she gripped a ballpoint pen in her hand so tight her knuckles were white. She began scribbling notes on the margin of the instruction manual.

Need attack locations. Where are kidnapped victims? She tapped her pen on the paper, creating small dots around what she'd just written. Being artistic was never one of her strong points, but with a few more clues she would easily connect the dots. *Does slave juice have lasting side effects?* Angela wasn't sure what compelled her to write the question, but if she was to free the people Mario had kidnapped, understanding as much as possible about slave juice would be helpful.

Correction—*when* she freed the people Mario had kidnapped.

"I have a better idea." Mario's accent had thickened. "You

show me how good you are and maybe I'll consider letting you play with my army."

"Is your army all you want me to play with?"

Mario laughed, and the sound faded into a groan. Angela didn't need too much of an imagination to figure out what they were doing. Running her fingers through her hair, she lowered her head, closing her eyes once again and resting her forehead on her palms. There wasn't much to listen to now, an occasional moan and shuffling sounds. She didn't want them fucking. She wanted them giving her information. No matter how many times she did undercover work, patience wasn't one of her strong points.

Although sometimes pillow talk provided very important clues, so far all the two of them were doing was grunting.

"Time for that shower," Angela muttered, having no desire to listen to the asshole fuck. Anything they said would be recorded.

Angela pulled clean clothes from the closet where she'd unpacked and arranged them the day she'd checked in. After showering she planned on finding out what Jake King was doing in her hotel. Her tummy quickened as the image of him staring at her in the lobby filled her brain. Sexual tension had shot across that lobby, and it grew stronger by the moment.

"He is going to find you," she whispered, a mixture of excitement and nervous anticipation twisting her tummy into a fierce knot, when Mario and the woman started talking again.

"So, do we have an arrangement?" the woman asked.

"Is this how you seal all of your deals?" Mario's soft tone didn't sound amused or exhausted. He sounded crisp and all business.

"Not all of them." There was a short scuffling sound.

"All you've convinced me today is you give one mean blow job and know how to fuck in the back of a car better than a lot of sluts I've been with."

"Go to hell," the woman hissed, sounding pissed. "If you're going to win this goddamn game you're going to need an army larger than—"

"Don't tell me what I need to do to win the game," Mario roared, interrupting her and pounding against something that created an annoying scraping sound. "The other players don't stand a chance."

What Angela wouldn't do to learn who the rest of the players were in the game. Her heart pounded so hard in her chest she could barely breathe. Even slow, deep breaths didn't calm her down. She was so close to learning significant information about the game. Suddenly she needed to call her father again. There was so much to fill him in on.

"God forbid I tell you how to do anything." The woman was undaunted. "What I do know is you can increase the size of your army tenfold with my drug and control them easier than you are now."

My drug?

Angela froze, her jaw dropping as her heart quit beating. The woman in the car was Evelyn Van Cooper, the inventor of slave juice.

"Well, I'll be damned," Angela muttered, reaching for her phone to try her father again.

The hotel phone next to her bed started ringing.

"What the hell?" she gasped. That phone hadn't rung once since she'd arrived at the Drake. No one knew her room number other than her father, and he would reach her on her cell, not on the room phone.

She stared at the phone sitting next to her bed, watching the small red light glow as it rang a second time. Mario and Evelyn had quit talking. Angela hadn't heard car doors open and close, but the phone ringing might have distracted her.

Angela reached for the phone before it rang a third time. "Hello?"

"Come to room two-twelve."

"What?" Angela whispered, her heart beating harder than it was a few minutes ago. "Who is this?"

"Think back a year ago and I believe you'll remember," a man's voice said.

"What will I remember?" she asked, managing a softer tone and sitting on the edge of the bed. She straightened her legs, looking at her painted toenails as a fluttering began in her stomach and quickly swelled throughout her insides.

"Maybe that you don't really live in Aldea."

Angela smiled, remembering the line she'd told Jake about where she'd lived. A year ago in Mexico seemed like a different world, a different life. Yet she remembered the evening in that nightclub as if it were yesterday. Jake had taken her out to the dance floor and shown off moves that had her imagining he'd be one hell of a good lover. He'd also been very easy to talk to. Within a couple hours she felt as if she'd known him for years. Granted, he didn't know she was a private investigator. His attentiveness and probing nature, the way he watched her and asked questions, had her suspicious more than once that he might be on to her.

It was fairly late in the evening when she'd told him what she knew about Marty Byrd being in Aldea, a small village south of Tijuana. The local girl Angela had been out with that evening, who'd had drinks with her and Jake and his brother, needed to leave shortly after that. Angela had really wanted to stay but knew if she had, she and Jake would have fucked each other. Instead, she'd taken a cab, leaving Jake behind. Jake had taken the information she'd given him and destroyed all evidence of the game and killed Marty Byrd when they had worked with the FBI and blown up Byrd's mansion.

"Room two-twelve," he repeated.

The black box was quiet. Angela ran her fingers through her hair. There was no way she'd go see Jake without showering first.

"Give me half an hour," she said, then hung up before he could argue or, worse yet, hang up on her. Letting out a frustrated moan, Angela headed to the bathroom. Already the throbbing between her legs was growing damn hard to ignore. "Control, girl. Goddamn control or there is no way you can talk to him."

All she had to do was keep their conversation on business. There was plenty to discuss. She needed to let him know there was a mark on his head. Not to mention he was going to explain what he was doing here. They would catch up; then she'd head out for her evening date with Mario. Although the last thing she wanted to do was leave the exciting sexual tension that sizzled between her and Jake to go to a monster who would likely grope and humiliate her all evening long.

Her heart fluttered as she turned on the shower.

Chapter Three

Jake glanced up from the couch when someone knocked
gently on his hotel room door. She'd said half an hour, but it
had been forty-five minutes. Did Angela primp and prepare
herself to come see him?

He stood, stretched, then tugged his shirt and smoothed
it out as he headed to the door. Patting his gun, which he'd
tucked into the back of his jeans, he leaned forward and
looked through the peek hole. He stared at Angela's profile,
distorted through the small circular glass. She looked both
ways up and down the hallway as if the chance existed she
might be followed. It was one of the negative aspects of their
line of work: having to be more cautious than most.

He unlocked and turned the handle, then opened the hotel room door. Angela Huxtable stared up at him with defi-
ant green eyes. Her long, thick black hair was damp and the
light reflected in it. He breathed in a hint of roses. Angela
had showered and cleaned up before coming to see him.
Something tightened inside him, and not just his dick. It
wasn't a familiar sensation, but he wasn't staring at just another pretty lady. Something about Angela made her stand
out, caused her beauty to be more unique and compelling,
and created a radiant glow around her that worked like a

magnet in drawing him to her. It also had had the strength to keep her in his thoughts for a year.

Angela entered his suite without a word, managing not to touch him as she glided past where he stood, holding the door. She paused in the middle of his room and turned to face him, not bothering to check out her surroundings but instantly snaring him with a hot and determined stare.

"Come on in," he drawled, taking his time closing the door and securing the dead bolt.

"What are you doing here, Jake?"

"Your dad didn't tell you? He hired me. I'm your backup, darling," he informed her, and enjoyed the hell out of her stunned expression. He took advantage of her shock to move closer. "Your father flew out to L.A. and personally hired me to help you out with the game," he added, lowering his voice as he studied her thick black hair.

It fell to the middle of her back, and the sleeveless pink blouse she wore helped offset its color. Her tan skin, green eyes, and slender figure with curves in all the right places made her a vision of beauty. But the hard, focused glare she gave him, beaming with intelligence and her willful nature, created an image of perfection he ached to know better—a lot better.

Angela didn't balk when he stopped close enough to reach out and grab a strand of her hair.

"My father hired you?" She didn't change her pose but continued staring at him, hands on her hips as she pressed her lips together in a thin line.

Jake let go of her hair and tried gripping her shoulders. Angela turned, walking to the window that faced the street below.

"Sit, Angela," he suggested, pulling out the chair he was going to guide her into before she slipped out of his grasp. "Bring me up to speed on what you've been doing here."

Angela wore blue-jean shorts that hugged her tight, round ass and ended just as that perfect curve met her leg. It was one of his favorite parts of a woman's body, the tender flesh on the backside and inner thighs, right at the top of her legs. They were legs he bet would squeeze the life out of a man as she came. He might have to fuck her just so he could work with her. Just standing in the same room, watching her ass in those short shorts, was proving to be one hell of a distraction.

She turned, staring warily at the chair he'd pulled out from the desk. "You sit," she instructed, her voice clipped. She continued flexing her hands into fists, then relaxing them.

Angela no longer looked him in the face. Her gaze would slip down his body; then as soon as he focused on her, she'd shoot her attention across the room. As if he wouldn't notice her checking him out. Hell, he would know how closely she scrutinized him with his eyes closed. The charge of energy in the air hadn't been there before she'd entered his suite.

Jake had guessed it when he'd captured her attention in the lobby. Neither of them had expected to see the other at that moment. What they got from each other wasn't guarded or covered up but raw, unleashed carnal desire. Sexual tension between two people wasn't usually so strong it charged the air between them at such a distance. Now, however, with not even a few paces between them, and the smell of her perfume and clean body wrapping around him and proving to be the strongest aphrodisiac he'd ever experienced, it was nice knowing he didn't suffer alone. Angela was fighting to maintain control.

"I don't mind sitting." Jake relaxed in the chair, straightening his legs, as he crossed one socked foot over the other. He would put her at ease, although he seriously doubted he'd be able to relieve the sexual tension. Jake wasn't a rapist, though. Not that she appeared overly worried about him attacking her. She put on a show of being pissed but Angela wanted to fuck him.

"My father made a mistake," she said flatly. "We can't work together, Jake."

He held her stare captive, probing into her milky green eyes, seeing emotions tumble over one another behind her mask of determination. It was on the tip of his tongue to ask why, but he wouldn't insult her. The reason why was incredibly obvious. It was charging the entire damned room and making his cock ache to stretch and swell.

"I think we can make it work." He spoke slowly, still staring into her eyes.

When she inhaled, the bra underneath her sleeveless sweater pressed against her breasts. Her V-neck collar allowed a glimpse of her cleavage. He let his attention drop to the view. Her skin color was as appealing as the rest of her, tanned but not quite caramel. She wasn't dressed to show off her features, but nonetheless they were easy to notice. It would be damn hard for Angela to be completely inconspicuous.

"We'll see." She took her time looking away from him. Angela wasn't shy. Her straightforwardness was as appealing as her bedroom eyes and every last soft curve on her incredibly enticing body. "First things first." She walked behind his chair, then came around him on the other side. "You're going to tell me what my father said you'd be doing while you're here. And know, whatever it was, I'm in charge here. This is my case."

Jake dropped his attention to the slender curves that sloped into her narrow waist. "Bossy bitch," he grumbled, and fought a smile when her jaw dropped.

"How dare you," she hissed. "Good grief!" She threw her hands in the air and spun around, causing her thick, long hair to fan across her back. "I knew it. This isn't going to work. There's no point in even trying. I'll explain to my dad. I don't need, or want, the type of backup you would offer. I need someone capable of focusing only on the case. I seriously doubt you'd be able to do that."

"The type of backup I would offer?" Jake understood her meaning. "This is your show, sweetheart. I'll do what you want." And he'd protect her. Again, he wouldn't insult her by stating the obvious. Angela knew he'd guard her with his life, as her dad had obviously known as well. Jake held his arms out, palms up, as he looked up at her, keeping his expression relaxed. "I'm offering my services. Use me as you see fit."

"I know damn good and well what you're offering," she sneered.

Jake watched her, deciding he would let her form her own conclusions and not sway them with responses she would choose to believe, or not, no matter how truthful they might be. And the facts were, if she didn't want to fuck him, he wouldn't press the matter. That had never been his style. Jake knew women, though. Angela was making a scene to cover up her own desires. Raging need damn near burned her alive. He saw the flush slowly spread across her face as she shot him fiery glances.

"Are you going to deny you're undressing me with your eyes?" She stopped in front of him, pressing her hands into her hips, and glared at him.

If he stood, he'd be head and shoulders taller than Angela. She was already on the defensive and he wasn't going to push her into a corner. So instead, checking his slight irritation, he stretched out his legs, forcing her to jump to the side so she wouldn't trip over them.

"You say I'm hands-on. I'm sure you know all there is to know about me, darling." He didn't speak too slowly, kept his voice flat, and only stared at her face as he spoke. Already, from what he knew of this case, Angela needed him. Jake doubted her father would be able to handle things if they got messy. Possibly Huxtable had reasoned that one out already. "According to your father, you were very aware of me, and my reputation, when we danced the night away in Tijuana."

"I gave you critical information and you proceeded to blow all evidence to hell and back," she accused.

"The FBI blew our evidence up, sweetheart. Our hands were rather tied with that matter." Jake had been falsely accused of worse. He smiled. "I'm sure if your father were kidnapped by an assassin you would have done the same."

She stared at him, her expression remaining chilled and tense. "And if things get out of control here, would you call the FBI once again?"

Jake stood, forgetting his effort to help Angela relax. She tilted her head back, staring up at him when he spoke.

"If a madman who prefers his women doped up on slave juice captured you, put your life in serious danger, and I wasn't able to get you out, you're damn fucking straight I would call in whatever authorities could help."

She searched his face, pressing her lips into an adorable pout before slowly looking down. Her gaze traveled down his chest and fire erupted inside him. She'd just pissed him off and he still wanted her. Angela might be right. Maybe they shouldn't work together.

"I heard your father was abducted in Mexico, but rumors suggest he allowed himself to be captured to get on the inside." She began pacing the length of the hotel room and continued shooting Jake hesitant looks. "That's what I've done, Jake. I'm on the inside, but not at the risk of slave juice being stabbed into my arm."

"Because you're getting cozy with some Italian warlord you think you're exempt from his slave juice?" he snapped. Jake was having trouble keeping his emotions in check around her, which bugged him.

"I don't know what you know about Mario Mandela, but let me tell you, he's not an idiot. Right now, my cover is secure. Mario knows I'm high profile because of the circles he believes I move in. He is under the impression my schedule is very full and I'm often in the public eye. If I strayed from my hectic schedule for even an hour, I would be missed. He won't risk the game and all it means to him just for me. Women don't mean that much to him. He is smart, though, and I'm covering my ass."

"I'm going to help cover that ass of yours."

When she tilted her head slightly and pierced him with those sexy eyes of hers, several strands of hair fell over her shoulder and drifted across her arm and breast. "I'm not sure you're the best man for the job," she mused, her voice suddenly soft-spoken, as if she was contemplating something pleasant, instead of deciding if she could handle having him up close and personal without getting too close.

"Why would your father think otherwise?" Jake asked. His fingers itched to pet her thick, black hair. It would be so smooth and silky. Her probing stare captivated him just as much as the rest of her did. When Angela met his gaze, staring hard and straight into his eyes, it was as if she saw past the surface and analyzed and discovered everything about him. As unnerving as the thought was that she might be able to see more of him than he wanted her to see, at the same time it was somehow erotic that Angela wanted to dig and learn more about him.

"I'm not sure." Her hard lines of anger began fading. "Sounds like he and I need to talk about this."

"Tell me about Mario." Jake wanted her talking, opening up to him. They weren't going to throw in the towel on this case over sexual desires. He was starting to think wanting each other might make them a good team. "How close have you gotten to him?"

"He took me shopping today." She looked mighty proud of herself.

"You move fast, sweetheart," Jake drawled. "When did you two meet for the first time?"

Her grin was wicked. "We met over the weekend at his private club I managed to get myself into, then seated myself conveniently under his nose."

"Sounds like I missed the good stuff."

"There isn't any good stuff with this case," she added quickly, her smile fading. "I'm under the impression he wasn't in town prior to that. I've overheard several of his phone calls, and although he was vague, I think he just arrived in Chicago. I wouldn't be surprised if he's been gathering his army." Her voice trailed off.

Jake got her meaning, though. Mandela was kidnapping people, just as his parents had been kidnapped earlier that year. Right before coming here, he and his cousin, Natasha, had learned that the drug Evelyn Van Cooper had developed, and used on his family when they had been in Arizona, was now being called slave juice. It wouldn't surprise him if Mandela might be using that drug, too.

"So tell me about Mario Mandela. What makes the man tick?" It bugged him that Angela was able to overhear Mandela's phone conversations. It had been his experience that when a perp let someone get close, they had ulterior motives. He kept his thoughts to himself for now, wanting to hear all Angela knew before drawing any hard conclusions.

"He's an evil bastard." She shivered and hugged herself, wrinkling her nose as she shook her head. "I've never been this close to someone so evil, so heartless, and so sure of themselves that they are doing the right thing. He has no conscience."

"He couldn't to be part of the game."

"Point taken," she said easily, shaking her finger at Jake. "I have successfully bugged the back of his limousine."

Jake was impressed. When she studied his face for a moment, then grinned, her expression lit up. "I've already got track running upstairs in my room," she offered, looking really proud of herself.

"You've got the ball rolling beautifully, darling," he praised her. "I'm seriously impressed."

Angela must have realized she'd relaxed too much, was actually enjoying having a conversation with him, and apparently decided she wasn't ready to let her guard down with him yet. That warm look disappeared and she pressed her lips together.

Angela stared at Jake, not saying a word. She took him in from head to toe. He was acutely aware of wherever she looked. When she lifted her attention to his face he swore he witnessed her mind switch gears.

"I'm going to head upstairs to talk to my dad," she announced, starting toward the door. "Mario is supposed to send his car for me early this evening. I'll be in contact with you before I leave and let you know what we've decided at that time."

"You aren't leaving yet." Jake was right behind her, reaching for her and dragging his fingers down her smooth, thick hair before she spun around, yanking the strands from his fingers.

"Rule number one is this is my case. You answer to me, not the other way around. I give the orders." She held her index finger up toward his face and straightened to her full height, which was probably somewhere around five and a half feet tall. "That is, if I decide we can work together. For now, I'm going to my room to call my father." When she took a step backward her hands were facing Jake, palms out, as if she were warding off some dangerous animal. "You aren't going to stop me and you aren't going to touch me."

"I'm not the bad guy here, Angela," he said, holding his own hands out in a gesture of surrender. He had no problem with Angela running the show. If she remained this skittish, though, he would have to work even harder to protect her.

When she let out a loud breath her body deflated. "You're right. I'm sorry. This case means a lot to me. I've come so far on it. And I'm really curious why Dad doesn't want to do backup and asked you instead," she mumbled, pushing hair behind her shoulder.

"Because of his missing-person case."

"I'm curious to find out what case could be more important than this."

"How often do you two discuss each other's cases?" Jake didn't know Huxtable and his daughter's relationship well enough to know whether he'd tell her everything or not. Angela's tone suggested she believed she knew about every case he had, though.

Angela tugged at her sleeveless sweater, stretching the knitted material over her breasts, then crossed her arms, showing off her cleavage as she leaned against the door instead of opening it.

"Lately all we've talked about is this case." She dropped her attention to her hands, unfolding her arms and staring at her fingernails, which were nicely filed and painted a bright pink. "I guess he could be working other cases right now without me knowing it." She didn't look up when she tucked her hair behind her ear. "I'm used to knowing everything he does, though," she added, sighing and shaking her head.

Jake sensed her sincerity. Angela was proud of her father, loved him, and more than likely believed she took care of him. Huxtable might be a hard-ass, but he wouldn't weigh her shoulders down with anything else while she worked this case. That meant he loved his daughter as much as she loved him. Maybe it was that tight bond that had sent him flying out to California, stuffing his pride the best he could and asking for help on his daughter's behalf, because he knew she was going in way over her head.

"What are your plans tonight?" Jake asked.

"To end the game," she said without hesitating.

"Nothing wrong with optimism." He noticed her hand on the doorknob again, but she wasn't turning it. He really didn't want her leaving. If she did, he'd probably boot up his laptop and start researching her. It would be a lot easier, and more enjoyable, learning about Angela from Angela. "Call your dad here," Jake decided, moving into her space and taking her hand off his doorknob. "It would be a good idea to hear your debriefing. I need to be brought up to speed on everything."

Her hand was soft, her fingers long, slender, and warm. Jake gripped her smaller hand in his, turning her as he did, and guided her back into his suite. When he ran his fingers down her back, he swore she shivered. Her silky black hair was thick, very straight, and had an enticing aroma to it he'd love to breathe in deeper, filling his lungs with it. Holding her hand and escorting her, his fingers and palm barely moving across her slender, perfectly arched back, damn near hardened every inch of him to stone. Jake needed to figure out how to work with this woman without sporting a hard-on every time he got close enough to smell her, feel the sexually charged energy she emanated, or touch her. Maybe it was the Chicago humidity affecting him. Jake didn't lose control around women, no matter how hot they were.

Angela slid her hand out of his when she once again stood near the chair where he'd sat. She stared at her hands, rubbing them together. Jake wondered if he affected her the way she did him. That was one hell of a scary thought. If it was the case, knowing each of them was defenseless around the other would either prove incredibly deadly or wear both of them out trying to fight it.

"And if you're in charge," he added, trying to relax her, especially if she was fighting to douse the fire burning alive inside her, "you're going to have to tell me what you want me to do."

"You're right." Angela glanced at him and her flushed cheeks were incredibly noticeable with her long black hair bordering her face. "I'll call Dad first, but stay quiet while I talk to him."

Jake gave her a salute, which she either didn't catch or ignored. Her expression remained serious, almost preoccupied, when she pulled one of the chairs out from under the round table near his windows. He sat facing her. When he stretched his legs under the table, he brushed his ankles against her smooth, warm skin. She sucked in a quick hiss but still didn't look at him. Instead she focused on her phone, scrolled down, placed her call, then put it to her ear. She was definitely fighting to ignore him.

Which proved to him Angela was as affected by his presence as he was by hers. Although Jake knew she would suffer along with him, somehow knowing this didn't boost his ego the way it usually did when he learned of a pretty lady drooling after him. He could speculate on the reasons or simply accept that nothing was the same with Angela as it was with any other woman he'd ever met or spent time with before.

"Hi, Dad," Angela said, her entire face lighting up as she leaned back in her chair. "How's your day going?"

Jake listened to father and daughter chat idly, playing catch-up. He saw a tight connection between the two of them, concern, love, and friendship. He also saw a new side to Angela. For a minute or two, she appeared to forget Jake sat facing her, watching her. Everything about her transformed, her pretty eyes glowing, her laughter melodic. He wouldn't have believed it possible for his insides to twist with even more turmoil and sexual energy so raw, not intimidated, and damn near unleashed, as if what he felt was right and even approved of by some unknown authority.

Angela looked up at him, shoving hair behind her shoulder

as her expression sobered. "He's sitting right across from me," she said, her voice still light, although that wary look was back in her eyes. "Why didn't you tell me you flew out to California? What if I'd needed backup?"

Angela nodded at whatever her father said. "True," she said. "You're right and you know I discuss every movement. How could you run backup otherwise? We didn't know for sure it would be quiet. You can't leave town again, though. Are we clear?" Angela smiled as her father probably sounded appropriately chastised. "And why do you have to take a missing persons case right now?"

Angela dragged her fingers through her hair as she listened to her father's explanation. "So what is the case?" she asked, resting her head on her hand and staring at the table.

"You're right," she agreed quietly, then after another moment stiffened, her expression tightening. "I just agreed with you, didn't I?" she argued. "And you know I can stay focused. I only asked about your case so I would know what you're doing."

Huxtable's voice was suddenly louder through the phone. Jake heard his name but didn't catch what was said. Angela had her phone pressed firmly against her ear, blocking his ability to hear most of what Huxtable said.

"Nothing will distract me from this case, except maybe not knowing what you're doing." She stressed every word. "Tell me about your case."

There was another brief pause as she listened to whatever her father was saying.

"We haven't discussed much yet," she explained, speaking faster now. "I'm going to bring him up to speed."

Apparently Angela decided not to argue against Jake working with her.

"I'm fine. . . . Yes, it's fine. Don't worry," she urged, her voice softening as she displayed her nurturing side. There wasn't a side to her that didn't make her glow and draw her sensuality closer to the surface.

"Dad," she breathed, sighing. "You know I'm going to worry more if I know you're working a case and don't want to talk to me about it." Her smile looked strained, and although she looked in Jake's direction, Angela wasn't focusing on him. He'd lost out to her father. "Yes, this is a strenuous case. You know I wouldn't argue that. It doesn't mean I'm incapable of being there for you. Why don't you want to tell me about it?"

Jake suddenly pictured his home and no one ever being able to pull off something on someone else or hold on to a secret for too long or try doing anything behind the rest of the family's back. Sometimes living with a houseful of investigators and bounty hunters was a royal pain in the ass. Jake managed not to grin when Angela's frustration became apparent.

"I'll call you later tonight before I go to bed," she said, her tone short. "I love you, too, Dad."

Angela stared at her phone, which she flipped around in her fingers, after hanging up. "Why would he not want to discuss his case with me?" she asked, still staring at her phone.

Jake wasn't sure. "You always know the cases he's working?"

"I'm the one who accepts or declines the cases he works."

There was definitely a controlling side to Angela. Even as Jake assured himself any trait like that in a woman would make him nuts, he couldn't look away when Angela looked to him for understanding.

"I can focus on this case just fine and also know the details of his case." She stood and walked away from the table. "Unless he thinks I would worry about whoever the person is who is missing," she said, snapping her fingers and marching back to the table and reaching for her phone.

"You know quite often in missing persons cases the person isn't really missing." Jake remained seated but eased his chair back enough to comfortably stretch out and cross his arms over his chest.

"Calling him back won't do any good. He'll point out I'm already not focused on plotting out my next move."

Jake had considered pointing that out and was glad she'd

figured it out herself. She picked up her phone and shoved it in her back shorts pocket. "I'm headed to my room."

Jake hurried after her when she did a quick march to his hotel room door. "I thought we were brainstorming, plotting. I need to know every development and where you plan to head with what you know so far." When he grabbed her arm he swore his world shifted. Everything inside him once again hardened, creating a steel barrier he wanted to pull her behind with him. It was a protective instinct, so strong and overbearing for a moment he couldn't move.

Angela didn't say a word but stilled. It took her a moment before she lowered her attention to where he held on to her. He swore he heard her mumble under her breath, "This isn't going to work."

"What?" he asked.

"Nothing." She pulled her arm free, then rubbed where he'd touched her. "Fine. Fine," she repeated, looking more nervous than a cat cornered and fearing capture when he remained where he was, trapping her between his body and the door. "I'm sure Dad told you everything when he hired you, but I'll go over what we know and where we are right now," she began, speaking quickly.

"Why does your father think you can't stay focused on this case if you know about his?"

"I'm focused." She pinned Jake with her captivating green eyes, as if proving her fact. "Are you?" she asked, her voice dropping a notch.

If she suddenly looked so captivating intentionally, as if determined to show him up, he couldn't be certain.

"What exactly does your father know about me?" he asked, holding his ground and her gaze.

"He knows about KFA."

"How do you know? The two of you discussed bringing me on board before your dad flew out to L.A.?" he asked.

Before he finished with his question Angela was shaking her head. "I had no idea he was pulling in new backup," she stressed.

He believed her. Angela relaxed, sensing he accepted what she said as the truth. She started around him. Jake grabbed her other arm, this time tugging enough to force her closer to him.

"What have you told him about me?" Suddenly he understood. Angela had shared what had happened, or, possibly better yet, what she wished might have happened with her father after she spent the evening with Jake in Mexico.

Angela looked surprised only for a moment before her mouth straightened into a thin line and the smoldering glow in her eyes changed when she narrowed them and glared at him. "I honestly don't remember if we discussed you at all," she said coolly. "Why does it matter?"

When she tried pulling her arm free, Jake didn't tighten his grip but instead yanked hard enough to make her stumble against him.

"Because, Angela," he said, his voice turning husky when he looked down at her and breathed in the enticing scent of her shampoo, "your father is concerned about your ability to focus. I seriously doubt a detective with his solid reputation would allow his daughter to take on a case of this magnitude if he didn't believe you were incredibly qualified to do so."

Angela didn't move, nor did she try looking up at Jake. He had an eyeful of incredibly shiny, satiny black hair traveling smoothly over her slender shoulders and draping over her back to her ass. He held her arm, feeling her solid pulse thump repeatedly against his fingers. She knew where he was going with this. Jake wished he knew how she'd react once he said it.

"That leads me to think you're usually quite focused. But for some reason, right now you aren't. Would you care garnering a wage as to why that is?" He put the question out there and waited.

Angela didn't move. "My father said if he started discussing his missing persons case with me, I would lose focus here but you have no idea how focused I am right now," she finally said, her tone sharp yet soft-spoken. The amount of control she exerted at that moment dripped in every syllable out of her mouth.

Jake shouldn't push it. Where would it lead them? He was here to work a case with her, an incredibly dangerous case where many would die if he and Angela treaded just slightly in the wrong direction.

He had to know. If he didn't push her, his concentration would be shot to hell with just the wondering of what might happen. This way at least both of them would place their limitations out on the table.

"How much did you tell your father about our might in Tijuana?" he asked. This time he adjusted her stance, taking both her arms and moving her so she faced him.

"You are so arrogant. There wasn't much to tell."

Angela fought for a second when he pressed his fingers under her chin, encouraging her to tilt her head and look at him. "I'm sure KFA's reputation wouldn't be what it is if one of you were completely incompetent," she murmured, then pursed her lips together as if she would kiss him. Her green eyes were bright. She was challenging his work and his nature.

"Did you tell him how it felt dancing with me all evening?" he asked.

His reputation was sound. Obviously Angela was a control freak and she might think she could keep him in line if she knocked him down a few notches. Jake could take orders just fine but sparring with him would result in only one thing. He had no problem showing her how competent he was.

"You're right. It wouldn't be," he said and brushed his fingertips down her cheek. "So you told your father we had a couple dances and that was it?"

Angela jerked backward, banging her backside against the door. When she instinctively moved forward, Jake captured her in his arms, pinning her against him. He ran his hand down her hair, feeling her shoulder blades stiffen when she looked up at him of her own accord.

"Why are you doing this?" she demanded, her tone not

quite shrill but, along with her expression, proof her frustration grew in leaps and bounds. "I swear, Jake. You're the one who can't focus."

Jake thought she'd push against his chest, demand her freedom. He hadn't decided whether he'd give it to her or not when instead of shoving against him, she gripped his shoulders. Suddenly Angela was stretched against him, her head tilted, her long, thick lashes fluttering over her smoldering gaze. When she licked her lips, moistened, then parted them, something clicked inside him. Angela stretched further, her lashes lowering, her lips still parted, as her fingers slid up his shoulders to the sides of his head.

She drew him to her, initiating the kiss without another word. Jake lowered his head, his attention on her mouth as he slid his hands into her hair, tangling the thick, smooth strands around his fingers.

"I told him everything," Angela whispered just as Jake's mouth captured hers.

Her lips remained parted and Jake eased inside her when he kissed her. The heat that greeted him damn near made him teeter with need. It was something he'd wished he'd done a year ago and gone back and forth on over the months after parting ways with her. If he'd known what she'd tasted like that night a year ago, he might not have let her go. Now, feeling her moist, soft lips open further for him and her nimble tongue willingly swirl in a dance of lust around his, Jake understood why the attraction between the two of them had been so noticeably intense.

He gripped her hips, pulling her closer while lowering his head and feasting on her mouth. She was soft yet firm. Her breasts pressed against his chest and he ached to cup them in his hands, feel how hard her nipples were.

God damn! Ripping her clothes off her and enjoying every inch of her hot, sultry body suddenly seemed the logical next step.

Angela's fingers moved over his arms to his chest. When he guessed she might try pushing away from him, he brought one hand to the middle of her back, pressing her even closer.

She arched into him, stretching her fingers over his taut skin. Her gentle touch, exploring and inquisitive, sent fire searing through his insides. Maybe it had been a while since he'd taken time to enjoy the erotic touch of a lady, but nothing any of the women he knew came close to matching how incredibly hot Angela was. And all they were doing was kissing.

She balled her hands into fists, still pressing them against his chest. Jake decided to end the kiss, allowing him the upper hand, before she gathered enough strength to push him away and claim she didn't want him. He wasn't sure he could handle her lie and was sure they would be the first words out of her mouth.

He nipped her lower lip before straightening and enjoyed her gasps as well as her lashes' fluttering open as she took a moment to focus on his face.

"I'm not going to fuck you," she whispered, her voice scratchy.

"I know," he said, and stroked the side of her head. Her hair was as smooth and silky as he had imagined and the picture of it falling down her naked body as she rode them both into explosive orgasms wasn't a vision he wanted to let go of.

"No. I don't think you do." She blinked, making no effort to back out of his arms but staring up at him as her thick, black lashes hooded her gaze. "You think I would lie and say that, blaming you for kissing me, and storm out of here. That isn't what I meant. I'm not a liar. I know you can't wait to fuck me and I admit I've been intrigued since I met you a year ago. But we're not going to have sex, Jake."

He easily could have gotten hung up on her saying she'd been intrigued since first meeting him. It was something about her relaxed expression and the way she spoke softly, as if the guard he'd ached to force her to let down was finally gone. She sighed when he ran his hand down her hair again. There was more and he wanted to hear her mind. Resting his hands on her shoulders, he held on to her gaze when she licked her lips and studied him.

"I can't be seen with you. You're a King. Mario Mandela knows who you are."

It wouldn't be the first time he'd hunted a criminal who knew too much about Jake. It was the price of his family's success. He wasn't so cocky as to not see he hadn't earned that type of reputation on his own.

"Who I am isn't going to change." Jake let go of her and walked into the middle of his suite, then crossed his arms and stared at her. "We aren't going to solve this case arguing over issues having nothing to do with Mandela."

"Which is exactly why I worry we aren't a good match to work on a case together."

"Because we want to fuck each other?" he asked softly.

She stared at him. "You're blunt, but okay. Yes. And I can't risk anything distracting me from this case."

"Do you know what the difference between a bounty hunter and a private investigator is?"

He loved her smile. It was more than just the curve of her full, moist red lips. Her entire face transformed when she grinned. Her eyes flashed, showing her amusement, and she tilted her head just a bit to the right, flashing her white teeth.

"Now you're redirecting." Her grin didn't fade. "What's the difference?" she asked.

"When a private investigator is on your tail, you know it. You see him, or her," Jake added, and watched her tongue dart over her lips. "A good PI knows how to build the trepidation, make their target sweat. That target will know in their heart the moment they slip up, they're snagged."

"And let me guess." She laughed and walked toward Jake. She tapped her finger against her cheek, more than likely trying to be serious when she obviously found him amusing. "A good bounty hunter is never seen."

She got close enough that Jake tapped her nose with his finger. "You're right, sweetheart."

Angela nodded and turned away from him. "That isn't going to cut it, Jake."

Snaking his hands around her waist, he pulled her back against him. Her smooth, round ass snuggled against him.

Blood drained from his brain, making him light-headed. Jake fought the urges inside him, using more strength to control getting hard when that hot little ass of hers continued moving against him. But he would make his point, and to do so he couldn't let her see how greatly she affected him.

"It's more than not being seen, my dear," he whispered, lowering his head and breathing in the perfumed scent in her hair. It smelled like coconut, but there was a lingering aroma as well that reminded him of roses. He imagined every inch of her smelled like that and fought an overwhelming desire to do whatever it took to find out if it did.

Jake pressed his lips against the side of her neck. Angela sucked in a sharp breath, and when he nipped at her warm flesh she gasped. He wondered how strong her reserve actually was with her insistence that nothing happen between them.

"You'll think I'm gone," he continued, straightening so he wouldn't be dragging her intoxicating scent into his lungs with every breath. "No matter how hard you search for me, you won't find me. You won't see me. But believe me, the moment you're in any kind of trouble you'll feel my arms around you like they are right now, pulling you to safety."

Chapter Four

It was almost weird how a man who stood so tall, with more brawn and sex appeal than should be legal, could appear so compassionate and concerned. It was damn unnerving. If Angela didn't know better, she'd swear Jake King was worried about her. Reminding herself of what she already knew about him, of his infamous reputation as being a player, as well as her dad's advice that a man like Jake would need a very tight leash in order to obey, Angela assured herself Jake was simply being himself, playing the field with the lady nearest him in his arms.

But there wasn't time to worry about that when her legs were suddenly as stable as wet noodles. She needed to get the hell out of there, but her body didn't want to cooperate. The most gorgeous man she'd ever laid eyes on had his hands on her, cradling her against him as if she meant more to him than anyone else in the world. If she couldn't think clearly when standing this close to Jake she was in serious trouble. There was no way they could work together. She'd miss every available clue.

He might be trying to convince her they'd never see each other, but she knew better. When they weren't in the field they'd be brainstorming—together. She knew as well, as any good detective would that without a solid plan, carefully thought out and every angle explored, solving a case could be damn impossible to do.

Which made all of this seriously suck. She would definitely have some words for her father once she could speak to him alone. All she wanted to do was grab Jake's massive arms and push him toward his bed. Exploring every inch of his perfect body sounded better than walking out of his room.

God! She was in serious trouble.

It was imperative she get Jake out of her system. And it was terrifying that in a matter of minutes he'd put her in this state of mind. He did the same thing to her a year ago, seducing her into lowering her guard until she was babbling out all the information she could think of to help him when he didn't even know that was what she was doing. It was disgusting.

Angela took a step backward and Jake let his hands fall to his sides. When she faced him her insides were so swollen with need she could hardly think what to say. The longer she remained here, the more the need would grow. It was a craving for something she'd never had before, yet there was knowledge inside her that without any doubt it was exactly what she needed.

"I can see your hunger."

Angela blinked, realized she'd practically been drooling while staring at the well-defined bulging muscle underneath his T-shirt. She snapped her attention to his face. "Go to hell, Jake."

"It's like seeing my own emotions in a mirror."

He was fighting off a grin, the bastard. Like she would stand there and amuse him just because he liked the idea of them being hot for each other. Angela needed to remind herself how many women he'd probably used that line on in the past.

That was it. Maybe if he kept talking like a pompous ass it would piss her off and turn her off. She dwelt on anger, forcing it to surface. It was the only way she'd walk out of there with any dignity.

"At the rate you're going, I doubt you ever see any of you inside me." The moment the words were out of her mouth, she regretted them.

Something darkened in his gaze. "Keep standing there and I will definitely see me inside you," he whispered, his tone dangerous.

The heat that swelled inside her was unbearable. "I see how it is." Angela shook her head, praying she appeared disappointed. "Looks seriously are deceiving. You're so strong and incredibly tall, but the truth is you're weak." She dared lifting her gaze to his face. Butterflies fluttered frantically as she stared into smoldering domination. No way he'd see her sweat, though. "The only way you can meet my terms is to insult me, so I'll storm out and leave you alone."

Jake cleared the distance between them too fast for her to react. Grabbing under her arms, he lifted Angela off her feet, holding her in midair so they stared into each other's eyes.

"I never said I planned on meeting your terms, sweetheart," he informed her. "You're hoping if you get pissed off it will soothe the fire that has already ignited between us." Jake lifted her an inch higher as if she were light as air. His thumbs pressed against the bottom of her breasts, torturing her even further. "I'm here to tell you it's not going to work."

"Put me down." She hated the pleading sound in her voice.

Jake lowered her until her feet were once again on the floor. He didn't let her go, though, and she hated thinking if he had she might have teetered backward. When his large hand gripped her jaw and fingers inched their way around her neck, it was as if he paralyzed her. Angela stared as his face moved closer to hers.

"You want me," he breathed, his coarse tone scraping over her already-too-sensitive nerves. "We aren't going to argue that anymore. But also, both of us want the game ended. We're going to work together, use our strength and knowledge as the professionals that we are, and end the game once and for all. And sweetheart, once this case is solved, I plan on enjoying every tantalizing inch of you."

Angela grabbed his wrist, which was so thick she barely

wrapped her fingers halfway around it. She sucked in a breath, blowing it out and reminding herself what she was doing here in the first place.

"That's enough, Jake," she said, her solid tone and conviction enough to douse the sizzling lust that had made the air thick. "I know about your playboy ways. Your reputation as a player might be as strong and solid as that of a bounty hunter. Obviously flirting and seducing women is such a part of your nature you might not be able to help yourself. And possibly that is the reason why you fucked up in Mexico."

"I didn't fuck anything up," he retorted, his voice suddenly so thick and dark it was impossible not to look at him. "And where have you heard about me? Because, sweetheart, if you're prone to listening to gossip, keep in mind over half of it is always wrong."

Angela swore she was working more undercover right now, fighting to keep her feelings and emotions under lock and key, than when she'd been with Mario and faked enjoying his attention.

"You're more intent on getting in my pants than you are on working this case." She walked out of his hands' reach, plotting her choice of words. If she left he might sense a victory. It was best to make sure he understood every rule. She needed to spell it out clearly so the gorgeous hunk staring at her would turn off his seduction skills when they were together. "I'm going to put everything in perspective for you." She straightened, clasped her hands in front of her, and stared him down, determined to see him simply as a tool to help solve this case and nothing else. "All you are to me is solid backup. Nothing else matters but this case. Do you understand me? Nothing."

The blank look he gave her in return did a weird number to her insides. Angela forced herself to stay on track. Now wasn't the time to dwell on any type of emotion, good or bad. Angela marched over to the door, this time determined not to look at him but to leave, head upstairs, calm down, and call her father back.

"Do you think I don't know why you've gone undercover?"

Jake used a tone she hadn't heard out of him before. It was deadly sounding, bone-chilling, and sent a rush of trepidation prickling over her flesh. "I already know about your case and why you're staying here, in this extravagant hotel, instead of at the small house you own."

She stopped in her tracks, forcing herself not to turn around.

"You're seducing Mario Mandela, working to get him comfortable around you, so you can take him down." Jake was moving, closing in on her. Every tiny hair on her backside stood at attention, as if the sexual charges radiating off his body created some kind of electrical response inside her. When he continued speaking, his voice was just above her ear. "You're calling me a player, a seducer, someone who isn't concerned with anyone's feelings but only interested in getting himself off. Well, lady, that isn't how it is. If all I wanted was to fuck you, I would have simply asked if you wanted to fuck. I'm not trying to trick you into thinking all I want is a piece of ass while I'm here."

"Don't even suggest I spend my time trying to manipulate and seduce men," she hissed. "Mandela is one of the lowest forms of life and I will do anything to take him down." She wouldn't fuck the bastard, though.

Jake moved closer to her. "And it might require anything to take him down," he said, his baritone deepening and sending chills rushing over her flesh. "You're a detective moving into waters so dangerous you very well might not make it out alive."

"You think I don't realize how dangerous this job is?" she whispered, staring at the door handle in front of her when she wanted to turn around and give him a piece of her mind.

"You're not going to do this alone."

"I never said I was. I thought I was working the case with my father."

Jake's phone buzzed and he moved away from her. Angela prayed he didn't see her sigh with relief and her body sag. She reached for the door handle, turned it, and pulled the door open. The door didn't have time to close behind her when Jake grabbed it and stepped outside his room.

"Angela," he said, making her name sound more like a demand.

She waved over her shoulder, refusing to look at him and damned if she'd run to the elevator. "I'll talk to you soon," she said, and pushed the button for the elevator.

His heavy footsteps sounded in the hall. Dammit! Would he seriously follow her to her room?

"That was a short call," she said, knowing she was snapping at him when he reached her side.

"I need your cell number and room number." Jake wouldn't give her the chance to claim not to have anything to write with or on. He shoved a small hotel suite notepad in front of her along with a pen.

She took it, jotted down her number, and shoved it back at him.

"Room number, too."

The elevator doors opened and she stepped inside. Jake faced her, holding the doors so they wouldn't close, although he didn't step inside with her. The look he gave her was enough to show her he would close them off inside this small space if she didn't give him what he wanted.

"I'm in room twelve-twelve."

Jake let go of the elevator door and it slid silently shut.

"Okay, Dad, what the hell is going on here?" Angela released all her pent-up frustration on her father the second he answered his phone.

James Huxtable didn't often find humor in situations. He wasn't a morbid soul, but he took life and all around him seriously and treated it with respect. He did the same with his daughter, using his calm, smooth, assuring tone that used to solve her world's problems when she was young.

"I thought you liked Jake King," he said.

"Dad!" Angela paced the length of her suite, slapping her hand against her hip. "He is the last thing I need right now. But Jake isn't what this is all about. Something is going on with you."

"I'm fine, Angela." He remained calm, which didn't confirm

or deny her suspicions. "All that matters is you stay focused. I'm sure I'll have things wrapped up on my end in no time, hopefully soon enough to help blow the game up once and for all. You can handle everything until I'm back by your side, right?"

It was on the tip of her tongue to answer. All she'd ever wanted was her father's acknowledgment that she was one of the best, top of the line, just like her old man. Angela might be young, but she'd pulled off some moves. The cops in their precinct and the D.A. had all acknowledged Angela's abilities to unravel a crime. But to hear this praise from her father, even in the form of him saying she could hold down the fort in his absence, was enough to make Angela jump on the bait.

She stopped pacing, looked up from the carpet she'd been scowling at, and stared across her hotel room suite.

"You know I can," she told him, but didn't feel the joy she knew would come when her father, the great James Huxtable, told her she was good enough to run lead on one of the most dangerous cases, possibly, in American history. "Something strikes me as odd," she continued, her tone flat.

"It's a tough case, I know." Her father had picked up on her suspicion that he would step away from this case. "The Kings are the best there is, or I wouldn't have pulled Jake in on this one. The fact that you two have already met actually works to your advantage. The second he saw your picture, he jumped on the case. He will protect you to death. I have no doubt."

Again her father had thrown her a curveball. The bait he dangled in front of her was damn near impossible to resist. Angela squeezed her eyes closed, fighting to remain focused. She desperately wanted to know every detail around Jake accepting the case after that small bit of enticing information her father had just offered.

"I'm sure," she forced herself to say. It was what her father wasn't telling her that mattered more than what the most gorgeous man she'd ever met thought of her. "Dad, why are you taking another case right now when we're ready to bring down the game?"

"It won't take long," her father said without hesitating.

Something unpleasant twisted in Angela's gut. The charged sexual energy between her and Jake still zapped at her insides. His aggressive nature and the look on his face when those elevator doors closed had left her weak with need. Angela managed to shove her personal desires out of the way as she collapsed on the edge of the bed.

"Who are you looking for, Dad?"

"No one. All you're to think about is the game, and Mario Mandela. One wrong move—"

"I know that, Dad," she snapped, interrupting him. "And you know that, too. Which is why I find it incredibly odd that you're focusing on another case."

"You need to brief Jake."

"I know what I need to do. Everything is under control."

"Good."

"Why won't you tell me about this missing persons case? It's not like you. You need to fill me in so I know what you're doing. That's how you taught me to work in our business, Dad. Always keep the other one informed, at all times."

Her father sighed. Angela's chest constricted. She held on to her cell tight enough to pinch the skin on her palm. Her mind raced, scenario after scenario playing out as she considered his complacent mood. His continual redirecting every time she asked who he was looking for made her worry even more.

"Who is the missing person?" she asked, her voice tangled with emotions.

"Marianna." This time her father spoke without ceremony. "Your mother called me several days ago to make sure your half-sister had arrived okay."

If Angela hadn't been sitting, she possibly would have fallen over. A small sound escaped her throat as she tried to speak.

"But," she managed, her mind unable to wrap around her father's response. She hadn't come up with any plausible answers her father might give her, but this one definitely did not compute.

"Your mother told me you two had been planning for her to visit us here in Chicago."

"Planning." Angela stressed the word. "We hadn't set a date."

"Marianna flew into LAX over a week ago. I confirmed she got off the plane in Los Angeles. The odd thing was that she didn't claim all her luggage. No one can say where she went after that."

"Marianna flew into LA." She didn't make it a question and still couldn't wrap her brain around any of this. Marianna wasn't missing. She couldn't be. They had talked daily online about Angela's half-sister that she hadn't seen since she was a teenager coming to Chicago. But Marianna was still in Buenos Aires. She had to be.

Angela hadn't checked her e-mail, or Facebook, since the day they'd confirmed Mandela was in Chicago. Angela had immediately been on his tail. Since then, there hadn't been time to chat with anyone. When her life was on hold, everyone else was supposed to know that. But how could Marianna have known that if the last they'd chatted, Angela hadn't been working a case?

"Yes, she definitely was on the plane to L.A., and she disembarked." Her father's matter-of-fact, all business—just the facts and nothing but the facts—tone grated on her nerves.

Angela was suddenly terrified that to her father Marianna was just another client. At the same time, it was also suddenly crystal clear why her father hadn't wanted to tell her. It made sense. Even though Marinna was from her mom's second marriage and her father had never met her, he knew how much Marianna meant to Angela.

Marianna was the radiant sunshine on Angela's cloudy day. She was the hopeful optimist to Angela's jaded world. Marianna was all that was pure, perfect, and untarnished. Talking to her online had always lifted Angela's mood, and over the past year as they'd gotten to know each other all over again, having her come stay with Angela and her father for a while had sounded like the perfect plan.

"We hadn't finalized her coming up here to visit."

The moment she and her father had determined a game player was in Chicago, Angela had forgotten about her own life and she'd gone undercover that evening after trailing Mandela around all day. Her personal life had faded in lieu of the investigation.

Angela moved to her laptop and typed frantically, willing her e-mail to open, and at the same time pulling up Facebook.

"I'll find her, Angela."

She barely heard her father trying to reassure her when her e-mail finally opened. Angela scrolled through a week's worth of junk mail and spam. "Damn it," she hissed, spotting Marianna's e-mail and clicking on it to open.

"What is it?"

"Marianna sent mail to me later that afternoon after we last chatted." Angela stared at the e-mail when it opened and read the excitement and happiness in Marianna's words. Her throat constricted and she swallowed several times before she could speak. "It says she managed to find a cheap flight out of Buenos Aires and she jumped on it since there were only a couple seats left. She flew out later that day," she finished, her voice going out on her. Every inch of her was too tense to catch her next breath. This couldn't be happening. "My God, Dad! Has she been missing over a week?"

"When your mother couldn't reach you, or Marianna, she called me. Marianna hadn't called to say she'd landed safely and she had promised her mother she would call the moment she had a signal."

Her father's words weren't registering in her head. "Mom called you and not me?"

Angela's parents had hated each other enough to reside in different countries after their divorce. Angela had moved with her mom to Buenos Aires, in Argentina. She'd been three at the time. Her father had sent letters often, and Angela always wrote back. When Angela had turned sixteen, she moved back to the states, leaving her younger sister, who'd been only eleven at the time, and her mother, for the exciting life of a detective's daughter.

"The night she called, I was parked in the car outside Enclave. I couldn't believe you got in to that club. The place was packed and I was watching for you, or Mandela, to come out, which had been hard as hell to do with a nonstop group of people hovering around the entrance. I would have sent the call to voicemail if I hadn't recognized the Argentina country code."

"Why didn't you tell me?" she demanded. Angela fought the urge to scream. Why the hell hadn't her father found Marianna yet? James Huxtable was the best out there and her half-sister had been missing over a week? It made no sense.

Angela pulled up the archives from when she and Marianna had chatted on Yahoo Messenger and scanned their conversations but saw nothing that indicated there was anything Marianna wanted to do in the states other than visit Angela. "Why didn't I check my mail before now? Do you have a trail on her at all?"

"Your mom called when the airline contacted her about Marianna's luggage."

"Her luggage?"

"She picked up one suitcase but not the other."

"That doesn't make sense."

"Her flight arrived at LAX in Los Angeles on Sunday morning," Angela's dad told her. "I've spoken with the airline and one of the stewardesses remembers her being on the flight. She said she remembered Marianna because of her excitement to come see her sister who she hadn't seen for seven years in the states. I've confirmed everyone got off the plane. Marianna picked up one suitcase but left the other."

"So she takes one suitcase off the luggage conveyer belt and leaves the other. Marianna wouldn't have just forgotten it. What was in the suitcase she left behind?"

"It was sent back to Buenos Aires. But according to the description, Mona told me that was the suitcase Marianna stuffed a photo album in, under her clothes. She'd glued an envelope inside the album that had cash and credit cards in it."

"Christ. She left it behind on purpose." Angela felt sick. Marianna was only eighteen, entering a country she'd never been to before, and so excited to embark on her new adventure. "She knew something was wrong. God! My little sister comes to see me, is barely in the U.S., and something terrible happens to her. Dad, where the hell is she?"

"I'm not sure," he said slowly.

Angela understood now why her father had hesitated to tell her that her sister was missing. This was even more of a distraction than Jake had been. Angela's anger peaked faster than her confusion had. She blew out an exasperated sigh, imagining wherever Marianna was right now, she was in serious danger and terrified. Marianna was the sweetest thing on earth, incapable of hurting a fly, and with a heart that was solid gold.

Angela voiced her fears. "Someone kidnapped her."

"How were the two of you communicating?" her dad asked instead of commenting.

"On Facebook, Yahoo Messenger, and e-mail."

"Can she send you a message there that you would get next time you got on the computer?"

"Yes."

"And there aren't any messages?"

"Nothing." Angela wanted to bust the case with Mandela wide open. She would quite possibly make serious headway tonight at his home. Ending the game would secure her reputation as an investigator, and save the lives of so many innocent people. She would have been beyond livid if her father had held out much longer and not told her about Marianna. But knowing had her torn up inside.

"She e-mailed her itinerary after our last chat. The e-mail didn't offer any information they didn't already know. After following Mandela from night club to night club and getting him to notice me, I then focused all my attention on settling in here at the Drake and making a show of being the rich prima donna to all of the staff. I needed my cover intact when he checked up on me. And you know he checked. What happens when you try calling her?"

"Straight to voice mail. I know it's pointless telling you not to worry. You do need to focus on Mandela and the game, Angela. Jake is there to protect you. Don't make his job too hard. I will find Marianna. At least I won't have to worry about you as much with Jake King on your side."

Angela never knew her father was that impressed with the Kings. Normally there were very few people in his profession whom her father thought much of at all. He wasn't conceited, but James Huxtable took his job seriously and didn't approve of anyone who didn't meet his high standards. She seriously doubted Jake had a clue how much of a compliment her father had paid him by seeking him out to be her backup.

"You really think that much of him?" she asked, unable to stop herself.

"I don't know him," her father said without hesitating. "KFA has a solid reputation."

"I just wondered. There are quite a few good candidates here in Chicago you could have asked to run backup."

"Not for you, there aren't," he said, his tone lowering as if this subject upset him. "Get yourself ready for your evening. I'll let you know if I head back to L.A."

"What leads are you working on?"

He didn't answer right away, which wasn't a good sign. Angela sucked in a deep breath, unable to get the painful lump in her gut to go away. Her little sister was out there somewhere, and they didn't know where.

"I'm trying to get permission to view the security camera footage that should show Marianna getting the one suitcase she left with, and if anyone was with her."

"Of course someone was with her. She wouldn't have left her suitcase with her money and credit cards in it if there wasn't something seriously wrong. Someone abducted her. She was taken the moment she got off the plane. You've got to view those security tapes immediately."

"I will. There is paperwork and procedure," he said, disparagingly.

"Paperwork and procedures can go to hell," she grumbled. "You need to find her, Dad."

"I will."

The firmness in his voice ended her tirade before she got going. James Huxtable was the best man to be looking for Marianna. It made Angela sick beyond comprehension that her little sister had been missing a week. There were many other families with the same sense of panic and grief, who also had loved ones missing, thanks to the game. As much as Angela wanted to jump on the next plane and trace Marianna's steps from the moment she got off that plane, she had to trust her dad.

"Why didn't you stay out in L.A. and look for her?" she demanded, getting a second wind and ready to scream and yell until something made sense to her.

"I'll be able to view the security camera footage online, once my request is approved. Hopefully, I'll get a good look at her abductor. Then I'll run his picture against pictures of anyone with a record, or who had been booked, or who has ever worked for a government agency or the many other types of employment that demand security photos as part of their policy."

"How long does it take to get approval to view the footage?" Along with worry and panic, Angela was pissed. She would kill whoever took Marianna if they so much as laid a finger on her.

"Airport security is a separate company and is not associated with the airlines. It was a lot of work getting through to the right channels so they would expedite matters. I hope to have access to them in the next twenty-four hours." Her father's tone relayed what he wouldn't voice. He was on edge about Marianna's disappearance. "But I'm here in Chicago to make sure my daughter doesn't disappear, too."

Chapter Five

Jake stared at his missed calls, glancing at each woman's name before deleting. It was a damn good thing his phone was on Silent. Angela would have thrown a fit if she'd known how many women had texted or called while Angela had been in his room. He deleted three texts without bothering to read them.

Angela claimed he was incapable of being with a woman without trying to seduce her. That wasn't true. Jake never had a problem separating work from play. He took both very seriously. Jake glanced at his phone and the screen that had gone dark. He wasn't sure he could separate the two when it came to Angela, however. Hell, he didn't want to. There wasn't any play when it came to her. But his urge to make love to her went far beyond wanting to play.

"She'll think she's another conquest on a rather long list," he said with disgust, deleting the last text message and tossing his phone on his bed.

How in the hell did Angela know anything about his personal life anyway? KFA's reputation was known nationwide. They'd been in the papers and on the news numerous times. KFA's track record was perfect. But Jake's personal life never hit the papers, TV, or even the Internet. He'd always handled his affairs with women very discreetly. There wasn't any way Angela had proof whether he played the field or not. She'd made an educated guess and hit it on the nose.

"Right on the fucking nose," he grumbled.

Angela was still on his lips. Hell, he could still smell her in his hotel room. The raw, unleashed energy pulsated around him. Jake knew how to switch gears, though.

He would call home, check e-mail, and take a long, cold shower. But not in that order. Jake stripped and headed to the bathroom, his thoughts already returning to Angela.

An hour later Jake sat in his boxers at the desk in the hotel room and booted up his computer while calling home.

"Dad, it's me," Jake said when Greg King answered after the first ring.

"Make it in okay?"

"Yup. I've been here an hour or so."

"Have you seen Huxtable? How about his daughter? She got a handle on that case to bring the game down?"

Jake pulled his phone from his ear for a moment when another call started beeping through. It dawned on him as he stared at the name of one of the ladies he knew in L.A. on his phone's screen that he hadn't given Angela his personal cell phone number.

He grunted at his father's comment. "Angela seems to have her act together." In more than one way although Jake knew his father didn't care what Jake thought of her personally. "I'll tell you this: she's bossy and demanding," he offered, figuring that summed her up well enough for his father.

Greg didn't miss a beat. "Damn. Sounds like you might have just met the perfect girl for you," he said, surprising Jake.

"The perfect woman for me would not be someone who is bossy and demanding."

His father muttered something Jake didn't catch, which was followed by his mother's cheerful laugh.

"I know this young lady is beautiful. I saw her picture, too. Does 'bossy and demanding' mean she won't submit to the famous King charm?"

"What woman could resist that?" Jake's mother said in the background, still laughing.

"That's not what I meant," Jake insisted. "Angela is bossy, but she's determined to pull off the case of a lifetime." He was defending Angela to his father.

"You two have your game plan all worked out?"

"Not yet." Although Jake wouldn't be surprised if Angela returned to him with every detail laid out. "We met briefly after I checked in. She went upstairs to her room. I just got out of the shower and figured I'd call you before checking back in with her."

"What happens tonight?"

"She is going to Mandela's. Apparently she's spent the past few days getting close to the man, working her way into his playground. She's planted a few bugs."

"She's moved in fast." His father let out a low whistle. "Stay focused on this one, Jake."

"I know how dangerous this case is. That's why I'm here."

"Your mother is worried," his father said tightly. "I am, too."

"Tell her I'll be fine."

His entire family had entered into life-threatening situations at times when a hunt got dangerous. Jake knew this case ranked right up there. He recognized the spike of adrenaline and knew soon he would be trailing Angela.

"I don't have to tell you how fatal it would be to let your thoughts stray while running a stakeout."

Jake's temper spiked at the insinuation his father was making. "I'm not going to make moves on her while she's under cover."

"Something about this girl appeals to you, *and,*" Greg stressed, "this case appeals to you, or you wouldn't be out there. Keep a few things in mind. The first one being bounty hunting is illegal in Illinois. If Mandela learns you're out there and decides to take you down and can't do it in his normal fashion, he'll use whatever means to stop you from tracking him."

"Point taken," Jake agreed, knowing his father was right.

"Here's something else for you to consider." His father paused and this time silence grew between them. Jake knew Greg was making sure his son was paying attention. It was a ploy his father had used for years. "I saw the picture of Angela Huxtable. She is an incredibly beautiful young woman. Obviously she has some pretty decent detective skills, too. I know how that combination appeals to a King man. But she got you thrown in jail once already. Mandela might not be your only adversary. She's worked this case for over a year now and probably believes she's closing in. From what you've described, she'll want the glory for solving this case. Jake, promise me, don't let your guard down. Take my advice on this one, Son."

There weren't many times when Jake would say his father was wrong about something. But in this case, Jake knew Angela wasn't that type of woman. She would be satisfied with solving the case. All the glory and hype and media attention wouldn't be her style. It wasn't something Jake thrived on either.

"Your advice is well noted, Dad. I'll give you a call tomorrow and update you on everything," Jake promised, ready to end the scrutinization of his personality. "Now let me talk to Mom so she doesn't call me later and accuse me of ignoring her."

There was one more call to make after talking to his parents, and he had a feeling his call was being expected. "Huxtable," he said, lowering his voice when the older man answered the phone.

"Are you with my daughter?"

"I'm not with her right now."

"But you know where she is, right?"

"I assume in her room."

"You assume?" Huxtable snapped. "This isn't a game, King."

"I don't play games. I'm not going to crowd her space when she insists on alone time, either. I was with her at the elevator and watched it climb to her floor after she left my room. I'm heading up there after I finish talking to you."

"My daughter is already making her game plan for the evening."

That didn't surprise Jake any more than the fact that Huxtable already knew his daughter was in her room and what she was doing in there. "I'll head up there to go over everything with her."

"Angela will insist on running the show. You let her do that, Son. Do you understand me?"

Jake had a feeling it didn't matter whether he understood or not, as long as he agreed.

Huxtable didn't wait for Jake's response. "She's spent a lot of time working this case and firmly believes her angle is the best one. You're going to go along with whatever she says to do. If you believe she's made a bad decision, contact me. I'll take care of it. Right now, if you cross her, it will only make matters worse. You'll do a lot better working with Angela if you do as she says and make sure she always feels she is in charge."

Jake shook his head, clearly seeing that "bossy" and "demanding" were genetic traits in this family. "I'll guarantee your daughter's safety and promise you no one will harm her." How Jake would do that was his own damn business.

"I know you will. Now give me your account number and I'll transfer some of your money into it right now so you can cover expenses while you're here."

"You'll deposit two grand tonight into my personal account. As soon as this case is wrapped up, you'll deposit two more. *An-n-n-d,*" he added, stressing the one word and drawing it out before Huxtable could say anything, "you will fax a contract of agreement to KFA. I'm not leaving this room to check on your daughter's whereabouts until I get a call from home letting me know the signed contract has come through."

Jake King was a pompous ass. Angela hated him. She hated Jake for causing her skin to tingle, for making her insides ache and crave his touch again. And right now wasn't the time to be thinking about another man, not when she was walking through Mario's living room. It was impossible not thinking about the man who'd entered her hotel room earlier tonight. Jake had respected her ideas, listened to her game plan, and agreed to almost everything she suggested. Angela almost had believed they could work together, until he'd pierced her with a gaze so compelling, so controlling and predatory, she'd almost forgotten to breathe.

"I'm going to tell you what I just told your father," Jake had said, moving in on her the way a deadly predator would stalk its prey. "I know how to take orders. But regardless of what you tell me to do, or not do, I will guarantee your safety. No one will harm you," he continued, his voice dropping to a low growl when he stopped in front of her, then brushed his knuckles down her cheek. "Your game plan is impressive, sweetheart. Sounds like you'll be in his home tonight. Just remember the image you've given Mandela, though. If you aren't out of there by ten, I'm coming in after you."

Jake wouldn't tolerate her sleeping with Mandela. It had been on the tip of her tongue to promise Jake she had no intentions of allowing the asshole to get anywhere near going that far with her. If she had made that promise, though, Jake would make more demands, insist she follow his instruction the next time, and the time after that. Angela wasn't about to let that happen. She'd remained quiet, staring up into his smoldering green eyes. Although she'd managed to maintain control verbally, when Jake had lowered his mouth to hers Angela hadn't been able to move. He'd swept her off her feet with a kiss so hot, so intoxicating and mind-blowing, he'd damn near made her come while standing there with his arms wrapped around her.

Which put her body in even more conflict. Marianna was missing. Her father suggested that if Angela knew her sister was out there somewhere, taken against her will, it would distract her while she was with Mandela. Instead she was acutely aware of her surroundings. And at the same time sending up repeated silent prayers that her sister was okay.

Angela paused in the middle of the living room, forcing herself to take in its contents. Her thoughts should be focused on everything around her, on Mario. She was here to do a job and nothing could prevent her from being the professional she knew she was.

"This way, *mi amore*." Mario took her hand and guided her across the large, pretentious living room. There was enough furniture in the room to turn it into several living rooms. "You're either love struck by my company or in awe of my home."

Angela caught him grinning at her, the smile on his face too intense to be sincere. She'd ran her fingers over the back of one of the couches, noting that the furniture appeared brand-new and as if no one had ever used any of it. She matched his smile and fought the urge to glance behind her when Mario looked past her. His black eyes gleamed as they did when his mood changed.

"Marco, the lady is drinking whiskey and Coke and I'll have my usual."

Angela turned to catch a man in a black suit nod once before disappearing from the doorway. He looked more like a security guard than a servant and she clutched her small handbag that held her cell phone and a small amount of cash, just a few twenties of emergency money in case she needed it. Her biggest treasure at the moment, though, was her phone. The prepaid phone had bogus numbers saved to it, just to make it look like a normal phone. But the only number called, or received, was Mario's. Hopefully Mario would never get the chance to look through her numbers, but if he did, nothing could incriminate her.

"You haven't told me which one it is," Mario said, taking her hand and bringing it to his lips.

"What? Oh." Angela didn't have to work too hard to blush but hoped Mario would think her distraction was due to him being so close to her. "Your home is breathtaking," she whispered, sounding enamored.

"So it's my home that impresses you and not me." He sounded sincerely disappointed.

This coming from a man who'd had sex with another woman earlier today. Angela fought off the disgust that rose like bile in her throat as she leaned against him and went up on her tiptoes. Mario was a tall man but nothing in comparison to Jake.

"I figured you already knew what I thought of you," she whispered, and nipped playfully at Mario's lower lip.

"A man loves being praised," Mario informed her, straightening and slapping her rear end hard enough for it to sting.

"And maybe a little rough, too?" She batted her eyes at him and caught his expression darken again.

Repulsion turned her stomach and she walked out of his arms, moving ahead of him as if she would explore his home without invitation. Mario was right behind her, wrapping his arms around her waist and pulling her back against him.

"No woman talks like that unless it's an invitation."

She twisted slightly in his arms, and when he tried kissing her she angled her face just right so he managed to peck at her cheek. He smelled of garlic and alcohol, and she wondered how much he'd already had to drink. "Not too rough, darling," she whispered. "I wouldn't want you to hurt me."

Mario stiffened and stared into her eyes. "Do you worry I might hurt you, *mi amore*?" he asked, his accent thickening as he pulled her against him. "Does it excite you, or terrify you, knowing I have the power to destroy?" he whispered, holding her against him as he spoke in a soft whisper into her hair.

If she laughed at him, he would be insulted. Tonight wasn't the night to learn what kind of temper Mario had. She'd gained enough of his trust to be in his home with him, and his preposterous questions wouldn't ruin it for her.

"Why do you ask me questions like that?" she asked, pressing her palms against his chest and pushing. She licked her lips and studied his face. The dark rage that appeared from time to time wasn't there. At the same time, his expression seemed more guarded than usual. He was testing her.

She just didn't have a clue what he wanted to know. "I already know you would crush and destroy anyone who would cross your path," she whispered, and relaxed her hands on his shoulders as she leaned into him. Then pressing her breasts against his chest, she managed to place a kiss on his chin without gagging. "You already know I wouldn't cross your path, though, or I wouldn't be here, right?"

"Sì," Mario growled. "Tonight you're here with me, in *casa mia*."

Mario's dangerous air and sexually crude manner probably had many women melting at his feet. Angela wondered how many took time to look deeper and notice the sinister edge that never completely left him. His lazy drawl made the hairs rise on her arms. She reminded herself again how incredibly careful she needed to be. One wrong move and Mario's suspicions would rise. A man in his position didn't get where he was by trusting too many people. She wouldn't flatter herself into thinking she would be one of the few he would let his guard down around.

The man in the black suit cleared his throat when he entered the room carrying two drinks. Mario gave him a scathing look, as if the guy had a lot of nerve interrupting them. The man didn't make a sound when he placed the drinks on a nearby small, round table. It was pushed up against the wall and, like so much of the other furniture in Mario's oversized house, appeared to have no purpose at all. Angela wouldn't be surprised if it was the first time anything had been placed on it.

The man disappeared as silently as he had arrived. Mario let go of her and Angela breathed a sigh of relief the moment he turned his back and picked up their drinks.

"Not many women read me as well as you do, Angela." The small blocks of ice clinked against her glass when Mario handed it to her.

"That's because I pay attention." She lifted her drink in a silent toast and sipped. It was a very good, expensive whiskey that was smooth going down. She hummed her approval and took another drink. The whiskey empowered her, relaxing her and building her confidence. "Now are you going to give me a tour of your home or do I need to go exploring on my own?"

"Is my home so much different than how you're used to living?" His probing look dropped down her body.

His focus was as subtle as Jake's, but instead of heating her insides Mario made a cruel chill rush over her. Angela sipped at her drink, returning his appraising stare. "The way a man lives says a lot about him," she offered, grinning over the rim of her glass.

Mario chuckled and drank from his bottle of beer. It was a brand she didn't know, but she wasn't a beer connoisseur.

He used his free hand to pet the side of her head. "I thought you already knew everything you needed to know about me."

She knew more about Mario than she had several days ago. Mario worked hard, albeit as a criminal, having moved up the ladder until he could afford to live a life of leisure. She didn't really care what had put the demonic edge inside him. Knowing it existed was enough. Something incredibly cruel, vicious, and hateful simmered just under the surface of this man. As gallant and cultured as he could appear to be, a good look into his eyes, at the way he kept his lips pressed in a thin line almost always and how he held himself, as if he might pounce on someone, or something, at any moment, told her even more about Mario Mandela.

If she were to sum him up in a few words, Angela would be able to say he was incapable of love. He truly hated most everyone he saw around him and associated with. Beautiful possessions were important to him but held no true meaning for him inside. Mario needed the world to see his wealth, but if anyone got too close to it, he immediately despised them. Angela might have been able to view him as a very sad man, but with so much evil threatening to be unleashed inside him at any moment, it made it easier for her to see him for whom he truly was, a cold-blooded killer with no heart or soul, who was capable of destroying anyone around him without feeling an ounce of remorse. Mario wasn't a man but a creature, mutated by events or circumstances that no longer mattered. The damage was done and irreversible. If it were up to her, creatures like him would be destroyed immediately.

"If I knew everything about you, where would the fun be?" she asked, grinning as she suppressed her hatred for him. "Show me your house, darling."

"Your wish is my command," he said gallantly, bowing and gesturing with his hand as he led them across the living room.

Mario was proud to show off all he owned and made a point of telling her how much everything cost him as he pointed it out. As they walked from room to room, he told her stories of his life. Mario had a gift for talking while telling her absolutely nothing. She paid attention, but his small anecdotes and tales of his youth or how he had obtained a certain vase or a painting on the wall were so romantic and entertaining she doubted any of them were true. They didn't fit with the man who told them.

The mansion was larger than anything she'd ever been in before. Angela paid attention and still wasn't sure she wouldn't get lost in the place. She did her best to create a mental floor plan as they moved from one floor to the next.

"You can see I don't use all the rooms," he explained, ending the tour in his incredibly large master bedroom. "I like having all the space, though. If family comes to visit I can put them up. I would never allow a relative of mine to stay in a hotel if they were in town. Not to mention, I hope to have a houseful of children someday."

She didn't miss his stab about her staying at the Drake instead of with family, and she ignored the comment about family, instead walking across Mario's bedroom, keeping a fair distance from the incredibly large bed in the middle of the room and pausing at his desk and the computer sitting on it. They had discussed why she was at the Drake, so she could entertain all her friends and not be around her father, whom she despised. Mario had made a show of disapproving, but her hunch with her choice of a cover had proved right. Mario was attracted to her even more after learning that although she was always surrounded by friends and attending parties and social functions, she didn't associate with any family who would worry about her.

"Do you have family visit often?" Angela opened her purse, aware of him watching as she pulled out lip gloss. She stared at him innocently while applying the sticky stuff to her lips. Wearing so much makeup sucked, but Mario almost drooled watching her paint her lips.

"Not yet." His gaze was locked on her mouth. "I've lived here less than a year and hope to move some of my family into the country soon."

Angela didn't know whether he meant that or not. She hadn't heard any mention while studying his MO about Mario having any family he remained in contact with in Italy. She wasn't sure it mattered. At this stage in her investigation she couldn't afford to discard any information about Mario, though, and made a mental note to bring up family again, just not the children part. If there were family members, Mario might use them to hide the people he'd abducted.

The man who'd brought their drinks appeared in the hallway. He lingered hesitantly, not once making eye contact with her but focusing on his boss. Mario took his time pulling his gaze from hers before giving the man a stern look.

"A moment, please," the man said, his accent thicker than Mario's.

Mario grunted but walked to the doorway, blocking her view of the servant.

Fingering her lip gloss, Angela opened her purse and carefully dropped the sticky stuff into a small sandwich bag she'd put in her purse earlier. Angela closed her purse, then slid the lid to the lip gloss alongside the front of the keyboard where it wouldn't easily be noticed. One of her listening devices was inside the lid. No one would notice it unless they looked inside the lid, which she banked on Mario not doing. If he discovered it, he would simply think she dropped it there accidentally. She'd just placed her first bug in Mario's home.

Clasping her hands behind her back, she studied the men at the door. Mario had shifted his weight, which allowed Angela a better view of the servant speaking in hushed whispers as he said something very quickly and in Italian. Angela couldn't pick up a word he said. The man in the black suit focused on Mario. The servant could easily switch his attention to her but never did. Angela decided that was strong loyalty to his boss. It allowed her to learn the man's features, put to memory his olive-colored skin and black, thick hair that was greased back. She imagined without the goop in his hair or the black suit he would look like a young thug. His hair was probably long enough to fall past his face. Put him in jeans and a T-shirt and remove the hair gel and he'd look completely different.

She shifted her attention to Mario. He wore dark jeans and black boots that accentuated his long, muscular legs. His black hair was long enough to give him that bad-boy look, but with enough charm about him to captivate those around him. Was that how he captured people to be in the game? Did he lure them in with charm, then abduct them when their defenses were down? As she returned her attention to the man listening attentively as Mario said something harshly under his breath, it hit Angela the two men were very similar in appearance.

As if they were related. Family.

Angela took a step toward them.

"Thanks for letting me know," Mario said loud enough for her to hear. He turned at the same time, his smile cold and without feeling.

Angela had never seen eyes so incredibly opaque, as if suddenly he didn't have a soul. But she knew he did. Mario had a soul so tainted and destroyed with death and destruction it surprised her it didn't glow with the evil swarming through every inch of his insides. Mario possessed the ability to suppress whatever emotion he was experiencing. She witnessed that as she stared at him.

"Is everything okay?" she asked, sensing something was wrong. Her curiosity was piqued, although she doubted she'd learn anything by asking.

The man standing in the doorway shifted his weight from one foot to the other, his expression strained. If the two men were related, it was clear why Mario was the man in charge.

"Of course," Mario said, his smile stiff. He moved across the room to her, reaching for her and wrapping cold fingers around her arm. "I guarantee you have all my attention this evening, but the curse of success is there is always business to handle."

She managed to remain relaxed and even snuggle up to him when he pulled her closer. "Keep me posted, Marco. That is all," Mario said, dismissing Marco with a wave of his hand but not looking over his shoulder. Instead, all of his attention was on Angela.

Marco looked at her for the first time before turning and leaving them. For a brief second she swore she saw intense hatred. Where Mario's eyes were marked, this man's dark eyes glowed with animosity and something else. She couldn't put her finger on it. When she tilted her head, curious as to what emotion she'd triggered in him, Marco looked away, turning and disappearing.

"What did he want?" She thought about commenting on Marco's odd look, just to see what Mario would say.

Mario cupped her face, not pinching her skin, but his grip was firm. "My work is personal. And I have promised you that it won't steal me away from you, *amore*."

He brushed his thumb down her cheek. Angela closed her eyes, hoping she appeared touched by his words and intimacy.

"I'm not some delicate bimbo who can't put two and two together," she said, keeping her voice soft as she blinked a few times before gazing up at him.

He'd relaxed his features considerably and looked sincerely

compassionate when he continued brushing his thumb alongside her face. "I don't believe I ever implied you were stupid or easy."

Angela smiled. "That's not what I meant. You've got business to take care of and I'm not so self-centered that I would be offended if you had to deal with it." She turned her expression sly, grinning up at him. "Besides, you don't make all this money by putting pleasure before work."

Mario grinned as well and slowly began shaking his head. "You're one hell of an impressive lady. Keep this up and it will be hard to keep things casual between us."

Angela reminded herself that he'd fucked another lady earlier today. Everything out of his mouth was a line stated for a reason. If he was suggesting their relationship might be moving to the next level, it could only mean one of two things. Either he really did believe she would only have sex with him if she thought she was in a relationship or for some reason he thought it would benefit him to have her closer to him.

"I'm only being honest." She stepped out of his arms and started toward the door. Looking over her shoulder, she caught Mario watching her ass. "And if I'm intriguing you enough to consider keeping me around for a while," she added, feeling her heart speed up painfully when his attention shot to her face, "show me why I should keep hanging around. Let's go see how you make all this money."

It didn't surprise her that Mario stopped her in the hallway. She prayed he didn't notice how damp her palms suddenly were when he grabbed her and flipped her around.

"I didn't invite you over to go over business matters," he said gruffly, holding her by her arms so she faced him. "Tonight is a night for lovers. By making love to you I will show you why you will want to stay with me."

She could handle this. Mario might be an incredibly dangerous man, but he didn't know she knew that. Angela had managed her way around many men in the past. There were times when she'd wondered if there were only so many pickup lines in the world and she'd already heard them all.

Mario's line was direct but not original. His intentions were to fuck her tonight, and she had no problem putting him off without turning him off.

"You will most definitely show me," she drawled. "Come on. Let's go outside." She enjoyed his moment of confusion and took advantage of it, working to calm down inside as she did. "Come on," she repeated, heading toward the stairs. "Where's your sense of adventure?"

Mario laughed, grabbing the back of her neck as he led her down the hallway.

"We were next to a bed and my lady wishes to go outside. You are original, *mi amore*," he said, continuing to laugh as he pulled out his phone and ordered more drinks for them out on the patio.

His bedroom was now bugged, and he had a computer in there. If only she could figure out how to put a tracking device on his computer, one that would track every keystroke. At the moment she wasn't sure how she'd pull that off, but damn, if she could, she didn't doubt she'd hit the gold mine. She had one more bug on her and needed to place it strategically outside his home. It wasn't obvious in what part of the house he would conduct business, though.

They moved across the living room, this time entering a part of his home he hadn't included in his tour. Angela glanced at an expensive-looking grandfather clock along the far wall. It was not quite nine and Jake had informed her he would give her until ten. Angela knew his words hadn't been an idle threat.

Mario opened sliding glass doors that led out to a large wooden patio. Large torches burned around the edges, which made it hard to see farther into the yard. But the thick smell of roses and honeysuckle made for a sweet aroma that Angela breathed deep into her lungs. Mario's home was magnificent, beautiful, and elegant. If it weren't for the evil lingering so heavily from room to room, this place would be close to paradise. Angela only had a moment to enjoy the richly perfumed air and inky black sky.

"Mario." An older man, also wearing a black suit, appeared

at the sliding glass behind the two of them. "This is important." His English was crisper than the younger servant's had been. "Mario," he repeated, deep lines in his face growing as he scowled at Angela.

"I already said it could wait." There was a fierceness in Mario's tone that even made the crickets too scared to continue singing.

Marco was already on the patio with a tray of fresh drinks. He glanced from the older man to Mario and continued holding the tray over the table. It was as if Marco had frozen, fear or extreme concern causing him to forget to place the drinks down.

"I don't think this can wait." The older man didn't look authoritative. He lowered his head as he spoke, as if offering reverence and respecting the man who wrote his paycheck and owned all the wonderful things around them. "You must hear me out now." At the same time, there wasn't fear in the older man's face, as there definitely was on Marco's face.

A cool breeze blew the tension around in the air. Nervous anticipation prickled over Angela's skin when she swore Mario growled at the older man. Marco shifted his weight, his uneasiness apparent and confirming Angela's suspicions that something wasn't right. The small, square ice cubes rattled in the glasses until finally Marco put the tray on the table. He then shifted his weight from one leg to the other, glancing at the door more than once, as if pondering whether he could escape before the deadly eruption occurred.

Hoping to hear something that would give her a clue what the men were talking about, she placed her hand on Mario's chest. "I don't mind waiting for you for a few minutes," she offered. "Your staff appears nervous about something."

"There isn't anything for them to be nervous about," Mario said, but didn't look at her. Instead he stared over her head at the older man behind her. "I do the thinking, and the plotting, around here. *Sei fuori linea, vecchio.*"

"*Stai pensando con la testa sbagliata.*" The older man sounded as harsh as Mario did.

Angela repeated what the two men said to each other,

wishing she knew Italian and praying she could remember their words so she could try to translate them later.

"You are dismissed, both of you!" Mario bellowed.

Angela jumped in spite of her efforts to remain calm. Instinctively she took her hand off Mario's chest. She took a step away from him and turned to look at the older man. There wasn't any way to figure out what they had been saying. The older man shifted his angry expression to her when she met his gaze.

"*Le troie sì seguono intutti le classe e colori*," the older man snarled, his pewter-colored hair greased back similarly to Marco's. He spoke with enough enthusiasm that a thick strand fell over his forehead when his expression turned hostile.

Marco froze, his jaw dropping. Angela didn't need to see Mario's face to know the older man's comment had outraged him. And she didn't need to know Italian to know she'd just been seriously insulted.

"What did you just say?" she asked the old man, unable to stop herself. The fury hanging in the air made it hard to breathe.

"That is enough!" Mario grabbed Angela, almost tossing her to the side as he lunged at the older man.

Angela couldn't have stopped Mario if she'd tried. She had a small handgun in her purse, but pulling it out would make matters even worse. Marco was already in the house and jumped to the side, apparently more concerned with protecting his own ass than the old man's.

"Mario!" Angela yelled, scared he would seriously hurt the old man. She didn't follow Mario inside but remained on the patio, staring into the house but knowing she had an escape route if needed. With all their backs to her, she reached in her purse, feeling the cool, hard metal of her gun. Her fingers were damp and shaky and in moments this explosion would be over. She wrapped her hand around a pen, instead, and pulled it out, clicking it open as she did.

"There is too much at stake," the older man said, not backing down when Mario lunged at him.

Mario took him by the arm, hauling him across the room. "That's my problem, now, isn't it? This is my money, my business, my fucking world!" His voice grew louder with each word, but then he continued, his tone dropping to a cruel, harsh, quiet baritone. "You'd be smart never to forget that. Or you'll be walking back to Italy. You aren't part of the game!" he added in a deadly whisper.

Angela almost didn't hear his last comment, but for whatever reason it hit the old man harder than anything else Mario said.

"You would never send me back to Italy," he insisted, making it sound more like an order than a plea. "And you know damn good and well I'm as much a part of this as you are. You wouldn't be here if it weren't for me."

"Twice in five minutes you misjudge a person's nature." Mario seemed to grow in size. His hands were fisted at his sides, and muscles bulged against his shirt. His presence was so commanding the room seemed to grow smaller, the walls closing in around them. "First you insult my *fidanzata* and now you underestimate me."

Marco was closer to Angela than Mario and the older man. *Fidanzata* meant "girlfriend." She wasn't fluent in Italian, but there were words she had picked up here and there. Marco shot her a speculative look, as if Mario's claim on her surprised him. She tried seeing the old man's face but couldn't. Mario was blocking her view.

Clutching her purse under her arm, she held the pen in a way so no one would notice it. It would record what was said for up to an hour. It was the best she could do to capture every aspect of this explosive conversation. She wanted desperately to see the old man's face but wouldn't move, for fear of disrupting them. The pewter-haired man was on the verge of losing his cool over something, and even if it meant enduring more insults she would record and translate later, she wanted to know what it was.

"If I ever underestimated you, then you wouldn't be here right now." There was a cold edge to the older man's voice. For a moment Angela thought it was Mario speaking, but as she stared at his back the man shifted his weight, giving her a partial view of the old man. The hateful fury lining his already-wrinkled face was intense. He raised his hand and poked Mario in the chest. "I encouraged you and bandaged your knees when you were a bambino."

"Take all the credit you want," Mario said, interrupting. "That doesn't change a thing today."

"It is proof I wouldn't make accusations if I didn't care," he hissed. "What are you doing?"

"I was trying to have a nice, relaxing evening!" Mario yelled. "You send Marco with questions because you can't figure out what to do, then dare imply I'm not thinking straight. There isn't one goddamn minute of the day when I'm not thoroughly thinking every matter at hand through. Not once have I entered into a business proposal without analyzing every angle. And see where it has gotten us?" He stretched out his arms, gesturing at their surroundings. "Are any of you worried about your next meal? Your clothes are quality and your lifestyle is plush. That is because of me!" Mario pounded his chest with his fist. "Now I suggest you both leave us before I suddenly decide to become less generous."

Marco and the old man hurried across the room and Angela thought the discussion was over. In spite of relief washing over her that it hadn't turned violent, nerves still ransacked her system and she was frustrated. None of them had said anything damning.

Her skin prickled when Mario turned his back on them and walked to her. His mask wasn't as in place as it usually was, and the raw, uncensored emotions surging through him twisted his expression into something terrifying and demonic. It would be the perfect time to make her exit, insisting the outburst had ruined their moment. But Angela wasn't sure whether suggesting she leave would set him off further or not. Besides, she wanted to know what the argument was about.

"Only God is perfect," the old man said, apparently deciding he would have the last word as he moved into the doorway leading to the patio from inside. "Win your game, Mario. But history is quite clear as to what happens to any man who suddenly believes himself omnipotent. You don't need zombies to win and you are making a mistake about her."

"I said shut up!" Mario moved across the room with enough speed Angela barely had time to react to what happened next.

He flew through the doorway, crashing into the old man, and the bloodcurdling scream that followed was a sound Angela would never forget.

Chapter Six

Mario stood in his observation room, one room he hadn't shown Angela, and faced the monitors on the wall. His breathing had slowed, and some of his anger had ebbed. At least enough so that the blind rage was gone. It wasn't his fault he'd slipped over the edge. If anyone knew what buttons to push, it was his family.

The goddamned bums!

He shook his head, heaving a sigh and running fingers through his tousled hair. Of all people, family were supposed to always have one another's backs. They were the ones who could be trusted, who would always be there, who would support one another through thick and thin. That was the code the Mandelas had once lived by.

If his father were still alive . . .

"He'd have done the same thing I did," Mario grumbled under his breath.

"What did you say?" Marco appeared in the doorway.

Mario waved a hand dismissively without looking over his shoulder. "Did you find her?"

"No." Marco didn't elaborate, nor did he move.

Mario studied the monitors. Images were hard to see at night where there was little light. A few of the cameras, those near the house, offered better views of the outside because of nearby floodlights. It would be smart to install more lighting. He had one hell of a security system, but cameras weren't worth shit when all they recorded was darkness. It was impossible to tell if anyone had moved through the yard and, if they had, which direction they headed once they were away from the glow of the floodlights by the house.

He wasn't sure what Angela saw or, better yet, what she thought she saw. There were more pending matters to address, but ensuring Angela didn't run scared for help was also a situation he'd have to take care of. As soon as he knew things were cleaned up here, he would put on a performance that would have Angela back in his arms and ready to spread her sexy legs for him.

"Did you take care of Uncle Petrie?" Mario turned to face Marco. There wasn't any reason to keep staring at the monitors. Angela wasn't going to walk back to Mario's house after running away from it.

"Yes." His younger cousin quit leaning against the door frame when Mario faced him.

"And how did you do that?" Mario ignored his cousin's puzzled expression and stood silently waiting for him to answer the question. It didn't matter that Mario had given specific instructions on what to do with Uncle Petrie's body; Mario knew his cousin was as smart as a brick. Not only did Mario have to spell out how Marco should handle matters, but he also needed to know the numbskull had followed his directions. Now wasn't the time for sloppiness or idiotic family members' risking everything Mario had worked so hard to accomplish.

"Just how you told me to," Marco said, suddenly defensive.

"Tell me exactly what you did." Mario shouldn't have to lower his voice, give his younger cousin a deadly look. His harsh stare brought the necessary results, though. It was a damn shame he had to be a bully to his own flesh and blood just to get an appropriate response. He imagined his padre had often felt the same way.

Marco tugged on the collar of his white button-down shirt. He wasn't wearing his suit jacket anymore and his sleeves were rolled up. Dressing for success helped make a man feel good about himself. It raised his self-esteem. Mario insisted everyone who worked for him be dressed to the hilt. He waited for Marco to explain how he had disposed of his own *padre* before deciding if he would reprimand him for coming to Mario looking like a slob.

"We put him in the bathtub, poured bleach until he was soaking in it, left him in it for ten minutes, and took him to the lake." Marco's gaze shifted as he stared at everything in the small observation room just to avoid looking at Mario.

"You didn't dry and dress him?" Mario asked.

"Yes. We did. You told us to dress him."

Mario nodded once. "Good. You wouldn't want your *padre* buried naked."

"He wasn't buried." The first sign of resentment appeared in Marco's eyes.

Mario held his younger cousin's gaze, shifting his weight to hold on to it when Marco tried looking away. "Lake Michigan is very much like the ocean, yes?"

Marco blinked. "Yeah, it is."

"Uncle Petrie loved the ocean, didn't he?"

Marco nodded.

Mario sighed. Marco was young, barely over twenty, but Mario was patient and he honored family. Massimo Mandela's brothers and sisters never had amounted to much, and their children were following in their footsteps. But Mario had learned well from his own *padre*, the one Mandela who actually had worked hard and broke his back doing everything he could to give his wife and children the best life possible. Family mattered more than anything, to Massimo, even when some of them were a complete waste of flesh.

Mario moved closer to Marco and slapped him on the shoulder. He didn't smile when Marco flinched before straightening to attention. Mario hoped Marco had learned something from tonight's events. Quite possibly he wasn't any better than his father, but Mario knew blood was thicker than water. He would be patient with Marco as long as Marco followed Mario's orders impeccably.

"You gave your *padre* the kind of burial he would want." Mario left the observation room, knowing Marco would follow him, like a trained dog, without Mario telling him to do so. "Now, Marco, you are the oldest son, right?"

"Yes." Marco was half a pace behind Mario, but it wasn't hard to miss the bitterness in his tone.

As much as Mario would like to think Marco resented being the oldest of a man who couldn't perform the simplest of tasks, Mario didn't get where he had in life by making false assumptions. Marco wasn't smart enough to see when he should feel humiliated and when he should be kissing ass.

"It is now your responsibility to take on your *padre*'s tasks. Is this something I can trust you with?" They climbed the stairs and arrived at Mario's room. Mario turned to face Marco, who remained in the doorway. "If you aren't ready for the additional responsibility, you may tell me. I won't ever punish you for honesty."

"You punished Father for his honesty."

Mario studied Marco. He straightened, bringing himself to his full six feet. Even as he puffed out his chest, there wasn't enough man facing Mario to make Marco a compatible opponent, mentally or physically.

Mario sighed, making a show of his patience being pushed. "Marco," he said, and tapped his finger against his lips. He began pacing, focusing on the carpet. With the simpler minds, visual effects were often more effective than words. He would keep it straight and easy for his cousin's sake. "Come in here and sit down."

Mario continued pacing as Marco crossed the room and sat in the chair facing Mario's desk. Mario remained standing, forcing Marco to shift in his chair so he could see Mario.

"It's important you share your thoughts with me. But I have a hard time believing you think your *padre* was punished for honesty."

"He told you what he thought," Marco blurted out, suddenly sounding like a whining child. "He cared for you as if you were his oldest son or he wouldn't have bothered trying to make you see how things were."

"And how were things?"

"If I tell you what my father told me, you will kill me, too," Marco said and set his jaw stubbornly, pressing his lips together as if he would say no more.

"I won't kill you," Mario promised, sighing. He was getting bored with Marco's tantrums and ignorance. There were only so many ways to spell something out for someone. "Why do you think I killed Uncle Petrie?"

Marco took his time looking at Mario. When he finally shot Mario a wary look, the anger no longer flared in his eyes. He seemed lost, confused.

"Tell me," Mario encouraged.

"Because of the *signorina* you had here," Marco shot Mario a furtive glance but then decided to give his attention to the carpet.

"I should tolerate any of you calling my dates sluts to their faces?" Mario had every intention of turning Angela into a very nice slut. It would take some time. Angela preferred teasing him and thinking she could get away with it. He'd considered giving her some of the slave juice, just to release the wild creature he knew existed under her properly bred composure. Mario didn't doubt for a moment, though, that he would reap his reward for patience if he held out a bit longer. Angela would be worth every minute of it. "I warned Uncle Petrie," Mario added coolly. "But not only did he insult my guest, he also insulted me."

Marco mumbled something under his breath.

"What was that?" Mario demanded.

"My *padre* sent me to you." Marco shifted in his seat. "I came here to warn you."

Mario spotted the lipstick lid near his keyboard and picked it up, spinning it in his fingers. The lip gloss she'd applied had been a glossy pink color, and as attractive as it had looked, he would much rather have seen her in a flashy red. He would suggest that next time he saw her. Stuffing the lid in his pocket, he returned his attention to Marco. "You told me you were concerned my guest wasn't who she appeared to be. I was very clear that we would discuss it later. While a guest is in my home isn't the time to go over their history."

"My *padre* was concerned for you, for your safety." Marco twisted his hands in his lap and stared at them. "We're pretty sure she's the daughter of a detective."

"What did you say?" Mario snapped, something deadly twisting inside him.

"The *signorina*," Marco explained. "We found a picture online. It's old. But that is what I came to tell you, to ask you," he corrected himself. "If you would take time to look at the picture."

"Show me." Mario would do more to her cute little ass than just fuck it if she was trying to take him down.

Angela put her hands on her hips and stared at the black box on the table in her room. "Why the hell did you quit?" she asked the inanimate object.

It didn't answer.

She paced around the table, staring at her surveillance equipment. Someone must have picked up her lipstick lid. Did they discover the bug in it?

"What did he come to warn you about?" She wanted to know. The conversation had stopped right after Marco told Mario why he and Petrie had interrupted his and Angela's evening. She was dying to know. Translating the Italian wasn't as easy as she'd thought it would be. When she typed the sentences into translating programs online, they didn't pull up anything that made sense. Angela tried various spellings of each word, which resulted in very bizarre sentences. Possibly Jake knew a little Italian. She expected him to show up soon, banging on her door and demanding to know what happened.

Angela hadn't tried looking for Jake when she'd raced across Mario's lawn, which had been quite the trek. She was sure she would go into cardiac arrest by the time she'd reached the street. Even as her heart had pounded painfully in her chest, Andrea had kept her cool and walked with purpose out of that neighborhood of mansions. She'd never looked over her shoulder, but the prickling down her neck might have been from Jake watching her.

Angela understood why he wouldn't have picked her up and given her a ride. It would have blown her cover if anyone else kept an eye on her as she ran like hell when Mario killed his uncle. Angela had walked ten blocks before grabbing a taxi back to the Drake.

It would be awkward seeing Mario again, although she anticipated that meeting happening soon. Mario had killed a man in front of her. He wouldn't let her walk out of his life now. She was surprised he hadn't tried making contact with her yet. More than likely, Jake and Mario would demand her attention at the same time.

In the meantime, she would listen to her bugs, learn what she could about Mario, and somehow validate his connection to the game. She needed something solid to instigate an arrest. It would be smart to call her dad soon, as well. There were no messages from him all evening. Not that he would tell her on voice mail if he'd substantiated any solid leads. Even if he had finally viewed the security camera footage, he might not have more than a picture, which wouldn't do them any good until they could match it with a name. She definitely had information to share with him, though.

The small black box began beeping. Angela jumped. "Shit," she hissed. Her nerves were frazzled. Maybe a drink would calm her, or even hot tea. It would be smart to stock up on a few supplies and keep them in her refrigerator. She had a microwave and a sink. Calling room service every time she wanted something would break her bank.

Settling for cold water, Angela propped herself on a chair in front of the box on the table. There were knobs and lights facing her, and she tilted the box, reading the label by each light and referring to her owner's manual.

" 'There will be one solid beep to indicate frequency change.

This will happen only when more than one transmitter is activated. After the beep, switch the listening channel.' " She quit reading and turned the small knob until it clicked. Popping sounded through the speaker. "God, I love these devices."

"Bobby!" someone yelled through the crackling.

Angela pulled her knee to her chin and wrapped her hands around her leg, resting her head and staring at the box.

"You need to feed the goons."

"What's the point?" a man asked, more than likely Bobby. "All they do is sit there like zombies. They aren't even pacing or talking anymore."

"Just because they're drugged doesn't mean they don't need to eat." Whoever was giving the order wasn't Mario.

"And isn't it your job to feed them?" Bobby complained.

"Not anymore. I've been promoted. You're feeding the goons now."

The goons were probably the people Mario had abducted for the game. A wave of excitement rushed through Angela. She almost jumped out of her chair. The people he'd kidnapped were there at his house somewhere.

"Look at you, Marco. Not an hour after tossing your *padre* into the lake, you assume his command with no remorse. Do you see what is happening?" Bobby sounded disgusted.

"Yes. I see clearly. You would, too, if you were smart," Marco hissed. "Mario will win the game. Do you know what the winner of the game receives?"

Angela stared at the box, her eyes burning from not blinking. She strained to catch every word. Recorded or not, this was what it was all about. Right here. Narrow in on the game and take it down, along with all of its morbid players.

"I'm going to own the world along with him," Marco said, his voice a hoarse whisper. "Mario isn't a monster. He's driven. And if you aren't, you'll end up like my *padre*. You have the choice. I choose to live."

"Like you could rule the word." Now Bobby was disgusted. "You don't even have a hold on your family."

"Feed the goons," Marco ordered.

"Feed them your own goddamn self."

Angela nibbled her lip, listening to the rustling sound coming through the speaker. There were a few grunts and silence. Already she could pin murder on Mario. There was enough proof, along with what she'd visibly seen, to get a warrant. Murder would put him away but wouldn't end the game. She had to hold out a day or so to learn more. None-theless, she wrote *lake* on the hotel note pad, which was on the table, and circled it. The body would be harder to find the longer she waited.

"Fine! I'll fucking feed them," Bobby panted, sounding out of breath.

"There are ten of them."

"I know that," Bobby hissed.

"Do you? You know the rules of the game you profess to despise?" Marco's accent was thicker, making him hard to understand.

Angela leaned forward, chewing her lower lip and closing her eyes so she could hear every word.

"Each player can have no more than ten pieces on the board at a time."

"If you behave, I'll show you the board."

Angela sat up so fast she almost toppled out of the chair. Gripping the sides of the table, she stared at the box. "Tell me where it is, baby," she whispered.

"How in the hell would you do that?"

"I've seen it," Marco said. "It's on his computer."

Angela was sure Bobby would be giving Marco a look of awe, just as she was to the box.

"Mario would kill you worse than he did your *padre*."

"Maybe. If he caught me. When he goes after that slut that was here, I'll take you to his bedroom and show you. It's pretty cool."

"Deal."

"Better hurry and feed the goons. He'll be heading out tonight."

Did that mean he would come looking for her tonight?

Angela could only imagine how many women he had parading around him. No wonder his family assumed she was a slut.

"So what's my best plan of attack now?" she mused, stretching and glancing around her room. She still expected Jake to storm in on her at any moment. She remembered him telling her she wouldn't see him unless she needed him but that didn't settle her nerves any. She shot another furtive look around the hotel room, focusing on the darker corners and staring at the dark shadow that loomed out of the bathroom.

"Marco!" A man yelled the name, his voice so audible it sounded as if he were right next to her.

Angela yelped, then slapped her hand to her forehead, exhaling loudly. "Lord, woman," she muttered under her breath. She was way too on edge. It was a damn good thing she was alone. She adjusted herself in her chair, putting her feet on the floor under the table and sitting straight, facing the box, and focusing on the small speaker.

"You know what Mario says about smoking on the patio." This man spoke with a polished accent, his voice calm and authoritative.

"It's been a tough evening. I doubt he'll deny me a smoke. Besides, I've been promoted. I have new responsibilities."

"Which you'll lose if you break the rules." Whoever spoke used a stern tone. He sounded like Mario but with a deeper voice; possibly he was older.

Interesting how the family Mario spoke of with such reverence and denied having in this country were those he used as his servants. It shouldn't surprise her. Turning his immediate family into hired help fit Mario's profile.

"Then don't tell him," Marco said, lowering his voice so that he sounded as stern as the man speaking to him.

"I won't. But Mario wants to see you. He sent me for you."

"Is he angry?"

"Of course. But I don't think at you. Come on."

Angela sat staring at the surveillance equipment, but several minutes went by without anyone speaking. She'd caught that conversation outside, on the patio, where she'd placed her last bug before running from the house and catching a cab.

If she were to go back to Mario's house and give the impression she wanted to talk to Mario and was upset, her presence would be justified. However, Marco wouldn't show the board to Bobby if she were there. Standing and stretching, she began pacing. Her next move could prove to be crucial in advancing this case.

There was one thing she didn't want to have happen: Mario couldn't come here. Taking time to change into a comfortable pair of shorts and tank top, Angela slipped into sandals and began cleaning her hotel room. Jake swore he would have her back, even when she didn't know it. Something told her that was true. As much as it unnerved her, there was also comfort in the thought that he was watching her wherever she was.

After putting her surveillance equipment away and doing a quick sweep of her room, making sure all was in order, Angela headed out, taking the elevator to the lobby. There would be witnesses to her leaving. Maybe she would even say something to the doorman. If Mario came looking for her, her absence wouldn't come across as odd.

"Good evening, miss," the night doorman said, bowing his head and looking at her solemnly with watery gray eyes. The old, thin gentleman was dressed in black tails, just as Benjamin did, but Angela hadn't seen this man before.

"Good evening." She didn't want to sound too cheerful. The doormen knew everything, saw everything, and reported it willingly to anyone who asked. She'd overheard Benjamin, the daytime doorman, gossiping with other guests since she'd started staying here. Although the doormen didn't do anything but stand at the door, since it oscillated or opened automatically, depending on which door you took, their position at this hotel was as icons. Angela knew this man would report her actions, behavior, and anything she said to him to anyone who might ask.

"Will you be needing a car this evening, miss?"

"I think I'm going to take a walk." She smiled at the older

gentleman, but he didn't return the smile. Instead, he nodded seriously. Angela decided a bit more information might be beneficial. "It's been a long day. I won't be out late. I thought I'd see if there was a coffee shop nearby. Just somewhere to go and relax and clear my head."

"Very good, miss. There are several shops nearby that I'm sure you'll find suitable. Feel free to call the hotel if you wish a ride back here." Although the door opened on its own, he still held his hand out, making a show of keeping it open for her when she stepped outside. "Be careful, miss."

Angela waved over her shoulder and walked onto the sidewalk outside. There was moisture in the air, as if it might rain. She felt it cling to her skin and hair almost immediately as she looked up and down the street, deciding which way to go.

Both sides of the street were lit up, and she finally chose the direction she was facing. There were several coffee shops, but Angela started toward a Starbucks sign across the street and a few minutes later was ordering a decaf espresso roast, since it was already getting late and she didn't want to be buzzed all evening. The rich, smooth blend went down easily as she sipped and stared out the glass windows.

Her thoughts continued lingering on heading back to Mario's. She would need to know when he left the house. It would help, as well, to be assured she wouldn't trip any security system around the house. The easiest way to do that would be to simply walk in through the front door. But if Mario wasn't there, she could demand to be allowed to wait for him in his bedroom. They already thought her a slut. If she were in his room, waiting for his return, she would have time to sit at his computer.

But what would she do once he returned? Mario would assume she was there to kiss and make up. Angela knew which direction that would go.

If she headed back to Mario's, she would definitely need backup in place. Just thinking about Jake watching her, every muscle in that perfect body of his tense and ready for action, got her hot. No matter how hard she tried thinking of him only as a partner, as a means to an end of the game, darker, tempting, enticing thoughts wouldn't leave her alone.

Why couldn't she have insisted on someone else for backup?

A man shouldn't be able to turn her on to the point where she couldn't think straight. It wasn't her style to lose control. She was honest by nature, though. Her anger and frustration were directed at her and not Jake, even if she let him feel the brunt end of it. Jake stirred something inside her differently than any other man had. It was almost as if she ached to surrender and allow all that brawn to overwhelm her. But at the same time an overwhelmingly powerful urge to make him submit, see only her, be completely unaware of any other woman on the planet, washed over her and intensified her already-feverish passion. No wonder she was frustrated and angry.

Angela finished her coffee, bought another one, and headed out of the store. In spite of drinking decaf, she was rejuvenated from the hot brew. It helped to convince herself laying out the pros and cons of Jake being her partner and covering backup would make it a hell of a lot easier to understand where to focus in order to keep him from manipulating her thoughts.

She strolled along her side of the street, taking her time returning to the hotel. It was damn hard not to glance around her. Was Jake really trailing her? As much as she wanted to believe he wasn't, he'd told her he would do just that. Jake didn't know she'd witnessed a murder earlier, or did he?

"Crap," she muttered, realizing she hadn't started her mental list intended to clear her head and calm her down.

On instinct she looked over her shoulder. Even at this hour, there were people on the street. They hurried, their heads down. Or small groups strolled in a cluster, chatting as they headed to their destinations. No one cared about her.

When she reached the hotel, she wasn't ready to close herself in her suite for the night. Raw energy still sizzled inside her, making her oversensitive to any noise around her and even to her clothes when they brushed against her skin.

At the next corner, she looked both ways before crossing and swore a large figure jumped into the shadows just across the street.

Angela instinctively slipped her hand into her purse where her gun was. Hurrying that way, she reached the spot where she'd seen the figure. It had been under an awning to a clothes store that was closed for the evening. There wasn't anyone there.

"Chasing shadows isn't going to help you any," she grumbled, adjusting her purse under her arm as she glanced around her.

She remained under the awning for a moment, staring at the mannequins dressed in cute outfits. If she was going to push this case forward, she needed to learn the details of the game. If she knew the next play or the play after that, it would help her prepare and know when to make her hit. Angela needed to know where the people Mario had abducted were, and she already had pretty decent confirmation that they were somewhere on Mario's property. She also needed to know who the other players in the game were. Once she had solid proof of all players, Angela could end the game forever. Could she buy herself enough alone time in Mario's room? Everything she needed to bring down the game might be on his computer.

If Mario was going to come after her, his limo would appear in front of the Drake. It would come from the opposite direction from where she stood. He'd either come personally or send someone for her. From where she stood, she could see the front entrance to the hotel. If Mario's limo showed up and he was in it, then he wasn't at home. But that wouldn't give her enough time to go to his house before he returned. Angela almost shrieked when her purse vibrated and her phone began ringing inside.

"What are you doing?" Jake asked when she answered on the first ring.

His deep baritone seeped into her brain like a warm aphrodisiac. Angela felt her insides swell and shifted her weight from one foot to the other, which caused her shorts to rub against her suddenly incredibly sensitive crotch. Her heart still pounded too hard in her chest, and if she didn't sound calm, in control, Jake would pick up on it instantly and he'd demand answers. He might decide to keep a closer eye on her.

Don't even think about where that might lead.

"You said you would always be watching me," she purred, keeping her attention on the well-lit drive in front of the Drake. There were no limos anywhere.

"I know where you are. What I don't understand is why you're standing under the awning of a closed store in the dark. That is, unless you have a second job you haven't told me about."

Angela's cheeks burned and she turned around quickly, half-expecting Jake to be standing right behind her. There was no one there. The side street was dark and quiet in both directions.

But when Jake laughed in her ear, the embarrassment plunging through her soon changed to anger. She wouldn't let him hold the stronger hand. "I'm heading back to Mario's," she announced.

"Miss him already?" Jake grumbled.

Angela smiled. She did hold the upper hand. Jake would have to comply with whatever decision she made on this investigation. His job was to ensure her safety, but he wasn't in a position to call the shots. That was her job.

"Desperately," she said dryly. "There are some new developments."

"There is a bookstore behind you," Jake interrupted. "Check out the fiction section."

"Why would I want to do that?" Angela waited for Jake to answer, but he didn't. She pulled her phone from her ear to see the call had ended. "Son of a bitch," she hissed, focusing again on the Drake before glancing down the street in the direction of the bookstore.

If Mario showed up and she wasn't in her room, he would think she got skittish and disappeared on him. Angela wasn't sure whether that would benefit her case or not.

The bookstore wasn't exactly what she expected. It was very large, with high ceilings and lots of shelves of books, DVDs, and videotapes. But it was an adult bookstore. Angela felt the eyes on her the moment she entered the establishment. Her guard went up immediately and she fingered the outside of her purse, feeling the hardness of her gun.

Rows of bookshelves crisscrossed one another, offering a fair amount of privacy for anyone wishing to browse. Angela walked past a couple men, both of whom failed miserably at being subtle when they gave her a curious once-over. She appeared to be the only woman in the store.

Her heart lodged in her throat for a moment when she spotted Jake, sprawled out on a love seat in the corner of the building. He was at the end of the aisle, his long legs sticking out, which would make it impossible to go past him without stepping over them. The love seat was barely noticeable under his massive frame. He leaned against one corner of the seat with his legs crossed at the other end. One arm was draped lazily over the back of the seat while he held a paperback in his other hand.

At first he didn't appear to notice her. He seemed rather involved with the story he was reading. Angela moved closer to him, looking for the first time at the books on the shelves. Some of their titles were rather alarming. She noticed a label above the books she glanced at—*Domination/ Submission.*

As she edged closer to the end of the aisle, it became harder to pay attention to the books. She pulled one out for a good show but was barely aware of the book. So much man sat within feet of her. Her body tingled, memories of him kissing her in his hotel room ransacking her brain. Suddenly it was too warm in the store. Her heart picked up a unique beat, pattering in her chest while her palms grew damp. The air was charged with sexual energy that had nothing to do with the amount of pornographic material surrounding her.

"Do you like the BDSM novels?" Jake asked, his voice barely above a whisper.

Nonetheless, Angela almost jumped when he spoke. She

shot him a scathing look. His shaggy brown hair bordered his masculine face, and intense green eyes danced with amusement as he stared at her over his paperback.

"Personally I lean more toward the threesomes," she told him, glancing at a title of a book in front of her at eye level. "Ever consider you and a good buddy of yours submitting to a woman and doing whatever she says?" When Jake's eyes sparked, his arousal apparent, Angela added for good measure, "Even doing each other while she watched?"

"Nope!" His aroused stare turned darker when he narrowed his gaze on her. "I don't mind a buddy joining me while a lady submits to my every command, though," he growled, the deepness of his voice causing the charged air to snap against Angela's flesh.

The corner of his mouth twitched and those damnable eyes of his were undressing her as she stood there. She'd give him two seconds to let her know why he brought her in here before she marched out of the store.

"You might find books more to your liking around the corner here." Jake pulled his legs in the best he could, implying she should come closer. He nodded to the other side of the shelf where she stood.

Angela started around the bookshelf. She hesitated when he moved his legs again. The brute would not trap her in the far corner. She could only imagine what type of peculiar fantasies might have been played out on that couch. Unfortunately, imagining what could be done in this semi-private public bookstore only made her blood pressure rise more.

If he were to trap her, she wouldn't be able to get away. The love seat barely held him, and if he pulled her down on top of him all of that brawn would touch her everywhere. She imagined no one stopping him or even watching while he held her captive, her body pressed against his . . .

Angela tripped over her own feet working her way around him and slapped her hand on his shoulder to brace herself. "Shit," she hissed.

"Can't keep your hands off me, can you?" Now he was grinning.

She was sure she growled. Even as she snatched her hand away, her fingers touched him long enough to crave all of that solid muscle even more.

"Go to hell," she whispered, finally making her way around the corner and finding herself blocked by two bookshelves. No one could see her except Jake.

"What have you learned?" he asked, his tone changing and sounding all business as he once again relaxed on the small sofa.

She studied his profile for a second as he raised the book, appearing to continue his reading. Angela sighed, her brain caught in a thick fog of lust. There couldn't possibly be a more infuriating man anywhere on this planet. Jake managed to unnerve her, create incredibly kinky images in her brain, and seemed more relaxed now than he had when she first spotted him.

It occurred to her no one could get to her now without passing Jake. He was her backup, her protector. And he was doing his job. Angela was safe in the store, and he was waiting for information. All was fine in the world of Jake King.

Damn him!

She stared at the books in front of her but forced her mind to matters at hand. "I've actually learned a lot," she began, choosing another book at random and flipping it open to an incredibly graphic sexual scene that immediately planted images in her mind. Except the characters were her and Jake. Angela pulled her gaze from the book. Like she would ever submit to being tied to a bed. She swallowed thickly. "The game has a board, like a real board game. It's on Mario's computer in his bedroom. He has ten people abducted because each player is only allowed ten pieces on the board." She whispered, speaking quickly, realizing she'd been dying to share what she'd learned.

"Damn." He breathed, not looking at her but focusing on his book. "Did you see the board game?"

"No, but there was an incident tonight," she continued. "I left his place upset and took a cab back to the hotel."

"I know." Jake didn't elaborate. "What was the incident?"

Sometime soon they would discuss exactly how he was staying out of sight. "A man was murdered," she whispered.

Angela swore Jake's knuckles grew whiter as he gripped the book.

"Mario killed one of his hired help. I managed to plant my bugs at his home, before it happened, and I slipped out of there during all the chaos," she continued, her heart slowly resuming its steady beat. Angela glanced in the opposite direction of Jake, then peered into the bookshelf, confirming there was wood behind the books and no one could stand anywhere on another aisle and see or hear her. "I left two bugs at his home and picked up new intel once I arrived at the hotel." Angela repeated the conversation she'd heard between the two men who'd been on Mario's patio. "I also learned Mario is coming after me. He might be at the Drake right now. I am going to take advantage of him searching for me and return to his home. While he's gone I'll wait for him in his bedroom. Hopefully that will give me enough time to search his computer."

"His computer will be password protected," Jake guessed, although he spoke as if it was knowledge he already knew.

Angela had thought of that but also remembered how confident Marco had sounded when he offered to show Bobby the board for the game. "I'm not sure that it is," she said slowly. "The hired help I met didn't appear smart enough to figure out someone's password. And if I have enough time, I can put a tracking program on his computer."

"How are you getting back over there?"

"I'll take a cab."

"What are you going to do when he returns?"

Jake glanced in her direction for the first time since their conversation began. She met his gaze and prayed he didn't see how wary she was of being alone with Mario in his bedroom. "I'm going to talk to him, ask how the older man is doing that I saw murdered, and make sure Mario believes I didn't witness a crime."

Jake didn't take his gaze from hers. Once again heat rushed over her, pooling between her legs. Angela couldn't look away. As much as she believed in her heart that Jake would provide the protection he swore to her that he would, she also knew that she was going to make a liar out of herself. Sometime soon, she would do more than just kiss Jake King. The longer she stared at him, the sooner she hoped it would be.

Chapter Seven

Jake didn't remain in his hotel room this time when Angela left to return to Mandela's home. He returned to the rental car he'd picked up earlier that evening and slid behind the steering wheel, closing and locking the car doors before turning on the engine. He opened the glove box and pulled out the tracking monitor that told him where Angela was—as long as the small, round pad remained on the back of her spine, just below the waistband of her shorts. Hopefully it wouldn't be detected. This way he could keep an eye on her from a fair distance without anyone thinking she was being followed. Hopefully Angela wouldn't let Mario get his paws all over her. The bug would stick to her like a good Band Aid and not come off, even in a shower, unless she seriously scrubbed her lower back. Most people didn't. They rubbed soap on their arms, shoulders, maybe the back of their neck, then let the water rinse it down the rest of their body.

His feelings about Angela should bug him more than they did. Jake damn near saw red just thinking about her being in that monster's arms. She didn't strike him as the type of woman who would sleep with the enemy. Jake could see in her eyes how badly she wanted to end the game, though. It made him want to stick to her side like glue until all of this was over.

Jake wanted to be at her side for other reasons, too. Especially after hot, mind-blowing sex.

He picked up on Angela's wariness, though, the moment she entered the bookstore. The way Angela looked at him after explaining what she'd do at Mandela's place remained burned in his mind.

Angela wanted him. Women came in all shapes and sizes, but lust burned hot the same in all of them. Jake had learned to understand that look straight out of puberty. Hell, when a person loved doing something, they became an expert at it. What bugged him were the overwhelming protective urges he felt toward Angela.

King men were protective and possessive. Jake had heard his dad say so enough times and seen his father and his brother show both traits around their women. Angela wasn't his woman, though. Jake wasn't used to running backup on an investigation. He was a bounty hunter for Christ's sake. That was probably why he was feeling all weird around her.

Angela didn't have him figured out yet. Not that Jake should be surprised. He didn't have himself figured out yet, either, especially when it came to her. It was one thing to feel that sexual pull when they first saw each other. And kissing her would naturally make him wonder and hope for what would come next. But damn it! He was scared there was something else there, too. It was easy to see it in her eyes, but he knew what he saw was also inside him. Hopefully it was just curiosity. Jake had never met a beautiful woman with a passion for the hunt, for unveiling a mystery, as strong as his. Angela's furtive glances stopped once she started sharing what she'd learned. Her pretty eyes flashed with the excitement that knowledge brought when clues began unraveling. The anxiousness that grew in his gut as she shared her information ran hot in her, also.

Angela had been doing undercover work for a while now. He'd done his research on her. She'd been a licensed private investigator for four years. She was twenty-three. She'd lived with her father since she was sixteen and prior to that with her mother in Buenos Aires. Investigating was all Angela knew. It was in her blood, in her heart, and in her soul, which explained why she became a licensed P.I. damn near soon as she was legally able to do so. Jake had more in common with Angela than with any other lady he'd ever been with. Maybe that explained his possessive reaction toward her.

Whatever his reaction toward her, it was definitely strong. Too strong to just be lust. Which terrified him. If he liked Angela, really liked her, why the hell was he letting her work her way into a murderer's bedroom? Her window of opportunity was so damn narrow her chances of getting out without being discovered were slim to nil.

They were in a dangerous line of work. What she proposed doing tonight, though, went beyond dangerous. It was deadly. Not only did she risk getting raped if Mandela discovered her alone in his room, but if he grew leery of her being there she could get seriously hurt or killed. Tonight he needed to be positioned just right so that if Angela's plan backfired, he could get her the hell out of there before anything happened to her.

As sexy and beautiful as she was, Angela was also intelligent. She would do whatever it took to solve this case, return the kidnapped victims to their homes, and end the game forever. She was stubborn and would lock horns with him just for kicks. That didn't bother Jake. And it surprised him more than a little bit that it didn't. All those wonderful attributes he saw in Angela spelled out one simple description—"high maintenance." Jake didn't do high maintenance.

What was it about Angela that had him thinking like this?

Angela and her father had made it clear she was in charge. That didn't mean Jake should let her make foolish decisions. Jake's gut twisted with nervous trepidation. Why the hell did he agree to let her go on this insane mission?

He slowed within a block of Mandela's home. This part of Chicago was one mansion after another, each of them sitting on prime land and far off the road. A few he couldn't see from where he sat. Mario Mandela's home, which he'd signed a twelve-month lease to rent, was visible from the road but surrounded by a very tall black rod iron fence. Tall, pointed spikes every few feet on the fence made the place appear very uninviting, if not intimidating. The place just looked like a cold-blooded, murdering Italian Mafia lord would live there. A managing company rented the place to Mandela. Jake hadn't been able to find out who actually owned the mansion. Furthermore, Jake couldn't find out much about the management company, Luxury Living, other than they weren't registered with the Better Business Bureau. It wouldn't surprise Jake if the management company and the owner of this place were both crooks.

What he had managed to get, after having the thought come to him to check to see if Luxury Living had a website, which they did, were the floor plans of the homes they had listed for rent. Jake couldn't tell from the ambiguity of the site if the home Mario was in was currently listed as being for rent, or if it hadn't been removed from the site since it had just been rented. It showed the site had last been updated two weeks ago, which was two weeks after Mario had moved in. What the site didn't display were availability dates on any of their homes. For all Jake could tell every home they managed had floor plans on this site. Definitely a shady organization!

Regardless, Jake had been able to print the floor plans to Mandela's home. The accuracy of the website or how scrupulous they were, or were not, wasn't his problem. Jake already had a basic idea of the layout of the yard surrounding the home, and where it would be hardest for anyone to see someone jump the fence. It would be a bitch getting over those black spikes in the tall rod iron fence, but not impossible.

Getting situated in the car, turning the monitor so he could see it, and adjusting the backlight on the screen so it let off minimal light, he got as comfortable as possible. He had endured more stakeouts than he ever wanted to and knew the most important part of waiting was not allowing himself to get stiff. If he needed to spring into action, the last thing he needed was a foot or hand going to sleep on him. He stretched his large body out as best he could and actually got rather comfortable. He would have to change positions every few minutes to keep the blood circulating.

It hit him he hadn't bothered responding to any text messages since the other day when he'd still been home. Jake pulled out his phone and stared at it. The day was almost over and he hadn't received any text messages. He hadn't answered the ones he had received yesterday or the day before. His women were finding other men who would give them the time of day.

As he stared out the front windshield into the darkness, Jake realized that it didn't bother him. He'd grown tired a long time ago of lining up so many ladies as if they were notches on a bedpost. Old habits die hard and it simply took him a while to come to terms with the fact. He needed to keep in mind his time here in Chicago was short-term, though. Jake would return to L.A. as soon as this case was wrapped up. So did that mean once he was home he would start searching for one woman to date on a steady basis?

That thought didn't appeal to him, either.

Sighing heavily, Jake dropped his phone in his cup holder between the seats. His rental car still smelled new, and the seat was stiff when he adjusted it to recline a bit. He tilted his head to stare at the monitor. His thoughts drifted to Angela approaching him in the bookstore earlier.

The shorts and tank top she wore had showed off her slender legs. Her top barely reached her shorts, giving him a peek at her stomach. It was flat, hard, and toned to perfection. Those spaghetti straps kept threatening to slip over her shoulders, which had distracted him from ogling her round, full breasts. And there was no missing those perky, hard nipples. His mouth watered just thinking about them. The rest of him was hard as stone, lust and something even more primitive, more possessive and predatory, coming from deeper inside him, stirred to life as he thought of her.

When she had neared him in the back of the store, her long dark hair streaming past her shoulders and down her back, a carnal urge had sprung to life inside him. Suddenly

he understood that urge. It was the need to protect, to claim
and make him her man.

Jake wasn't sure how he knew what he was feeling. He
tried remembering the last time a woman drew so much out
of him and couldn't. Possibly his mother, but that was a completely different group of emotions. That was how he identified what he felt, though. He would kill to protect his family,
and already, after having met Angela a year ago and now
being with her again for less than a day, those feelings burned
as strong inside him as the need to impale her and experience
her soaked heat wrapped around him.

"God damn," he hissed, straining to adjust his vision to
see outside. He glanced at his rearview and side mirrors,
looked over his shoulder, and surveyed the land outside in
front of him. He appeared to be completely alone.

Appearances could be deceptive, though, which was why
he needed to remain alert. Sitting there with a boner and
imagining how incredible having sex with Angela would be
made it harder to focus on his job. This wasn't the first time
he'd done surveillance work. It was often a long, boring part
of the investigation. But it was necessary and could be the
most important part of the job. He was there to protect Angela. God only knew what might happen to her if he weren't.

Jake focused on the small, round dot that blinked on the
screen, showing him where Angela was at this moment.
The dot was moving. She'd found her cab and was coming
to the mansion. He straightened, watching the dot and shifting his attention to his surroundings outside until he finally
spotted headlights.

A city cab passed him, slowed, and stopped down the
street in front of the rod iron gate blocking the entrance to
Mandela's mansion. The cab door opened and Angela stepped
outside. Her hair lifted off her back from the breeze as she
walked to the gate, took a moment studying it, then found
the small box on the side that would announce her presence.
If her plan worked, she would be inside the gate soon. Jake
would have to get closer, too.

He would have preferred time to get a very accurate layout of the outside of the home. Knowing where all the security cameras were was a plus. Many times homes like this, as well as small businesses, and even at times larger businesses when they were trying to cut costs, or were just plain greedy with their cash flow, had fake security cameras. Jake had learned early on in the job how to tell if a surveillance camera was for real, or just a deterrent and didn't actually record or transmit anything.

Jake stared at her rear end, watching as she shifted her weight from foot to foot and waited. Angela's black strands curled at the ends, right above her ass. The shorts she wore hugged her hips and accentuated her nice curves. After a minute it appeared things weren't going as Angela had planned. She lowered her head, causing her long hair to fall forward and block his view of her face. Angela pushed the button on the box and said something, although Jake couldn't hear her from this distance.

When Angela returned to the cab, Jake exhaled. His nerves were wound tight. Even though he'd been prepared to get up and personal with that house while she was inside, it didn't bother him a bit that she'd have to find another way to gather her intel. He didn't want her alone with Mandela. When they met back at the hotel, Jake needed to convince her of a better way to release all those abducted people and take down Mandela.

Mario tapped his finger against his lips as he stared out the tinted window. Tomas pulled away from the Drake, not saying a word as he merged into what little traffic there was at this hour. Mario didn't mind the silence. Half the reason he'd kept Tomas on was because the man never said a word. He dutifully did as he was told without questioning Mario. If only his family could be so efficient.

He searched for the remorse for what he had done to his uncle but couldn't find any. Mario offered his sweat and blood to give those around him a good life. Even when he told himself Uncle Petrie was trying to warn Mario about Signorina Torres, Mario knew he'd done the right thing.

Uncle Petrie screaming that Angela was a slut simply confirmed the old man didn't have a clue how to be professional. He'd become a liability. This wasn't the old country, where everyone yelled at one another. In America, yelling sent people into shock. As it had Angela, causing her to run.

Mario continued tapping his finger, wondering if her running wasn't the result of something else. Possibly she'd taken advantage of Mario's uncle's outburst to flee the scene. Which she would have done if she was guilty of something.

In Mario's *padre*'s time, it would simply be a matter of finding her family. Blood proved a lot. Mario's *padre* always had told him that. Family was everything. Know the family and you know the person.

Mario leaned back, envying how simple things had been in his *padre*'s time. Mossimo Mandela had married the most beautiful woman on the planet. They had five children and Mario knew his *padre* regretted that Mario wasn't his first-born son. Of course Mo Sr. mourned Mo Jr.'s death. A father did that sort of thing. But Mo Sr. never had questioned how his son died. Mario's *padre* never sent his men or anyone from the village down to the river to investigate how it could be that such a strong teenage boy could die where he had. The undercurrents could get deadly, but they were a ways from the ocean. The river didn't flow as fast where Mo's body had been found. That death had been necessary, just as Uncle Petrie's death had been. From the day after Mo's oldest son perished, drowning in the river, Mo had kept Mario at his side. It was their secret, one they never discussed. Mo Mandela was quite possibly the smartest man on earth. Mario knew it and so did Mo. Mario never brought up his older brother's death, and Mo never asked questions.

"So what would you do now, Padre?" Mario whispered.

Tomas didn't turn his head or give any indication he heard Mario speak. Mario glanced at his cell, which was still perched on his knee. He'd come looking for Angela, and she'd gone back to his house. The *signorina* perplexed him and got his dick harder than stone.

Who would return to a scene that she'd run from in terror?

It would have been one thing if she'd called the police, frantic that she'd just witnessed a death. Mario could have handled that. The American judicial system was too easy to work around. Money was everything, and Mario had plenty of that.

"But you didn't return with the *polizia,* did you, *signorina*?" he mused, and continued tapping his finger against his lips as he tried figuring out the sexy black-haired *seduttrice.* "So why did you return?"

What would provoke a person to return to a scene of a crime? Mario let his memories slide backward until he sat on the stool next to his *padre*'s desk. Padre would lean back in his wooden chair that was worn in a concave pattern from years of him sitting there. His hands would be clasped behind his head, forcing those thick black waves that were laced with silver to push forward and border his round face. Padre would puff on his pipe, angling his gaze so his black, watery eyes focused on Mario, on his favorite son.

"*Che cosa succederà ora*?" Padre would ask in his husky, influenza-inflected voice.

Mario always straightened when asked that question. His *padre* cared what Mario thought. Mo saw the intelligence in Mario and helped it blossom. Mario would predict the next action, or step, in whatever they'd been discussing. It might have been town politics or how to reprimand one of his *fratelli o sorelle.* Mario had enjoyed deciding the appropriate punishment for one of his siblings. Mo Mandela was a strong advocate of corporal punishment, which usually kept most of the Mandela offspring well behaved. As Mario grew older, deciding the best outcome for the people in his town appealed to him more. He'd almost been a man when he and his *padre* had argued heatedly about the best way to govern the people.

That had been the day Mario and his *padre* had screamed and yelled at each other until Mario's father burst out into a fit of coughing. Mario had gone to the tobacco pouch, shoved his *padre*'s pipe deep into the pungent leaves, then brought the deadly tobacco to his *padre* and forced him to inhale until it killed him. But not before Mario had learned everything his *padre* had to teach.

It had been an honorable death. Mossimo Mandela had died where he was master of his *terra,* which was much better than dying slowly in *l'ospedale.* Nor had he faded away to nothing, no longer able to command his world, or protect and provide for his family. Mario knew his *padre* looked down on him from heaven with love and pride. *Il mio unico figlio generato.*

"What should happen next?" Mario repeated the words in English his *padre* had always asked him. If only he could ask his *padre* that question now.

Angela had been standing next to Mario when his uncle began his rant. Mario had leapt into the house when his temper had erupted. Uncle Petrie had collapsed to the floor after Mario had broken the old man's neck. When Mario had turned, Angela was gone. Marco had just stood there, dumbfounded, staring at a corpse that wouldn't move instead of paying attention to Angela, who was quite capable of flight.

"You didn't go to the *polizia* if you returned alone." Mario pondered this, staring at his phone. Marco had sounded too excited, already too full of himself with his new rank and authority. Marco was a hypocrite, mourning his *padre*'s death yet thrilled to have his job. And he was an idiot for not paying attention to Angela when he should have been. "So now the moron calls and tells me she's at the gate," he grumbled, thinking too little too late, an American expression he was rather fond of.

Angela had even suggested she wait in Mario's bedroom, not wishing to be in the way of the staff, until Mario returned.

It had been a tempting offer and one Mario had almost accepted. "There is no brain in balls," he murmured, one of of his *padre*'s favorite expressions that translated well into English. And also one Mario's *madre* despised. Mario credited himself for thinking on his feet. There was no reason for Angela to be in his home if he wasn't there.

Regardless of how many times his *padre* had encouraged him to marry, Mario knew himself well. Mo Mandela had been many things and even in death had his honor. Mario would swear on his *padre*'s grave that he never once cheated on Mario's *madre*. He also knew himself well enough to know he wouldn't be able to take that matrimonial oath. One woman simply wasn't enough.

Which was why Angela would wait for his return and enter his home with him. She wouldn't get so comfortable at his home that she felt she could come and go as she pleased. No *donna* would ever work her way into Mario's world and feel she was part of it. Angela was around because she intrigued him. He wanted to fuck her. They weren't friends and never would be. Mario saw clearly, even when he was a *bambino*, how his *madre* was his *padre*'s weakness. Mario would never allow an Achilles' heel. Not when the world was so dangerous.

Besides, he needed time to dissect the information Marco had show him earlier.

Mario had conducted the search on Angela Torres after first meeting her at the country club. Her story had seemed believable, which was why he had questioned it. Not to mention she was new on the scene. He wasn't paranoid, but a man could never be too cautious. Diving into something just because it was hot and sweet could blindside a man. Mario knew he wasn't perfect, but he strived to make as few mistakes as possible. Angela had been witty, charming, and very flirtatious the first time he'd met her. Her behavior hadn't changed. But Mario always did a thorough background check on any bitch he decided he wanted to fuck.

When Mario did a background check on Angela, the only flag he came up with was that there was hardly any information on her. Which would make sense if her story was true. She'd received most of her education from being tutored while living in her parents' different homes in Europe and in America. Mario had confirmed her mother was in Buenos Aires, which was where Angela said she was currently residing. Angela had recently come to Chicago to spend time with her father. She had told Mario if she gave both of her parents equal time each year it helped ensure her monthly checks from each of them continued coming in.

His uncle had run a background check on a local detective.

It was a project Mario had given the old man, one to help him learn how to be comfortable using a computer, and as well, it was always good to know what all local law enforcement was doing. Uncle Petrie had reported every little thing about any officer on the force and detective in the area. It had gotten old. No matter how much Mario tried emphasizing he only wanted to know if any of them were involved in local scandal or if there was ever news on their family, his idiot of an uncle continued hurrying to tell him every little detail about all law enforcement in Chicago.

When Uncle Petrie had sent Marco to Mario's bedroom, with Angela alone in his room with him, Mario had started wondering if Uncle Petrie would ever learn. It was easy to see why Mario's *padre* had little use for his brothers. And there were six of them. Mario had grown up with Uncle Petrie and Uncle Enrico. Both of them were a lot younger than Mario's *padre*. Mossimo Mandela had helped raise his youngest siblings. So where was the appreciation?

It was another lesson Mario learned. Family mattered more than anything, but when they became a handicap it was his duty to eliminate them. Nothing would tarnish the family name. Uncle Antonio was proof of that. He was the firstborn Mandela son. Mo was next in line. That hadn't stopped Mario's *padre,* and it hadn't stopped Mario. Something had happened between his *padre* and Mario's uncle when Mario had been in his late teens. He remembered the night well. His *madre* had cried for his *padre* not to leave the house. Mo had been stern, even going as far as to tell Mario to take care of his *madre*. When Mo came home he refused to discuss what had happened, but Mario never saw Uncle Antonio again.

It was how life worked. Mario had worked closely with Uncle Petrie, even when he knew the old man was skating on Mario's coattails. Uncle Petrie didn't have hard jobs. Mario never gave him too much responsibility. And Mario paid him well to sit around and be a useless bum, which he was very good at being.

Wouldn't it just figure the one time he came to Mario with a bit of news worth biting his teeth into he would present it at the most inopportune time? What the hell was Mario supposed to do with Angela: leave her alone in his bedroom? Like hell!

Uncle Petrie was thickheaded enough not to figure that out. He pressed and pressed, even after Mario instructed Marco to have his *padre* hold on to the information until he could come to them. It wasn't until after Uncle Petrie's death that Mario sat down and took a look at the old article his uncle had found online.

He had sat at Uncle Petrie's desk and stared at the article that was still pulled up on the old man's computer. Mario couldn't help wondering if he'd made a terrible mistake with Angela. Unfortunately, there was no way to know for certain. Uncle Petrie had been convinced, obviously. Marco seemed to believe it to be true as well. The short article was about the nationally recognized private detective James Huxtable, who lived right here in Chicago. The picture was seven years old and the article didn't name the daughter. Mario had stared at the picture for a long time. Huxtable stood next to his teenage daughter, both grinning recklessly at the camera. The teenage girl was pretty, her soft curves just starting to form and her thick black hair tumbling down her front in two neat braids.

Mario was pretty sure Angela had green eyes. It looked like the kid in the picture had the same stubborn jaw line and pouty lips that would soon turn into a seductress's alluring mouth. Angela dressed to show off her cleavage and the rest of her hot body. Mario didn't spend a lot of time looking at her face. One of those programs that did age enhancement would make it a hell of a lot easier to decide if the kid in the picture and Angela were one and the same.

This was a matter he would research further on his own, though. Not only did he not want any of his family, or hired help, thinking Mario was considering that he might have been wrong in killing Uncle Petrie, it was a delicate matter that he best handle discreetly. Not to mention, the old man was better off dead.

However, if Angela was, in fact, Huxtable's daughter,

then she wasn't rich. Which meant it was probably not a coincidence that they met. If the little *puttana* was investigating him on behalf of her *padre*, Mario would have some fun
with the bitch before killing her. Or maybe he'd hold on to
her and make her part of his army.

Due troie sono meglio di uno.

"Is that picture of you, Signorina Angela?" Mario bit back
a smile as he thought about adding to his *puttana* collection.

A few minutes later Mario stepped out of his limo as
Tomas held the door for him. Marco hurried across the large
six-stall garage.

"We couldn't get her to wait," Marco said, out of breath.
"She was *une l'molto arrabiato.*

"What?" Mario hadn't decided whether Marco's busy-
body nature was an asset or an annoyance just like his dim-
witted intelligence. "The signorina drives back to my home
but refuses to wait ten minutes for me to return? Why was
she so upset?"

"I did everything you told me to do," Marco complained.
"The *signorina* said she was too upset to wait and not be
alone. She said if you didn't want her in your bedroom that
was fine with her," he finished, winded, then rocked on his
heels as if he were pleased to relay the message to Mario.

"That's fine." Mario waved him off. All that mattered was
Angela wasn't there. As to why she was upset, he could
wait to find out. There wasn't any proof that Angela Torres
was James Huxtable's daughter. If she was, though, she'd
lied to him. It wouldn't have bothered Mario if her father
was an investigator. Hell, that might have made fucking her
even hotter. What mattered was the truth.

It had been easy enough to verify Mona Torres lived in
Buenos Aires. As for Angela's father, her *padre*, Juan Torres,
an investor, whom, according to Angela, loved to play the
American and European stock markets, he was a bit harder to
validate. Torres was a global player and someone Mario
would love to know. Not as someone dating his daughter. *Ni-
ente affato!*

Mario would love picking the man's brain. He didn't want,

or need, a mentor. Very soon Mario would be close to one of the wealthiest men on earth. Money was power, and ensured control. Mario wouldn't be one of those *idioti* who lost his fortune because his government didn't know how to maintain a budget. Thinking globally was the right move. Angela's father was a smart man to do the same and knowing his secrets would be advantageous as Mario worked his way to the top.

If Angela had lied to him, she'd dishonored him. No *puttana* anywhere would ever believe she was smarter than Mario Mandela.

If Angela was lying and her father was Huxtable, Mario would have to give her credit for being one smart bitch. Fabricating a lie that would grab Mario's attention and appeal to him to the point where he dwelt on the lie more than trying to verify it was fucking impressive. He would learn the truth, though, and soon.

Mario headed out the side door of the garage and followed a brick path to one of his outbuildings. Right now, there were other matters to deal with. Marco chased after him as if he were the family dog, eager to stay close to his master in case he might get a treat.

"Where is Bobby?" Mario stopped and did an about-face fast enough that Marco almost tripped over his own feet.

"I'm not sure." Marco took the necessary steps backward to get out of Mario's space but stuttered and wrung his hands like an old woman as he searched Mario's face. Marco looked worried. "He might be in the kitchen or he could be in the stables. Am I in charge of him, too?" Marco brightened with his last question, looking hopeful.

"Find him." Mario ignored Marco's question. He needed to plot out the next couple days, and wanted someone with half a brain to take instructions. "Send him to me." Mario left Marco standing on the walk and headed to the outbuilding.

Bobby Anderson was a bum. Over a year ago Mario had run into the man scrounging through a Dumpster. Mario wouldn't have believed a human being could stink so bad until he met Bobby. The moment he saw Mario's limo, Bobby had started pestering Mario for a job. He had promised to do anything, no chore would be beneath him, if Mario would give him a hot meal and a place to sleep. Mario had agreed to Bobby's terms. The man had proven to be a damn good employee.

Mario pressed the buttons on the security pad outside the metal door to the large outbuilding, then let himself inside. Reaching for the light switch on the wall, he flooded the large room with fluorescent light.

"Army, stand at attention!" he barked, his voice echoing off the high ceiling as he gave the order.

Ten men and women leapt to their feet and stared straight ahead. Mario would have to hand it to Evelyn, her slave juice was impressive. His army had come to attention when he'd ordered them to do so before, but they had glared at him with hatred. Now they stood tall and proud. There was no hatred, no resentment. None of them cared that they were in cages. They had no concerns at all. He was the only one doing the thinking in this unit.

"Our first battle starts tomorrow," he informed them, not bothering to raise his voice this time. It didn't matter whether they heard him or not. Tomorrow morning they would fly out, their first attack being here in America. The game was the most thrilling venture Mario had ever embarked upon. The stakes were high, but winning would give him absolute power and control. Every leader on this planet would answer to him. And all it would take was strategically planting his army and training them to kill without hesitation. He smiled at the men and women standing in their cages. There was no way Mario could lose.

"Mr. Mandela."

Mario couldn't help smiling. He'd told Bobby in the past to call him Mario. He turned, facing the man, who was probably close in age to Mario. He knew everything there was to know about Bobby. The man had worked at a plastic factory straight out of high school, held on to the job for ten years, and lost it when the factory laid off almost all their workers. Bobby had tried to find another job. When Mario met him that night a year ago, Bobby had lost his car, his apartment, and his girlfriend. To this day Bobby would solemnly tell Mario he didn't have the rank to call Mario by his first name. Bobby was old-school. His loyalty and admiration held more weight with Mario than all the blood his family could offer.

"Bobby, how are you doing tonight?" Mario used the same soft voice he'd used on his army a moment ago.

"Very good, sir. How are you?" Bobby didn't look at Mario's army. He didn't suggest he knew anything about Uncle Petrie's death. The man stared directly at Mario, appearing calm and without a care in the world, and his question sounding sincere.

"I can't complain." Mario continued smiling. It was a line his father always had used and when he'd been alone with Mario had explained that complaining never got a man anywhere, but action did.

"I can't complain, either." Bobby moved his hands behind his back, his blue eyes sparkling and his tousled sandy blond hair making him almost attractive. Recently, Bobby had taken to shaving every day, which impressed Mario even more. Before, with the unkempt whiskers, Bobby had looked like a bum. Now, give the man a suit and he'd probably pass as a businessman. "What can I do for you, sir?"

Bobby never waited to be told what to do. If he wasn't doing something, he asked for a task. Again, another admirable trait.

"Our army looks good." Mario had a good feeling about including Bobby in planning his attack.

"Thank you, sir. They are shipping out to Kansas City in the morning, correct?"

"Yes, they are." It was a small attack, and one easily won. The bombing of the building in the midwestern city wouldn't garnish much attention. The winner of the attack, the one who succeeded in getting their army to perform the attack first, and successfully, would move on to the next battle in St. Louis, then Minneapolis and after that, Dallas. The final American battle was in D.C. Once all twelve buildings, each in a different city, were blown up, the federal government would pay heed and listen. It was rather ironic the game was set up to conquer the United States first. Mario would have chosen the Middle East or several European countries. He didn't mind owning the U.S., though. It was a gluttonous nation but powerful nonetheless.

As if reading Mario's thoughts, Bobby also smiled. "They will be petty attacks at first. But your army is top-of-the-line. I'm very confident, sir, that you'll win this country within a week of playing."

"I am, too." Mario laughed along with Bobby. "I need you to take care of some things for me tonight, though," he added, shifting gears and turning from Bobby.

"Anything you say, Boss," Bobby offered, the smile still in his tone.

"I know."

Mario walked between the cages where each of his men and women still stood perfectly straight and at attention. They would remain that way all night if Mario didn't tell them to lie down and sleep, which they would need to do soon. The slave juice rewired their brains. Mario wasn't sure how the drug worked, and honestly he didn't care. He had tested it to his satisfaction while in California. As perfect as the drug was, humans were very flawed. Run them into the ground and they would collapse. Several of the game members had tried using slave juice on their army and had made that mistake, which inevitably had wiped out their army and forced their elimination from the game. Mario had stepped up and was now a player on the board game. He would go to any means to win.

Mario wrapped his fingers around one of the bars to his hot little *puttana*'s cage. She stood motionless, staring straight ahead with large, dark brown eyes. Her thick, black hair was as long as Angela's although his *puttana* was much younger, barely legal. She was the tenth member of his army, and definitely the youngest.

"My pretty little *puttana*" he sung under his breath as he wagged his fingers in between her cage bars. His dark-skinned *buena* simply stared at him. "Do you remember committing murder, my pet?" he whispered, leaning closer to the cage bars.

"What?" Bobby asked.

Mario shook his head. "Nothing. Just having a conversation with one of my soldiers."

Bobby chuckled. "She's hot as hell."

"Yes, she is. Maybe after you take care of a matter for me, you can spend some time with her. We can order the rest of our army to all watch," he suggested, and caught Bobby grinning. "It's always work before play, though."

"Of course." Bobby nodded at the young woman standing at attention in the middle of her cage. "But shouldn't you enjoy the *signorina* first?" he asked.

It was strong proof of loyalty when a man understood his lower rank and assumed his boss should enjoy the spoils of war instead of him.

"She's a bit too young for me," Mario said, looking at Bobby. "Now a younger man like you—"

It was probably the first time Bobby had ever interrupted Mario, although he did it with laughter. "You know as well as I do we're about the same age," Bobby said, still chuckling.

"We might be at that." Mario left his *puttana* and patted Bobby's arm as he started toward the outside doors. "I want you to go up to Uncle Petrie's room. Box up all of his things. Maybe we'll donate them to charity. Let me know if you find anything valuable, though."

"Yes, sir."

"While you're up there, the computer is opened to an article about a local detective. I want you to take a good look at the teenage girl in the picture on that page and tell me what you think."

"Is there something wrong with her?" Another quality about Bobby: he admitted when he was confused. Not once had he made a mistake while working for Mario. It was because Bobby didn't take on an assignment without completely understanding all parameters.

"Not at all. Just tell me what you think after looking at the picture."

"Yes, sir."

"That's all."

Bobby nodded and left Mario alone with his army. Mario walked over to the cage where a young police officer he had abducted from right here in Chicago stood with her hands relaxed at her sides. "Are you ready to help me conquer the world, *mi amore*?"

"Yes," she said, her tone breathy.

Mario laughed. She would have agreed if he'd asked her to take off all her clothes and do cartwheels.

"Which one do you think is hotter?" Mario asked the *giovane*, who was in the cage between the cop and the young *puttana*.

Each cage was six by eight feet and six feet in height. He had them built into the outbuilding; his intention at the time was to make it impossible to break out of them. The slave juice took away that worry. Mario probably could leave all the cages unlocked and none of his army would go anywhere. As effective as Van Cooper's drug appeared to be, Mario didn't take chances.

The *giovane* glanced at the cop, since Mario had gestured to her. He looked at Mario and said nothing.

"Does not compute?" Mario sneered, then laughed. "*Idioti*."

Slave juice didn't allow whoever was under its influence to reason. Instructions had to be kept as simple commands. Mario had taken the time to work with his army while they were on slave juice. He had experimented with many different forms of commands. And although it was likely his competition on the board game would assume slave juice would make their army into obedient slaves, and they wouldn't take the time to confirm just how it worked, Mario was prepared for anything the other players might bring on.

"At least you're a sexy *piccolo cogna* when you stare blankly at me with those large, pretty eyes of yours," Mario said as he walked over to stand in front of his young *puttana*. Her eyes weren't too large for her oval-shaped face. She blinked once, flashing long thick black lashes at him. Mario thought he had detected a bit of a fiery nature the day he'd given her a big, friendly hug at the airport before injecting her with slave juice.

It had been as easy as he'd been told it would be. The syringe and needle were smaller and more slender than a pen. Coming up behind the *signorina* as she waited for her luggage, Mario had wrapped his arms around her. He'd hugged her and slid the needle into her pulsing vein at the side of her neck. He had told her to hush and she hadn't cried out, or even uttered a word. The slave juice was one hell of a fast-acting drug. He hadn't wasted any time escorting her out of the airport and had intentionally kept his head lowered or his back to all security cameras he had noticed.

"How much of your brain is still working?" Instead of telling her to move toward him, Mario reached into the cage, took her arm, and pulled her up against the bars.

The young *signorina* hadn't been the *donna* Mario had been told he would receive, and that he'd paid dearly for. There were those who were very skilled at finding men and women who were young, healthy, in good shape, and wouldn't have anyone looking for them if they suddenly disappeared. It was unbelievable how many traveled, having told no one they'd left their homes, and had no one waiting for them at their new destination.

Mario paid $500 on the delivery of an acceptable man or woman. The people he contracted to handle supplying his army worked hard for their money. With this particular purchase for a woman arriving at the Los Angeles airport, his contact had found a newly divorced lady flying out of Mexico City into L.A. At the last minute she was a no-show. His contact was on a different flight, intentionally arriving at a different part of the very large airport.

It wasn't until after his contact landed, and had a signal on his cell phone, did he learn of the no-show and was able to call Mario. The *donna* had fallen through but would a young *signorina*, a college student traveling all the way from Buenos Aires, do instead?

The young *signorina* spoke and understood English and was very conversational with the stewardess, explaining that she would have to find another flight after landing in Los Angeles. Her half-sister had a very busy job and hadn't yet confirmed when she would be able to meet. Since the last time the *signorina* had checked, her half-sister hadn't yet read her e-mail telling her that she was coming to visit. All that told Mario was that his little *puttana* wasn't shy and was able to strike up a conversation with a stranger. She had spoken openly enough that his contact had overheard and discovered she was a perfect candidate for the game.

A crazy thought struck Mario as he stroked his *puttana*'s smooth tanned arm. She pushed her full lips into a puckered pout and continued staring at him.

"*Puttana*, tell me your name."

"Marianna Torres," she said, and blinked again.

Chapter Eight

Jake stifled a yawn. He never bothered counting how many times he'd leaned against the side of a building, waiting for something to happen. It was well after midnight, and he wasn't sure what he expected. He hoped nothing. This was the best way he knew to learn the battleground, though. If all went well, he'd return to the hotel and draw a diagram of Mario Mandela's property, highlighting areas where Jake could get on and off the property without detection.

As locked up as the place appeared, it wasn't that hard getting over and past the tall iron fence. After driving around Mario's property on narrow blacktop roads, Jake had slowed near the front of the house in time to see a long black limousine enter through the black gate and head to the house.

There were cameras along the roof of the house, and Jake doubted they were fake. He'd been loitering next to a large outbuilding behind the mansion but didn't want to risk stepping into the line of fire. The cameras might pick him up, and Jake hadn't ruled out the possibility that other security might exist, too.

All he'd determined so far was that he could get over the fence from the backyard without being detected and that standing alongside the back of the outbuilding appeared fairly safe. He needed to push further, determine a safe route to the house. It was his job as backup to have a viable route in and out of there if necessary.

Jake kept his back against the building as he moved sideways, repeatedly glancing from side to side to make sure no one approached. Perspiration trickled down his neck and back as his nerves grew hyper-sensitive to any sound around him. By the time Jake reached the front of the outbuilding he swore he could hear the breeze brush over every blade of grass in the yard.

He put to memory each tree and shrub around him. He made a mental pattern of the row of windows on the first and second floors of the huge, rambling home. Jake glanced down the length of the building and also studied a large wooden patio that spread across most of the back of the house. There were floodlights on the corner at either end of the house that appeared motion sensitive. Where he stood, though, was shrouded in darkness. Motion-sensitive lights weren't around the entire property, just next to the house. The two lights attached to the house didn't quite reach each other. Unless those cameras fixed at the edge of the roof were equipped with night vision, Jake would be safe as long as he remained in the dark shadows looming around the yard and house.

If the cameras could pick up movement in the dark, someone would have detected him by now. Mario Mandela was cocky enough not to use the most sophisticated monitoring system. That or the cameras came with the house, since Mario was renting, and possibly had only simple features. There might be monitors inside that could be viewed, and possibly Mario had employees who kept an eye on them. The guards would see only what the quality of the cameras allowed them to see.

There were bristly bushes along the wall against the front of the building. They didn't stand as tall as Jake but were a foot or so from the steel siding. Jake stepped away from the building, taking in the heavy-looking door that appeared to be the only entrance. A structure this size could store a hell of a lot. Or if the person who lived inside the elaborate mansion was involved in shady, criminal activity, this building would be perfectly suited to hide his criminal activities.

It would especially suit to hide people who'd been kidnapped and possibly drugged. Jake's heart started racing even faster. He kept a tentative eye on the house and sliding glass doors leading inside at the other end of the patio as he moved toward the entrance of the outbuilding.

There was an expensive-looking security panel next to the outbuilding's entrance with a number pad on it. A password was required to enter the building. Adrenaline peaked inside him, making it damn hard to stand still.

With such an expensive-looking security pad installed next to the door, Jake would bet cold, hard cash the people Mario kidnapped and would force to play in the game were inside this building. All Jake needed was proof.

A small voice in the back of his head reminded him he was here to ensure safe passage on and off of this property so he could properly protect Angela. He was doing that. But if while here he could pick up a solid lead or two, he wouldn't turn down the opportunity.

Someone whistled and Jake almost choked on his heart when it swelled into his throat. He lunged behind the prickly bush, moving to a squatting position as he stared wide-eyed into the darkness. Annoying thorns scraped his bare arms and tugged at his shirt. Jake would endure the minor aggravation to prevent being discovered. If whoever whistled had seen him, he would need a damn good reason for sneaking around back here, or he would have to attack and blow his cover. Either way, the situation just went from exhilarating to dangerous and deadly. Jake might have to seriously injure or kill whoever was out here in order to return to the street safely.

Every muscle in Jake's body cramped while he remained frozen, only his eyes moving frantically as he searched the yard. The person whistled again, this time carrying a soft tune while walking across the yard. Jake watched the shadow

take form and studied the tall, lanky blond male as he sauntered across the wooden deck and into the yard. The man
wore jeans and a T-shirt, was possibly in his early thirties,
with hair that once might have been buzzed short and appeared to be growing out.

Jake continued putting the man to memory, guessing him
to be around six feet and under two hundred pounds. The
man reached the outbuilding and stopped at the door. He
pressed buttons on the keypad. It was dark and Jake couldn't
swear by it, but he thought the man pushed four buttons on
the keypad. There was a solid beep and the man reached for
the handle. The door opened into the building.

For a moment the yard was flooded with light. "I found
boxes and sorted through everything," the man offered cheer-
fully before the door closed behind him.

Which meant there was someone else already inside the
outbuilding. Not that Jake hadn't already guessed there were
probably a handful of prisoners in there. But the blond guy
had reported in to someone, letting them know he'd finished
some task that involved sorting. Mario might be in there.

Jake swallowed the lump in his throat and took his time
straightening. He wasn't as young as he used to be. This line
of business took its toll on a body fast. His muscles stretched
and threatened to cramp when he took a second to arch his
back and press the balls of his hands against his lower back.
It was more than likely time to get the hell out of Dodge.
He'd laid out a good feel for the property and would be a lot
more comfortable the next time Angela came here. Before
he left, though, there was one more thing he wanted to do.

Many brand-name security pads possessed the same type
of ten-key pad. They also often came with a precoded password that many people didn't bother to change. Jake crept
along the front of the building, continually casting a watch-
ful eye over his shoulder and toward the house until he
reached the door to the outbuilding. The security pad was a
common brand name Jake had seen many times before. It
was one of the secrets of his trade, but quite often Web sites
for these keypads had manuals on them that could be down-

loaded. The manual might say what the preprogrammed password for the lock would be.

It was almost midnight when Jake got out of the shower. Digging through his suitcase, he pulled out clean jeans and a T-shirt. His stomach growled and food sounded really good but so did sleep. There were a few good years left before he needed to worry seriously about all the crap he put into his system. Jake wasn't a fanatic when it came to watching his health. He didn't smoke, didn't drink all that often, and for a man under thirty he figured he had at least a few more years of eating when he wanted and keeping odd hours.

Jake grabbed his phone, punching in the numbers as he headed out of his hotel room. It might be late, but there were things to discuss and figure out. "No rest for the wicked," he said under his breath as Angela's phone rang in his ear. A lady who didn't have some sappy love song as her ringtone. That said something about her character right there.

"Where are you?" Angela sounded like she was whispering when she answered, her soft, raspy voice making him think he might have woken her.

Images of her lying naked under sheets with all that long, thick black hair tumbling over her bare shoulders as she rolled over on her pillow, her cheeks flushed, got him hard as hell by the time he reached the elevator.

"I'm going to be in your room in seconds."

"Like hell! It's too late." It sounded as if she tumbled out of bed.

Jake stifled a grin as he pushed the button to take him to the lobby. "Meet me at the bookstore. Opposite corner this time. Go to the second booth." He ended the call, not giving her time to refuse his location.

Regardless of what Angela might think, the bookstore was a perfect meeting place. Sometimes the seediest of locations were the safest. Especially when their perpetrator was a high-class criminal. Mario would turn green with envy if he were to learn Jake planned on spending time with Angela in a private booth in an adult bookstore watching porn. Hell,

Jake couldn't wait. Maybe all the booty calls had grown old, but getting kinky with a hot lady during a peep show would never turn him off. Not as long as he could breathe.

"How do you keep your hours?" Jake grinned at the night-time doorman, Albert.

Albert Rodney ran his vein-covered bony hands down the front of his black tuxedo jacket and nodded formally to Jake. Although Rodney had to be close to seventy, with greased-back silver hair that offered the impression the man hadn't found a hairstyle that suited him since the fifties, he was sharp and formidable. A good ally to have. Jake bet very little slipped past the old man who stood at the main entrance appearing unobtrusive.

"Where else would I be paid so well to do absolutely nothing and be able to flirt shamelessly with beautiful ladies?" Albert extended his hand, making a show of holding open the automatic door that wouldn't close even if Albert were to move his hand. "What I want to know is why one of them isn't on your arm, sir?"

"What did I tell you about that 'sir' crap?" Jake said, keeping his voice low. He hadn't narrowed down who was the night manager yet and didn't want to get Albert in trouble. Pulling a five out of his jeans pocket, Jake slipped it to the doorman. "And trust me, Albert. I plan on having a lady on my arm really soon."

"I have all the faith in the world, Jake," Albert said, lowering his voice toward the end of his sentence.

"Same here." Jake offered Albert his classic crooked smile, and the old man winked at him. "Tell me something."

"What's that, Jake?"

"You know who Angela is, don't you? A young lady about my age with long black hair?"

"How could anyone not notice such a beautiful creature?" Albert spoke in awe, his cool, serene tone educated, with just a clip of an eastern accent to it. "Miss Angela is a rare gem. If you don't mind me saying."

"I agree completely." Jake reached into his back pocket, grabbing the doorman's attention immediately. He kept his attention on Albert's face as he watched Jake's movements when he pulled out his wallet and removed one of his business cards. "This is just between you and me, okay?"

Albert lifted one of his bushy gray eyebrows after reading the card, then slipped it discreetly inside his coat pocket. "Always, Jake. I'm always discreet."

Jake believed him. "I want you to let me know if she leaves the hotel. Just call that number. Can you do that for me?"

"Of course. It might not be the moment she leaves, but I can use a phone when I go on break."

"How often do they give you a break around here?"

"The Drake takes very good care of me," Albert said proudly. "I sit and relax a bit every hour. They know I don't abuse the privilege and I know there isn't anywhere I would rather work. It's the best type of relationship to have. Too many don't realize if they take care of those around them, they will be taken care of as well."

"Words to live by," Jake mused.

"I can tell you that your lady left twice earlier this evening. She wasn't gone very long and has been in the hotel now for a couple hours."

"Do you know where she went?"

"It isn't my place to pry." Albert frowned at Jake as if the insinuation he would know what everyone did who stayed at the hotel insulted him. "I do believe both times she went out for coffee. The second time she returned was less than an hour ago and she carried two large cups from Starbucks."

Jake immediately wanted to know why Angela had bought two cups of coffee. "And that was less than an hour ago?"

"Yes." Albert answered with enough conviction it wouldn't be surprising if the man marked some people's arrivals and departures by the clock.

"She'll be coming downstairs here in a few minutes."

"It will be a pleasure seeing her."

"Yes, it will." Jake grinned at Albert and swore the old man winked at him. "I'll find out if she has anything to say to you when I return."

"Very good, Jake." Albert nodded and continued holding the automatic door as Jake headed out into the night.

It only took a couple minutes to walk around the corner to the bookstore. The establishment was open twenty-four hours a day, and the clerk behind the counter sat perched on a stool, his nose stuck in a worn-out-looking paperback. The rent for this place, in this part of town, couldn't be cheap. Jake was curious how the store kept their doors open. This was his second time here, and both times the shop had been practically void of customers.

The clerk didn't look up when Jake moved between the aisles and headed toward the rear of the store. When he reached the unmarked brown doors along the back wall, Jake turned, glancing over his shoulder. Neon lights blinked in the store window, illuminating the words "Vanity Bookstore." He no longer saw the clerk perched on his stool, and there didn't appear to be anyone else in the store.

Jake looked around the store, easily seeing over the many aisles of paperbacks, DVDs, and videotapes. Satisfied the store was empty, he turned his attention to the three doors in front of him, each one opening into a private booth where a porn movie could be watched privately. Above each door was a lightbulb, and the sign on the wall explained the light's being on meant the booth was occupied. None of the lights were on.

Jake opened the middle door and stepped inside. He stood in a six-by-six-foot space, around the size of a large closet, complete with a fake roof to offer some semblance of being soundproof. To his right was a wooden bench, built into the wall. In front of him was a TV screen, also in the wall. A coin box was next to it with a knob that offered several selections to watch.

Jake dug into his pocket, pulled out several one-dollar bills, and fed them into the box alongside the TV. He let the movie that whoever had been in here last start playing. It was on to create noise and make it harder for anyone outside to hear him and Angela talking. Jake stared at the small screen and watched an incredibly skinny blonde with very large breasts start giving a man a blow job. The screen could be bigger and cleaner, but Jake got the gist of what was going on.

His dick got hard as he imagined Angela on her knees in front of him with her moist, hot mouth wrapped around him. He jumped at the sound of the doorknob turning behind him.

Jake leapt to the side, watching the door open slowly. When Angela hesitated, not stepping inside, he stepped around the door, placing his hand over hers on the doorknob.

"Come in," he said in a husky, low voice, taking Angela's hand and wrapping his fingers around hers.

Angela's hand was cool, her fingers slender and long. She ducked backward and tried pulling her hand free. "What?" she began.

"Angela," he whispered, keeping her hand in his and dragging her into his arms.

When she was against him, Jake closed the door and clicked the lock on the door handle into place.

"You wanted me to meet you in a peep show room?" she demanded, sounding indignant.

"You agreed to meet me here." If he continued holding her in his arms while she twisting against him, they'd get very little discussed. Although as he moved his hand over her back and all of that long, thick black hair tumbled over his arm images of it flowing over her naked body while she rode him made it damn hard to think about anything else. "Sit," he told her, releasing her but taking her arms and guiding her forward.

Angela freed herself, but there wasn't anywhere to go in the small room to allow her space. "You want me to sit there?" she asked, glaring at the bench built into the wall and running the length of the wall. "Do you know what people do there?"

He assumed the question was rhetorical. "I have a vague idea," he said dryly.

Angela rolled her eyes, the glow from the TV casting shadows over her face. "This is one hell of a place to meet," she grumbled, crossing her arms and glaring at the small TV screen.

Jake noticed her features soften immediately. She was drawn into the porn. Maybe Angela wanted Jake to believe she was all business, but there was kink in her, too. He saw it as her features relaxed and her eyes glowed as she stared at the set. Angela was a complex woman. Jake was going to enjoy learning the different angles to this sultry investigator. One side of her became very apparent as her cheeks flushed and she continued staring at the small TV. Angela didn't want him to know her level of perversion. Possibly she wasn't aware of how obvious it was. Her cheeks remained flushed and her breath slowed as she inhaled deeper, trying to hold on to her control. He wasn't sure how much longer he could wait until he shattered that control.

Since she seemed intent on standing, Jake sat on the bench. When he stretched his legs out, Angela was forced to move closer to the set or he'd have his legs on either side of her. She turned her back on the TV and pursed her lips, studying Jake's face. Her nipples were hard, which made for one hell of a mouthwatering view.

"Where were you this evening?"

Jake took his time raising his attention to her face. "Exploring Mario's property."

Her eyes grew wide. "You were at his house? When?"

"After you left in your cab, I waited for Mario to return and head inside, then decided to learn the layout of the land. I need to know the best ways in and out of his property."

She nodded once.

"There's an outbuilding," Jake continued.

"I've seen it."

"Have you been inside?"

She shook her head. "No. I saw it from the patio earlier tonight."

"Could you give me a layout of the inside of his home?"

She looked like she'd blow Jake a kiss as her gaze dropped. She was either giving his question some thought or taking in his body. Maybe she was doing both. Long strands of hair slid forward over her shoulder and parted around her round breasts. Her nipples were still hard and poked against her tank top. There wasn't much room in the small booth. But there was enough to fuck her until she couldn't take any more.

"I think so," she answered slowly. "It's a big house, but he gave me a tour."

Jake gave himself a mental shake, glancing past her at the TV he could only partially see with Angela standing in front of him. "I'm sure he did," Jake muttered, willing himself to focus on Mario's house, on where his army was, and making sure Angela didn't put herself in a position he couldn't get her out of. "Do you know how many people are working for him?" he asked, knowing of three so far.

"The tour ended in his bedroom," she added, her expression not changing although it sure looked as if there was a challenge in her eyes. "And I'm not sure. I saw three, but one was killed while I was there."

"I want to create a blueprint of the inside and outside of his place."

"We can do that," she answered, looking away from Jake for the first time.

"Now tell me about this murder you witnessed." That grabbed her attention. "Don't leave out any details."

"Okay," she said slowly, turning as if she might pace but realizing taking a step in any direction would be futile. There simply wasn't enough room to do anything other than watch porn, masturbate, or get laid if someone was lucky enough to have a willing partner in there with them.

Angela let out a slow breath and again searched the walls around her. Jake wondered for a moment if she might be claustrophobic. She didn't look comfortable and possibly her hard nipples distracting him made him overlook the obvious, which was that she didn't seem to like being in here with him at all.

"Is something wrong?" he asked, keeping his tone calm, speaking quietly and nonconfrontationally.

"Actually, yes, there is." Her tormented expression disappeared and she suddenly looked pissed. "I don't have a problem going over this case with you," she began, and held her palm up, blocking his view of her breasts. "But there isn't any space in here. If it's your intention to have us in here so I couldn't think straight with your body sprawled everywhere so I can't even move without running into you, I don't think it's fair play."

"I asked you to meet me here because it's quite possibly the safest place for us to talk and still be close to the Drake." It never crossed his mind that Angela was equally tormented by his body as he was by hers. "You witnessed a murder tonight. Do you honestly think Mandela is going to stay home and sleep soundly without knowing beyond any doubt you haven't become a liability?"

"Point taken." She straightened, hugging herself, and stared at Jake. Her gaze was flat, though. She was definitely shoving every emotion and reaction to what he just said to her under a thick carpet.

He didn't have a problem giving her the time she apparently needed to relax. He was all she had right now. That meant trusting him implicitly. Jake couldn't think of a better place than this small closet-type booth where no one would seek them out or bother them. As long as he continued pumping dollar bills into the box next to the TV, they could stay in here all night and not be bothered.

Jake straightened, pulling his legs in so she didn't have to step over them, and patted the bench next to him. "Sit," he instructed. "Tell me about the murder you witnessed."

"If there were regular lighting in here I bet you'd be able to see all the stains in that wooden bench from . . ." She let her sentence break off, not finishing it, but giving him a quirky smile as if trying to make light of the fact that many men probably sat and masturbated here.

Jake pulled off his shirt. "Allow me to be a gentleman." He shook his shirt out and placed it on the bench next to him, making a show of ironing it smooth with his hand.

"Jake!" Angela hissed, her hand going to her mouth. Then she coughed and accepted his offer as she planted her cute butt on his shirt. Her legs were pressed tightly together, and her hands were clasped at her knees. "That wasn't necessary," she mumbled.

"Just trying to make you comfortable."

"You took your shirt off," she spit out.

"That makes you uncomfortable?"

"How would you like it if I took my shirt off?"

His grin must have answered her question.

She pointed an accusatory finger at him. "Exactly. I doubt you'd care much about hearing about a murder if I didn't have a shirt on."

"I'm willing to test that theory."

Angela rolled her eyes. "You wouldn't care if you lost."

"I don't see how I can lose on that one."

The apprehension on her face disappeared as she stared at him. Jake saw the smile in her eyes before it played at her lips. "You're impossible," she muttered. "Has anyone ever told you that you're a lost cause?" She shook her head, her green eyes glowing with amusement. "If there was a Playboy Anonymous I would strongly recommend you work the steps."

Angela had already informed him that his reputation didn't impress her. He doubted it would impress her if he told her it had been almost three days since he'd talked to another woman. And he'd scare the crap out of her if he mentioned she was the reason why.

"Tell me about the murder," he grumbled, leaning his bare back against the scratchy wooden wall behind him.

"It actually started in Mario's bedroom." She slapped her palms against her bare legs and relaxed, matching Jake's position and facing him. "He'd just finished giving me a tour of his home. It didn't surprise me we ended up in his room and *believe me* . . ." Angela stressed, but hesitated for a moment, hooding her gaze as she stared at her fingers. She didn't look up when she continued. "I admit being preoccupied for a minute on what to say, or do, to get us the hell out of there. However, when one of his goons in a suit came to the door and the two of them spoke for a few minutes, I was able to leave a bug at his computer."

"What started in Mario's bedroom?" Jake really didn't want to hear about her being in Mario's bedroom, even though she made a point of telling him she didn't like being in there. Forcing his emotions to the far back of his head, he focused on what she said. "And what kind of bugs are you using?"

"An argument of sorts. I could tell Mario didn't like what Marco, his manservant, said to him. And they're the brand my father has always used. They record what's being said, so I'm not missing out on anything by being here with you."

"Good. And how did you know it was an argument?"

"'Argument' is probably a strong word." She nibbled her lower lip, watching his face. When her gaze dropped to his chest, her cheeks flushed. She sucked in a deep breath and blew it out just as loudly. "Marco wanted Mario to come with him and Mario continued telling him it was a bad time."

"I'm sure."

She made a face at him. "So of course I encouraged him to go with Marco. I tried to show him I was an understanding girlfriend and knew sometimes work got in the way of fun."

"So now you're his girlfriend?"

"No, no." She waved off Jake's question. "It was a good excuse to get out of the bedroom."

Angela straightened her legs and they brushed against his. Jake leaned forward, placing his hand over her thigh. "If you're giving him the impression your relationship is anything beyond casual, I need to know," Jake said, aware his tone had turned menacing. It was the last thing he wanted to hear, but he would handle it. He could cover her ass regardless of what tactics she decided to use with the Mafia bastard. Jake hadn't known Angela long enough to make any claims on her. Maybe if he forced himself to believe Angela was the kind of lady detective who didn't think she was doing anything wrong if she acted like a slut undercover, he could cool off the heat she'd created inside him.

"I have to make him comfortable around me if I'm going to learn where he is storing the file that has the board game on it for the game. As well, I need to know where the people are he's abducted. I need to get them out of there before taking him down. You know that."

He did know that. "Tell me about the murder."

"Fine. As I said, I could tell Mario wasn't happy with whatever Marco told him. We went downstairs and to the patio. We were barely outside when an older man appeared and started yelling at Mario in Italian."

"What did he say?"

Angela shrugged. "I wrote it down the best I remembered when I got to my room. But I don't speak Italian. I know he called me a slut."

"The old man called you a slut?" Something unexpected hardened inside Jake.

Angela noticed it. She bristled. He still had his hand on her knee and didn't realize he'd tightened his grip until she straightened.

"It's part of the job," she offered quietly. "Trust me. I've been called worse and by a lot better than that old man."

Angela didn't try removing Jake's hand but instead pushed her hands against her thighs as she looked down and blew out a breath. "I shouldn't have said that. The guy is dead and I'm not one hundred percent sure why."

"Keep going. Tell me what happened."

When Angela began sharing the events from earlier that night with him, Jake studied her, listening to every word but watching her eyes darken or brighten, according to whatever emotion she experienced. There was a strong passion running through her when it came to working this case. Unfortunately, that just made her even hotter and sexier.

"I got the impression something had happened. Marco was adamant about showing whatever it was to Mario, but he didn't want to leave me."

She got more comfortable sitting next to Jake. When she crossed one leg over the other, Jake moved his hand but then rested it on her knee again once she was situated. Angela kept talking, getting excited about her story. She didn't pay attention to him touching her, or she didn't mind.

"More than once I told Mario he could go tend to business and that I wouldn't mind. He insisted the night was for the two of us and his work could wait."

"Are you sure Marco said he wanted to show something to Mario?" Jake asked.

Angela continued staring at his hand on her knee. "I think so," she muttered, then looked up at him with a small smile. "Yes. I'm sure he said he needed to show Mario whatever it was immediately. It was one of the few things said in English, which is why I remember. When we were on the patio, the older man showed up. He didn't speak to Mario the way Marco did. I mean there wasn't the same level of respect. He spoke more as if they were equals. And at one point, Mario threatened to send him back to Italy if he didn't leave us alone. I'm pretty sure his house servants are his family. Marco and Mario have similar features."

Jake remembered the blond guy walking across the yard and entering the outbuilding. If he was related to Mario, it certainly wasn't by blood.

"The old man told Mario it couldn't wait."

"What couldn't wait?"

"Whatever it was they wanted him to know, and that they were insistent he come see." Angela met Jake's gaze, staring at him for a moment. "I kind of got the impression it was about me, the way the old man kept glaring at me. That or he blamed me for Mario not wanting to see whatever it was at that moment."

"And you don't have any idea what that was?"

Angela brushed a strand of hair away from her face as she shook her head. "I really need a crash course in Italian," she said, dropping her attention to Jake's bare chest and licking her lips. "The old man started yelling at Mario in his own language and he said something about me. Like I said, I wrote down what he said when I got to my room and the main word that stuck in my brain was the word *puttana*, which means slut."

Jake looked away from Angela. It dawned on him the sound from the TV had stopped and he stood, digging into his jeans pocket for some more bills. "So the old man didn't like the fact that you were there. You were distracting Mario from something they felt was important and needed his immediate attention."

"I think so. Or it was about me." She watched Jake feed the bills into the coin box. "If it was about me I guess I'm grateful Mario didn't find out what it was, because a few minutes later the old man was dead."

She'd uncrossed her legs when Jake turned to face her after selecting another movie to play. He caught her staring at his lower back or maybe his ass. She shot her gaze to his face the moment he looked at her, and again licked her lips. Jake swore she looked hungry, and could easily change the subject to them. He stood facing her for a moment, aware of his dick threatening to grow in his jeans.

It was her mind that turned him on as much as her body. He'd never cared before to learn anything about the women he saw before Angela. If the lady put out, that was all that mattered to Jake. The women he had seen in the past understood that and seldom asked him about his work, either. Angela was different. Mental, as well as physical, stimulation appealed to him more now than it had before. Damn, he'd been a shallow bastard.

"We need to interpret whatever it was the old man said to Mario."

"I was going to do that."

When Jake sat next to her she moved and pulled his shirt out from underneath her. "You should put this back on," she said, shoving it at him but not meeting his gaze.

"You don't mind sitting on the bench without it?" He tried not to sound too amused.

She sent him a scathing look and stood, dropping his shirt in his lap. "I'm going back to my room," she announced, turning to the locked door.

Jake didn't hurry to stop her but moved easily enough that he had her in his arms before she could unlock the door. "Why does it bother you sitting in here with me?" he whispered into her hair.

"You're half-naked and porn is playing in the background and you want to know why this bothers me?"

Jake chuckled and turned her around to face him. She wasn't amused and showed him as much when she smacked her fist against his chest. He put his hand over her fist, keeping it pressed against his chest. Her skin was soft and warm and he liked her touching him. Even more so, he was very aware of her breath quickening when he lowered his head to hers.

"I already know why it bothers you," he whispered, using his free hand to tilt her head back. She didn't try pulling her fist away from his chest but resisted when he pressed his fingers under her chin. "Angela," he whispered.

"Jake," she complained.

She wasn't telling him no. And he knew why. His fiery little detective wanted him possibly as much as he wanted her. It was the same fire the two of them had ignited a year ago in Tijuana, and it hadn't fizzled out during the time they'd been apart. Maybe a good portion of it was curiosity, but Jake swore he detected something else, something that went deeper than anything he'd felt for any other women he'd ever been with.

Jake cupped her chin with his hand, leaned her head back, and brushed his lips over hers. "You're not leaving yet," he said, his voice suddenly so husky with need he sounded raspy.

"I'm not fucking you in here," she informed him, her thick black lashes batting over her milky green eyes when she tried focusing on him.

He had the sense not to laugh or smile at her demand. "That's fine," he said, and pressed his lips against hers again.

She tasted so good. When he let go of her fist and pulled her against him, Angela didn't try pushing away. The sigh she released was music to his tormented brain. He pressed his tongue between her lips, and she opened for him, fully surrendering as her hands went up to his shoulders.

Jake ran his hands along the slender curve of her back, feeling drunk from the taste of her. He started a slow, seductive dance, moving his tongue around hers and enjoying the mixture of coffee and peppermint in her mouth. When he gripped her ass, pressing her against him as his dick stretched and throbbed, aching to be inside her, Angela gasped. He held her firmly as she arched against him. Her breasts were so full and round. Jake imagined ripping her top from her body and sucking each nipple until she came. The way she gasped and sighed as he feasted on her mouth, he knew the sounds of her coming for him would be enough to tear him apart.

Angela dragged her fingernails down his arms and moaned into his mouth. He started thinking he could make love to her here and she wouldn't fight him. But he'd honor her request, if it killed both of them.

Jake broke off the kiss and was rewarded with a view to die for. Angela's hair streamed down her back. Her nipples were hard as rocks and poked through her tank top. One strap had slipped off her bare shoulder and draped around her arm, giving him a better view of her cleavage. But it was her face, her thick lashes fluttering over her dazed expression and her flushed cheeks a beautiful rose shade, that caused something to tighten in his chest. For a moment he couldn't breathe. She was the most beautiful woman he'd ever laid eyes on, let alone held in his arms.

"You're so damned beautiful."

Angela's gaze cleared and she stared up at him, almost wary.

He hadn't meant to say that out loud. Women knew they were beautiful. They used their ways and wiles to seduce men, to taunt and tease them. Telling them they were gorgeous allowed them to manipulate men, to take advantage of the need burning in a man and to use sex to control men.

Whatever had tightened inside him shattered when Angela smiled. She blinked and licked her lips and continued grinning. "Thank you," she whispered, sounding anything but her usual demanding self.

He let her move out of his arms and accepted his shirt he'd apparently dropped on the bench. "Here's what we're going to do," he said, needing to focus on business so he wouldn't melt in her arms and demand they continue where they left off a moment ago. "I want you to stay here."

"Stay here?" She frowned, apparently not liking that idea.

"Only for a minute," he assured her, pulling his shirt over his head. "I'm going to leave and make sure no one is looking for you. Stay in here until I call you. Once I know no one has stopped by the Drake searching for you, I'll call and let you know it's okay to return to your room."

"And if someone is looking for me?" She looked skeptical.

"Then I'll come back for you."

Chapter Nine

Angela locked the door after Jake left, clutching her purse and feeling reassured at the hardness of her gun. She pulled her phone out and stared at it. She had a signal. The small cubicle didn't allow enough room to do anything. Except what it was designed for. She stared at the TV screen built into the wall. A woman arched her back while on her hands and knees and licked her glossy red lips while a large man fucked her from behind. Angela imagined Jake taking her the same way and immediately her body reacted. The swelling between her legs grew so intense she sat, dropped her phone back in her purse, and pressed her knees together.

Angela no longer cared what had been done on this bench. She had worse problems than where her ass was sitting. This whole thing sucked. Jake was beyond any doubt the best-looking man she'd ever laid eyes on. If he had any idea how cruel it was of him when he yanked off his T-shirt then he was definitely a coldhearted man. She'd been forced to talk shop while staring at his perfectly sculpted body. And there was no way he didn't know how much sex appeal he possessed.

"Damn it," she sighed, dropping her head in her hands and dragging her fingers through her hair.

No one forced her to do anything. It had been all she

could do to keep her hands to herself and not molest him. God! She wanted him so badly her pussy throbbed to the point of distraction. Not to mention they were so close sitting next to each other in this little sex room. Knowing what others had done on this bench, in this room, sure didn't help matters much. If she got her mind on the case for a minute, one glance at the TV set and she was right back to undressing him the rest of the way.

"Which is probably exactly what he wanted," she said out loud, blowing out an exasperated puff and standing. Granted, Jake did initiate the kiss. "Lord, what a kiss," she mumbled. Who would have known a man could make her damn near come just by kissing her?

Angela's phone rang and she almost jumped out of her skin. It took a minute to drag it out of her purse. She stared at the area code and phone number. Jake hadn't given her his number. She could only guess this was him. "Hello," she said.

"I confirmed Mandela's driver has been by for you with his limo." Jake was all business.

It was easier matching his tone, and frame of mind, on the phone. Angela didn't have to stare at his perfect body. "Tomas," she said. "How did you find that out?"

"I have my sources."

"And do you bribe the doorman, too?"

His silence answered her question and she smiled.

"Head on out of there. I have my eye on you. Mandela's limo isn't here now."

Angela opened the door and stared at the quiet bookstore. The windows facing the street were black and reflected her image as she moved through the store. She never would have guessed there were so many sub-genres of porn, and if she weren't so preoccupied with Mario seeking her out she might have taken time to browse.

Mario wasn't going to quit searching for her. The sooner she convinced him she hadn't seen anything, the better. If she played this out, laying low and making herself impossible to find, eventually Mario would put a mark out on her. In his eyes she'd witnessed a murder, making herself a liability. He wasn't going to leave her alone. There wasn't any walking away from this.

Angela nodded at the clerk behind the counter, who barely took time to look up and acknowledge her. "I think I should call Mario," she said once she was outside on the sidewalk. This late at night wasn't safe no matter what part of Chicago she was in. Her heart rate accelerated as she picked up her pace and headed around the corner to the Drake.

"Agreed," Jake said without hesitating, which was surprising. "Head to your room first. We're ironing out a game plan. You're treading in really deep water now."

"Where are you?" she asked, although she didn't want to glance around and appear nervous. When she came within sight of the glowing entrance to the Drake, with its high brick overpass, she eased her steps.

"Enjoying that hot little ass of yours sway back and forth," he growled in her ear.

Angela shot a furtive glance over her shoulder before she could stop herself. Jake's chuckle in her ear sent shivers down her spine. Her skin broke out in goose bumps, but she wasn't cold. Far from it. At the moment she was searing hot and growing annoyed.

"Fuck you," she grumbled, having half a mind to hang up on him.

"I plan on it." His deep baritone sealed his promise and made her knees weak.

Angela almost stumbled when she hurried across the circular drive of the Drake. And she did hang up on him. That would show him. Jake didn't believe her promise that they wouldn't have sex while working on this case any more than she did. She was practically panting and a warm sensation traveled over her when Albert opened the door for her. Jake was a son of a bitch.

Albert's warm smile made it impossible not to smile in return.

"Have a nice evening, Miss Angela?" he asked, his grin broadening.

If Jake had given the old man any indication where she'd been, she'd kick his muscular ass. "It was okay," she offered. "Any messages for me?"

"Quite a few actually, miss. You're quite the popular lady."

"Oh?" she asked, taking in the quiet lobby as she stepped through the door before facing Albert. "A lot of people were looking for me?"

"Two actually. Both just kept returning. You know, my dear, dragging on several gentlemen isn't always as entertaining as it appears."

Angela couldn't help grinning at Albert's concerned expression. He thought she was playing the field, with men calling for her. If only that were the truth instead of being so far from how things really were. She had to be careful how she responded, though, since her cover was to make everyone believe she was an unscrupulous spoiled rich girl who was content digging her nails into the bad boy Mario Mandela.

"You're a sweetheart to care about me," she said, batting her lashes at Albert and feeling like the floozy he probably saw her as. "But someone was looking for me other than Mario?" She frowned, shaking her head. "Do you know who?"

"You're right about Mr. Mandela. He sent his car by for you a couple times. But there was also a gentleman who is staying here at the hotel who asked about you."

"Real big guy?" She held her hand up in the air but knew she didn't come close to offering an accurate measurement of Jake.

"It's been my experience, miss, if I may offer a small amount of wisdom without offending?"

"Of course. What were you going to say?" Angela dropped her hand and stared into Albert's eyes.

"As I said, it's been my experience that gentlemen willing to pay for information on a lady are usually doing so because they wish to control and possess her."

Angela's jaw dropped and she snapped it shut but leaned closer to Albert, breathing in the faint smell of Old Spice, which made her think of her father. It was an odd sensation, since Albert certainly wasn't talking about her father when he mentioned two men. She knew exactly who Albert was talking about. She also knew why both men would want information on her. Or she hoped she did.

"Both of them paid you to keep an eye on me?" Now she whispered, too.

Albert chuckled. "I'm an old man and more of a fixture around here than an active employee. You flatter me suggesting I could keep up with a beauty as active as yourself."

"And you're a bad liar," she said, smiling but narrowing her gaze on him. "Don't try to make me think for a moment that you can't tell me everything that goes on around here."

She thought Albert blushed, but his wrinkled, hollowed cheeks were pasty enough it was hard to tell. He straightened, though, his expression growing serious.

"When two men are that determined to know a lady's whereabouts, it's because they feel a strong sort of possessiveness toward her. Now if you don't mind my saying, I see danger in one and a strong sense of possessiveness in the other. If you mix the two . . ."

"It would be one hell of a mess," she finished for him.

"Tread carefully, Miss Angela. Your men may not quite be as they appear."

A car pulled up into the circle, its headlights beaming on the two of them for a moment. Angela heart pounded viciously in her chest until she confirmed it wasn't Mario's limo.

"Duty calls," Albert said, patting her arm and grinning, appearing relaxed and completely in control.

Angela gathered inner strength and smiled easily at him. "Thank you," she said, slightly upset there wasn't time to learn more of his thoughts on Mario and Jake.

A few minutes later her hotel door closed silently behind her, automatically locking. She kicked off her shoes, leaving them at the desk and walked to her bed, climbing on to it and collapsing.

"It's about time you got here," Jake said as he appeared from around the corner by the bathroom.

Angela shot to a sitting position, managing to free her

gun from her purse by her hand and aim it at him before she acknowledged who spoke to her.

Jake brought his hands out from his side slowly. "I didn't mean to startle you," he said, his gaze riveting on the gun.

"Crap, Jake." Angela was pissed and relieved all at once. She lowered the gun, her hands shaking when she dropped it on top of her purse. "You scared me to death. What are you doing here?" Her senses returned to her with her next breath. "How did you get in here?"

Jake gave her an impish grin when he pulled a card key out of his jeans pocket. "It was in your shorts pocket."

"What?" She didn't understand. "But I used my card to get in here."

"Apparently you had both cards on you." Jake shrugged and dropped the card key on the table by her surveillance equipment.

"Wait a minute. How were you watching my ass if you were in here?"

Jake moved in on her, reaching the edge of the bed and leaning over. He pressed his fists into the bedspread. Long, corded muscles bulged in his forearms. His shoulders flexed and chest muscles rippled under his T-shirt. "An ass as hot as yours doesn't leave the mind easily," he growled, lowering his gaze to her breasts.

God! He was 100 percent flirt. She was staring at a purebred playboy and knew without giving it thought that she was desperately out of her league. Her life was all business. The men she had dated behaved in a civilized manner. Angela made the first move if she decided they were worth her time. Jake wasn't even bothering with the first move. The look on his face made it clear he was coming in for the kill.

Maybe in his world women fell at his feet, willing to do whatever he wanted. In her world, though, when she chose a man, he fell at her feet and begged to do whatever she wanted, Angela pulled her knees to her chest and scooted back on the bed. It might have been a king size, but with a man the size of Jake, there wasn't enough space to escape him. His eyes blazed like rare emeralds when he grabbed her ankles and pulled her back into his arms.

"Damn it," she cried out, and slapped her hands against his warm, steel chest.

"What did Albert say to you?" Jake braced her with one hand pressed against the middle of her back. His fingers crawled into her hair, tugging until she let her head fall back and stared into his smoldering gaze.

"Albert?" she asked, blinking until Jake returned his attention to her face. "Who is Albert?"

"You know who Albert is." Jake captured her mouth, demanding entrance and impaling her with his tongue.

Angela barely had time to capture her breath before he began making love to her mouth. His fingers moved up her spine, caressing and pressing into her flesh, which proved to be almost as erotic as the way he kissed her. As sturdy as he was in holding her against him, his other hand moved delicately down the side of her head. When he brushed his fingertips against her cheek, all the while instigating a dance with their tongues that ignited flames of passion deep inside her, it was all she could do to hold on.

Maybe they were in different leagues. But that didn't mean she lacked experience. Jake used his body as his weapon. He possessed skills most men didn't even know existed. Jake might be one of the best bounty hunters, with too much sex appeal for his own good, but his skills vanished when it came to women.

Not his sexual skills. Angela wouldn't argue they were off the charts. She was barely able to maintain control of her own mind as he created sensations inside her she wasn't sure she'd ever felt before. But he plotted, brainstormed, and analyzed a case before beginning his hunt. Jake wasn't brainstorming and analyzing her. He dove in, all aggression and demanding. Angela needed to tame this virile beast.

If she could manage it. Angela turned her head, fighting to catch her breath and make her brain work. Instead of breaking off the kiss, Jake made a rumbling sound in his throat as he ran kisses along the side of her face to her ear.

"Jake," she cried out, her entire body jerking as he raked his teeth down her earlobe. When he teased her inner ear with his tongue, the swelling between her legs exploded into a pool of moist heat.

"You don't have a clue how sexy you are," he whispered, his words torturing her as much as his tongue did.

"I think I have a clue," she mumbled, although she was lying. She should be focusing on taking the upper hand, not on learning how he reacted to her touch. Exploring his body wouldn't help her tame Jake, but it sure as hell caused the heat smoldering inside her to grow into a pressure ready to explode almost immediately.

"Are you going to tell me what Albert said to you?" Jake's voice was raspy and his breath hot against the curve just above her collarbone. With each kiss, each nibble and scrape of his teeth against her flesh, he moved closer to areas that swelled, screaming for his attention.

"I don't think I will," she admitted.

Her hands were under his shirt. There was an odd sense of power as her fingertips explored and his muscles twitched under her touch. Angela barely had time to catch her breath, let alone clear her vision, when Jake let go of her long enough to rip his shirt from his body. She didn't even register where he threw it when he grabbed her tank top and as easily pulled it over her head, tossing it wherever he sent his shirt.

"Now is as good a time as any for you to learn something," she began.

Jake cupped her breasts. Angela grabbed his wrists but wasn't able to get her fingers to wrap around them and meet. She was even less successful at stopping him when he tugged on her already swollen breasts. He squeezed her nipples between his fingers and Angela's world toppled to the side, taking all her coherent thought with it.

"I would have to agree," he grunted, not taking his attention from her breasts. "And I plan on learning more than something, darling. I'm going to learn everything about your body, where you're most sensitive, where you're ticklish, what gets you off, and what doesn't."

"That's not what I meant." This was quickly becoming the wrong time to show Jake how he needed to act around her. Unfortunately, she couldn't tell him his behavior turned her off. Her pussy throbbed and was so damned soaked, she felt her come on her inner thighs.

"You're very sensitive." His crooked smile was mischievous.

"Jake!" Angela would not lose this battle. She pressed her hands flat against his chest. Tight small curls of chest hair tickled her palms while his solid heartbeat matched the throbbing between her legs. There wasn't any way she could push Jake backward if he didn't want her to. "Lay down," she ordered.

Her expression must have given her away. Jake's grin faded and his expression grew serious as he dropped his hands. "You're going to run the show?" He sincerely sounded surprised.

It was time for his first lesson. "I've always run the show," she whispered, and gently pressed against his chest.

It was an odd moment for Albert's words to come to her. *I see danger in one and a strong sense of possessiveness in the other.* She could only guess which man held on to which trait. If anything, both men were dangerous and possessive. But to give in to either would put her at the mercy of that man. She would lose control.

"All right, darling." Jake stretched out on the bed, his head touching the headboard and his feet at the edge of the bottom of the bed. "I'm yours to command," he added, raising his arms and strapping his hands behind his head. His brown hair was tousled and his expression once again mischievous. This was all a game to him.

"I can only imagine how you've mastered such skills." She really didn't want to know how many women it took to make a man as confident and convinced of his abilities as Jake was. "You're not mine and I'm not going to command," she tried explaining.

Jake pressed his lips together as his body tensed. "They aren't skills. What's happening here isn't something we've plotted out and now are putting into action." His jovial look was gone, and the man staring up at her looked dangerous, intelligent, and incredibly focused. "This is new territory for me and for you, which is why you want to maintain control."

He moved his hands and gripped her waist, lifting her and easing her on top of him, until her legs straddled him.

Angela straightened her arms, flattening her hands against his chest. "You're seducing the hell out of me," she accused, pushing and sliding backward. They couldn't do this with Jake determined to manipulate her thoughts and insist her desire to control was to cover up some deeper longing.

Jake grabbed her arms, keeping her from getting too far away from him. "Don't try and make me think you don't want me."

"I thought we'd already established there was mutual desire." The fog was still there, drifting around her senses, but she felt a remnant of control return to her corner. "This isn't a good idea."

"You believe that?" He wasn't letting her go.

Angela tried twisting out of his grasp and ended up struggling against him. Wrestling with Jake would only put her back in the middle of that fog. She ended up with her back pressed against his hard chest and his muscular arms wrapped around her. The two of them knelt on the bed, and Jake lowered his head so his curls brushed against her cheek.

"You're so damn hot and I bet if I were to check right now you're soaked as hell, too," he whispered against her face.

Angela stiffened. "Soaked" didn't begin to describe her current state. "Don't you dare," she whispered, but made the mistake of turning her head to look at him.

Jake raised one hand and gripped her neck, using his fingers to pin her face and keep her gaze locked with his. "If you believe both of us should restrain and not ease our pain and desire for each other, I have a right to know."

Instead of making her think of an answer, he stretched her body against his, both of them on their knees with his legs on the outside of hers. He kept her head turned and slowly brushed his lips over hers. It was barely a kiss, but she made the mistake of fighting him. Jake came back for more, pressing his lips against hers, and once again applied incredible skills as he made love to her mouth. She was stretched against his torso, on her knees, leaning back into him while they devoured each other's mouths. When his hand eased inside her shorts she stilled.

"Trust comes with time, sweetheart. I understand that. You're accustomed to being in charge and not letting go. Tonight, let's just enjoy the release of mutual cravings." His voice was raspy and scraped over her raw senses the way his teeth and fingertips had tortured her flesh.

As he spoke, his hand slid over her pelvis. Instinctively she tightened her abdomen, giving him easier access. In spite of her mind demanding control of this situation, as Jake had just suggested, her body was more than willing to ease the path to pleasure and satisfaction. His fingers parted her moist flesh, and his eyes opened wide, staring at her in astonishment. Even at close range, they locked gazes and both forgot to breathe.

"You're smooth." He spoke with a reverence that was empowering.

Angela sucked in a breath and swore she could taste him as she took his scent deep into her lungs. Shaving was a personal vanity. She knew men liked it, but she loved how it felt, too. The smooth, hairless skin heightened her sexual experiences, when she had time for them. And it kept her feeling clean. At the moment, though, she was so wet his fingers slid easily deep inside her.

"This isn't . . ." *a good idea.* Angela didn't get the entire sentence out of her mouth.

The only hint she had was a slight twitch on the side of Jake's jaw before he thrust his fingers deep inside her.

"Holy crap!" And her world erupted.

His fingers were long, thick, and took her to new heights she hadn't known she'd been missing out on until now. He thrust again, then one more time, each time he impaled her a very macho grunt escaping his lips. With his fourth thrust, which was as premeditated as the ones previous, a dam

broke inside Angela. Wave after wave of pent-up desire
rushed through her, streaming fast and wild like a narrow
river heading for a very high waterfall. She tumbled over,
free-falling and seriously unsure if she'd recover from her
orgasm and ever be the same again.

Giving Jake this unhindered control would put a strain
on their relationship. Just as Albert said, Jake was very possessive. It would make him think he could call all the shots
and simply tuck her under his wing. Letting go and giving
him that power would be the biggest mistake of her life. Although the way his arms had tightened just enough around
her when her orgasm hit, how he allowed her to ride it out,
and with his continual impaling, thrusting until the pressure
was fully gone, was not only the most incredible experience;
it was hot as hell.

"You're so soaked." Jake nipped at her ear. "My sweet baby
needed to come."

His baby?

Jake plunged deep inside her, applying the same amount
of force and aggressiveness that had pushed her over the
edge a moment ago. Hell, she was still basking in her after-
math and he shoved her right back into a state of turmoil and
swelling pressure.

"Damn it! God!" Angela would have tumbled over if he
weren't keeping her pressed against his body. Besides, his
hand in her shorts braced her. Instead of crashing to the bed,
both of them leaned forward slightly. His fingers plunged in
an altered course, hitting a spot that was seldom touched.
Her orgasm peaked so fast it stole her breath. "Jake. Oh shit!"

Her world exploded in an array of warm colors, every
sensation suddenly heightened as she started plummeting,
sliding into an explosive state of satisfaction that gripped
and held on to all of her senses. Angela felt her orgasm tear
through her and, try as she did, she couldn't stop it or control
its strength.

Which was what she usually did. It didn't hit her until the
intensity of her ride began to ebb. No man ever made her
come until she was ready for release. Angela controlled her

orgasms, just as she controlled everything else in her world. It allowed for few surprises but kept her world manageable.

"Next time you come like that, it isn't going to be with your back to me." His deep chuckle raked over her nerves.

Already he was assuming control. If she weren't so sated right now, Angela was positive she would have a comeback that would securely put him back in his place. Just because he got her off better than she could do herself. And although he'd made her come when she'd instructed herself not to, that didn't make him the boss.

As soon as she quit floating and the intense pleasure causing every inch of her to tingle receded, she would make sure he knew that. No matter what Jake King thought about her, now that he'd just given her one hell of a memorable orgasm, Angela didn't answer to any man. Nor would she ever. Although maybe, possibly, if Jake was nice about it, she might let him make her come like that again.

Chapter Ten

"We've got work to do." Jake held Angela's limp body against his, feeling the strong thumping of her heart between her swollen breasts.

Jake had never made a woman come the way he just had with Angela. As tortured as he was physically at the moment, with his cock engorged and the urge to rid her of her shorts and impale her soaked pussy, a strange sense of calm and intense satisfaction seeped through him as well. It made for a strange mix. Maybe her demanding nature had its effect on him. Getting her off satisfied him in a way. He definitely wanted to fuck her for hours and hours, but as late as it was getting, they needed to start laying out their game plan. He was a bit surprised Mandela hadn't figured out her room number and come pounding on her door.

Angela blinked, shifted, and tried twisting in Jake's arms. He reluctantly pulled his fingers out of her moist heat and dragged them up her flat abdomen. They were sticky and wet, and he fought the urge to lick her come from them but wasn't sure what Angela's reaction would be to that. It was another odd sensation that her feelings and thoughts meant so much to him.

His family had been right. It was worse than a humbling

revelation. The past few years he'd gallivanted around, lining women up as far as the eye could see. The women had used him as much as he used them. He didn't know a lot about any of the ladies he spent time with, other than contact information and small bits of useful knowledge, such as which ones preferred to be on top or enjoyed giving blow jobs. Jake forced himself to face the whole truth. He'd been worse than an alley cat on the prowl.

Right now, as he stared at Angela, all that mattered was her pleasure. His cock was harder than steel. It rubbed against his boxers and jeans and was uncomfortable as hell. And he didn't care.

Well, he cared. No way would he consider himself converted from prick to saint in the matter of time it took for Angela to come twice. If she were any other woman, he would probably take advantage of her dazed state to strip off the rest of her clothes so he could get himself off.

Jake ran his hand over Angela's long, black hair, stroking it away from her flushed cheek. He'd seen other women with hair as long. Her hair tickled his chest and was thick and silky. It was a nice contrast against her creamy white skin. He'd been with many women who were a lot tanner than Angela, women who dedicated time daily to ensuring their tan remained dark and their skin healthy. Jake doubted Angela gave a lot of thought to how dark or light her skin tone was. He'd been with women who'd had breast implants and with women who barely had breasts. Angela's full, round breasts were natural and her nipples large. They were perfect and again he would be surprised if she worried about their size or shape.

When his hand was no longer in her shorts, Angela slid off him and let her legs fall off the side of the bed. She sat on the edge, hunched over, and dragged her fingers into her tangled mane.

"I didn't ask for this." Her voice was raspy, as if she was out of breath.

"Ask for what?" Jake combed her hair with his fingers

and she arched her back, tilting her head so she stared at the ceiling.

She gave him a hard look over her shoulder. "I didn't ask to come."

He grinned. "Consider it a gift."

She sighed, shaking her head, and stood, gathering her hair at her nape and pulling it free of his hand.

"I'm going to take a shower. Jack off if you want, but I'm not going to watch you do it. When I get out, we'll order food and I'll play back what the surveillance equipment has recorded so far." She walked away from him as she spoke and didn't look over her shoulder as she shut herself in the bathroom.

Like hell he would jack off. Whether she asked for it or not, Angela hadn't told him no. She didn't hold back and didn't get angry with him for what he'd done. Jake knew a sated expression when he saw it. Maybe he'd been a male slut for too many years, but those years had taught him a thing or two about women. Angela wasn't a manipulator or a schemer. She wasn't a player, and although he believed she was damn good at acting and handling undercover work, that didn't make her an expert as a sexual prima donna.

Jake stared at the closed bathroom door as a grin played at his mouth. Angela meant something to him. He hadn't understood what until now. She thought keeping him in a state of yearning, of wanting her and not having her, would keep him in line. If the little lady believed she could maintain control of him through sex, she'd definitely bitten off more than she would be able to chew.

Jake stared at the table with the small black box and manual next to it. Angela had top-of-the-line equipment. She'd already planted bugs inside Mandela's house, one of the most notorious and elusive criminals in this country. Working with Angela would be more than fun. "You're a challenge," Jake whispered, and realized why she intrigued him as much as she did.

Angela wasn't boring. She challenged him. And that was what held his interest. He walked around the table, got comfortable in one of the two chairs, and turned the black box so he could study the knobs on it. The volume was turned down, and he adjusted it until crackling sounds popped in the small speaker.

"You really are the best boss I've ever worked for." A man's voice came through the speaker, his words breaking in and out and static crackling as the guy laughed.

"You'll never find a better job, Bobby. I guarantee it."

Jake leaned forward, turning the volume up when he recognized Mario's Italian accent. There was a notepad and pen on the table, and Jake grabbed both, sliding them closer as he leaned into the box, straining to hear everything said.

"I think I actually believe you." There wasn't a shred of accent in this man's voice, yet he'd said he enjoyed working for Mario. Maybe it was the blond Jake had seen walking across the yard earlier tonight. "Although I did have a boss right out of high school who hooked me up with one of his favorite hookers because he didn't want a virgin working for him."

Mario laughed loudly, his thick baritone coming through the speaker clearly. Jake wondered where Angela had placed the bug to allow it to pick up these two men's conversation so easily. There were advantages to being the son of a cop who'd been a detective for twenty-five years before switching careers and becoming a bounty hunter. Jake's dad had taught him quite a few tricks of the trade. One of them being how to listen to bugged conversations. Jake would bet these two men were outside. When people were inside they tended to speak in softer tones. As Greg King put it, everyone is taught at a young age to use their indoor or outdoor voice. As well, there was a very slight echo that could almost always be detected with decent recording equipment when a person was speaking in a room. Jake squinted, focusing on their words. He didn't hear an echo.

"You were still a virgin when you graduated from high school?" Mario was still laughing. Whoever Bobby was, Mario sounded relaxed with him.

"Hell no, man." Bobby chuckled and made a snorting sound.

"But after high school I headed east for a while. I was new in town. It was a chance to get laid and I figured when my boss gave me a hundred-dollar bill to give to the hooker, she had to be good."

"A hundred dollars, huh?"

"I gave her fifty."

Mario laughed again. "A man after my own heart. What town was this?"

The question was slipped into the conversation, but Jake pictured Bobby's face sobering. There was only a brief silence.

"Baltimore," Bobby said, not letting the silence last longer than a second or two.

"You didn't mention Baltimore on your résumé."

"You're right. I figured if I put down too many towns you'd think I was a vagrant and unable to keep my nose clean enough to stay in one town that long."

"So you went from town to town dodging the law?" Mario was serious now.

"I almost wish I could say that was the truth. It would make me sound more like an outlaw." When Bobby laughed, it sounded sincere. Mario didn't laugh with him this time, but Bobby didn't sound daunted as he continued. "Honestly, Boss, I went from town to town quite a bit after I got out of school. I never got busted for anything. I just got bored with the scene and I guess I was searching for my niche."

"I think I understand," Mario said slowly. "All of us have a gift we're given and with some of us it takes a while to learn what that gift is. I think you've found it here, yes?"

"I think you're right."

"I'm always right, my friend."

"So what do you think my gift is?"

"You take orders well and know when to ask questions and when to keep your mouth shut."

"That isn't a gift. That's common sense." There was a squeaking sound, like a door opening.

Jake realized he gripped the pen hard enough so that his knuckles were white. He forced his hand to relax and prayed the two men wouldn't walk away from the bug without saying something he could use as a lead.

"You're good at taking care of my army. And as you can see, I know how to show my appreciation when one of my employees shows loyalty and respect."

"I enjoy the job." Bobby chuckled again and it sounded as if he slapped Mario on the back. "And I sure as hell enjoy how you show your appreciation."

"She's one hot piece of ass, isn't she?"

"You know I always did like them submissive and willing," Bobby said, still chuckling.

Jake cringed. His guess was that Bobby, or both of them, had just fucked one of the women Mario had kidnapped. They needed to confirm where Mario's army was soon.

"Sleep well tonight," Mario said, his voice sounding farther away. "Oh wait," he added, coming in clearer. "What did you think of the picture on Uncle Petrie's computer?"

"The girl? Do you think she is your lady? There is a resemblance."

"I thought so, too. What do you suggest we do about it?"

"You're asking my advice?"

"I would like your input, yes."

There was a brief silence and Jake rubbed his palms down his jeans. Would Mario be referring to Angela as his lady already? In spite of Jake's stomach twisting in a cruel knot as his entire body hardened instinctively, keeping an open mind was imperative. He didn't blink as he stared at the small black box.

"Say something that will make sense, damn it," Jake grumbled to the box. He snapped to attention, sitting upright in the chair when the two men continued talking.

"Go pick up the detective. If she's his daughter, she'll come forward to save his ass." Bobby barely paused for a breath when his voice deepened, suddenly sounding cruel and hateful: "If she does come running to save her daddy, you know what you must do."

"Don't forget your place," Mario hissed, his accent thickening, which made him sound mean and heartless.

"Trust me. I know my place. You have one hundred per-cent of my loyalty. But unlike the rest of your staff, who would all die for you, I will always be on my toes, thinking, because I plan to live with you."

Mario's laughter sounded twisted, if not demonic. "Very good. Which is why you're here talking to me right now. As long as you never forget where your paycheck comes from."

"Not only would I never forget that; I also know you don't fire your employees."

Jake guessed Bobby meant Mario killed them if they crossed the line, as the old man Angela saw murdered ear-lier tonight had done. He leaned forward, holding his breath and wondering if Mario would incriminate himself. Murder, kidnapping, terrorism—enough charges to put the bastard away for life, if not give him the electric chair. That was if they could make the charges stick.

"Keep talking, you son of a bitch," Jake hissed, and fisted his hands on either side of the box.

"I don't believe in liabilities," Mario said, suddenly sound-ing calm.

When Bobby laughed, it was as if he'd just been told a good joke. Jake fought the anger simmering inside him. He needed a cool head to nail these assholes to the wall.

"I like working for you, Boss." Bobby quit laughing and it sounded like the door opened once again. "I'll get on the detective. It would probably be best to take care of that to-night."

"Make it happen."

The squeaking sound was followed by a dull thud. Jake stared at the box. It grew silent in the room until Jake was able to focus on water running in the bathroom. Angela was taking a bath. He jumped out of his chair, wired and pissed as he reached for his phone. She would be pissed if he stormed in on her, but Angela needed to know what just had transpired. No names were mentioned, but Jake would be surprised if there was another detective in Mario's life who was the father of a lady he was spending time with. Jake barely glanced at the time when he placed his call.

"Do you know what time it is?" James Huxtable sounded pissed as hell. His voice was thick from sleep, though.

"I believe it's almost one in the morning," Jake said coolly. "Wake up. I need to talk to you." He could be as gruff as Huxtable.

"I am awake," Huxtable roared into the phone. "Why are you calling?"

"Because you're about to be kidnapped."

Jake relayed the conversation he'd overheard and explained that Angela had planted the bug. By the time he finished, the water was no longer running in the bathroom.

"This doesn't sound good," Huxtable said slowly, the sharpness in his tone gone.

"It wouldn't be hard to track this Bobby character," Jake said. "I'm sure I could even catch him in the act of kidnapping. That wouldn't incriminate Mandela, though. And it sure wouldn't implicate him in anything concerning the game."

"What's the kidnapping of one man when a much larger bust hovers in the wings?"

Jake glared at the floor, gripping his phone hard enough to snap the thing in two. "Grab a few necessities and get out of there. I need your home address and I'll head that way to cover you."

"Got this all planned out, do you?"

Jake didn't realize he'd started pacing until he stopped in his tracks. "Before Mandela and his henchman started discussing the possibility that a rather old picture of your teenage daughter found on the Internet might actually be of Mandela's lady, the two men were discussing the sex they'd just had with one of the women Mandela kidnapped for the game."

"You have proof the abductees are there?" Huxtable sounded interested for the first time since they'd started talking.

Jake didn't let out the sigh of exasperation building inside him. Huxtable acted as if his life weren't in danger. Regardless of what the man thought, he wouldn't be able to hold off some hired thug if he came to Huxtable's house. Henchmen like that didn't knock on the front door and ask you to come with them.

"Maybe. I'll have physical proof by tomorrow," Jake offered, but continued before Huxtable tried swaying the conversation further off the issue at hand. "The two men were spending time with one lady they'd kidnapped and were talking about her, and their time with her, when they walked within range of the bug your daughter planted."

Huxtable swore under his breath. Jake dragged his hand through his tousled curls. His hair was tangled and he doubted he made it look any better. "We already knew they were despicable assholes," he grunted. "You need to leave your house. Give me your address."

"I'm a step ahead of you, boy," Huxtable said, his stern tone returning. "I've already left the house. They won't find me and in the meantime I want to know what picture they found on the Internet of Angela. To the best of my knowledge, there are no pictures of her anywhere on the Web. Nor have there ever been. Even her mother agreed to that."

"I don't know," Jake said. His gaze shot to the bathroom door when it opened.

Angela stepped out, a white towel wrapped around her body and another wrapped around her hair. She padded barefoot to her suitcase and squatted, pressing one hand to her chest to hold her towel in place while unlocking her luggage and rummaging through it.

"I'll do a search, but the picture has already been discovered. I need to make sure her cover hasn't been blown."

"What?" Angela gasped, managing to balance herself while keeping the towel in place. "Who are you talking to?" she whispered, searching Jake's face.

An overwhelming urge to touch her, to protect her and destroy anyone who even thought about causing her harm, forced his chest to tighten. He couldn't breathe. The sensation rushing through him had that much strength.

"You're damn right you do," Huxtable snapped. "Regardless of whether that picture is of her, or not, they now suspect

Angela. You make sure you tell her this changes the entire picture."

"Is that Dad?" Angela asked, her eyes widening. "Why are you talking to him at this hour? What's wrong?"

"Is that Angela?" Huxtable asked at the same time Angela spoke. "Let me talk to her."

"Yes," Jake said to Angela. "It's your father." Jake turned his back on her when she stood, reaching for the phone. "Angela doesn't know about this yet. I'll explain and have her call you."

"I need to know my daughter is safe." Huxtable didn't yell this time, and the concern in his voice came through stronger than his stern tone.

Jake cut him off before the older man implied something he might regret. "Your daughter is safer than she would be anywhere else," Jake growled into the phone. "And I think you know that already, since I'm with her because you encouraged it. Actually, you demanded it. Where are you headed?"

"I'm getting a room tonight. It's too late to go anywhere else."

"Call me as soon as you've checked in." Jake didn't usually hang up on anyone without saying good-bye. In this case, he made an exception.

"What the hell is going on?" Angela demanded, throwing her arms out in frustration when Jake snapped his phone shut. She lowered her arms and grabbed her towel when it started to slide.

Another time Jake would have enjoyed the incredible display of her breasts and how the towel pressed them together. He might have even grabbed her towel, yanking it off her body, and endured her show of anger just to have her naked. His protector's instincts were at full mast, though. Her almost-nude body didn't just make his dick hard but also drew the powerful need inside him in, hardening every inch of him.

"Your surveillance equipment records, right?" He walked

over to the table and began messing with the knobs on the small black box.

"Yeah. Why?"

"I want you to listen to a conversation that took place why you were in the bath."

Angela returned to her suitcase and the closet, dropping her towel with her back to him and sliding into a terry-cloth robe.

"Don't mess with it," she ordered, her calm tone all business as her shiny black, unbrushed hair tumbled down to her waist.

Angela reached around him, sliding the box in front of her, and sat in the chair where Jake had been while she bathed. "What did you hear? And why did you call my dad, or did he call you?" she asked, glancing up at him while the small box hummed in front of her.

"I called him." Her robe was tied at her waist but loose at the shoulder. From where he stood, he had one hell of a view. "You'll understand in a minute. I want you to listen, and while you do, I need a laptop."

"Go ahead." Already she focused on her box, frowning and chewing on her lower lip as she rewound, paused, and rewound again until she hit part of the conversation.

Jake sat in the chair opposite her, pulling up the Internet on her laptop. "Rewind a bit more. That's around the middle of the conversation."

"That's Mario. I don't know who he's talking to," she said, picking up the pen off the notepad and clicking it open and shut as she pressed the button on the box. "What are you doing on the computer?"

"Apparently there is a picture online," he began when Angela pushed Play on her box.

Static popped only for a moment before the man who'd been talking to Mandela, possibly the blond, began speaking: "You really are the best boss I've ever worked for."

Angela looked up at Jake, her milky green eyes wide as her moist lips parted. Jake loved how her face lit up; the thought of learning something new, picking up a solid lead they could play through, showed in her expression, and she glowed from the excitement of it.

Jake nodded at the box. "Listen," he instructed, and typed *Angela Torres,* the name she'd given Mandela, into the Internet search bar. Nothing came up. Jake tried spelling her name several different ways and still came up with nothing. Then he typed in *Angela Huxtable*, since the connection to the picture had been through Huxtable. Links filled the page. A quick scan didn't show any pictures.

Mario and Bobby started talking about the woman they'd just left. When they implied having just had sex with her, Angela gasped and shot an outraged look at Jake.

"Fucking pricks," she said under her breath, slapping her pen down on her notepad.

Mario and Bobby kept talking.

"What did you think of the picture on Uncle Petrie's computer?"

"The girl? Do you think she is your lady? There is a resemblance."

"His lady?" Angela whispered, and all color drained from her face. She stared wide-eyed at the black box as she gripped her bathrobe and tightened it around her as if suddenly she were freezing. Her lower lip started quivering as she listened to Bobby promise to take care of the detective that evening. There was the sound of a door opening and closing and silence followed.

Angela sprang out of the chair as if something had just bit her. "Crap. Oh my God! Crap!" There was a wild look on her face when she stared at Jake. "You heard this live and immediately called my father?"

Jake nodded, standing slowly. Angela looked pissed as hell. He started around the table, but she shook her head, long damp strands of hair clinging to her robe, looking tousled and adding a wild air to her already-outraged expression.

"He's okay, baby. I promise." That tightening in his gut returned when Jake brushed her hair over her shoulder. "I've taken care of him for now."

Angela spun on Jake, her fury finding a target as she

stabbed him in the bare chest with her fingernail. "I am not now nor will I ever be your baby. Babies are unable to take care of themselves, require complete care and attention. If you ever suggest that is how you think of me again, no matter how big you think you are, I will kick your ass." She glared at him, her breathing coming hard as she squinted, narrowing her gaze on him. "Are we clear?" she whispered fiercely.

"*Sweetheart,*" he began, stressing the word as he took her pointed finger in his hand and wrapped his fingers around it, holding her hand when she tried pulling it free. "We're very clear and I apologize for allowing you to think I believed you were incapable of anything. You're quite easily the strongest, most capable woman I've ever met."

She stared at him, not saying a word. Her anger didn't sway, but she didn't lash out again. Jake wasn't sure if she knew how much he meant what he just said, but right now wasn't the time to dwell on it. Angela was pissed her father was in danger, an emotion Jake understood very well. Anytime family met the radar of a perp, fury could blindside rational thinking.

He treaded lightly, knowing he needed to keep her focused but aware if she thought he was coddling her she'd explode again. "How far does your father live from Mario?"

She blinked, frowning. "Probably twenty minutes or so. Why?"

"Within less than ten minutes of that conversation ending, your father was already gone from his house and heading to a hotel for the night."

"Which hotel?"

"He didn't say. Once he's checked in he's calling me back."

"Huh." Angela marched across the room and grabbed her phone. After punching in a number, she began combing her hair with her fingers as she stared at the floor. "He's not answering." Angela sucked in a breath and pulled the phone away from her ear to stare at the screen before listening again. "It went to voice mail."

"Don't leave a message."

"I wasn't going to. He'll see the missed call." She hung up and lifted her gaze to Jake's, searching his face for a moment. "Why did you say not to leave a message?"

Jake shook his head, unwilling to explain that his antenna was tuning in on something that wasn't ringing right to him. "Where did you leave the bugs at Mario's home?"

Angela dropped her phone on the table and walked to her suitcase. She dug through it and pulled out clothes, rolling them in her hands and hugging them against her chest when she straightened and faced Jake. Her expression was still tight and angry.

"There is a bug in Mario's bedroom, next to his computer. I left the other one on the table outside the sliding glass doors on his patio. That is where Mario and Bobby were talking. I don't know who this Bobby person is, though. Mario had several house servants. All of them were in suits and all looked like they were related to Mario or at least men he'd known from his home country."

"When I was scoping out his place I saw a tall blond, probably a few years older than me. He was in jeans and a T-shirt. I watched him enter the outbuilding where, I'm willing to bet good money, the people Mario's abducted for the game are being held."

"We heard Mario and Bobby talking as they came up onto the patio, probably after leaving that outbuilding. I never got a really good look at it. Mario has floodlights on either side of his house facing the yard, but the way the light streams, it doesn't quite reach the outbuilding."

"I noticed that, too. At first I thought it might be because Mario was renting and it was how the owners of the house had set it up. But now I'm thinking it might be intentional. It takes the attention away from that outbuilding by shrouding it in darkness."

"Which Mario would definitely want if he was harboring captives that he's drugged and plans on using for terroristic activity with the game." Angela headed into the bathroom and pushed the bathroom door closed.

It didn't click shut but remained ajar. Jake walked toward

it, trying to figure out why it seemed like something wasn't right. "Try calling your father again," Jake suggested, standing outside the bathroom. His attention riveted to the floor when her bathrobe crumpled just inside the door. "He should have called us by now if he'd checked into a room."

Angela was combing her hair with her fingers when she pulled the door open. "What do you mean, if he checked into a room? That's what he said he was doing, isn't it?"

"Yes. And he was pissed when I called him, which at first I didn't question since it was almost one o'clock in the morning."

"What are you saying?" Her hair was still fairly wet and shone black as night as she worked her fingers through it. Apparently she didn't think she was going to bed anytime soon. The jeans she wore hugged her slender hips and clung to her legs like a second skin. They were faded and looked comfortable. She'd tugged a sleeveless pink blouse over her head, and some of her hair was still stuffed under the collar. "Dad doesn't usually wake up grouchy, but you probably shocked him when you called."

"I told him to wake up and he said he was awake," Jake said, replaying his conversation with Huxtable in his head.

"Of course he was awake. You'd just called him."

"Call your dad." Jake backed away from the door to let her out and gestured toward the table where she'd left her phone.

Angela grabbed a brush off the counter and headed out of the bathroom. "You don't think that Bobby guy got to Dad before he made it to a hotel, do you?" She was brushing her hair and looked over her shoulder, her mouth puckered into a circle as she searched Jake's face.

If any of Mario's men were after Huxtable, he was in serious danger, whether they'd caught him yet or not. "Your father told me he'd left the house before we finished our phone call with each other." Jake stared at his phone and Angela's on the table next to the surveillance equipment. "I listened to the conversation between Mario and Bobby as it took place. It wasn't even five minutes later when your dad was no longer at his home. And he didn't give any indication anyone was following him."

Angela picked up her phone, her damp hair shrouding her face as she pushed numbers.

"Wait a minute." Jake grabbed her phone out of her hand.

"What?" she gasped, more surprised than pissed as she looked at Jake, confused.

"Something isn't right here. Your dad hasn't called. He wouldn't tell me where he was going."

"They wouldn't already have him?" Angela's tone rose as she spoke.

Angela loved her father; the bond between the two of them was tight. Jake didn't need to see the two of them together to guess what Angela had with her father was close to what Jake had with his.

"I don't see how they would have him. I just talked to him." Jake kept her phone in his hand and walked around the table, picking his phone up, too. He stared at both of them, knowing Angela was watching him. "Is your father so arrogant he would think it wasn't crucial for me to know where he was going?"

"My father isn't arrogant," Angela snapped. "He might be confident. He's the best there is. But mister, he isn't any cockier than you are."

If he weren't so focused trying to work his brain around this he might have smiled at the expression on Angela's face.

"If I were dodging someone who'd just decided a mark should be on my head, I'd let my backup know where I was." He gestured with the phones in his hands, ignoring her comment. There was a difference between being cocky and simply knowing you were good. He'd tell anyone that, but changing the subject would make him lose his train of thought and there was something not right with everything that just had played out. He needed to figure out what it was. "So if you don't tell your backup what you're doing—"

"You're my backup."

"I'm not his," Jake finished, staring into Angela's milky

gaze. "So if he'd plotted to do something, he might not have put either of us in the loop."

"What?" she whispered.

"Maybe it wouldn't cross his mind to do it." Although it was a rather stupid move. Jake kept that thought to himself, though. "All I know is that if he were checking into a room he would be checked in by now. I can't think of any hotel that would be this slow."

"Unless he thinks our phones aren't safe." She glanced pointedly at the cell phones Jake held in each of his hands.

Jake held his phone up, capturing her tentative stare at the same time and holding it as he spoke. "There is a scrambler in my cell phone, as there is in all of our phones with KFA. Anyone who tries tapping in on our phone conversations will be blessed with a high-pitched, incredibly annoying whine in their ear." He grinned and Angela cocked one eyebrow and tilted her head, giving him the impression she found him either amusing or annoying. Jake was sure he was both, although at the moment he was serious. "Is your phone censored at all?"

"That's a track phone," she explained, nodding at her phone in his other hand. "It's not my real number. I started a new account when I took up residency here. If Mario does a search on me, and I was sure he would, there would be no way he would be able to trace my true identity. Does Dad know your phone is scrambled?"

"Well, obviously you weren't thorough enough." Although when Jake had done a search on her real name, he hadn't found any pictures of her.

When she sucked in a ragged breath, her gaze faltered as she looked away from him. "What picture do you think he's talking about?"

"I've been looking," Jake said, returning his attention to the laptop screen.

"You didn't find it? I guessed that was what you were doing on my laptop when I was listening to Mario and Bobby's conversation. And I don't have a clue what picture they were talking about. There shouldn't be anything anywhere on the

Internet that connects me to my father." Before Jake could say anything, Angela marched around the table and held out her hand. "I need to call my dad. Let me use your phone if it scrambles phone calls. We'll search for the picture after a bit. First we secure my father."

Jake placed his phone in her palm but then wrapped his fingers around her hand with his cell in it when she tried pulling away. "Your father doesn't know my phone is scrambled. He might not answer and that might explain why he hasn't called back. If he feels he's being hunted, he might cut himself off from us to protect you."

"I have to know he is okay." She wasn't pleading. There was a firmness in her tone Jake was growing accustomed to hearing. Her father might be an arrogant son of a bitch, but something told Jake he seldom crossed his daughter.

Jake let go of her hand. "Call him."

Angela punched numbers into Jake's phone, then slowly lifted her gaze to his when she put his phone to her ear. He heard it ring, once, twice, three times, as their gazes remained locked. Her anxiety climbed with each ring. Huxtable wasn't going to answer. It was damn near impossible that Mandela would have snagged him considering the time frame. Jake couldn't kick the feeling he was missing something, though.

"Damn it," she whispered, ending the call when it went to voice mail and slowly lowering his phone. Angela snagged her phone from Jake, giving his phone back to him, and punched numbers again.

Jake reached out and stroked her damp hair over her shoulder, enjoying the cool silkiness of it. Angela didn't stop him; in fact, she barely appeared to notice the gesture as she chewed her lip and focused on his chest as she listened to the phone ring.

"God damn it!" she cried out, tossing her phone on the table when no one answered. "Where the hell is he?"

She began pacing but stopped when she neared Jake. "You're the bounty hunter. You're part of KFA. My God, you're damn near a household word," she said, narrowing her gaze on him as if that were an accusation. "Find my dad,

Jake. We're not brainstorming or searching for a damned picture until I know he's okay." Her expression more than challenged Jake. With a look, Angela showed him she actually would try kicking his ass if he countered her.

Once again, that tightening in his gut hit him. It spread to his chest, making it hard to breathe for a moment. He would go out in the night and track Huxtable down, whatever it took to calm that frantic look on her face.

"Can you think of a reason your father would lead me to believe he just woke up and it not be true?"

She blinked, exhaling. "I'm sure there could be many reasons."

"Think, Angela. I need to know where to start hunting." When she noticeably relaxed, the tightness inside him grew hot, spreading throughout his body faster than he could take his next breath.

"Okay," she breathed, giving him a quick smile that might have been anything from gratitude to an apology for her offhanded comment. Her milky green eyes showed the turmoil flooding her system. Angela was holding on by a thread and unwilling to show him how much this turn of events affected her. "When he's working a case," she paced to the other end of the room and took her time turning around as she continued speaking, "which is what he's doing right now—"

"You know where he is right now?" he demanded. "What the hell?"

"No!" Angela snapped, her voice sharp. She shot a hostile look at him.

"You aren't making any sense."

"I don't know where he is." Angela looked at him, her expression lined with worry. "Jake, please find him."

He knew at that moment he'd do anything to make her happy. He should take time to analyze the emotions ransacking his system, but now wasn't the time.

"I will, sweetheart," he promised, closing the distance between them. "But you aren't making sense. You said something about his case . . ."

"Yes." She tucked damp hair behind her ear and appeared to be focusing on his neck. "The missing persons case for Marianna."

"Yes."

"I know he's finding my half-sister." She walked around him, still not focusing on him. "Marianna and I grew up together and he knows how much I love her. When I was sixteen, I moved here to live with Dad, and Marianna and I fell out of touch. She was the perfect little sister. I remember I missed her terribly at first, but Dad and I got to be so close, and I fell in love with the mysteries he would share with me. As soon as I was able, I started working with him, which was long before I was legally able to work a case. Dad would let me do the little things, although they didn't seem so little at the time. I would write down all the clues, or lay out clothes he would wear while undercover. I remember how important that made me feel." Her back was to him when she sighed, lost in her memories. "But Marianna was the perfect kid sister. She never was too far from my thoughts. So when we started talking on the computer, we were instantly best friends and I loved her to death all over again. She is still so absolutely perfect."

"Has your father shared any leads with you? Has he mentioned where he was with this case?"

Angela made a snorting sound and looked at him. "He didn't even want to tell me he was looking for her. He thought it would distract me from this case."

Jake knew damn good and well how it felt to have family members in danger during the heat of a case. More than once they'd been hot on a trail, ready to crack everything wide open and bring down their guy, when one of them had gone missing. It was one hell of a distraction. Each time it had happened, it had created a fever of intensity in him that burned so hot he would have done whatever it took to bring his family home and back together. He wouldn't go there, though. This wasn't about him.

He didn't realize he'd been scowling at the ground until Angela cursed under her breath. She spun around, turning on him. Jake moved in on her but she warded him off with her hands.

"When Dad is hot on the trail, or is ready to break that big lead, he forgets about the rest of the world. He'd forget to eat if I didn't put a sandwich in his hand as he was hurrying out the door," she said, her eyes suddenly bloodshot. "He really is amazing. Watching him in action can be breathtaking at times."

"So maybe he's hot on the trail of his missing-person case?"

Angela opened her mouth to answer when her cell phone chimed and vibrated across the table at the same time. She jumped on it as if it were alive and she needed to catch it before it ran off.

"It's Dad," she sang out, giving Jake a toothy grin as she answered it before it rang twice. "Where in the hell are you?" she snapped, her smile disappearing so fast Jake wouldn't have noticed it if he hadn't been watching her. "Dad!" she shouted, but then pulled the phone from her ear, staring at it with a mystified look on her face.

"What did he say?"

She looked at Jake, frowning. "He said he was fine and not to worry about him, then hung up."

Chapter Eleven

Angela fought the covers when her undercover cell phone woke her up from a troubled sleep. She had been haunted by dreams of Marianna and her dad. Marianna was crying out to Angela, begging for help. Then her father was next to her, insisting she not worry. In the next instance both of them were gone. Angela had never felt so alone. So incredibly alone. No matter where she looked she couldn't find either one of them. She was all by herself. Angela woke up with a knot in her gut. Her phone was still on the table and her room was cold as she hurried to grab it.

"Hello," she grumbled, her voice rough and her mouth too dry. Her heart still pounded in her chest, with her dream still fresh in her mind.

"Where did you go last night?" Mario asked.

Angela went blank as she fought to remember what excuse she'd planned on giving Mario when she talked to him next. She'd prepared a script in her head she would play out in order to convince Mario she had seen nothing other than a fight between him and his hired help, which had upset her terribly. The trauma from her dream prevented her from remembering the convincing words she'd planned to use on Mario.

"What time is it?" she asked, instead of answering him, and headed to the bathroom.

"It's early." Mario didn't sound upset. He didn't sound anything, which caused the knot in her gut to grow. "We need to talk."

"Okay." After she drank about a pot of coffee. She stared at her tangled hair and the extra-large T-shirt that hung crookedly on her. "I need time to wake up, Mario. I didn't sleep well."

"Because of me." He wasn't apologizing for upsetting her, was he?

It hadn't crossed Angela's mind that Mario might try to convince her no one was killed last night. That thought didn't wake her up completely, but it definitely zapped her brain, giving her somewhat of a kick start.

She rubbed her face with her palm and sighed. Some of the lines she planned on using on him came to her as she stood barefoot on the cold bathroom tile. "Not completely," she said, taking her time answering. It would make her sound more sincere. "I know we both agreed we were in this for fun and the adventure," she began, pausing and listening to the silence on the other end of the line.

Mario's willingness to hear her out could mean a couple things. Maybe he was waiting to hear if she would comment on his murdering a man in cold blood. Or, if Mario believed he'd found her picture on the Internet, he'd hear whatever she planned on saying to him, then calculate how to use it against her, which he'd do in person. His MO didn't suggest he'd make idle threats. When Mario struck, it was with venom meant to kill.

"And you've been nothing but honest with me since we first met," she added, leaning against the counter and staring at her bloodshot eyes. She couldn't remember what time it had been when Jake had left or even crashing. "I know you have to be ruthless sometimes in order to control the business you run," she finished, deciding leaving it vague over the phone and keeping the conversation open would make it easier to pick up where she left off once her brain was awake.

"I'm coming to you. Be ready. We'll discuss this more in person." There was no emotion in his voice. His baritone was dark and sounded ruthless.

"I need a shower and time to get ready. Give me an hour."

Although she was grateful that he agreed, forty-five minutes later she still didn't feel ready to take him on. Her dreams had taunted her until she woke up again. After showering, dressing, and downing her second cup of hotel room coffee, which was mediocre at best, she still didn't feel coherent.

Staring at her destroyed bed, she thought it looked as if she'd had wild sex in it the night before. Images of Jake filled her mind along with memories of him getting her off with his fingers while he held her in his arms.

"Jake," she whispered, her voice still scratchy. It was barely eight in the morning, but she needed to let him know she was heading out. She'd demanded he find her father. It wouldn't surprise her if Jake were already hot on her father's trail. Suddenly she was frantic to talk to him. Bounty hunting was illegal in Illinois. Granted, he wasn't going after anyone for a bounty, but Angela knew there were cops in Chicago with serious attitudes.

Angela admitted she no longer wished to work this case alone as she listened to Jake's phone ring. It wasn't because she was suddenly scared of Mario after seeing him kill a man in cold blood, with his bare hands. Mario was capable of stealing people from their lives, drugging them, and making them kill and possibly get killed, all so he could win a damned game. Angela had known how dangerous this case would be before now.

Jake was an asset now that danger closed in around her, but she enjoyed going over the evidence with him. He brought good insight to the table. The way his expression had been pinched with excitement when he told her he'd overheard a conversation the night before, while she'd been in her bath, had almost turned her insides to jelly. He'd seemed larger-than-life as he'd brainstormed what bugged him about her father's phone call, his deep green eyes as vibrant as they'd been when he'd gotten her off on her bed.

Angela had come damn close to unloading her fears about Marianna on Jake. She was guilt-ridden over her half-sister and, so far, had kept all of her worries to herself. Jake had seen how emotional Angela was last night and had almost pulled her into his arms. If she had let him wrap those strong arms around her, Angela would have lost it. She didn't doubt for a moment he would have consoled her. It would have been so nice to unload on him. Angela imagined where opening up to him would have led, and not because Jake was such a playboy. More than likely she would have instigated sex, then she'd be even more guilt-ridden today. Or would she have felt better?

She shivered. There wasn't time to dwell on Jake's skills in bed. Although when there was time she definitely planned on learning what else he was good at doing.

"Good morning, darling," Jake answered after the fifth or sixth ring. His deep, raspy voice crawled into her system like a warm blanket, making her instantly hot and swollen and wanting him now. "It's early. Everything okay?"

"Are you awake?" she asked, surprised he was still asleep. Maybe he hadn't slept well either.

"Part of me is wide awake."

She heard the smile in his voice, and her body reacted even as she fought not to grin at his implication. The swelling between her legs started throbbing. What if she left her room and traipsed down to Jake's room? He wouldn't kick her out of his bed. And Mario would still be around, still angry and threatening, once she and Jake were done. It would be so much nicer starting her day by giving in to her needs and enjoying hot, wild sex.

"Mario is going to be here in a few minutes to pick me up," she said instead of giving Jake any indication that his subtle comment had affected her at all.

"Where are you going?" His lazy drawl was gone. Jake was all business.

She pictured him sitting on the side of his bed, probably naked, his hair tousled and a thick shadow across his jaw. The image made her weak in the knees as desire spread throughout her. Suddenly it wasn't cold in her room anymore. A fire had ignited inside her after just a few seconds of talking to Jake on the phone. Her needs went beyond physical. It wasn't rocket science figuring that out. She ached to discuss Mario's call with Jake, as brief as it had been. There were often clues hidden under everyone's nose that were easier pulled out when time was taken to analyze every aspect of a situation or conversation. Angela was falling for Jake's mind as well as his body.

"I'm not sure. He didn't say. But we're going to talk about last night. He brought it up already on the phone, and when I told him I didn't sleep well last night he suggested it was because of him."

"If you need me for any reason, send me a text. It doesn't have to say anything. Text one letter or one number, anything. I'll know that means you're in trouble and I'll be by your side in the next minute."

Angela knew he wasn't exaggerating, and it was on the tip of her tongue to ask where he would be while she was with Mario. She jumped, her heart lodging in her throat, when there was a firm knock on her door.

"Someone is at the door," she whispered, suddenly annoyed that Mario hadn't given her time to enjoy her fantasy of seducing Jake. Not that she would have played it out, but it was a hell of a lot better thinking about making love to Jake than it was playing mind games with Mario.

"Be careful. I'll be close, very close," Jake told her, his tone deepening with his promise.

"Don't let him know you're near," she said, focusing on her door. There was a click in her ear. Jake had hung up on her. Angela pulled her phone away from her ear, staring at it for only a second before hurrying to put it in her purse. If she'd hurt Jake's feelings he would get over it or discuss it with her later. Right now, she had work to do.

She really hoped he wasn't mad at her, though. Damn it.

There wasn't time to fall for the damn brute when her head needed to be incredibly clear to remain a step ahead of Mario. The first place she and Mario were going would be to get more coffee, good, strong coffee.

Angela was almost to the door when she did an about-face and studied her suite. All of her spy equipment was put away. The place wasn't spotless but didn't look as if she was trying to catch a criminal, either. Her heart was beating too fast in her chest, and she felt jittery. But something told her not to leave anything that could possibly incriminate her anywhere, even after she left. She'd hidden her surveillance equipment behind her suitcase in her closet the night before. The hotel room was wired to capture anything that was said in here on tape. But if someone broke in here while she was gone and found her equipment, it wouldn't matter whether a conversation was recorded or not. There was another solid knock when Angela dove to her closet floor, yanked out her suitcase, pulled out her clothes, and brought up the false bottom. She almost hurled her equipment into its hiding place, her hands shaking, then closed the false bottom and tossed her clothes back inside the suitcase.

"Crap!" Angela almost tripped when she spun around again, yanked her purse open, pulled out her phone, and switched it to Silent. The last thing she wanted was to miss a call from her father. But like him, she knew phone calls couldn't interfere with her investigation. "And neither can your frazzled brain."

Straightening, she ran her hands down the snug-fitting sundress she'd chosen for the day. There was a third knock, this one a bit louder and more persistent, but Angela paused in front of her full-length mirror, taking in her appearance.

She hadn't washed her hair this morning but instead wrapped it in a bun while showering. Nonetheless, it was damp and frizzy. But it hung straight and was tangle free. No one had ever convinced her she looked better with her thick mane falling almost to her rear. Angela much preferred it up. Wearing it down made her look relaxed, more carefree. Right now, she definitely needed all the help she could get pulling that look off. She did a final twist, ran her hands over her rear, and made sure her dress was straight. It was a bright pink sleeveless dress with a high collar, tapered at the waist to show off her figure, and ended just above the knees. If only she felt as sharp as she looked.

"Fake it, baby," she instructed herself, holding her head high and exhaling slowly as she took her time walking to the door.

Angela unlocked the door and opened it, taking a step backward, and started to point over her shoulder. "Just let me get my—," she began, expecting Tomas to be standing in the hall.

"Did I not give you enough time to get ready?" Mario stepped toward her, his dark eyes pinning her with a hard, condemning stare. He didn't like being left to wait in the hallway.

"Mario." She almost smiled and caught herself. It was time to put on the performance of her lifetime. If Mario didn't believe 100 percent that she thought she had witnessed a fight and not a murder, her entire investigation, all the work she'd done over the past year, would go up in smoke. Angela relaxed her expression, not moving but tilting her head when he stepped into her space. "I expected Tomas and was struggling with my zipper," she lied, holding Mario's gaze.

"This morning will just be you and me." Mario moved in on her, touching her shoulder, then guiding her back into her suite.

Or he would have if Angela didn't step to the side, gripping the cold doorknob, although the metal warmed quickly in her damp palm. She was far from cold, but the heat that surged through her while talking to Jake was far from the same sensation she experienced now as her flesh burned where Mario had touched her. She felt repulsed, disgusted, and fought the urge to step out from under his touch.

Angela found herself against the wall, still holding the door, when Mario let go of her and sauntered into her room. He wore khaki pants and an expensive-looking button-down shirt. His black hair curled at his collar and the casual loafers he wore aided in his footsteps being silent as he continued moving through her suite until he stood next to her table, where the night before she and Jake had sat and listened in on Mario's conversation with his henchman.

"You're upset." Mario turned to face her. "Close the door, Angela. We're going to talk. I much prefer your beautiful smile over this frown I see right now."

If they stayed here, she wouldn't get her coffee. It would seriously suck, remembering every line she'd rehearsed in the shower, if her brain sunk back into its fog.

Angela let the door close but remained in front of it, clasping her hands in front of her while once again trying for a calm, relaxed expression. She hadn't realized she'd been frowning. "I'm not sure staying here is a good idea. I'm not properly prepared to entertain, Mario," she offered, and gestured with a wave of her hand as if one look at her suite would explain to him what she meant. "And I intended for you and me to go to coffee. You didn't give me time for room service, and the coffee in the room is mediocre at best." She wrinkled her nose, making a face she would despise on another woman, as if any problem were someone else's job to fix.

"*Mi amore,* you are quite spoiled," he said, his tone a deadly purr. Mario walked to her windows, pulled the cord, and made the curtains flutter open. "Look at this view. I find this rather to my liking." He shifted his attention to her bed and moved farther into her suite. "I'm glad you told me you didn't sleep well last night."

"What?" She was forced to follow him or she'd lose sight of him. His eyes were so dark they looked black, and his face was twisted in a rather demonic glare. But he was purring almost affectionately when he spoke to her. His tone contradicted his appearance.

"If you hadn't, I might be jealous, thinking you didn't sleep alone. Your bed is rather torn up."

If he expected her to apologize for the condition of her room when she hadn't thought they would stay here, he would be disappointed. "I'll call Housekeeping." Knowing someone would be interrupting them soon sounded like a solid plan. She grabbed the phone before Mario could say anything, pushed the button, and gripped it to her ear, keeping her back to him as it buzzed in her ear. "Yes, room twelve-twelve. I'm entertaining this morning and need House-keeping here immediately to clean the room." Her spoiled tone was enough to make her puke and didn't impress the woman on the other end of the line, either. But the woman told Angela she'd have someone there soon and hung up.

"That wasn't necessary, *mi amore,*" Mario grumbled, his voice even more threatening with his soft, slow drawl. "Unless for some reason you're suddenly nervous to be alone with me."

That was her cue and she'd rehearsed the tar out of this moment in her head ever since leaving his house the night before. Angela spun around, her jaw dropping, then closed it slowly as she started toward him.

"Do you think I'm some stupid hypocrite?" she asked, keeping her voice as soft as his had been. "I told you I understand what you do and am cool with it." As quickly as she'd sounded accusatory, she changed her expression, shifted her weight to her other foot, and waved her hand at him dismissively. "My father has had to make an example to his employees before. You aren't that different, you know."

Mario found the glass doors that separated the bedroom area from the living room and gestured for her to enter her bedroom. Since this also shut them off from the closet where her suitcase was, Angela obediently left the phone by her round table and joined him, not saying a word when he closed the doors, closing them in the master bedroom.

He didn't say a word as he made himself comfortable on the love seat in the corner of the bedroom, then pulled out his phone. "Tomas will bring us coffee. Sit," he ordered, patting the space next to him.

She didn't know his game but reassured herself that he didn't know her game, either. She moved across her room, still barefoot but knowing the dress she wore would appeal to Mario. One glance at his face and she knew he was paying attention to how her outfit hugged all of her curves. She didn't have to sleep with the enemy to use sexuality against him.

"There is a Starbucks across the street," she offered, sitting on the couch next to him and twisting to face him, with her back in the corner at her end.

Mario nodded, gave Tomas instructions, and clasped his phone shut. He placed it on the coffee table, then rested his hand on her knee. If either of them looked straight ahead and not at each other, they would be able to stare at her destroyed bed, the bed where Jake had made her come harder than she had in her entire life. It hit her Mario probably chose this location with that view intentionally, believing if she had slept with someone else, it would rattle her and expose her guilt if made to sit facing the scene of the crime,

"Did you resolve the problem with your hired help last night?" she asked before Mario could say whatever he was about to say. She needed to lead this conversation. "I'm sorry I ran out on you, but men fighting have always upset me. I've always hated it," she added, wrinkling her nose again in a look she had discovered Mario interpreted as indicating her being spoiled.

This time he didn't comment on her being spoiled. He was probing, studying her, and making no qualms about the fact that he was doing so. If she remained steady under his gaze, he might grow even more suspicious and start believing she was raised around interrogations and not businessmen making deals with their fists.

She sighed loudly when he remained quiet after a moment. "I just said I was sorry I ran out," she whined, feeling like an idiot and sounding like a child. All part of the job, she told herself. "Maybe next time when your men are out of line and bugging you, take them away from me and then make them obey you." She puffed out her lower lip, tilted her head slightly, and stared him in the eye.

"I don't want you to worry about any of this anymore," he said, his voice gentle.

"How could I not when you wouldn't let me back into your home last night?" She threw her hands up in the air and let them fall and slap her legs. It would be one hell of an acting job to pull off a temper tantrum, but if it would convince him her intelligence wrapped around social events and shopping she would damn well do it.

"I wasn't there, *amore*," he crooned. "My staff has already been instructed to allow you inside if I'm not there and make sure you are made comfortable until I return."

She seriously doubted any of that was true. "There is nothing worse than disobedient staff. I'm sure you have the matter under control, but if you don't, I can get you references to replace your house servants." She banked on him turning down her request, since she didn't have a clue where someone would hire maids and butlers.

"That won't be necessary." Mario placed his hand over both of her hands. His skin was cold and smooth, not warm and a bit rough like Jake's. "Like I said, this isn't something you will worry about. The matter is well under control."

"Good," she said, and moved her hands farther down her legs. He tightened his grip on her, but at least his hand wasn't so close to her crotch now.

"I have a question for you, and I'll know whether you answer truthfully or not."

"Sure." She shrugged with one shoulder as she studied his face. More than anything she wished the coffee or Housekeeping would arrive.

"Who is your father?" Mario asked.

"You know who my father is." She blurted out the line she had come up with if he asked her that question. "Are you doing business with him?" she asked, her eyes going wide as she leaned forward just a bit, as if excited to learn new gossip. Holding the pose for only a moment, she leaned back against the love seat and forced herself to look determined. "Nope. I don't care if you are," she announced. "I hate him. I told you that already."

"I'll get more to the point." He tightened his grip, pinching her fingers together and piercing her with a look that made her feel a twinge of nervousness for the first time since sitting with him. "Is your father a detective?"

Angela stared back at Mario, holding her facial expression as she stared blankly at him. No way would she let him catch her off guard. Men like Mario played on throwing out the unexpected, maneuvering their prey into a corner, and pouncing the moment their target's defenses were down. What they never seemed to take into consideration was that all criminals seemed to use the same tactics for intimidation. She'd rehearsed this conversation in her head several times before going live with Mario now. It was a plan of attack her father had taught her years ago. There was never a way of knowing exactly what a criminal would say, but with good forethought, several plausible comments or questions could be predicted. It was imperative to rehearse not only her responses but her body language during the conversation as well.

"Yes," she said, nodding once, having decided last night confirming her father was a detective would be the best way to maintain her cover. It would also be the last answer Mario would expect her to give, which helped her hold on to the lead. "But you know that already."

"I know that now," he said, not hesitating, although it seemed something shifted in his gaze. "Why is it something you kept from me?"

"I haven't kept that from you. His success makes him a hard secret to keep," she mumbled, sounding disgusted. "If I could keep the world from knowing I'm his daughter, I would do that." Angela laughed, watching Mario's expression change, the hard lines dissipating as he continued studying her. "Wait a minute," she continued, her nerves relaxing as her confidence built and she finished her lines. "Don't use me to get to him, please. He's such a worm." She turned her hands under Mario's, knowing this was where she needed to be a bit affectionate. Her stomach twisted when she squeezed his hand and his fingers quickly intertwined with hers. "I already know you're much more intelligent, quick on your toes. If my father is giving you grief, he doesn't stand a chance against you. You can handle him," she finished, whispering her last sentence as if she were seducing Mario. "He doesn't even handle his investments as well as you do."

He hadn't expected her response. And she'd known he wouldn't, which was why she'd decided it was the best angle to go with. Tomas couldn't show up with that coffee soon enough.

Mario laughed and for the first time his focus dropped to her breasts.

"I'm not concerned about what your father thinks of me," Mario said, sounding amused. He released her hands and began stroking her leg. "You, *mi amore,* are all I'm worried about."

"Mario, don't worry about me," she said. "I know how to take care of myself."

"I'm not so sure about that." His phone rang and he reached for it, answering it without saying a word. Then standing as he closed the phone, he opened the glass doors and disappeared toward the hotel door.

Angela followed him, closing the glass doors again, this time shutting them in the living room half of her suite. Mario let Tomas into her room and took a cardboard box with tall cups in it from Tomas. She hurried forward, grinning easily at Tomas, and slipped one of the cups out of Mario's hands.

"I'm leaving town and I've decided to take you with me," Mario announced. "I've researched your father and although I know you aren't a detective, and wouldn't possess any of those skills, someone like your father would keep a very close rein on those dear to him. You tell me you two aren't close, but that doesn't mean James Huxtable wouldn't have a vested interest in what his daughter does and who she associates with. When I travel, I would like you at my side. We will make good traveling companions, and knowing you're safe with me will resolve any issues that might arise otherwise."

Jake pulled into the driveway and stared at the stucco house. It was well kept, with a screened-in front porch and brick path that led from the curb to the porch stairs. Angela sat with her hands clutched together in her lap, staring out the window. She'd been quiet most of the way over here. Mandela's conversation had upset her, although she'd tried making light of it, even going as far as bragging up her acting skills when she told Jake how Mandela had looked stupefied when she had admitted her father was a detective. It had been a good move on her part but didn't buy them very much time. First, Mandela thought he was taking Angela out of town, which would happen when hell froze over. And second, which was equally as important, Mandela wouldn't leave Huxtable alone now. If anything, Mandela would track him down with more energy and motivation now, using him to keep Angela at his side and behaving how he wanted her to behave.

"Ever been here before?" Jake asked, studying her profile.

The moment she snapped out of her thoughts, she pursed her lips, then turned to meet his gaze. "Never. And he's going to hear about it, too." She shook her head, looking more disgusted than pleased.

A few of the bricks were loose in the path up to the house, and there was a really simple doorbell system in use. The moment Jake stepped onto the porch steps, several dogs started barking frantically inside.

"May I help you?" a woman asked when she opened the front door and stared at Jake, then Angela, through the dark screen door. The woman didn't give any indication she suspected who Angela was, which was interesting in itself.

"I have an appointment," he said, repeating the words Huxtable had instructed him to use when he'd arrived. Jake hadn't mentioned bringing Angela along, although Huxtable never asked whether she would be there or not.

The woman could have been somewhere between forty-five and fifty-five. Jake had never been really good at guessing an age with ladies, especially when they kept themselves in good shape, as this woman obviously did. There were silver streaks in her hair, which was straight and curled under at her neck. She wore a T-shirt and shorts, and when she used her leg to block the two dogs and open the screen he noticed not only that she was barefoot but also that, judging by her muscle tone, she probably did a lot of bike riding, jogging, or both.

"Umm, yes. Okay, come in," she said, sounding hesitant. The pensive looks she shot him and Angela were curious. If this were her home, Jake would think she'd be accustomed to people coming here with appointments, unless Huxtable had just set up shop with this woman. "The dogs are harmless," she offered, leading the way across the screened-in porch and into the house, leaving Jake and Angela to find that fact out for themselves.

The dogs quit barking without instruction when they followed the woman into a dark, small living room. Jake prayed she was right about her pets and focused his attention on her, instead of the two dogs.

"I'm Jake," he began.

Angela was doing an incredible job of remaining quiet, his requirement for her coming along, since he'd arranged to meet Huxtable without mentioning anything about Angela. She'd balked at first but finally promised she wouldn't say a word until they were alone with her father. The look on her face showed the torture she was enduring. Angela watched the woman like a hawk, barely aware of the dogs, and probably was biting her tongue to keep herself from lashing out with a hundred questions as to who this woman was and what she was doing in Angela's father's life.

"He's back here." The woman kept walking through the living room and disappeared down a hallway, gesturing for them to follow.

Jake and Angela competed with the two dogs for hallway space as they followed her.

"One moment," the woman said, holding her finger up at the two of them before disappearing into a room with its door open.

The dogs followed her, their long black tails still wagging, although they were quiet except for their nails clicking against the wooden floor. Angela crossed her arms, glaring after the woman, before turning to Jake and blessing him

with the same disgusted look. Grinning at her would probably make it too hard to hold on to her silence. Jake didn't
want Angela's presence made known until they were with
Huxtable. The woman didn't act as if she knew who either of
them were, which meant Huxtable hadn't told her. Jake
would find the reasoning behind that soon enough, mainly
because he had a feeling it would be the first thing Angela
demanded to know.

There were pictures on the wall, and Jake squinted and
stared at the printed and framed poses of the woman, who'd
let them into her home, standing with a couple children at
different ages. The same children were also in pictures by
themselves, one of them, the girl, standing in front of this
house wearing a graduation cap and gown.

"Do you mind giving us a few minutes alone?" It was James
Huxtable asking the question, but his tone was so gentle and
soft-spoken.

Jake snapped his attention away from the pictures, but
Angela was already marching to the door. The woman blocked
the doorway when she appeared, and for a moment she and
Angela sized each other up. The woman didn't want them
there. Jake didn't know what Huxtable had told her about
him, but whatever it was, she didn't approve.

Jake placed his hands on Angela's shoulders, standing
behind her and inching her back against him to allow the
woman to leave the room and get around them with her duti-
ful dogs in tow.

"Thank you," he said politely, and the woman nodded.

"Come on in and close the door." Huxtable's demanding,
cocky tone had returned. Maybe Angela did know a different man than Jake did. Apparently Huxtable saved his good
side for the women in his life. "Have a seat." He gestured to
a wooden chair across from the cluttered desk that he sat
behind.

When Huxtable looked up and saw Angela, his strict expression disappeared and he stood, moving around the cluttered desk as he extended his arms and pulled her in for a hug.

"You had the good sense to bring her after all," Huxtable

said over Angela's shoulder, focusing on Jake for only a moment before blessing his daughter with a look filled with love and admiration. "Good. We have a few things to discuss."

"Yes, we do." Angela didn't just use her bossy tone on Jake. "Who is that woman?" she hissed, pointing in the direction the woman had headed when she left the room.

Angela's father didn't appear daunted or even upset at his daughter's tone. He returned to his chair behind the desk and waved at the two of them to sit.

"A friend," he stated, giving Angela a steady look for a moment longer than necessary. "Anne lets me use this room to work when I'm here. It was her husband's office before he died and since has also been used for storage." Huxtable leaned back in the chair and folded his hands over his belly. "She's not on our list for discussion." He allowed only a moment of silence to follow his order before continuing. "As you can see," he started again, giving Jake his complete attention, "no one knows I come here. It is for the protection of all those involved. And as you also noticed, I'm sure, Anne doesn't know a lot about Angela. For your protection, my dear," he offered, and it appeared the comment would appease his daughter, who was quite obviously sitting there fuming. "I don't have to tell you that your average person isn't equipped with the skills to avoid an interrogation from a criminal, be it casual or painful."

"How long have you known her?" Angela demanded.

Huxtable didn't bend to Angela's commanding nature, which was impressive, because at the same time her aggressive nature didn't appear to bother him at all.

"For now, I'm under the radar," he finished, his features softening as he gazed at his daughter. "You need to believe I'm not in danger and not to worry about me, sweetheart," he added, giving no indication he knew he'd intentionally ignored her question, which had her seething even more. "There is something I'm going to share with you, though. And as well, I want to be updated on your case. Would you care to begin?"

"There are two bugs placed at Mandela's place right now,"

Angela jumped in, her voice calm, collected, as she leaned back and matched her father's position when she relaxed her hands across her middle and her elbows on the sides of the chair. "His limo is also bugged. The equipment I'm using is working fine," she added. "Last night, though, we recorded the conversation that gave us the edge in handling Mandela when he acted today."

Huxtable nodded. "Did you find the picture on the Internet they were talking about?"

If Angela was upset by her father's all-business attitude, she gave no indication. She responded with the same relaxed tone, debriefing as if this was how they handled their cases every day, keeping emotion out of it and laying out the facts. It was impressive as hell but would never work in Jake's family. The whole lot of them were too hotheaded and weren't afraid to speak their minds.

Angela glanced at Jake and he got the uncanny sensation she was giving him permission to speak.

"No. And I looked." Jake had been the one to search the Internet. "Angela Torres doesn't show up online. Now Angela Huxtable does, but there isn't a picture of her to be found anywhere. I ran a search under your name as well," he said, nodding at Huxtable. "You appear online about as much as I do. Angela has taken on quite a few cases in the four years she's been licensed. If I understand right, she's solved most of her cases."

"All of them," she cut in.

"If I were checking her out," Jake said, not looking at Angela but focusing on her father, "I'd find it a bit interesting that nothing shows up at all under the name Torres and what is online under 'Huxtable' is all less than a year old. That in itself might be interpreted as suspicious."

Huxtable waved his hand in the air. "There just wasn't time. Angela worked hard to create enough history so when a background check was done on her it wouldn't be a blank slate. Creating accomplishments that could be found online wasn't as imperative as having information pop up if a background check was run. Mandela would care more if she was ever arrested or who might have pulled her credit than if she attended this social function or won an award."

Jake wasn't sure he agreed with that, but the point was moot, since obviously they'd already searched the Net and found her.

"Jake was on Mandela's property late last night and believes he knows where the kidnapped people are," Angela announced, changing the subject.

Huxtable nodded. "So he told me. Confirm or deny that ASAP," he ordered, then leaned forward and gathered papers on his desk, straightened them, and put them down. "Is there anything else?" he asked, shifting his attention from Angela to Jake, then back to his daughter.

"You know there is," Angela said under her breath, her voice seething with emotion.

Huxtable didn't look angry. The cocky bastard was well hidden in front of his daughter. "For now, my dear, know that I'm safe. What matters is the success of our cases, right? Our personal lives can't ever interfere."

Jake watched Angela as she focused on her father. He couldn't tell if she held her tongue because Jake was in the room or if this was her and Huxtable's normal way of communicating. For a moment Jake felt a twinge of jealousy over how well Huxtable controlled his willful, aggressive daughter. Jake had the satisfaction of seeing it could be done, though.

"There is something we do need to discuss." Huxtable stood, remaining behind the back of the desk and staring at the incredibly cluttered room. Stacks of boxes along the walls made it appear a much smaller room than it was. "I have news on my case," he began. When Angela leaned forward, suddenly incredibly interested, Huxtable continued, speaking just a bit faster. "Your sister is officially being reported as missing, in her country and ours."

"Oh God," Angela muttered, leaning back and pressing her fingers over her mouth. "You haven't learned anything?"

"It's what I haven't learned that is very interesting." Huxtable sat again, frowning as he seemed to ponder how he would word what he planned on saying next.

"Tell me," Angela said, guessing her father hesitated with not such good news.

"I've shared with you the facts. She disappeared at the airport. She never picked up her luggage. No one witnessed anything that could have been considered an abduction, an argument, or anything at all out of the normal. There are food courts where Marianna would have been after coming off the plane. All employees working that day have been interviewed and shown pictures of her. No one remembers a thing."

"She didn't just disappear." Angela stated the obvious.

"Of course not," her father said, once again using his gentle tone. "Yet she didn't struggle with whoever took her. She didn't try and grab her luggage, nor has anyone called requesting to have it sent. Her luggage was shipped back to your mother."

"LAX has security cameras." Jake moved to the edge of his seat, caught up in the brainstorming of an impossible case. They were always the most exciting when there were no clues. "Also, the employees working at the airport entrances need to be interviewed. All the exits are also under full-time surveillance."

"The order to view the surveillance cameras came through. I've viewed them already. Marianna left the luggage pick-up area with a man. He was tall with black hair, just like Marianna's, and appeared to know her."

"What makes you think he knew her?" Angela demanded. She was gripping the edge of the desk with white knuckles and so focused on her father she didn't even blink.

"He hugged her when he first saw her."

"Well, who the hell is he?" she yelled.

Huxtable stared at his daughter, his voice as intense as his expression. "I don't know."

"What do you mean you don't know?"

Jake wasn't focusing on Huxtable any longer. He faced Angela, itching to stroke her hair, rub her back, touch her somehow. They weren't sexual desires but something deeper, drawing up from far down in his gut. All that mattered was calming her down, not seeing her so distraught and upset.

"Did you get any facial recognition at all?" he asked, keeping his voice low.

Angela shot her attention to him as if she'd forgotten he stood next to her.

"His back was always to the camera, or his head was down, focusing on Marianna."

"Do you think he was intentionally avoiding the cameras?" Jake asked.

"Could be. It looks as if all of his attention were focused on her. Honestly, she left so quickly with him, without fighting him, it really appears she was glad to go with him."

"That's impossible!" Angela stated, gesturing wildly with her hands. She took a step backward as if she might start pacing, remembered how closed in they were around the desk, and settled for slamming her hands down on the edge of it. "She doesn't know anyone in this country but me!" Then, fisting her hands at her waist, she glared at her father, then turned her head and looked up at Jake, blessing him with the same accusatory look. "One of you better find her right now," she said in a harsh whisper. "Or I will."

"I have a curiosity," Huxtable said calmly.

"A curiosity?"

Angela turned to Jake. "A curiosity is when there are no clues, which because there are none creates a clue."

Since he'd never heard of the term he guessed it was one Angela and her father had made up. Jake started brainstorming over what no clues might point toward.

Huxtable saved him the time. "We know she knew no one in this country, yet she leaves the airport with a man who is holding her affectionately, or so it appears. He walks up from behind her. Marianna never looks over her shoulder at him. He simply comes up from behind and wraps his arms around her. It's impossible to tell if she jumped, acted startled, or even tried to resist the hug. He is a lot taller than she is and, with his arms around her, hides any reaction she might have had to his embrace. He keeps one arm around her and moves the other to pull her hair back from her face. The next moment, she turns away from the luggage area and

leaves with him. She never hugs him in return, nor does she
once look up at his face. It doesn't appear that she says anything to him at all. If someone abducted her right off the
plane, she would have fought, loudly, if she could. Yet she
didn't. There were a lot of people working who could have
seen something, yet no one saw anything unusual."

"So whoever took her said the right thing to scare the crap
out of her and make her leave with them without a fight,"
Jake offered.

"Possibly," Huxtable agreed. "Marianna had her clothes
with her. One of her suitcases was still on the conveyor belt.
She had quite a bit of cash stuffed in her suitcase that she
didn't take. Whoever took her didn't care about her luggage."

"They didn't take her for money," Angela cut in, pointing
her finger at her father as her face lit up with excitement.
"But also," she added, her voice growing quiet, "they didn't
care if she had clothes with her."

"That's right." Huxtable nodded. "Whoever he is, he
knew how to make her not fight, didn't want her for money,
and didn't care if she had a change of clothes. Anything
else?" He looked from one of them to the other.

Jake didn't care for the feeling that he was being treated
as the student, being judged if he could see the obvious and
not so obvious.

"Let me think," Angela said, tapping her finger over her
lips. Her straight, black hair streaming down her back and her
bare shoulders with her pink sleeveless blouse complemented
each other. She narrowed her brow, giving her father's question serious thought.

"Someone could have drugged her." Jake didn't take his
attention off Angela, and her attention snapped to his.

Her eyes widened. "No," she whispered.

"It's a curiosity," her father said quietly.

Suddenly Jake understood where their thoughts were
headed. "You think she might have been abducted to be part
of the game."

"We don't know how many players are playing the game."
Huxtable leaned back in his seat. "The fact that it's been

kept out of the news proves to me the FBI is still working this one, but I've managed to find out there has been a significant increase in public kidnappings. No ransoms have been requested. The person taken goes without a struggle."

"They're being drugged with slave juice, then escorted away from wherever they are." Angela hugged herself, leaning forward, and looked like she might be sick. When she slowly turned her head to look at Jake, there was something akin to terror in her pretty eyes. "You're going to find out who is in that outbuilding immediately."

Chapter Twelve

Angela stared at the picture of Marianna her mother had sent. The last time she'd seen her half sister, Angela had been sixteen and Marianna eleven.

"She's beautiful." Jake stood over Angela, nodding at the eight-by-ten in her hand. There was sincerity, a glimpse of true compassion, and pain in his eyes.

Angela nodded. "Absolutely gorgeous," she murmured, still not trusting her voice.

After seeing her father and learning he had a girlfriend, Angela and Jake had returned to the Drake to prepare for the rest of the day. Mario planned on picking her up at five, which would be the time when Jake returned to the property and learned who was in the outbuilding. Angela prayed, and at the same time was terrified, that Marianna was in that outbuilding. Just remembering the conversation that had been picked up between Mario and Bobby from the bug she'd planted outside made her sick. They had implied they had had sex with one of the ladies in the outbuilding. It made Angela's blood boil and made her frantic to free the people inside. If there weren't so much at stake, she would march over there, guns in both hands, and demand entrance into that building. Hopefully within less than twenty-four hours, all the kidnapped people would be free. If her little sister, precious and perfect Marianna, was tarnished in the slightest way, Angela would kill Mario with her bare hands.

"She's not in there," Angela repeated to herself in a feeble effort to keep herself sane and focused.

If Marianna hadn't been abducted by Mario, had another of the players kidnapped her? Or maybe some random lunatic had walked up to her in the airport. If that were the case, they hadn't done a thing to find her. If Marianna had been abducted for the game, at least she would be free soon. They were so close to a bust she could taste it.

Angela was making herself sick thinking about the different possibilities. She needed to focus on something else just so she could be at her top performance. Marianna would be free sooner.

"We need that board game, if there is one," Jake said, once they were settled in her hotel suite. He'd removed his shirt and kicked off his shoes. What was it about that man wearing nothing but faded, well-worn blue jeans?

"There is." Her voice cracked and she dropped Marianna's picture on the table but continued staring at it. This was her father's missing-person case. Her mother had called him, not Angela. Regardless, it was her case now, too. No way would Angela allow Marianna to be in that monster's clutches for a minute longer than she had to be.

"Angela." Jake reached for her hand, pulling her to her feet, and grabbed her other hand when she would have brought Marianna's picture with her. "We're going to find her. She's going to be okay."

More than likely if the tables were turned, Angela would have said something similar to him. She still wanted to strike out, demand to know how he knew everything would be fine. Jake pulled her closer, then let go of her hands and began stroking her face.

"We'll go over our plans, follow them, and all of this will be over soon," he assured her.

It wasn't what he said but how he said it that did something to the fierce knot that had been in her gut since she had left her father. This time Jake didn't pounce on her mouth, impaling her as if he were starving for her. It was more as if they melted together, the two of them fusing from scalding heat created out of existing cravings and a new desire to cleanse the negative energy zapping inside both of them and replace it with courage and motivation.

She'd created this hunger in both of them. If she'd made love to him last night, possibly all of this would be out of their systems and they would be content plotting and creating the master plan to bring down Mario and find Marianna. They were organized. Both had shared what they planned to do come five o'clock. It hadn't taken more than an hour after returning to the hotel. The time between now and then was meant for the two of them. They would create a bond through making love, and it would secure their ability to perform, work together, and end the nightmare the game had brought down on too many families.

Angela's insides quivered. A quickening tightened in her womb, increasing the aching throbbing she'd endured to a full, raging pulse that demanded compensation now. There wouldn't be any teasing or torturing this time. She sensed Jake knew that also. His touch was different from last time, his movements more relaxed, although determined.

Jake's strong hands were all over her, pressing her against him, stroking her already-too-sensitive flesh. When he cupped her bottom, lifting and thrusting her against his hard dick, tiny sparks of passion exploded all over her. She was teetering between the reality of now and a world so much more sensual. A world with no problems other than learning what would make her explode and what would make him come.

"Jake," she said, uttering his name on a breath.

"Yes, sweetheart?" He hadn't called her baby since she'd snapped at him about it. Jake might be more trainable than she'd originally given him credit for being.

"We should . . ." The words wouldn't come out.

"Yes, we should." Jake scooped her into his arms, nestling her against his chest while he held her as if she were a small child.

Angela wasn't skinny. She wasn't fat, but she knew she wasn't light as a feather. Which only proved how strong, how confident and sure of himself, Jake was. She damn near slid down his body and melted onto the bed that had been made with fresh throw pillows tossed at the head of it. The firmness of the mattress did little to help her regain any stability. She collapsed against it, her head sinking between two pillows and the bones in her body giving way to the insurmountable heat surging through her.

It took a minute for her to recognize the ringing as coming from Jake's phone. Instead of cursing the interruption, Angela gave thanks that she had a moment to take a deep breath and return some oxygen to her brain. Jake stood at the edge of the bed, his hands on his hips, and stared at her. He didn't move to answer his phone.

"There's no one I want to talk to right now," he told her, his expression strained as need visibly ransacked his system as much as it did hers. He stood where he was, ignoring the ringing, and began taking his pants off.

Angela heard the phone ring a third or possibly a fourth time but couldn't pull her attention from Jake's face. Her heart beat so fiercely it was hard to concentrate. She wanted to tell Jake not to hold back, to let go and take her, making love to her however his natural desires and cravings demanded. At the same time, something in the back of her head warned her that Jake was a very tall man, well over six feet. He was incredibly muscular and very strong. If he released all of his pent-up passion and desire on her, would she be able to handle it?

The thought of trying was so intense the room almost turned sideways on her. She sucked in a deep breath.

Jake must have misinterpreted her sigh. "I'll set it to Silent so it can't interrupt us again." Even though he spoke with clarity, he took his time turning away from her.

Angela couldn't remember ever craving a man to be rough with her. She preferred a bit of control in her sexual encounters. She wanted her man to be a man but not to step over that line of her knowing she was in charge of her own body. With Jake, she wanted him to release that energy she saw burning out of control inside him. She wanted to fight him and have him restrain her and impale her with all that fury and unleashed need.

Images of Jake doing just that damn near made her roll off the bed when she moved onto her side. If she didn't get a grip, she would be panting and drooling.

"N-n-o, w-w-wait," she stammered, her senses barely managing to break through the thick fog of lust in her brain. "Don't put it on Silent. Check to see if its my father." Once Jake had told her father that his phone had a scrambler on it, her father immediately decided Jake's phone would be used for all calls.

Jake glanced at his phone and shook his head. "It's not. He's already dished out his orders. I doubt he'll contact us again unless we wait too long to report back in. And he wouldn't expect us to pull everything off before nightfall."

Jake's stormy green eyes burrowed deep into her soul when he left his phone on the night stand. There was something about this giant man who moved so gracefully and stealthily. It turned him into a deadly predator and one so beautiful, so incredibly loaded with sex appeal.

"Who was it?" she asked, fighting for clarity as, her attention shifted to the bulging roped muscles in Jake's biceps and forearms when he began crawling onto the bed.

"It was nobody." There was a rumble in his voice that matched the skilled seducer as he moved in, forcing Angela to lie back as he continued crawling until he was on top of her. "Clear your head, sweetheart. We're going to have your sister back in no time. But we can't do anything until Mario leaves at five. Until then, it's just you and me."

The throbbing between her legs was becoming a desperate pounding as blood rushed into the most sensitive part of her body. It excited and scared the crap out of her at the same time that Jake read her like an open book. They really hadn't known each other more than a couple days. Angela never had sex with a man until she knew him really well. Oftentimes getting to know them too well turned her off because she became acutely aware of all their annoying traits.

Jake started teasing her sensitive flesh just above her collarbone. It made her want to curl her toes to the ceiling. At the same time one of his hands made its way under her shirt, finding her breast and cupping it, tugging just enough to make her eyes roll back in her head. Jake's skills included making her come without making love to her. She had guessed his list of skills was endless. Excitement twisted around inside her with the knowledge she was about to find out.

Jake moved her bra out of the way with a solid swipe of his hand, then pinched her hardened nipple. Shock waves rolled over her, shooting straight down her middle. If she could have rolled over and cried out, begging him to stop and demanding he keep going, she would have. When she opened her mouth, she didn't have a chance to make a sound before Jake pounced on it, impaling her with his tongue as he continued torturing her too-sensitive nipple.

Angela didn't realize her hands were stroking Jake's back until taut muscles twitched under her fingertips. She dragged her fingernails down the length of his bare back as far as she could reach, enjoying how solid and inviting his body felt.

Jake growled into her mouth, his tongue swirling around hers in some erotic dance she didn't know but picked up on right away. He broke off the kiss in mid-swirl, leaving her gasping and barely able to focus.

"What?" she mumbled when Jake straightened.

"Your clothes," he grumbled, his words raspy and laced heavily with need. As he spoke, he moved his hand away from her breast but kept it under her shirt as he pushed it up to her shoulders.

Angela didn't have to lift herself off the bed to remove her shirt. Jake took her arm, pulling her into a sitting position but remaining on top of her so that her nose was almost touching the tight curls on his chest. She breathed in his rich, musky all-male scent, then got a whiff of her fabric softener when the shirt went over her head. It was promptly tossed to the floor.

Her shorts were yanked off with one solid sweep. She hadn't bothered with underpants. Now she didn't know whether she regretted the few clothes she'd had on or not. The look Jake gave her when he released her and let her tumble back on the bed stole her breath.

"Infatuated" didn't quite describe it. "Enamored" maybe. Definitely "pleased." Angela gazed up at him, letting her vision blur, which made the moment all the more erotic. As exposed as she felt lying naked under him, the way he devoured her with his eyes, letting her see how hungry he was, made her feel sexy, desirable, and anxious.

"I've dreamed about this," Jake confessed, his attention shooting to her face the moment he spoke, as if needing to see her immediate reaction.

She smiled. It would be cheesy as hell to admit she'd imagined this, too. A lot. More than he needed to know. Jake already reeked of self-confidence and his skills were off the charts. Stroking this man's ego was hardly necessary. It was odd how at that moment it dawned on her how very much alike Jake and her father were. She would consider it high praise to tell either of them that and didn't doubt for a moment both would see it as an incredible insult.

So she smiled, keeping her thoughts to herself. "You aren't dreaming now, darling," she drawled, and swayed her hips against him but stilled when his thick cock greeted her, rubbing against her inner thigh.

"I can't wait to find out if your steamy heat is as intoxicating as it was in my dreams."

Did he really dream about her? Jake said the most romantic things. He could also utter daring sexual comments Angela wouldn't have the nerve to say out loud. Hell, she wouldn't confess she'd dreamed about him all night the night before. His skills should be terrifying her and not making her grin like some dumb twit straight out of high school.

She tried matching his smooth, confident air, using the training she had learned working undercover over the years.

"You'll have to let me know if it does." At least she sounded confident and at ease.

"Trust me, you'll be the first to know." Jake stepped out of his boxers.

When his phone rang again he cursed under his breath. Her vision cleared and she watched every inch of him tense, causing muscles to bulge throughout his body.

"It's Dad." Angela leapt to the side of the bed.

Jake picked up his phone, scowled, and sent it to voice mail. "No."

"Well, then you're mighty popular."

"It's not the kind of popularity I want." Jake dropped the phone on the bedside table before crawling in next to her.

"Who was it?" She rolled to her side, fighting the urge to cuddle against Jake.

So much sexual energy charged the air between them she worried the heat surging off his body would scald her alive. At the same time, she sensed his tension. He wasn't as care-free and grinning as he was when they started. His expression had hardened as if he worked to mask his emotions from her.

Jake was an intense man. In spite of his casual attitude and the way his eyes glowed with a hungry passion she couldn't wait to know firsthand, he didn't fool her for a moment. Maybe his phone ringing so much should bother her, too. What if there was a lady for him back in California and she was desperately trying to reach him?

There wasn't a spoken commitment between him and Angela. There wasn't any commitment at all. She didn't do one-night stands and she sure as hell didn't have sex with married men or men in commitments. She wasn't the kind of woman who could make love to a man just to enjoy the physical release. There had to be an attraction. And it had to be mutual interest that would possibly take the two of them somewhere more permanent.

So what the hell was she doing now? She wanted Jake. God, she'd wanted him a year ago when she'd first laid eyes on him. Something about Jake turned her on physically and emotionally. He hadn't given any indication that her feelings for him were mutual. The only thing he'd made obvious was that he really wanted to fuck her. But fucking and making love were different.

If Jake was the kind of man who could bring any lady to her knees, that very well could mean he'd done just that with women back in California. And there were women. Jake's roguish playboy personality was so well established there were comments about it in some of the articles she'd read about KFA.

The look he gave her was too focused, too deep and determined, for her to believe he would look at any other woman that way. He might have skills, but he wasn't shallow. She felt his emotions right along with his lust.

But what were the emotions she was sensing? Were they all driven by one hell of a sex drive and an insatiable lust that he didn't keep hidden from her?

She lifted herself to relax on her elbow and blinked to focus on his face. That hard look was still there. His green eyes focused on her, but they were opaque, not glowing as they did when he teased her or when they discussed the case. It was those moments she enjoyed with him, when his passion flared, not only for her but also for the hunt. They were two souls with so much in common, but if there was another side to him, encouraged and fine-tuned as a result of him being so incredibly appealing, having sex with him might be her biggest mistake ever, Angela would give him a piece of her heart, and he wouldn't give her anything in return other than incredible sexual satisfaction.

When he didn't answer but continued staring at her, torturing her with the nearness of so much carnal, unleashed sex appeal reverberating off his tall, overpowering body, she decided to probe a bit harder. "If you need a minute to return a phone call, I won't go anywhere. I promise," she offered, moistening her lips and studying him for his reaction.

"It's simply a friend who doesn't know I'm out here." Jake slid his arm under the curve of her neck and pulled her on top of him. His hooded gaze made it harder to read how he felt about the interruption. His attention was on her breasts as he adjusted her against him.

His cock immediately danced between them, stretching and throbbing. Angela's insides swelled. She was already soaked, but as she stretched her legs, straddling him, she felt the moisture cling to her freshly shaved flesh.

"Your skin is so incredibly soft," he said, changing the subject before she could question him further.

Call it the detective in her, but immediately she was curious whether this friend was a man or a woman. Angela was about to make love to Jake. That made it somewhat her business. She had a right to know if another woman was trying hard to reach him when Angela was ready to become intimate with him.

"Every inch of you," Jake continued, dragging his hands down her back until he reached her ass. He cupped it, stretching and spreading her open further as he kneaded her flesh. His fingers inched closer to the source of her heat. "Damn," Jake growled, his eyes glazing over as he finally met her gaze. "Already I can feel the heat, and how wet you are," he added, lowering his voice as he grumbled the last words. "You're going to scald me alive," he added, lowering his attention to her mouth.

"You know, I can feel you, too," she said, and wiggled her hips against him.

Jake growled, the sound rising up through his chest and vibrating through her at the same time that his dick thrust up and poked her in the belly. This was how it would be for now. They hadn't known each other long enough to voice any type of commitment. Her brain was quickly fogging over with lust and the overwhelming need to ease him inside her and experience what all this raw sexual being could offer her. Angela had to leave it at that. Nothing more. If as they continued spending time together they determined there was something between them to explore, than they would discuss it at that time. For now, at this moment, she would do something she'd never done before: experience sex as a physical pleasure and not as uniting two bodies together when their minds had already melded.

"What are you thinking, sweetheart?" Jake asked.

His question surprised her. She'd just convinced herself to keep her thoughts out of this and take it on as a physical release and Jake tried probing her mind along with her body. He was making her teeter back and forth between the physical and emotional.

The only thing to do was control the moment and guide him to where she wanted him. "I'm trying to decide how I'm going to take you," she said, lying through her teeth but knowing if she kept it physical she wouldn't be eaten alive with worry that she was making a big mistake.

"Is that so?" He lifted one eyebrow and searched her face, the glow returning in his gaze. "I would have said you were wondering if this was the right thing to do or not."

Damn him for reading her mind so well. Especially when he'd turned into a blank slate for her. She let herself drown in his intense gaze. The man was as powerful intellectually as he was physically. That really appealed to her.

"Are you suggesting I'm the kind of woman who would change her mind once I was sprawled naked on top of you?" she challenged.

Angela felt a wave of control grip her. She liked how Jake appeared in pain, overwhelmed with hunger that ate at him until her giant, muscular man was damn near putty in her hands.

He tried moving his hands and preventing her from rising off of him but didn't succeed. Angela pushed herself to a sitting position, still straddling him. The position had his dick dangerously close to her entrance. It pulsed and danced, continuously moving and trying to grab her attention long enough to distract her. This new position also made Jake move his hands, which helped her hold on to her yearning for him to be inside her and allowed her to tease him just a bit longer.

Jake gripped her breasts, bracing her and at the same time squeezing and tugging her sensitive flesh. Waves of need washed over her, and she arched into his touch, refusing to let her brain focus on any regret that might come after they were through. If this was just physical, she would make the best of it and take as much as she gave.

When he chuckled, it pulled her out of her thoughts and she looked down. Her hair streamed over her shoulders, covering her breasts and his hands and shrouding her with long, black locks.

"I know you want this as much as I do, but you're so damn wet I think you might be torturing yourself as much as you are me." He lifted his hips off the bed, causing her to fall forward. Jake grabbed her, held her in place, and rubbed the tip of his cock against her smooth flesh. "I promise there won't be any regrets, darling," he whispered.

Angela gripped his forearms, embracing the strength and power emanating from his body. She used it to fuel her confidence. But looking down to see his face when he spoke wasn't as simple. If she moved at all, he would slide inside her. She wasn't prolonging their torture, but there was the smallest part of her brain still arguing with her. Even though she was sure she wanted to go through with this and knew backing down now would piss him off, she wasn't so insecure or meek that she wouldn't take on his temper if she decided this wasn't the time or the right thing to do.

That's when she realized she wasn't holding herself off of him. Jake was holding her up. He was keeping her from sliding down on him. "Are you saying that to me, or to yourself?" she asked, and moved her legs so she regained control of when she would lower herself onto him.

Jake growled, and for the first time she noticed frustration in him and not sexual need. He moved her, causing her to roll onto the bed next to him. Her head found one of the many pillows and she sunk into it. Jake tangled their legs together as he nestled into her, pulling her up against him so when she inhaled, his masculine scent wrapped around her.

"What is it about you?" he asked, his expression torn as he brushed hair from her face. "You annoyed the crap out of me when you wouldn't make love to me the other night. Now I'm holding back until I'm positive you want me. I need to know I'm really who you want," he whispered, his voice gravelly.

He wasn't smiling. Possibly since meeting her, Jake was sharing a part of himself he didn't let many see. His expression seemed raw, almost vulnerable. Angela was hit with an overwhelming urge to reach out, stroke his apprehension away, and assure him she wanted this, too. But hadn't she just been ransacked with emotions that warned her against doing anything that might go against what she viewed as right?

She jumped at the sound of Jake's phone ringing.

"God damn it," Jake cursed, rolling away from her and moving to sit with his back to her as he grabbed his phone.

For a moment, Angela thought he might hurl the phone across the room. Roped muscle flexed in his back, showing off his incredibly perfect body. Without seeing his face Angela still knew he was ransacked with more than just frustration. Some more primitive emotion warred inside him. She pushed herself up against the pillows, wondering for a moment if it wouldn't be best to get dressed.

"What is it?" he snarled, answering his phone and using a tone harsher than he'd used before.

It shouldn't surprise her that the carefree Jake would have a serious side to him. Apparently he also had a fuse that could easily reach its limit if pushed far enough. She didn't know if the phone ringing repeatedly sent him there or if turmoil over making love to her when they didn't have an established commitment ate at him as it did at her.

If the latter was the case, it made Jake damn near the most perfect man she'd ever met. Something twisted around her heart as she stared at his backside and worked to understand the man sitting naked on the edge of her bed.

"There's no one out there I want to talk to," he said, sounding really angry. "And last time I checked, you weren't my answering service. Why are you calling to tell me this? Is there something work related you called to talk about?"

Angela perked up, his words confusing her. She wanted to know who he was talking about but, even more, what messages were just given to him that he didn't want to receive.

Apparently someone was desperately trying to reach Jake and he didn't want to talk to them. Her chest constricted. If there was unfinished business in Jake's life, it would create tension between them.

There was something sizzling between them. It had been since the beginning when they met a year ago. But nothing mattered as much as finding Marianna and ending the game.

"What? Wait a minute," Jake said, moving off the bed and stalking to the other side of the suite. Muscles flexed in his legs as he walked. His back was taut with roped muscles stretching underneath his smooth flesh. But it was his mannerisms that created anxiety inside her. As she watched while he listened to whoever was on the other end of the call, it was obvious the call upset him as much as his phone ringing over and over again. "Natasha, since you're obviously calling to make a point, spit it out and say it. I don't want to hear any messages."

Angela saw his profile when he turned. Whoever Natasha was, Jake wasn't pleased with her. Angela wasn't sure she'd ever seen him this angry.

"Either tell them not to call anymore or let them know I'm not interested. I don't really care." Jake blew out an exasperated sigh and ran his hand through his hair, messing up the curls around his head. "That's none of your business. I'm just not interested anymore. No, not in any of them."

Jake listened to Natasha a minute longer, then mumbled something and hung up his phone. For a moment he glared at the ground; then moving toward Angela, he didn't make eye contact as he grabbed his clothes and dressed.

"You deserve the best, Angela," he muttered, straightening his shirt and heading toward the door. "That sure as hell isn't me."

Chapter Thirteen

Jake sat in his parked car, killing about ten more minutes before the sun began disappearing on the horizon. Angela had left with Mario, and the last Jake spoke to her it had been on the phone, her tone all business. She would text him, sending a 1 if she was returning to the Drake and a 2 if Mario took her to his home. If there were an emergency, she'd text 0.

He hadn't even seen her before she left. Which was his fault.

Jake hadn't expected Angela to run after him when he'd left his suite. He had told himself the phone ringing nonstop had ruined the moment, but inside he'd known the truth. It still rose like a ruthless bile, forcing him to face up to it when he really didn't want to.

Angela was crawling under his skin when no other woman had ever been able to do so. This wasn't the first time he'd met a lady and not taken her to bed right away. Oftentimes building the suspense until they did fuck simply prolonged the excitement and, finally, the thrill of the act. With Angela, he felt as if he'd already waited forever.

But when Marla tried reaching him, then April, women he hadn't seen in well over a month, he'd taken his frustration and embarrassment out on his cousin. And she'd fed his pride to him on a spoon, which she'd shoved deep down his throat. Natasha was tired of taking calls for him, saying whatever it took to get the ladies off the phone. He should be flattered that so many women were persistently trying to reach him, but instead he was ashamed.

If Angela found out women were trying to reach him while he was busy falling head over heels for her, she wouldn't speak to him again. That thought did worse than leave an unpleasant taste in his mouth. The trepidation tightening in his gut damn near made him sick to his stomach. He wanted Angela, more than sexually. Jake wanted her as his woman. He'd never felt this way before, and it was scaring the crap out of him.

"The hell with it." Jake opened his car, which was parked down the street from Mandela's, and tugged on the black shirt he'd put on along with jeans and comfortable tennis shoes. He was dressed to climb, fight, run, and duck into cramped places. And it was time to focus on doing that and not where he stood with Angela.

It was so muggy, Jake's shirt stuck to his body. Even after he had sat with the AC cranked in his rental car all the way over here, perspiration beaded on his forehead. Part of it was nerves. He couldn't afford to stress over Angela. Not right now. Everything was about to blow open; the sizzling energy just under his flesh told him as much.

He hadn't waited more than fifteen minutes after Angela left to head out from the Drake. Mandela had already left his house. Jake slowed and cut off the road into a nearby cluster of trees with thick grass that appeared well maintained growing in their shade. As soon as he'd walked around the curve, the intimidating-looking estate came into view. He stared, confused, at Mandela's place.

A small procession was leaving Mandela's home. Two nondescript black SUVs, possibly Excursions, although Jake couldn't be sure from this distance, pulled out of Mandela's driveway. A moving truck, not the largest there was but a good-sized one that might be used to move several pieces of furniture or a dozen people or so, followed the SUVs onto the street. Jake stared at the taillights of the truck as the black rod iron gate automatically closed and locked itself with a clang. It was time to make his call. Jake shifted the car into drive.

His rental wouldn't make it in a high-speed chase. The little four cylinder was good for long-distance traveling or allowing tourists to get around the town they were in. Fortunately, that moving truck wasn't in a hurry to get where it was going.

His suspicions mounted as he watched the truck leave the gate. They were moving all of the kidnapped victims. He could stay where he was and investigate the outbuilding after they left. Or he could go with his hunch and follow the truck and SUVs. He didn't have much time to decide. On an impulse, Jake sprinted back to his car.

He kept a safe distance and didn't turn on his lights until he passed the gate. As he glanced down the narrow black paved road on the other side of the security fence that led to Mandela's mansion, Jake spotted a man standing just inside the gate. For one brief moment the two men locked gazes. Jake hadn't turned on his lights so he could get a better view of Mandela's property. The man pulled something off his waist, and for an instant Jake clenched, gearing up for an attack. The guy put the object to the side of his head. He was calling someone. The only thing to do was play the friendly idiot. Jake waved and turned on his headlights.

He couldn't swear to it, but Jake thought the man was Bobby. It wouldn't surprise him if the guy was calling to worn them of a tail. Jake wasn't sure how that moving van would be able to pull off shaking Jake free. Unfortunately, though, he couldn't see the two black SUVs in front of the truck.

When they neared the on-ramp for Interstate 190, Jake slowed to merge into traffic. The car behind him didn't. Bright headlights damn near blinded him, hitting every mirror in his compact car.

"Son of a bitch," Jake hissed, squinting and pulling off the merge. The truck in front of him hit the interstate and immediately merged through traffic. Jake couldn't tell whether the SUVs were still in front of him or not.

As the vehicle behind him, which very well could be one of the SUVs judging by the size and positioning of the headlights, continued tailgating Jake, he began thinking he'd made the right call in following the truck. Although with the driver behind him hell-bent on making Jake's driving experience hell, it was harder to focus.

"Damn it!" he howled when the truck took the next exit.

Jake was in the wrong lane. He'd grown up in Los Angeles and learned to drive in some dangerous traffic, but that also meant he knew when not to pull off a jackass move and try hard-lining it across the lanes to make the exit as well.

"Son of a bitch!" he yelled, slamming his hand against the steering wheel as he continued in his lane to the next exit. The chances of finding the truck once he was off the interstate were nil to none. "Crap," he seethed under his breath. "Fucking headlights."

That's when he realized the SUV had backed off. Jake glanced at his rearview mirror, searching for the vehicle. There were a lot of cars behind him and around him. None of them were much larger than the vehicle he was in.

"What the fuck?" He focused ahead of him, watching the exit signs and the large green signs overhead.

Jake squinted at the cars ahead of him, then, on an impulse, picked up speed. He ignored the next exit and instead began pacing a large black SUV. It was an Excursion. There wasn't any way of knowing if it was the same vehicle that had left Mandela's mansion, but if it was, and the truck had taken an exit to lose Jake, his hunch was right. They were transporting the kidnapped victims to another location.

"The airport," he said, his insides pumping with adrenaline as he moved to the middle lane, ready to cut to either side if he needed to make a quick exit.

The SUV continued on its course for another fifteen minutes or so. Jake could only guess the second SUV had gotten on Jake's ass to distract him so he wouldn't be able to follow the truck. When the truck got off the interstate and lost Jake, the SUV had either followed or slowed drastically, allowing enough cars in and around Jake to prevent him from seeing his tracker. That didn't mean all vehicles might not have the same destination. If it was the airport, O'Hare was one of the largest airports in the world. It would be worse than finding a needle in a haystack if Jake didn't stay on the ass of at least one of the vehicles.

There wasn't any proof he was following one of the SUVs that had left Mandela's. Jake could be wasting his fucking time. Nothing sucked worse than a wild-goose chase. If he was following the right SUV, it would try losing him, too, if he gave himself away. Jake held back a safe distance, allowing a few cars in front of him, but tracked the black SUV that was maintaining a good clip in the right lane.

When he started seeing signs for the airport, his heart began thumping in his chest. There was something exhilarating about taking on a chase blindly. Obviously it was better when he had a good clue where his perp was headed. But when Jake didn't, pursuing at high speed, knowing anything could happen at any moment, was beyond invigorating.

Jake glanced at the digital clock on his dash. Almost an hour had passed since he'd left Mandela's, which meant Angela was well into her evening by now. If Jake speculated too much on how her night was going, it would possibly be all the diversion he needed to lose his possible perp. No way would Jake call off this chase and admit defeat until he knew beyond a doubt the SUV in front of him had nothing to do with Mandela. Something told Jake it did, though.

He jumped at the sound of his cell phone vibrating. Without radio or any other diversions, his phone sounded exceptionally loud. Jake grabbed it, not taking his eye off the road, and glanced at the screen while bracing it against his steering wheel.

How are you doing? The message was from Angela.

Worried about me, sweetheart?

Another advantage of growing up and learning to drive in the big city was that Jake could text and drive without taking his eyes off the road. He also knew it was against the law. Jake placed the phone next to him, not looking at the screen as he returned her text message. He wasn't sure if she was worried about him or not. Jake was worried sick about her. He was in uncharted waters with Angela and botching the hell out of it so far. He needed to analyze his feelings for her and what he perceived as her feelings for him, although he had never dwelt that much on any lady before. Worse yet, he couldn't afford the time. All of his attention needed to be on what he was doing now. Jake grabbed his phone and sent a second message.

How is your dinner date?

Mere seconds passed when his phone buzzed again. *Relocated.* Jake stared at the one-word message. Was Angela telling him the kidnapped victims were being moved? He kept the phone at his side as he typed: *Where?*

Silence grew too loud in the car. He waited as every inch of him remained tense. Jake white-knuckled the steering wheel. The black SUV ahead continued at a steady speed, and his phone sat next to him, silent.

He wasn't any better off than he'd been a few minutes ago. Although he knew Angela was okay and able to send a text message, hopefully without feeling her life was in danger by doing so. He still hated not knowing the details of where she was and what she was doing.

"Yes!" he said out loud, damn near cheering, when his phone vibrated. Jake grabbed it, positioning it in his hand so he could see the screen while keeping an eye on the road. He stared at the message, reading it several times over, although it didn't make any more sense regardless of how many times he stared at the screen.

It's a trap.

"It's a trap," he muttered out loud, and diverted his attention to the road ahead of him when a car cut him off. "What's a trap?"

Another time he would have chewed out the driver and possibly cut into the other lane, then accelerated just to show the cocky driver who'd slipped in front of him that Jake wouldn't tolerate rude driving. This time, though, he slowed slightly, looking past the car in front of him to the black SUV several cars ahead and in the right-hand lane. Signs overhead announced the airport exits would begin a few miles ahead.

"What are you talking about, sweetheart?" he asked the dark silence around him. Did she mean somehow whoever had seen Jake drive past Mandela's driveway had tipped off Mandela and the drivers in the truck and the SUVs? If so, maybe Jake was being led on a wild-goose chase while the other SUV and truck were headed in a different direction toward their destination.

There was no way of knowing. But Angela knew. He glanced at his phone, needing more information. Lowering it to the seat next to him, Jake typed his message.

Where's the trap?

This time the response came almost immediately: *Turn around.*

What if Angela wasn't sending the messages? Jake stared at the screen. He'd been positive of what he'd seen when he witnessed the truck and black Excursions leaving Mandela's. It made sense they would move the kidnapped victims, and doing it at night fit the bill even better. Although Jake could have remained at Mandela's, scoured the place once the trucks and SUVs left, it would have surprised the crap out of him if he'd found the kidnapped victims. Now that they were almost at the airport, turning around seemed ridiculous.

"Unless you're following the wrong black SUV," he mused, focusing on the tail lights of the SUV and trying to determine if they were the same make and year as the vehicles that had left Mandela's driveway. Jake really hadn't seen any of the lights other than those of the truck.

The black Excursion took the next exit without signaling.

"Crap!" Jake swerved into the next lane, hit the far-right lane, and made the exit. "Don't fool me twice!" he snapped, his heart pounding in his chest.

He slowed, taking a look at his surroundings. There was a

convenience store on the corner when he stopped at the intersection. Otherwise, they'd exited on the far edge of the airport. Most people would take one of the exits ahead of them if they were going to park and head to one of the terminals.

The SUV headed forward, past the convenience store. A sign next to the road indicated there was long-term parking ahead one and a half miles. Jake waited until the SUV had driven a fair distance before he proceeded through the stop sign.

It was easier to focus once the lights from the convenience store were behind him. The road ahead was straight and dark. Lights illuminating the parking garage and roads leading away from it looked like those of a fat, squatty Christmas tree. Between him and the light show, it was a field of inky blackness. Jake cursed when the brake lights flashed on the black Excursion. Already he knew their game. A few moments later it pulled off on the side of the road ahead of him.

"Want to play a bit of cat and mouse?" It wasn't exactly Jake's favorite game. He preferred his perps to be a bit more aggressive and not quite as crafty. But that didn't mean he hadn't played the game before. "Annoying as it might be."

The Excursion pulled off the road, coming to a complete stop. Jake drove past them, not slowing or giving any indication that it mattered to him one way or another that they'd stopped. The Excursion remained on the edge of the road. They thought they were going to make him sweat it out. What they were really doing was giving him a chance to explore a bit, learn the playing ground.

Angela had sent the text warning him of a trap. Bobby, or whoever was standing in the driveway when Jake drove by, had tipped off the others. He'd lost the truck when it was warned Jake was trailing them. Obviously they were getting close to their destination. It was imperative they throw Jake off their track or somehow inhibit him so he wouldn't learn what they were up to. Not that Jake didn't already have a real good idea what was going on.

His headlights sliced through the darkness until the parking garage grew closer. It was one hell of a large cement beast, gaudy and almost hideous looking with white flood-lights piercing through the night around it. Jake squinted against the night until he spotted the row of lights.

"Runway," he whispered, glancing at his phone.

His thoughts drifted to Angela. If Mandela had arranged for his kidnapped victims to be transported tonight, why was he spending the evening with Angela?

"So he can't be connected with them if this transport is busted," Jake answered his own question, and glanced in his rearview mirror. "Except that I followed them here from his house." Which made Jake an annoying liability.

If he called the cops now, arranged for the bust when Mandela's men tried transporting the kidnapped victims, Mandela would very likely walk. Angela would be his alibi.

"And I never confirmed the kidnapped victims were in Mandela's outbuilding." Jake slowed when he neared the parking garage.

There weren't headlights in his rearview mirror. The Excursion hadn't passed him, which meant they were sitting it out with their headlights off. Somehow he needed hard-core proof; then he needed to call the police. He didn't have any connections in this town, nor would he be honored or respected as a bounty hunter. At the same time, he couldn't allow so many victims to be transported just because he didn't have all the proof he needed. He'd stared at Marianna's picture long enough he believed he'd be able to spot her. If she was on that truck, Jake wasn't leaving until he had her away from Mandela.

Jake ran his fingers through his hair, grumbling as he entered the parking garage. He would have to hoof it if he was going to throw these goons off his ass. Which meant paying to park, then hoping he could get close enough for visuals before all the action occurred. Jake pulled into the first empty stall, parked, then jogged through the parking garage to the exit. He ignored the attendant in the booth and curious looks from drivers coming and going from the garage. None of them gave more than a glance at a man running through a parking garage in an airport.

A few minutes later, the muggy night damn near suffocated Jake as he sprinted into the dark. He'd guessed right. The SUV turned on its lights and finished its trek, passing Jake without seeing him as it followed the road to the runway. It didn't surprise him a bit to see the second SUV and truck appear a few minutes later. As much as he hated calling in before the game took place, there wasn't much else he could do. Too many innocent lives were at stake. And he *knew* those kidnapped victims were in that truck. He'd bet his career on it.

It took ten minutes on the phone with Chicago PD before he reached a detective who not only listened but also got rather excited about making the bust after Jake explained the story to him. After confirming his name and number, Jake finally got off the phone and moved closer, creeping through thick, wet grass that soaked his socks and shoes as he fought to see what he needed to see.

The two SUVs pulled to a stop on either side of the truck. Jake gripped his phone, ready to snap pictures the moment they began unloading their cargo. A small private jet sat on the runway. The lights from the jet and the runway provided enough light to get a clear picture when men started moving around the truck. Chicago PD better show up before the plane took off. Jake would rather deal with the victims here than have to accept that cops in another city would take over and Jake wouldn't be part of the bust. It sucked he couldn't contact Angela to warn her what was going down. Although it seemed Mandela spoke openly in front of her, from what Jake had witnessed so far.

Jake didn't recognize any of the men who now hovered around the truck. Worse yet, he didn't understand a word any of them were saying. They talked and laughed easily with one another but were speaking Italian. He could stumble his way through a Spanish conversation. And as much as people said the two languages were alike, at the moment, Jake would beg to differ.

He watched the men's actions instead. If he weren't paying so close attention, his phone ready to snap pictures of any incriminating evidence, he might not have spotted one of the men holding a long, thick object in his hand.

"Shit," Jake hissed, slamming himself against the hard ground when the man turned on his large flashlight and flashed his beam in Jake's direction.

The jovial tone of the men changed and they sobered, continuing to chat quietly among themselves but all focusing on the beam that one of them aimed carefully at the field between them and the parking garage.

They'd guessed Jake's plan. He lay very still, arching his neck so he could keep an eye on all of them, and didn't move an inch as he prayed they wouldn't detect him lying in the grass. It wasn't the first time he'd gotten so damn close to being popped by his perp he could taste it. His heart pounded in his chest and every inch of him was bathed in sweat as he stared at the five men. A couple of them moved closer to the edge of the runway, squinting against the darkness as they searched for him. Although it was probably only minutes, Jake swore he lay with his body pressed against the grass and dirt watching all of them for what seemed more like an hour. He was even more convinced that the kidnapped victims were in the truck with the care the men took to make sure he hadn't come out of the garage.

For a few minutes, when the beam of the flashlight traveled over him, Jake was positive they'd found him. He was carrying, in excellent shape, and more than willing to take on all five of them, if needed. It wouldn't look good if the PD showed up and he was battling for his life against the five men, but he'd do what he had to do to make sure those kidnapped people were freed tonight.

He didn't bother exhaling until the beam of the flashlight passed him by and swept over the ground far to his right. The men finally decided Jake wasn't in the field lying in wait. They turned their backs to him and once again began talking among themselves as they headed toward the moving truck. Jake dared move, although he remained lying on the uneven ground and shielded the light from his phone with his hand as he checked to see how much time had passed since he'd ended the call with the Chicago detective.

Detective Mike Ames had given Jake his cell phone number, which Jake had ready to redial if needed. He would only have to push one button to put the call through. He hated not being able to reach Angela. As much as he ached to brief her on the pending bust, he would have to rely on her experience to be able to ride with the knowledge when it became apparent to her that her date was suddenly not a happy camper. Jake speculated the man would be enraged. Angela already had shared with Jake what Mandela did when he got pissed. If the asshole laid one hand on Angela, Jake would rip the man to shreds.

Jake's heart began thumping all over again when several of the men jumped into the back of the truck and handed down what looked like a large metal crate to the men standing on the ground. Whatever it held, it was heavy. Jake watched the men strain and one of them jump out of the truck to assist the two on the ground. The three of them moved slowly around the truck, carrying the crate between them as they headed to the waiting airplane.

The moment they walked into the light, Jake snapped his first shot. He couldn't risk using the flash and prayed the pictures would come out. His phone had a decent camera on it, but he was losing daylight fast. The crate was made out of thin, metal bars. They were hauling Mandela's army as if they were dogs. It reminded Jake of the kind of crates he'd seen at the home of one of the ladies he used to visit who owned Great Danes. She always crated her dogs when he came over.

Jake blinked, giving himself a quick mental shake. He didn't want to dwell on time spent with any of the women in his past. The only good thing that came out of that closed chapter in his life was knowledge that he'd never spread himself around like that again. He wasn't sure why it mattered so much to him that he convince Angela he wasn't a player, especially when she was in Chicago and he was in L.A. He couldn't be a bounty hunter in Chicago.

But Angela could be a private investigator in L.A.

Jake almost laughed out loud. Instead he grumbled under his breath. He'd had a lifetime of hearing how cocky and arrogant he was. He was absolutely losing it if he thought he'd be able to convince her to give up her life and move to L.A. with him.

He knew he wouldn't regret it if he did convince her to give him a chance.

Once again he reminded himself that now wasn't the time to dwell on Angela. Although he couldn't help worrying about her as this scene played out, he needed to focus on his actions right now. What mattered was grabbing the best proof he could to nail Mandela to the wall.

He snapped another picture when the men started climbing the stairs with the crate to load it on the plane. One of the men in the truck yelled to the others at the plane and began waving his arms when a line of cars appeared at the intersection with the convenience store and started coming toward them.

Jake's gut twisted as adrenaline flooded his system. The cavalry had arrived. He squinted at the cars, watching them come closer, and moved to his hands and knees when two of the cars turned on their lights. Red and white lights flashed across the field, turning the scene into a surreal setting. The five men started shouting at one another in Italian as they hauled ass to their SUVs, not that they had a chance to escape.

Jake pulled his gun, shoving his phone into his back pocket, and started across the field. The moment one of the men spotted him, they pulled their guns. Jake wasn't sure if he fired the first shot, but his aim proved better. One of the men fell to the ground, howling loud enough to wake the dead as the squad cars surrounded the SUVs and moving truck.

Suddenly there were uniforms everywhere. Jake reached the edge of the field, anxious to see for himself what was inside the truck. He needed to find Marianna. The pain on Angela's face when she'd learned her younger half sister was missing had torn at his heart. If he could return Marianna, bring Angela that happiness, it would be worth risking a bullet or two.

It didn't surprise him that the men surrendered easily. When he pulled out his badge, which identified him as a Californian bounty hunter, the local PD wasn't as impressed as he'd hoped.

"Back off, mister," one of the uniforms informed him, pushing Jake in the chest to prevent him from approaching the truck.

"Man, I called this in," he argued, but looked past the uniform and searched for someone in plain clothes. "Where is Detective Ames? I spoke with him on the phone."

More cars showed up and the cop who'd pushed Jake away from the truck turned his attention to his backup as more uniforms flooded the scene.

Jake tried stepping around the cop, his attention on the entrance to the back of the moving truck. He caught a glimpse of more crates, stacked on one another, when the cop who'd pushed him grabbed his arm.

"Look, man," he snapped. "Back off or I'll cuff you, too."

"I tipped off your department," Jake argued, yanking his arm out of the cop's grasp. "Where is Detective Ames?"

"Are you Jake King?" a tall man in a suit asked, adjusting his tie as he made eye contact with Jake. The man said something to the cop that Jake didn't catch, but the uniform seemed more than willing to leave Jake alone with the man in the suit. "Make sure we have every inch of these trucks and SUVs dusted and gone over with a fine-tooth comb," he ordered, and the cop nodded once before trotting off to assist with reading rights to the men who'd barely made it to the SUVs before they were detained.

"I take it you're Detective Ames," Jake said, edging closer to the back of the truck. His stomach twisted with revulsion when another officer flashed his light into the back of the truck. "Son of a bitch," he mumbled under his breath.

"I'm Detective Mike Ames," the suit said, dragging Jake's attention back to him. "Mind if you show me some ID?"

"Not at all." Jake handed over his badge, then stepped around Ames and stood at the back of the truck, staring at the large dog crates that held men and women, all whom appeared to be drugged. They were mostly lying in fetal position, stacked on top of one another, and judging by the smell hadn't been bathed anytime recently. "Good God," Jake uttered, outraged at the sight of the victims who'd almost been hauled off to commit some terroristic act.

"Mind telling me how you knew about this?" Ames asked, handing Jake's badge back to him. "Not to mention what you're doing in our fair city."

"We've been investigating the game for a while," Jake began. He focused on each crate, searching for Marianna.

He glanced toward the road, as did Ames, when a couple more cars approached. Jake shifted his attention to Ames in time to catch his frown turn to a scowl. Ames left Jake standing there and moved around his crew. He walked up alongside one of the two cars as they came to a stop behind the farthest squad car.

With lights flashing and cops around him talking and yelling orders to one another, while others, who apparently spoke Italian, were Mirandizing Mandela's thugs and loading them into the backs of the squad cars, the scene was quickly becoming a distraction. Jake wanted to check out everything before it was tagged and processed in as evidence, but at the same time Ames' behavior grabbed his attention. The detective didn't appear pleased with the arrival of the two unmarked cars.

Jake didn't make a habit of stereotyping people, but the men who climbed out of the cars and joined Ames had FBI written all over them. The way Ames was suddenly upset, then resigned as he shook his head and stepped to the side, allowing the new arrivals to join the crime scene, suggested he'd just lost this case before he even had it.

Jake would be next in line. He held less rank than the detective in a town that wasn't his own and with a rank not acknowledged in this city. Diverting his attention back to the scene, he stepped closer to the back of the truck, leaning into it without touching anything to get a better look at the men and women lying in the cages.

"Mr. King, I need to advise you to back off." One of the men who'd just arrived flashed his credentials in Jake's face.

He didn't bat an eye at the FBI insignia and barely registered the agent's name. Memories of their case in Tijuana and how the feds had stepped in after Jake's mother called in for backup to the police flashed before his eyes. At that time, KFA had helped bring down one of the players in the game but wasn't able to end the game once the FBI stepped in and took over. Obviously the feds were still on the case. Jake wouldn't condemn their agency but at the same time wouldn't see history repeat itself. As much as he hated it, he stepped away from the truck.

"You're welcome for the phone call," he offered, stepping away from the truck and holding out his hands in mock surrender. "Or let me guess, you've been on the trail all along but would have allowed these men and women to be hauled into battle in order to make the bigger bust."

"Where is your car, Mr. King?" the agent asked, sizing Jake up, then straightening and squaring his shoulders, as if puffing himself up to possibly six feet would do any good in trying to intimidate Jake.

Jake didn't ask to be six feet, six inches tall, but because he was and had been since he'd been a teenager no one got under his skin, unless it was to annoy him. This agent would do a good job if Jake spent much longer asking questions and getting no answers.

"I parked in the garage."

"Where are you staying? I'll need your contact information and your departure plans out of the city before you leave." The agent pointed with his thumb to the other agents, who had remained by their cars, still talking to Detective Ames. "If you'd give your information to Special Agent Robinson," he stated, then walked away from Jake without another word, dismissing him and heading over to the squad cars where Mandela's men were being held.

Jake didn't join the detective and other agent. Instead he returned his attention to the back of the truck, counting the crates inside. The men and women in the crates were all dressed, wearing jeans and T-shirts, nothing that would make any of them stand out. There were black and white men and women, one lady who appeared Asian, but Jake didn't see anyone who matched Marianna's physical description or her picture. He continued studying all the victims he could focus on while standing outside the back of the truck.

Whoever had put them in the cages went to some effort to make them as comfortable as possible, considering the fact that they were in dog crates. Jake guessed Mandela didn't want them suffering from body cramps or injuries while they were being shipped out. He would want his army in top shape when they attacked the other player's army. Jake scanned the inside of the truck, not sure what he was looking for but trying to find anything he could before being ordered away from the scene.

Headlights shone in zigzag patterns across the runway and the field. Although direct light didn't flood the back of the truck and Jake didn't have a flashlight, he was able to study the contents of the truck and noticed two small plastic totes just inside. They were to his right, and he hadn't noticed them since his attention was directed upward at the stacks of dog crates. There didn't appear to be locks or any way of locking the plastic totes. Jake glanced around him at the continuing scene of arrests and detectives and FBI men talking. He wouldn't have more than a minute before someone was ordered to scour the truck and document everything inside. More than likely they were waiting for paramedics to arrive before touching the kidnapped victims. Jake banked on that assumption and pulled his shirt up, wrapped his hand inside the edge of it, and lifted the top of one of the totes. He wouldn't get his fingerprints anywhere on the evidence.

There were several notebooks inside the first tote. Jake looked around him again, nervous energy pulsing inside him as his excitement peaked. What he wouldn't do to find clarification of the game, the needed documentation that would allow Angela to nail this case. If he had it in his power, he would get this for her. Angela had come too far, risked her life too many times in the hands of that monster, to have this case yanked out of her hands by the feds.

Jake's fingers were wrapped inside the edge of his shirt, which was damp from his sweat. DNA samples could be picked up and were used too frequently these days. He let go of his shirt, wiping his hands on the outside of it, and frantically searched for something that would help him open the notebooks. He had to see what was inside.

Jake stared at a pair of thick garden-type gloves. "What fucking luck!" The excitement nearly buzzed inside him as he grabbed the gloves and slipped them on. They even fit. And with hands his size that was a small miracle. He opened the first notebook and gawked as he began reading.

Chapter Fourteen

Angela excused herself from the table, finding the interruption as odd as Mario apparently did. He gave her a strange look, and she shrugged, then followed the waiter who'd asked her to come with him to the front lobby. Nerves prickled down her spine. There was a handgun in her purse, which she clutched to her side. She and Mario had just finished their dinner and over an hour of useless small talk, and it struck her as curious that Mario made no effort to join her when the maître d' came to their table and informed her there was an important phone call waiting for her on the house phone.

"Right this way, madam," the maître d' said, gesturing when they reached his narrow podium, where he stood and greeted guests.

Angela glanced at the house phone, which was next to the podium. Everything inside her tightened, and the prime rib she'd found exceptionally good suddenly churned in her gut. The expensive wine she'd sipped at throughout their meal began gurgling as her nerves spiked to a dangerous level. The restaurant was well air-conditioned, and throughout the meal she'd been chilly, almost wishing she'd brought a sweater.

"That way?" Angela paused in the lobby, ignoring the handful of couples who apparently didn't rate being seated right away. She frowned at the maître d', who turned to face her, his expression masked from years of training.

"Forgive me, madam," he said in a low, calm voice. "If you please. There is a private room through these doors."

"And there is a phone right there." She pointed at his podium and dug her heels in. Clutching her purse, she ignored the trickles of perspiration that beaded along her spine. Her heart thumped too hard inside her chest. She prayed her expression matched the maître d's, one of cool, calm confidence. "Is there someone waiting for me in that room?" she asked, staring the maître d' in the eye.

Which was the only way she spotted the flicker of hesitation that flashed there. "Madam, I'm simply following orders."

Angela stepped closer to the gentleman, who was probably somewhere around the same age as her father. "Who is waiting for me in that room?" she whispered, staring at his face.

"I was simply asked to bring you to them." The maître d' faltered, shifting his weight and tugging on his tie. "They asked that I not say who they were with in order to offer you protection." He was whispering now, too. "But madam, they have badges."

Badges? Criminals didn't usually carry badges, unless they were forged. Angela swallowed the lump in her throat and nodded once at the maître d', adjusting her handbag under her arm but unzipping it. She wasn't sure how quickly she could pull her gun out of it, but she'd be damned if she'd made it this far only to take a few knocks backward. They were on the edge of discovery. She could feel it sizzling in the air.

Mario had spoken openly on his phone when it rang, ignoring her from across the table and growing angrier by the minute as he spoke with the person on the other end of the line. Angela was positive Mario was being told that while they were moving his army someone had passed by his house and started trailing them. When the person talking to Mario called in the tag, it came back as a rental. Mario didn't bat an eye at a tag being called in. Apparently he had some damn good connections, not that learning that surprised Angela. She'd thought of excusing herself to powder her nose but worried her timing might be off. So she'd sat across from Mario, digging into her purse and pulling out her compact, then powdered her nose, or made a show of doing so, while staring into the small mirror and ignoring him. When she'd put the compact back, she'd slipped her phone onto her lap. Angela was able to text Jake while keeping her attention on Mario. After Mario got off the phone, it was as if he struggled to make conversation. Angela repeatedly got the uncanny sensation that he was killing time. It crossed her mind more than once that he was establishing an alibi, using her, so that his kidnapped victims could be moved and, if caught, the cops wouldn't be able to tie him in on the bust. He would have been at dinner with her.

Angela stepped around the maître d', but he hurried to follow her and opened the door he'd indicated for her. Then moving to the side, he offered a gallant bow when she entered a small meeting room. The door closed silently behind her with a click that almost made Angela jump. She stared at two men, both in dress shirts and black slacks. They had the Bureau written all over them.

"Are you Angela Torres?" one of them asked, stepping forward as he reached for his badge that was clipped to his belt. "I'm Special Agent Terry Baldwin and this is Special Agent Richard Peel."

Angela managed to nod as she stared at the badges both men produced. For the moment, she remained silent about them calling her Torres and not Huxtable. All it told her was they were connecting her to Mario. Her fear shifted to anger fast enough that she almost teetered. Straightening, she relaxed her grip on her purse but kept it under her arm. It would be the worst nightmare if the FBI stepped in, took over after all she'd done, and removed her from this case. If she showed her frustration, something told her the inevitable would happen faster. She straightened, maintaining her cool.

"This is rather odd," she said, and flashed them both

a toothy smile. "Why are you asking to meet me in this room?"

"You're dining with Mario Mandela." Special Agent Baldwin didn't make it a question.

"Is that a crime?" she asked.

"You're going to return to your table, inform Mandela that you have a family emergency and need to leave immediately." Baldwin sounded calm, although he ignored her question. His eyes were a bright blue, which made him appear friendly in spite of his closely trimmed haircut and nondescript gray suit that spoke of distance and mystery.

"Now why would I tell him that?" She adjusted her purse, hugging it against her stomach when she crossed her arms and tapped her open-toed high-heeled sandal on the plush carpet. "What's going on here?" she demanded.

"We know you're working undercover," Baldwin explained. "I don't know what information you might have gathered at this point, but we'll debrief you later. Right now, you will tell Mandela you must leave."

There wasn't any point in playing these two. But she still hesitated. "May I see your badges again, please?" she asked, holding on to her smile as she looked from Baldwin to Peel. Peel's gaze had traveled down her but shot to her face when she raised an inquiring eyebrow. "Please," she repeated, deciding she could make a few demands here, too.

This time she took the badges from both men, who relinquished them reluctantly. There were a few things she'd learned over the years. One of them was how to distinguish fake badges from real ones. She studied the insignia behind each of their names.

"Do you two have additional IDs?"

"Ma'am, this matter can't take much time," Baldwin stressed.

"You're right. Your driver's licenses, please?" she asked, adjusting the strap on her purse and shifting it to her shoulder. She held their badges in one hand and held her other out, letting her smile fade as she waited for them to confirm they were who they said they were.

Baldwin sighed, sounding put out, and pulled his wallet out of his back pocket. He opened it up, keeping it in his hand, and held it up to Angela's face.

Angela compared the information on the badge to the driver's license. She was already pretty sure the badges were legitimate, but if Mario was trying to bust her, this would be one hell of a way to go about doing it. Baldwin held up a Washington, D.C., license. Peel did the same. Their information matched.

"What do you want?" she asked, deciding they could go to hell if they wanted verbal confirmation that she was who they claimed she was.

"I just told you." Baldwin took back his badge and secured it to his belt, then shoved his wallet in his back pocket. "Tell your date you're leaving."

"He will want to take me wherever I go."

"That's fine. If he insists on returning you to your hotel room at the Drake," Baldwin said, narrowing his gaze on her and giving her a look that said they knew all about her. "Let him take you. If for any reason he diverts his course and tells his driver to take you somewhere else, we will have him pulled over. While the police are detaining his car, you will insist you don't like cops and tell Mandela you'll grab a cab. You'll slip out of the car before he can stop you. If he tries to detain you, the officers who pulled him over will prevent him from doing so and let you go. Do you have any questions?"

"Quite a few." Angela flashed her smile at the two of them, although she doubted it looked sincere. They were busting up her investigation, which pissed her off more than she would let them know. All she could do was go along with them. "I don't like this," she added, sighing. "I've put in just over a year learning everything I could about the game." She held her ground, studying both their blank expressions. "I don't want to be ordered off this investigation."

The look they both gave her let her know they'd heard that line one too many times. Angela opened her mouth to ask what they were planning on doing. Whether they liked it or not, she was on the inside. Angela wasn't opposed to working with the FBI. It sure as hell beat being tossed to the side and not getting any credit for a year of dedication to the investigation.

"We don't have any say in that matter, miss," Peel informed her before she could say anything else. He didn't sound apologetic or concerned. He just stated the facts. "We're following orders and you need to do the same."

Neither one of them needed to threaten her with arrest. Angela understood how it worked. They were FBI. If they wanted the case, they took it. Even the local cops could lose a case to the FBI if the Bureau decided it would be that way.

Angela turned around and strutted out of the room, outraged and upset at the same time. At least returning to their table didn't require she mask all of her emotions. She really was upset when she explained to Mario that there had been a family emergency.

"My father's secretary just contacted me. My grandmother has had a stroke."

"Why did they call the restaurant and not your cell phone?" Mario asked, the question sensible, which was why she'd immediately brainstormed to come up with a believable answer, and a clever one, too, at that. Especially if Mario did know more about her than he'd let on.

"My sister is the only one I've told about you," she offered, sliding into her chair and clasping her purse in her lap. "She doesn't live with my father, either, but has been visiting these past few months. When Grandmother collapsed, she told my father's secretary where we were dining."

Mario accepted her explanation without a blink of an eye and did insist on returning her to the Drake, as she'd anticipated. He didn't alter his course, and fifteen minutes later his limo pulled under the awning outside the front of the hotel.

Mario hadn't said a word during their drive, nor had he touched her. Her insides twisted further, although he made no show of sharing his thoughts with her or taking anything out on her. The limo stopped and he placed his hand over hers before she turned to the door.

"Before you start apologizing," he began, giving her a knowing look with his piercing dark, opaque eyes, "remember family always comes first. I'll call you later."

She hadn't planned on apologizing but bailing quickly. "I'm sorry. I can't help saying it." She offered a small and, she hoped, sincere-looking smile. "Your concern for family is admirable. Unfortunately, my family isn't worth being too concerned over." She held on to her cover and watched to see his expression change to disapproval, anything. When he kept his feelings masked behind his grave stare, Angela guessed something else was preoccupying his thoughts and probably he didn't mind getting rid of her since he might not need an alibi any longer. "I would much rather spend the evening with you than pacing sanitary hospital hallways. But I couldn't say no, now could I?"

"Of course not." He let go of her hand. "Dinner was quite enjoyable, *mi amore*," he said, lowering his voice as he brushed his knuckles down her cheek. "I didn't get to discuss our travel plans. You will come with me while I travel on business, yes?"

"It sounds fun." Angela's going along with whatever he said at the moment would allow her to get out of the car faster. "Give me a call later."

She managed to step out of the car. Albert was there, holding the car door for her and gallantly offering his hand, although if she leaned on the old man Angela would bet they'd both topple to the ground. Mario looked noticeably pleased when he strutted around the back side of his limo and came up to her, ignoring Albert, who moved out of the way easily.

Mario wrapped his arms around her waist, pulling her up against his body. "You are an incredibly beautiful woman, *amore*," he whispered, lowering his lips to hers.

Angela wouldn't be surprised if the FBI was watching. If the agents were, they probably had been for a while. They would know she'd never kissed Mario before. Although she despised the chaste kiss, she allowed it, then lowered her head, ending it easily.

"I need to go," she said quietly.

"Of course." He released her and moved to the back door Angela had hopped out of. Tomas was already standing there, a quiet giant, as still as a statue and not focusing on either one of them but patiently waiting for his boss to climb in so he could close the door.

Albert caught her eye and smiled. She started toward him, seeing how anxious he was to help escort her inside. When she turned to tell Mario good night, he'd already returned to the backseat and Tomas was sliding into the driver's seat. She watched the long, regal-looking vehicle pull out of the circular drive in front of the Drake, then glanced around, trying to look casual but shifting her attention from car to car. There was no way to tell whether anyone was watching her or not.

And honestly, what had just happened? Neither agent at the restaurant had told her officially to leave the case alone. One of them had mentioned something about debriefing her, but she'd been left with no specific instructions. If the FBI pulled her off the investigation, did they find Jake, too? Somehow, she didn't see that scene going down well at all.

Albert escorted her through the doors to the hotel, and she managed to slip away from him without too much small talk and start across the lobby. Angela pulled out her phone and texted Jake. She typed: *Drake,* stared at the one word, and pushed Send as the elevators opened on her floor. She stared down the hallway toward her suite at two men who were leaning against the wall. They straightened when they spotted her. One of them cupped his hand to his ear, and his mouth moved, indicating he was talking to someone. Her phone buzzed in her hand. She stared at the message.

I'm dodging suits. How about you?

Crap.

She responded: *Big-time*. Then without giving it much thought, since she barely had a minute before agents would be around her, she added to the text message: *Did you find my sister?* Angela clicked Send and dropped her phone into her purse.

"Angela Torres?" A middle-aged man, who sounded friendly, flashed his badge in her face as she approached her room. He moved in next to her, lowering his voice, when she pulled out her card key to unlock her door. "Or should I say 'Angela Huxtable'?"

The last thing she wanted was anyone seeing FBI outside her hotel suite. For whatever reason, the FBI was all over her. If she made a show of cooperating, maybe they'd let her stay on the case. She'd heard where it had happened before. Private investigators had been known to assist the FBI from time to time. Her best guess was they'd been working the case as long as she had, clear back to Tijuana. Now that everything was building to a head, they were moving in to claim the action. It wouldn't look good for the feds if a local private investigator made the bust on such a large criminal activity as the game. God forbid she steal their limelight.

"We need you to come with us." The agent put his hand out, blocking her from sliding her card through the lock to open her door.

She glanced at the agent speaking, then at his partner, who now stood on the other side of her. "I'm not going anywhere dressed like this," she said, keeping her voice calm. "Not to mention, I'm sure you understand that I can't leave with you. It would blow my cover, which would not only put my life in serious danger but cause Mandela to run, or alter his plans. If you're here, I'm guessing you realize how close I am to shutting down the game for good."

"We have confirmation that Mandela is driving in the direction of his home. He doesn't suspect anything, or maybe he has other matters that are more important than you," the second agent offered.

Angela shrugged. She was being polite. They didn't need to be pricks. "I'm not leaving with you." She ignored the agent's hand and slid her card key into her lock. "And I am changing clothes. I would appreciate it if you didn't stand outside my suite while I do so." She pushed open her suite door and stepped inside, turning to face them. Neither one of them would be able to say a word in their reports about her not being cooperative or being rude.

The agent who was wired cupped his hand to his ear again. It was nice to see that even the FBI didn't have perfect equipment. Obviously it was hard for him to hear whoever was on the other end. He mumbled something under his breath, listened as he stared at the floor, then responded. "Roger that," he said, reaching for her hotel room door at the same time when she would have let it close in their faces. "Miss Huxtable, we need a bit of your time. I'm sure you don't wish to interfere with national security and I know you understand the importance of this investigation, since you've been on this case for over a year now."

His smug grin didn't intimidate her. "It sounds like you've known where I've been for quite a while then," she said, keeping her expression serious as she placed her hand on the door. "Another hour won't hurt anything. I'm changing clothes."

"If you make any attempt to flee, or to contact Mandela, it will be viewed as interference with this investigation," the second agent told her.

"Now why the hell would I want to jeopardize this investigation?" she snapped, about done with all of their pompous attitudes. "Unlike you, I don't care who slaps on the cuffs. As long as this nightmare ends. If you have any idea how despicable the game is," she ranted, barely managing to whisper, and deciding not to mention her desperation to find her sister. If they thought Angela's interest in the investigation was too personal, they'd yank her off of it even faster. She snapped her mouth shut, pressed her lips into a thin line, and gave each of them a reprimanding stare "I just need a few minutes to change."

The first agent braced his arm, keeping his hand flat on the door and preventing it from shutting in their faces. He reached into his shirt pocket with his free hand and pulled out a card. "Call my cell as soon as you've changed clothes. We'll wait for you in the lobby."

Angela nodded, accepted the card, and took her hand off the door. "Fine. I'll call you. And thank you. You try spending an evening in heels. You'd want out of them, too."

The agents' expressions didn't change, but the one took his hand off the door. It closed quietly, the lock clicking into place. Angela leaned against it, staring into her dark suite as she let out a loud breath.

"Well, this sucks," she muttered, kicking off her shoes and pulling her phone out of her purse at the same time.

This was her case. If Jake proved where the kidnapped victims were, and especially if they were drugged, she was almost guaranteed an arrest.

Angela walked through her suite, taking her time looking at everything as she tried remembering how she'd left the place. Jake had her so worked up and upset when he'd stormed out, informing her she deserved better, and had left her naked on the bed. His end of his phone conversation had made no sense to her, yet she'd applied so many different possible meanings to it, she'd been sick to her stomach by the time she'd left her hotel suite, she had almost forgotten to put away her equipment. The suite appeared untampered with, but the FBI would be able to enter and do as they pleased in here without her knowing.

Heading to her closet, she squatted in front of her suitcase and shoved her clothes aside. All of her surveillance equipment appeared to be just as she'd left it. She pulled out the small black box and turned it on, holding it in her hand as she reached for her sweeper. It wouldn't hurt to go over her room and make sure no new bugs had shown up while she'd been gone. Even if the FBI possibly had equipment that was more top-of-the-line than what Angela owned, it brought some peace of mind when there didn't appear to be any listening devices hidden anywhere around her. The black box grabbed her attention, though. Mario was having one hell of an excited conversation with someone in Italian.

"Good God! Slow down," she hissed, unable to catch even a word here or there.

Mario was coming through loud and clear. But he spoke so quickly Angela couldn't catch more than a word or two and even then didn't have a clue how to spell them to enter them into her online translator.

She changed clothes as she listened. The only thing she could confirm was that Mario was pissed as hell. Angela didn't need a translator to figure that out.

Once she was in comfortable shorts, a tank top with a jogging bra on underneath, socks, and tennis shoes, Angela pushed the button to call Jake.

"Are you at the hotel?" Jake asked when he answered, not bothering with hellos. It sounded as if he was driving.

Suddenly it seemed another lifetime ago when he'd left her lying naked on his bed after his phone wouldn't stop ringing. At the time it had seemed such a big deal; now she didn't find herself caring. They'd reached out to each other when their investigations hit rough waters. If they were in a relationship, that was how it would be. Although it was also how good partners treated each other.

"I just got here. What's going on?" Once she had an update on his evening, she could then tell him about hers. Angela needed him to explain what had happened on his end. Maybe it would make her end make more sense.

"I'm coming back from the airport. We just made a bust."

"What?" she yelled into the phone. "What bust? What are you talking about?"

"We need to talk in person." Jake sounded too calm. Too serious and in command.

Angela's skin prickled. Something was seriously wrong. "That's easier said than done. I thought you had a scrambler on your phone."

"I do. So the suits are on your ass, too?"

"Unfortunately. I bought a few minutes by insisting that I change clothes. The FBI provided an escort back to my hotel room from the restaurant where Mario and I were," she offered. There wasn't time to drag everything out of Jake.

"But what kind of bust are you talking about? Mario wasn't arrested."

"Okay, let me think." Jake didn't answer her question. "The feds are all over you, and they're all over me. We need to debrief."

"I agree with you there." She began pacing, glaring at the carpet while gripping the phone to her ear. "There were two agents at my door when I came up to my room. They're waiting in the lobby for me."

"Listen to me, Angela." Jake's voice was deep, raspy, as if he'd just gone through one hell of a workout. Images of all that muscle, taut and glistening with perspiration, brought her pacing to a halt.

"I'm listening," she said, her voice cracking. Thinking of Jake like that would make concentrating another story. And there wasn't time to lust over a man who possibly had a long list of women wanting him right along with her.

"Neither one of us has broken any laws. The FBI wants us out of the way so they can claim the glory when they take down the game. But you can walk away from those agents and they aren't going to arrest you. We need to find a place to meet."

"You didn't hear me. They're waiting for me in the lobby," Angela stressed.

"Here is what you're going to do. Put on plain clothes, nothing revealing. Wrap your hair up around your head. Do your best to make yourself as nondescript as possible. You're a breathtakingly beautiful woman, Angela. It's very easy to pick you out of a crowd."

Angela didn't say anything. She didn't want to admit how his words affected her. She caught herself staring at herself in the mirror, though, listening to his deep baritone stroke her senses.

"Wash off all that makeup, pull that luscious black mane of yours up, and take the service elevator down to the back side of the Drake. Leave through the kitchen if you have to. Don't be afraid of the FBI. They don't want us on the case.

You don't want to talk to them. Keep your confidence up and don't let them intimidate you."

Angela snapped out of her trance. "The suits don't intimidate me," she informed him. "No one does. And fine. I'll be behind the Drake in a few minutes. But you aren't coming here. Not if they are on your ass, too."

She needed control of the situation, and in order to achieve that she needed all the facts. Obviously Jake was worked up. He needed to explain in detail what had happened to instigate this bust.

"Here's what we're going to do," she said before he could speak. "I'll grab a taxi here in a few minutes." There wasn't a lot of time to think this through, but Angela couldn't come up with a better idea. She prayed she wasn't slitting both of their throats. "Type this address into your GPS." Angela gave him her home address.

It really did surprise her that she made it out of the Drake, flagged down a taxi, and half an hour later was walking up the dark steps to her front porch. She hadn't been home in almost a week, and somehow entering her home made everything from the past week seem distant somehow. It wasn't, though. Angela headed across her dark living room to her thermostat and adjusted it so that her central air kicked on. Not only was this case erupting all around them, but dodging the FBI would make matters more complicated also. She and Jake needed to talk, though. Once they both knew everything they had to share, she had no problem seeking out the agents. It made more sense to do it on her time, when she was prepared.

Not to mention she needed to find Marianna. If Jake had found her, it would have been the first thing he told Angela. Jake wouldn't hold information like that from her. They could be wrong about Mario abducting Marianna.

She peered out the front window when a car pulled up out front. A moment later, Jake stalked up her walk, appearing larger than life when he stepped onto her porch.

"I don't think it's a good idea to stay here very long," she told him when she closed the door behind Jake.

"Where are we?" he asked, squinting against the darkness.

"My house." Something darkened in Jake's gaze when she lifted her gaze to his. "We needed somewhere to talk. I'm sure they will look for us here, but hopefully we have enough time to debrief each other first."

Her insides reacted to him moving into her space. Taking a step back seemed to show him as much. Angela walked through her house, not bothering with lights. They couldn't give any indication someone was here. His car was registered to a rental agency and as long as Jake hadn't been followed, it could be parked there for any of her neighbors. Most of the houses on her block didn't have driveways, including hers. However, if the FBI already knew he was driving it, there wasn't any predicting how long until they showed up.

"Did you check out of the Drake?" He was right behind her.

Angela paused in her kitchen. Her house smelled musky, but her AC unit was new and doing a damn good job of cooling the place off. Unfortunately, it didn't appear to be working on her insides. Just knowing how close Jake was behind her created a heat that surged into a raging fever within seconds. Jake might think she deserved better. Already Angela was thinking of several ways to show him it couldn't get better than the two of them together . . . naked . . . orgasm after orgasm.

Crap!

"Not officially," she managed, clearing her throat as she opened her refrigerator although there wasn't a damn thing in it. She'd cleaned it out before going undercover. "But I brought everything with me."

"I saw your suitcases at the door. Maybe we can talk while we drive." Jake grabbed her arms, pulling her backward before turning her around. He held her against him. In spite of how much taller he was than her, it seemed she easily molded against him. Jake grabbed the mass of hair she'd twisted in a knot at the back of her head and tugged. "I shouldn't have run out on you earlier."

"Why did you?"

"I was an idiot," he snarled, lowering his head and nipping her earlobe.

"Really?" she snapped. "So now we pick up where we left off?"

Jake didn't let go of her hair. "Sounds like a damn good idea to me," he whispered, his face hovering just above hers.

"So all you want is lots of sex?" She wasn't sure why she was pursuing this. They needed to be discussing the case.

"At the airport, after I'd been told to clear out and the place was surrounded by uniforms and suits, all that mattered was gathering what evidence I could so you could make this bust. I'm not going to let them take that away from you. Now why would I do that for you, Angela? Why would I risk spending a night in jail for you?"

"I don't know," she whispered, her mouth suddenly too dry.

"I do." Jake seared her mouth with a kiss that sent her world tumbling upside down. He demanded entrance, impaled her with his tongue, and made love to her mouth with so much feeling and emotion that Angela swam in it.

If the power existed to make him stop, it was washed away as he held her in his arms. Jake leaned over, causing Angela to lean backward. Her back was damn near parallel with the floor, but she didn't care. There wasn't a safer, more comfortable spot in the world than being wrapped in his arms.

Jake had skills. Incredible seductive skills. Angela didn't consider herself a novice, but letting go, allowing him free reign to devour her and show her the emotions and feelings he just implied he had for her, would have had her floating over the floor anyway.

There was a tiny voice in the back of her head telling her she was making a mistake. Solve this case, bring down the game, and part ways amiably. That was what she should do. Angela didn't listen very well. Instead, she dragged her fingers over his shoulders until his curls tickled her hands.

His hair was soft, tousled, and crawling through it as she opened up more for him was the final act.

They'd reached the most dangerous part of this case. And now it was worse. Whereas usually when the law was called in after Angela pieced all the clues together, this time it only added to the perils surrounding them. She would have to worry about Mario and the FBI. Doing so by Jake's side sounded a hell of a lot better than doing it alone.

"I want you," Jake growled when he left her mouth and started a scalding trail of kisses down the side of her face to her neck. "Don't tell me no, darling, please."

"No" didn't seem to be in her vocabulary at the moment. "My bedroom is—" Her words got stuck in her throat when Jake lifted her into his arms.

"Where?" He walked out of the kitchen.

Angela pointed, feeling weird and at the same time incredibly loved when Jake sprinted up the stairs, He pushed open the first door he came to at the top of the stairs.

"No. That one." Angela pointed again. "You don't have to carry me."

Jake was on a mission. He ignored her comment, kept her cradled in his arms, and headed toward the door she indicated.

All that virile muscle was too much. Every inch of him was hard and toned. Roped muscle flexed against her as he moved. He pushed open her bedroom door, walked to her bed, and placed her on it.

"Undress." His voice was muffled as he pulled his shirt over his head.

Angela moved to her knees, reaching for the T-shirt she'd put on and grabbing the end of it. She froze as Jake tossed his shirt to the floor and kicked off his shoes. They'd been naked before. And it was dark in her bedroom. But her eyes adjusted and she drank in the view of him.

Jake was more man than any woman should have a right to. Every inch of him was fine-tuned, like a well-oiled machine. His torso and shoulders were tan, and a spray of dark hair made his naked chest even more of a mouthwatering feast.

"If you care about those clothes at all you better take them off." The warning edge in his tone was full of dark promises of everything Jake was capable of being.

And with a body like that, skills that he'd mastered long before meeting her, and a passion that made his eyes glow, Angela turned into all thumbs as she struggled with her shirt.

It made it to the floor along with her shoes. Her voice was scratchy, but she forced herself to be practical: "Do you have a condom?" In spite of her justifiable anger when he'd left her earlier, his eagerness to be with her made her feel more desirable. "We really should practice safe sex." She flopped back on her bed, messing with the zipper on her shorts. There were other women out there who possibly would hate her for being with Jake, yet he looked at her as if she were all that mattered in the world.

"I bought some the other day." His curls fell around his face when he glanced down and peeled off his shorts.

She was about to ask when he had bought them, curious as to what would have made him do so. Was he that confident that he'd be able to seduce her?

Angela didn't know how to handle his easy manner and confident skills. She was always the one to instigate sex and call the shots in any relationship she'd been in over the years. Jake hadn't forced himself on her. She was doing this because she wanted it. But he wasn't singing out his desire to remain by her side, either. Although he insisted his actions during the bust were done out of stronger feelings for her, Jake hadn't elaborated. She was starting to feel as if it were impossible to control love.

Love?

Her body ached as she stared at him. She swelled and was wet instantly as she took in his nakedness. Jake didn't rush her as she thought he would. She pushed her shorts down her legs, along with her underwear, pulling her legs to her chest until she had them off.

Jake took them from her as he crawled onto the bed. "Tell me you want this," he said, dropping her clothes off the side of the bed, then caressing the side of her face. "I want you to be sure."

His expression was strained and it made her heart swell until she could barely breathe. "I don't want to be a notch on a bedpost."

Even when he smiled, Angela swore there was pain on his face. "There's no way," he uttered, coming over her like a calm giant. In spite of the hesitation he suggested existed, Jake didn't falter as he brought his face to hers. "I don't know how to describe this, Angela," he said on a breath, then teased her lower lip with his teeth.

He gripped her hip, adjusting her underneath him although he never once pressed his body against hers. As he braced himself over her a fiery heat scorched her body with the two of them naked, so close, yet not quite touching.

"I don't, either," she whispered, and lifted her head, wanting more than just teasing.

Jake was the sexiest man she'd ever laid eyes on. He was also one hell of a good partner. If there was something igniting between the two of them that was stronger than the lust surging through her body right now, she wanted to explore it.

Would Jake really want to try to have a relationship with her?

Was that something she was willing to consider?

Jake caught her gaze and held on to it as he ran his hand up her body, adding to the heat already boiling her alive. Wherever he touched her, sparks ignited just under her flesh, building the pressure between her legs. They stared at each other, and she watched his pupils dilate. The way he watched her made her believe her thoughts must have been written all over her face.

"I want this to work." He made the promise as he pressed his cheek to hers, forcing her head to the side, then began nipping at her neck. His teeth scraped over her sensitive flesh. "You won't regret this."

Angela wanted to curl her toes. She wanted to lift her body off the bed and press it against his. She ached to wrap her legs around him, force him down, and draw him deep inside her.

Jake cupped her breast, wrapping his long fingers around her flesh. When he tugged and at the same time pinched her nipple, sharp streaks shot through her.

"I'm not so far," she gasped. Angela grabbed him, digging her nails deep into solid muscle, and held on for dear life. She swore she saw the lightning flashes that shot over her body and straight between her legs.

"You're sensitive. I like that." He purred like a satisfied cat and lowered his head, treasuring his new discovery as he began torturing one nipple and then the other.

Jake lapped at her hardened peaks, moistening them, then breathing hot breath over her puckered flesh until she swore she'd melt underneath him. But as he eased himself down, moving with the skilled prowess of a seasoned hunter ready to enjoy the spoils of his riches, his hard, swollen dick brushed against her leg.

Angela dragged her fingers through his hair, lifting her head and watching as he sucked her breasts. Such a simple act, yet capable of doing things to her that sent her insides spiking to dangerous levels. The pulsing between her legs, the heat scouring her alive, and the pressure that continued building until she was positive she'd explode any moment brought her both pleasure and pain.

Jake didn't hurt her. Even when he dragged his teeth over her nipples, creating sensations that rippled over her body, she held his head firmly where it was, demanding silently that he continue with what he was doing.

He continued feasting on her breasts. Angela wasn't paying attention to how she squirmed and moved her hips, anxious to relieve the pressure but enjoying every minute of it building. Jake slipped his hand down her belly, caressing her flesh until he cupped her pussy. His dick did a wicked dance against her leg as he parted her soaked flesh and groaned.

"You're so wet," he said, scorching her with his hot breath

when he spoke with her nipple in his mouth. "Angela," he breathed.

With every caress, every kiss, ever tender bite, Jake tortured her worse than he'd ever know. All the feelings and sensations wrapped around one another until she couldn't separate them. When he sunk his fingers deep inside her, Angela gritted her teeth, fighting not to let go but knowing at the same time she would lose the battle. He moved his fingers, twisting them and caressing her insides until he found that spot.

It was a spot Angela wasn't sure had ever been touched before. "Jake!" she howled, slapping her hands on the bed beside her. "God! Crap!" she howled, arching into him as wave after wave of pressure released inside her.

"That's it, sweetheart. Come for me. God, you're beautiful." His words floated toward her.

She thought her eyes were opened, but as flashes of colors erupted before her, warm lavenders that quickly exploded into bright, radiant mahoganies, she blinked, aching to see him watch her. When she managed to focus, the sight of his face created another sensation that damn near did her in. Angela wanted to laugh and cry at the same time. Her orgasm continued releasing as he thrust his fingers deeper inside her, twisting them so his knuckles scraped the sensitive soaked flesh that clamped down against them. But the expression on his face, the way his eyes glowed with awe and adoration, and the slight grin that tugged at the corner of his mouth when he caught her staring at him created yet another, different type of sensation that constricted around her heart.

"I want you," she gasped, and watched his green eyes grow brighter.

"Wait a minute, sweetheart. You just came really hard."

She loved the sound of his baritone. And the way the corner of his mouth turned up, making his grin crooked, gave him a roguish look that was as hot as what he was doing to her body.

It was hard to talk, but she didn't want to wait. Angela

lifted her hand, which felt lighter than the air, and curved into him as she reached for his dick. When he slipped his fingers out of her, trying to stop her, the sigh that slipped out of her made him pause. At the same time, it allowed her to reach for him.

"Now," she whispered, her voice scratchy.

Chapter Fifteen

Jake swore his eyes rolled back in his head when Angela wrapped her warm fingers around his cock. He grabbed her wrist, ready to tell her she wouldn't get her wish if she touched him like that much longer. But she tugged, and every inch of him lurched from the pressure that tightened his balls and made it impossible to speak.

"Turnabout is fair play," she said, her soft, alluring tone still husky from her orgasm.

Jake glared at her, or tried to, but her soft smile and the radiant glow on her face simply added to the gentle torture session she administered. He couldn't remember when he'd last gone so long without having sex. Although he didn't regret turning down the many offers he'd received before leaving California, it made him more vulnerable than he'd ever felt before.

Something told him it wasn't from lack of sex, though. His vulnerability wasn't physical but from raw emotions, feelings that were too exposed. With a word, a wrong look, an indifferent action, Angela would destroy him. He'd never been this exposed to a woman before. She controlled everything about him. He swore he wouldn't be able to breathe if he didn't know beforehand that she was safe and happy.

When had everything about Angela started mattering more than anything else in his life?

Angela loosened her grip, which allowed a small amount of oxygen to return to his brain, but then her fingers began caressing his shaft. Slowly, deliberately, and with the most temptuous gaze on her face, Angela pulled his dick, commanding his movements with the slightest of gestures.

"You're either climbing on top or rolling on your back," she informed him, and pressed her thumb into the sensitive flesh just below his swollen tip.

Jake hissed in a breath, trying again to grab her wrist, remove her hand so he could regain control of the situation. It was all he could do to reach next to them, to the floor where their clothes were in a pile, and find the condoms in his shorts pocket.

She grinned. "Apparently I'm not the only one with sensitive parts of the body." She was gloating, completely in control, and rubbing it in his face.

Jake growled. It was the best he could do. She might think him nothing more than a Neanderthal, but at the moment he didn't care. There was only one thing he could do, and with what little oxygen nestled in his brain it sounded like the perfect plan to him.

Jake pulled her hand from his dick, lifting himself over her as he pushed her hand over her head and kept it there. "You asked for this, darling," he informed her, taking her legs and bringing them up to his chest. He ripped one of the packages open with his teeth and freed the lubricated latex. If she was surprised at his skills in slipping it over his dick while keeping his attention on her, she didn't show it.

He let go, leaving her feet to rest on his shoulders as his dick found her entrance. The heat radiating from inside her worked as a magnet, drawing him closer. She would never know how she still controlled the situation in spite of him cheating and taking advantage of being bigger and stronger than she was.

His cock weighed half a ton. His balls were pinched so tight the pain streaked right up the middle of him, like an intense flame scalding his insides. It was a mixture of pain and pleasure too intense to describe but one that robbed him of all senses other than burying himself deep within her tight, soaked, slick walls. He wanted to know that pleasure more than he wanted his next breath.

"You're not playing fair," he heard her say.

Angela twisted underneath him, moving her legs so that her silky smooth skin brushed against his chest and arms. But it was that soaked heat, that promise of pleasure, that took over his brain. Her pussy pressed against his balls and the underside of his dick, and Jake's entire world turned upside down.

He gave into the control she possessed over him, wanting nothing more than to see her satisfied. Angela nibbled her lower lip, watching him. And he saw her through a thick haze of lust. All that dark hair of hers that had managed to loosen from the knot at the back of her head now pooled around her face. She was the goddess of all temptresses, the vision of all that was beautiful, and the woman who would do him in.

Jake didn't want to think beyond the lust. He didn't want to let the emotions and feelings that simmered just under his sense of reality surface and cause him to think about more than incredible sex. But he couldn't help it. Jake had no desire to share with her the depths of his promiscuous path in life before meeting her. But if she would have him, by God, Jake would swear to her that he'd make her happy as long as they were together. If she would only agree, he knew neither of them would ever regret it.

"You might be bigger and stronger," she informed him, twisting again underneath him. One of her legs slid down his arm, and she wrapped it around his waist, nudging his spine with the heel of her foot and trying desperately to bring them closer together. "But I have a few tricks of my own."

Angela rubbed her pussy against his dick, stroking him with all that soaked heat. Something made his focus clear. It had to be her grin. She stared up at him, smiling as her eyes danced with amusement and enjoyment. The look on her face hit him too hard. It shouldn't have. Grinning and laughing during sex were natural. It was fun, pleasurable, a way to express feelings that otherwise might never be voiced. And it hit Jake harder than if he'd just been punched in the gut that this was a type of sex he'd never enjoyed before.

"Angela," he breathed, wanting to share his revelation. The words weren't there. The emotion was too new, too raw.

But she smiled. She ran her fingers over his flesh, stroking and learning his body while her eyes glowed and her cheeks remained flushed with a shade of red richer than a perfect dark wine. Jake couldn't remember ever watching a woman smile, let alone laugh, when he fucked her. They were always posed, their expressions tight and their full lips puckered into a pouting expression as they grunted and hissed vulgar comments, encouraging him until he came.

Had he ever made a woman come and then not cared if he received the same favor? How many firsts were there with this woman?

Jake didn't want to think about what he'd done, or hadn't done, with any other woman. There was no point dwelling on the simple truth that until this moment he'd never truly understood the pleasure given from making love. The reason was so clear it slapped him in the face with the truth of it.

"You're beautiful." He pushed his dick inside her, feeling like a fool for failing so miserably in expressing what he felt inside.

"And you're gorgeous," she said, but then cried out when his dick slid deep into her heat.

He filled her, stretched her, and drowned in the intense fire that wrapped around him and throbbed as so many tiny muscles threatened to suffocate the life out of him. There wasn't any stopping it. Usually when he did a lady for the first time he asked her if she liked it fast or slow. This wasn't doing a lady for the first time, though. This was Angela, the woman he feared had just stolen his heart and damn well knew she'd done it.

"God, yes! Oh damn!" Angela wrapped her legs around Jake, clinging to his shoulders with her hands, as a moist sheen made her flesh glow.

"You feel so good." He wanted to tell her, share with her

how perfect this was. As desperately as he'd wanted her since the moment he'd met her, Jake never knew it was because this was where he belonged.

He should be terrified. This was when men hauled ass, clinging to their bachelorhood and determined to hold on to what they considered freedom. Jake wasn't sure why any man would feel that way. Not if they experienced what Jake was feeling right now. Any man in his right mind would know, the moment he plunged into the woman who felt different than all the others, the instant he felt that tug that lured him into her heat as if he were finally coming home, that nowhere would feel as right as this did. Jake knew without bothering to give it more thought that Angela was the woman for him. He wasn't losing a damn thing.

As he plunged into her heat, soaking his balls and wanting more of Angela with each thrust, he swore he finally was free. He'd found his other half and wouldn't have to worry about being single ever again.

Jake blinked, doing his best to focus on Angela as she tightened around him, searing him alive with that hot, incredible pussy of hers. Her smile was still there, but she panted, her face and body glowing as her breasts bounced from their lovemaking.

"Don't stop," she said on a breath, searching his face as she reached for him. "Please, just keep doing that."

"That feels good?" He wasn't going too fast, but it wasn't painfully slow, either.

"You have no idea," she murmured, her thick lashes bobbing over her eyes and finally draping them as she closed her mouth and smiled. Angela hummed, dragging her nails over his chest as if she branded him, marking him with some invisible signature that would forever make him hers.

"Tell me." If he knew her thoughts, had a clue that this was as incredible for her as it was for him, maybe he could find the words he needed to say.

"You feel so good," she said quickly, letting the words spill out of her as she exhaled. "It's better than good." Her fingernails scraped over his shoulders. "Jake, it's perfect."

"Open your eyes." He watched her lashes flutter again.

"It's thick, just long enough. I don't know. It's perfect." The words spilled out of her again, and her lashes kept fluttering.

"Angela." His blood was boiling. The intensity of keeping this pace, focusing on it because it was what she wanted, antagonized him. There wasn't a better form of torture in the world, but nonetheless the tightness in his balls was hint enough his time was about up. "Sweetheart, look at me," he said again.

She stared up at him, her mouth twitching as her breathing grew raspier. The pressure was growing inside her again. He'd bet it was hitting that breaking point just as it was with him. If there was anything he would take from his years of enjoying so many different ladies it was knowing how to read when they were about to climax. Angela was right there.

"Come with me," he told her, watching her gaze shift as she stared into his eyes. "Let go and let me take you over the edge." He never spoke that way when he fucked other ladies. With Angela it felt right, though.

And when she gave him another one of those toothy grins he wasn't sure he'd make it until she climaxed. "You're tight, darling, and so wet. Feel how you cling to me. I want you to come so hard that you drain my entire soul into you."

"Okay," she gasped. "Go faster," she added, barely able to speak as she tried to breathe.

She didn't have to suggest it twice. Jake impaled her and she arched into the thrust, her round, perfect breasts bouncing and her nipples so hard his mouth watered at the sight. But it was her tight pussy, so silky smooth like hot velvet. He thrust deeper, feeling himself swell.

Heat deep inside him began spreading as she soaked him, drenching his balls, his cock, and every inch of her. They were so hot together, so damned perfect. The friction would burn him alive, but at the same time he wished it would never end. There wasn't any stopping it, though, now that they'd started climbing. The sensations that sweltered inside him, tumbling over one another until the explosion was imminent, tore him apart.

Jake threw his head back as every inch of him hardened and finally broke free. He came harder than he'd ever come in his life. If the condom survived their lovemaking session he'd be damned surprised.

"Oh my God!" Angela said, still breathing hard. "You're amazing. Lord, that was the best . . ." Her words trailed off and she didn't look up at him.

"We're amazing." He tried not to swell with pride over the words she almost had said. There wasn't any way he would force her to finish her sentence. In truth, if she had, it would only be fair to tell her she was the best he'd ever had as well.

He rolled to his side, needing to remove the condom that did somehow manage to stay on him but wanting just a minute to cuddle with her. "Once we catch our breath, we need to shower."

"I won't argue with you there." She turned to her side, resting her head on his shoulder as she placed her hand over his heart. "We should get moving," she added, but relaxed even more next to him.

It would take nothing to fall asleep with her in his arms. She felt so good there, every inch of her warm, her flesh glowing, and her hair tumbling past her shoulder and over his arm. He wanted to hold her, search for something to say that would bring out her thoughts and feelings at the moment.

As his head cleared, though, and oxygen slowly began filling his brain, Jake knew discussing any of his feelings at this point would make him sound like an idiot. They just had some really hot sex. Maybe to him it was truly making love, bonding them together and pulling them into a much closer, tighter relationship than they'd been in prior. It would be easier to show her that he felt that way instead of trying to put all of that into words. Somehow he'd keep her by his side. He wasn't sure how at the moment, but it wasn't something that needed to be talked out right now, either. Right now they would shower and bring each other up-to-date.

"Come on, sweetheart," he said, pulling both of them to a sitting position.

Angela remained completely sated, allowing him to move her but making no effort to do anything but remain cuddled next to him. "I am," she said, then sighed. "I guess it's time for the real world now, right?"

Something tightened in his gut. Even as he let go of her and let her move to the end of the bed, where she stood, stretched, and showed off how sexy she looked, basking from incredible sex, he wanted to pull her back into his arms. What they'd just shared had been real.

"That's funny. I don't remember leaving the real world." He stood, staring at her round ass and how her hips were slender but not too thin. Her narrow waist and flat tummy were firm but not gaunt. When she looked over her shoulder at him, gathering her hair and once again twisting it into a knot at the back of her head, the silhouette of her in the dark showed off how hard her nipples were.

"You know what I mean." The smile she gave him now didn't glow like the ones she'd offered when he made love to her. "The sex was incredible. More than incredible. I could sing your praises all night. But I'm sure you've heard it all before."

Angela bent down to grab their clothes, scooping the entire pile into her arms. He wanted to grab her, force her to admit it was more than sex. The emotions he'd sensed streaming from her before, were now in tight check. She'd covered them up, apparently believing he would somehow hurt her otherwise.

"Before doesn't matter," he said, following her when she left the bedroom and walked across the hall to a small bathroom.

"Well, some of it does. Tell me what you meant when you said earlier that suits and uniforms were all around you as you struggled to gather information to help me nail this case." Angela dropped their clothes on the closed toilet seat lid, then reached around her shower curtain and turned on the water. Once again, she didn't bother with lights.

The darkness suited him fine. Just as it suited him to discuss the case. There would be time later to open up to each other and share their feelings. He would damn well see to it.

"What I meant was that I called the crime in," he began. "I talked to a Detective Ames and he was excited as hell to come flying down there. Of course once he did, his uniforms didn't want me anywhere near the crime scene. It took more than a little bit of work to get close enough to take a good look at the kidnapped victims."

"Did you see Marianna?" Angela was stepping into the shower but turned quickly, her eyes wide as she asked.

He hated disappointing her. "No, and I almost got hauled down to the jail when I ignored the cops and kept looking for her."

They didn't take long in the shower, although she had good, strong water pressure and Jake would have enjoyed soaking under the hot pellets of water for a few. Instead they each made quick work of rinsing away signs of their lovemaking while Jake shared with her what had happened from the point when he arrived at Mandela's house, to following the two black SUVs and large truck across town, and finally to how he'd crawled across the field.

"Thank you for risking so much," she murmured, grabbing the towel hanging on her towel rack and handing Jake a folded towel that was on a shelf over her toilet.

"This is what we do, Angela."

"I know, but you were ordered away from the crime scene yet persisted so you could try and find Marianna. That means a lot, Jake. Not to mention you called the cops when you knew what their take would be on bounty hunters. And Detective Ames is a good man, by the way. My father has worked with him for years."

"There wasn't any way I could let them lift off with all those kidnapped victims. Too many families have been heartbroken for who knows how long since each one of those people went missing."

Angela sighed. "You're right. Good call."

She left him alone in the bathroom, not saying anything

else. After dressing and feeling incredibly rejuvenated, Jake found Angela in her living room, standing in the darkness and peering out front around her closed curtains.

"They're going to find us," she said, not turning around. "What did you find on-site during the bust, anything?"

"Actually, yes." Jake pulled his phone out of his shorts pocket. "Obviously I couldn't lift evidence, although I was tempted."

"What?" She turned to face him, her thick black hair damp and falling down her back. She'd changed clothes and the plain blue T-shirt she wore and blue-jean shorts couldn't hide her incredible figure. If she was trying for nondescript, it was probably the closest to it she'd be able to pull off.

"I took pictures." He held up his phone and watched her stare at it.

Angela's green eyes were bright even in the dark room. The way she stared at his phone, as if she could pull from it every image he'd photographed, was fascinating to watch.

"I only had a couple minutes at the back of the truck." Jake pulled up the images on his phone, and Angela moved next to him. There was a hint of rose about her, as if she'd sprayed perfume on after dressing. Did she do that for him?

"They're hard to see. What is this?"

"It's a picture of all the dog crates in the back of the truck."

"Where all the kidnapped victims were," she said, remembering what he'd told her and nodding slowly. "I can't tell how many are there."

"Do you have an e-mail address I can send these to?" he asked, flipping to the next picture for her, which was a shot of the men loading one of the crates into the plane. "They'll be easier to see on a computer screen."

She was pure-blood detective, every inch of her honed in on learning every clue, dissecting every bit of evidence. Watching her nibble her lower lip, look at the pictures he'd taken, then raise her attention to his face made him hard all over again. It didn't matter if Angela wore top-of-the-line, brand-name outfits or simple shorts and a T-shirt, there was an air of erotic beauty about her that was breathtaking. She was the perfect combination of beauty and brains that he never realized he'd been searching so hard for all his life.

"The glow of the computer screen would give us away. I'm actually surprised no one has shown up here yet."

"I'd like to think they're busy questioning Mandela."

"Wait a minute." Angela hurried around him to her luggage, grabbed one bag, then almost ran up her stairs, calling over her shoulder, "We'll use my laptop. We can set it up in my bedroom closet. That way the glow won't be visible outside."

A few minutes later Jake was e-mailing all the pictures he had taken to Angela, who was downloading them as they entered her in-box. She sat cross-legged on her closet floor, which was a fairly large walk-in.

"You know this closet helped sell me on this place," she offered, looking up at him with the same grin she'd given him when they were making love. It was a grin of passion, and he swore anytime he would see it on her face he would immediately be hungry for her. "I never thought it would be this useful for detective work, though," she added, laughing. "We need to set up my spy equipment, too. If there is anyone at Mario's home, maybe we can get a clue what is going on right now."

"Okay. That's all of the pictures." Jake shoved his phone into his pocket. "I don't think I can sit on the floor in there with you. But I'll grab your equipment. Where is it?"

"Nothing about you is small," she said, and color washed over her cheeks. Blushing didn't seem to bother her. He was still blessed with that incredibly vivacious smile.

"My mom fed me well." He shrugged and grinned at her.

Angela stared at him a moment, her smile fading but the glow in her eyes remaining. She was processing something about him, and he wished like hell he could get into her thoughts. The moment passed, though, and she returned her attention to her laptop. "There's a false bottom in my black suitcase. My listening devices are in there."

When he returned to her bedroom a few minutes later, Angela had shoved all of her hanging clothes to the back of the closet, almost doubling the space. She still sat cross-legged, her fingers hovered over the keys, and grinned up at him.

"Is there enough room now?"

She wanted him sitting in here with her. God. Jake almost felt light-headed from the pleasure that swelled inside him. "Let's see," he said, entering her walk-in closet and managing to sit on the floor by the door and put the equipment he'd brought upstairs in between them.

They worked silently next to each other, situating the monitoring box and opening pictures. Within minutes, they had the most cramped detective office Jake had ever imagined seeing. And they were up and running.

Jake switched channels, flipping from the bugs on the patio to the bugs in Mario's room. He started thinking the one she'd put in his room might be dead or discovered. There wasn't any sound coming from it at all. He heard a hum from the one on the patio. When he switched over to the one in the limo, it was silent as well.

"Oh my God! Jake," Angela cried out, reaching for him and grabbing his arm. "I don't believe it. Crap. You've done it!"

He stared at her, tried glancing at the laptop, but didn't have a chance when she damn near knocked it off her lap as she tried leaping over the equipment on the floor between them and into his arms.

"You're the best, the absolute best!" She laughed, managing to wrap her arms around him.

"So you've told me," he answered with a lazy drawl, and held her to him. "What wonderful thing have I done this time?"

She slapped at him playfully when she pulled away, then rebalanced the laptop on her lap. "These pictures. One of them was a page of links. I was going through them and look!" She pointed at the screen.

"Crap," he hissed, staring at a sign-in page. "Is that what I think it is?"

"It's the game," she said in awe.

"And we don't have the password."

"Once we break into this we'll have all the answers. I'm sure of it."

"But we don't know the password."

The image of Earth, spinning on its axis, kept the screen from going idle. Next to it in a thin black cursive font were the words *"Who shall rule the world?"* As the Earth rotated, different countries were highlighted. Underneath the spinning world was a place to enter a screen name and password.

"The program might be set up to lock-up if you enter the wrong password more than a few times," Angela pointed out. "You know, the way financial websites are usually set up."

Jake typed in *Ruler* for a screen name and *number one* as a password. A cartoon image appeared next to the boxes where he typed the information and pulled a gun on him, firing and causing the screen to melt.

"Oh my God," Angela gasped. "No!"

In the next second, the screen reappeared, informing him he got the screen name and password wrong. "I'm going to bank on the fact that the FBI is trying to break into this Web site, too. Assuming they've gotten it wrong the first few times, hopefully our little cartoon gunman will be patient with us."

"I hope you're right," Angela whispered. "Try Mandela as his screen name."

"Any suggestions for a password?"

"Umm . . . try 'family.'"

"'Family'?"

Angela shrugged. "Mario made a big deal of how important family was to him."

"Which is why he killed his uncle in cold blood," Jake grunted, but typed in *family*.

This time the screen didn't melt. Instead the cartoon gunman appeared, blew on his smoking gun as the words appeared below telling them they got the password wrong.

"His screen name is Mandela!" Angela shrieked, so excited she jumped. The laptop slipped in her hands, and she grabbed ahold of it, bracing it. "Okay, now for the password."

"Try 'Italy,'" he suggested.

Mandela wasn't the family man or loyal patriot. The

password wasn't "Italy." He'd filled Angela with a bunch of crap, and although Jake knew she despised the monster, it was hard not taking some things at face value when the person saying them sounded so sincere.

"I have an idea," Jake said, and leaned over the listening equipment again, reached in front of her, and typed on her keyboard. Sucking in a breath, he tapped the mouse, and the screen changed. Her laptop hummed and the two of them stared at the screen, silence building in the small closet.

"Oh my God," Angela whispered, her shock apparent as she stared at the screen slowly downloading on her computer. "What was the password?"

"I'll tell you later." He'd just proved Mandela was the grotesque monster Jake already knew him to be. "This is one hell of a program," Jake said, changing the subject.

Angela looked over her shoulder at him. "What was the password?" she asked again.

If Jake thought he'd found a woman he could protect from all evil, Angela was letting him know with one hard, cold stare that wasn't the case. "Tell me," she demanded, her eyes darkening with her tone.

"The password is 'AngelaMustDie.' One word. Each new word starts with a capital letter."

Angela blew out a long breath, shaking her head slowly as she stared into Jake's face. "Sure sorry to disappoint him," she grunted, then returned her attention to the screen. "Not only am I going to live. I'm going to watch that bastard rot in hell."

Jake's insides swelled. "Pride" didn't quite describe the emotion that swelled throughout him. Angela was tough as nails and softer than silk. At that moment, she reminded Jake of his mom. Worse yet, he never would have thought a woman with such attributes would turn him on so much. His mom would have a field day with that one. Jake groaned inwardly and shoved the image of his mother's gloating smile out of his head.

"Here's the map. It is a board game!" Angela didn't shout this time, but her excitement was apparent. "The players. Jake, look, there are the names of the players."

Jake looked. Mandela was player number three. Player number two was Brutoli. There was only one other player, player number one. Jake stared at the name, Cooper.

"Evelyn Van Cooper," Angela said out loud, voicing his thoughts. "And player number two?"

"Brutus Brutoli," Jake said, already shifting his attention to the rest of the board game.

"Now we have all the names. If Marianna is with one of these monsters we're going to find her!" Angela shot a hard look at Jake but returned her attention to the laptop, opening a new search bar page.

"What are you doing? We need to see if the board game shows where they're going to attack next." Jake reached for the laptop.

Angela moved her shoulder, turning at a slight angle to block him, although she didn't appear to focus on her actions. "How is 'Brutoli' spelled again? What is his first name again?" she asked, flipping to the game, then back to her new search bar. "I'm going to find out everything there is to know about these sons of bitches. Hopefully we can figure out where they have their armies set up. Once we know, we go into both camps and take them out. Maybe Marianna will be with one of them." Angela stopped for a breath and looked up at Jake. "It sounds sane to be able to pull that off within the next twenty-four hours, right?"

Angela jumped and he pulled her against him protectively when a loud knock on the door downstairs shook the entire house.

"Open up! FBI!" someone yelled outside.

Chapter Sixteen

Mario opened his own door when Tomas parked the limo in front of his house at five o'clock the next morning. He'd spent the entire evening at police headquarters, being drilled by one detective after another. During the early hours of the morning two FBI agents had begun questioning him, both looking as if they'd just woken up and showered. He still had the stench of their aftershave clinging to his nostrils.

They'd let him come home, which meant one thing: there wasn't enough information to nail him to the wall. And the idiots had everything they needed to send him to prison for the rest of his life. Yet another reason why he loved the American judicial system. They couldn't hold him. They couldn't beat him into a confession because he might sue them. This country protected criminals so well he could kiss the ground.

He'd been careful. So damned careful. Mario had spent years building up his life to become part of the game. Hell, before the game even existed he'd watched the best of the best, learned from their mistakes, and pulled himself out of poverty to become one of the wealthiest men in the world. He didn't get here by making mistakes.

But he'd made one. It only took one. His padre used to tell him that. Just one mistake can destroy an empire. Mario's padre would quote memorable historical events to Mario to prove his point. He should have been the one here, sitting on top of his empire. The old man got sick, though. He never got the opportunity that Mario now had. But his *padre* would be proud. Mario's *padre* would see all Mario had done and would tell everyone in heaven of his perfect son.

Enough!

Mario wouldn't dwell on the past. He walked slowly and deliberately to the door of his house. Tomas, who was an amazing silent giant, moved around Mario nimbly, reaching the door and opening it for him.

"Go to bed, Tomas," Mario ordered, not bothering to look over his shoulder at his chauffeur but closing the door.

Marco stood from the couch where he'd been sitting when Mario entered. His expression looked torn and weary as he studied Mario. Bobby was also there. The blond man stood slowly, not looking as anxious as Marco. Bobby studied Mario with a wary expression.

"How are you doing?" Bobby asked.

"I feel like hell," Mario grunted, shifting his attention from Bobby to Russell Pierce. Mario had instructed Pierce to wait here for him, having heard he'd been the one with the flashlight and had missed King lying in the grass, waiting to attack. Bobby had been the one to tip Mario's men off, informing them they were being followed from the moment they'd left his house. King wasn't that great of a bounty hunter. Apparently, though, Mario's men were idiots incapable of pulling off a simple assignment. How hard was it to haul zombies? King was probably gloating like a damn fool. All he'd proven was that he could capture morons. From what Mario had heard at the police station, King had almost gotten himself arrested as well. Bounty hunting was against the law in Illinois. Mario was okay with the bastard not being arrested. He looked forward to killing King. Mario had yet to decide how he'd kill him. All he knew so far was that the death would be slow and painful.

Mario glared at Russell, needing someone to take his anger out on right now. "Did you intentionally ignore King lying in the grass watching you?" Mario asked, moving in slowly as he watched the idiot start to tremble.

"What? No, sir." Russell shifted from one foot to the other nervously. "I helped drive the truck to the airport. Bobby said to be prepared in case we were followed, so we split up—"

"Mario only wants a 'yes' or 'no,'" Bobby barked, glaring hatefully at Russell Pierce. "He didn't ask for you to shovel out excuses for the sloppy work you've done."

Bobby yelling was as annoying as Russell spitting out nonsense and bullshit. Mario stormed out of the living room, ignoring their questioning looks and knowing none of them would move an inch until he returned. Not if they knew what was good for them. He stalked down the hallway to his office.

His eyes burned as he headed around his desk, then reached underneath the middle drawer to push the button hidden there. A panel slid out and Mario entered the code on the number pad. There was a soft clicking sound. Mario eased the number pad back into its slot and opened the drawer below it that he'd just unlocked. There were important documents in the drawer but nothing as important as what he had in his bedroom. A smart man never kept all the secrets to his fortune in one spot. Reaching underneath the documents, Mario pulled out his gun.

His people were chosen carefully, paid well, and treated better than most hired help was treated. Mario knew how to develop loyalty among his men. That didn't mean there wasn't an idiot among the group. Just one wrong move and Mario's entire world had blown up around him. Someone had to pay.

Mario stopped as he entered his living room, his hand at his side holding his gun tight enough it pinched his fingers. But the cold metal reassured him the strongest and most skilled prevailed. Those who were weak always perished. He glanced around the room, then focused on Bobby, who took his time meeting Mario's gaze. The man's expression was guarded, but Mario swore he saw something. If he didn't know better, he would say it was annoyance.

"Where is Russell?" Mario asked, facing Bobby. Bobby hadn't spent the last few hours being interrogated in a police station. The motherfucker had nothing to be annoyed or upset about.

"He just left." Bobby was giving Mario a strange look.

"Why did he just leave?" Mario yelled. Putting a bullet in Russell's head might have helped Mario sleep better tonight.

"I suggested Marco call it a night, too," Bobby continued, his stance relaxed as he spoke conversationally. "Everyone wanted to make sure you made it home safely, but we have an early day tomorrow. I sent them all off to bed."

"Is that so?"

It was quite possible pulling Bobby so close under Mario's wing had made the man a bit too cocky. It wouldn't be the first time a right-hand man had turned into a monster, the result of being pampered and treated as an equal by his boss. Mario took his time pulling his attention from Bobby before turning his attention to the hallway.

"Marco!" he bellowed, yelling loud enough his voice echoed off the walls.

His cousin might be a moron, but he knew when Mario said to jump, he better damn well do as he's told. There was the sound of footsteps hurrying down the hallway, and in the next moment Marco appeared in the doorway, his tie removed and the top button of his shirt undone.

"Where were you all evening?" If Russell ran like a fucking coward, there would be another scapegoat to blame. Mario would see to it.

The last thing he could do right now was sleep. There were too many things to do. The first one being eliminating the weak link in his household. Mario had been too soft, too generous. His men were about to learn that only the strong survived.

"I've been here ever since the police released me." Marco began wringing his hands. "Why did they send us home, Mario? They took your entire army and just let us walk. That scares the crap out of me." His accent grew thicker as he started whining. "I didn't say anything to them, though. I promise you that."

"I believe you." Mario was sickened by his younger cousin's whiny attitude. He had half a mind to shoot Marco just for being a baby.

"They sent you home because they don't have all the information they need yet to arrest you. They're going to watch and wait for one of us to fuck up," Bobby offered.

Mario let both of them see his gun as he stuffed it inside the back of his pants, then headed out of the living room once again. Bobby was right behind him. It didn't surprise him a bit that Marco snuck off to lick his wounds and feel sorry for himself. He was pathetic.

"I can't fucking believe this," Mario snarled, reaching the top of the stairs and heading for his bedroom. "Who is it, Bobby? Tell me right now."

"What?" Bobby didn't enter Mario's bedroom but leaned in the doorway. There was a gray shadow around the man's face, proof he had been up all night, too. Otherwise, though, he watched Mario with a steady gaze, all of his emotions well in check.

"Do you know how humiliating it is to be detained by the police while I'm out in public?" Mario needed to yell, although he didn't feel any better after doing it. His eyes still burned, and anger still tore at him. "How did King get wind of all this going down? What put him at my driveway the fucking moment everyone is leaving with my army? I want to know right now who the fuck messed up!" he bellowed.

Bobby either had the good sense to remain quiet or just wasn't sure what to say. Mario glared at him, content to take his wrath out on the man even if he was one of his better employees.

"Why did you let Russell leave?" Mario demanded, stalking over to his desk and staring down at his computer.

"No offense, Boss, but he's not one of your more competent men. I figured the more sleep he got the better he'd work for you tomorrow." Bobby said, remaining calm and not moving from where he stood in the doorway.

"Well, I want him back here right now." Mario slapped his hand down on his desk. "Cancel my flight to Dallas. Has Angela called?"

"Do you think Angela could be the one who tipped off the police?"

Mario scowled at the items surrounding his computer. Something didn't look right. Staying up all night was starting to take its toll. His anger was still burning his insides alive, though. He lifted his gaze slowly, taking his time glaring at Bobby, who still lounged in Mario's doorway as if he didn't have a care in the world.

"Now how the hell would she do that when she was with me all goddamn evening?" he hissed. He needed to throw something. There had to be something he could break. A slow, methodic thumping began in his brain, settling in around his temples. If he didn't get rid of this anger, he'd be suffering a migraine. That was the last thing he fucking needed.

"She was with you all evening?" Bobby questioned.

"What the hell kind of question is that? And why are you challenging what I say?" Mario demanded. He yanked his gun out of the back of his pants. The hard metal was rubbing him wrong. "Don't you think I would know where the fucking woman was, especially when she was with me?"

Bobby didn't flinch when Mario began waving the gun around. "Boss, maybe if you lie down awhile. I'll stay up, keep an eye on things. You know as well as I do that at least one of us needs to be on his toes if the feds come sniffing around this place."

"They come sniffing around here and I'll blow their fucking brains out for trespassing." Mario didn't care whether he made sense or not. He had just about had enough of Bobby's calm, cool tone. This wasn't a time for relaxed stances in doorways. "Quit standing there like a goddamned idiot," Mario barked, waving his gun at Bobby again just to see if he could get a rise out of the man.

Bobby dutifully straightened and took a step toward Mario. "All right, Boss. Whatever you say. What do you want me to do?"

At least the man knew when to act humble. Not that Mario didn't know it was an act. Bobby probably wanted Mario to crash so he could get him out of his hair for a while. Well if Mario wanted to rant and rave, he was damn well going to do it. This was his house after all. He paid the man's salary, and Mario paid him well.

"What's missing here?" Mario asked, returning his attention to his desk. He stared at his computer, moved the mouse, and watched his desktop appear. The computer appeared undisturbed, which was a damn good thing. The programs on this computer could incriminate him and fry his ass. Which was why he kept the board game on this computer and had the entire thing password protected. In fact, he'd just changed the password earlier this week. And he hadn't told a soul what his plans were for his hot new girlfriend once he arrived in Dallas. But he'd spelled it out clearly enough with his new password. "Wait a minute," he grumbled, putting his gun on his desk and gripping the back of his chair. "Where are my backup flash drives?"

"What?" Bobby asked, taking another step closer.

"My backup flash drives!" Mario yelled, which caused the thumping in his brain to increase. He pointed at his desk. "They are always right here. Who the hell has been in my bedroom?"

He caught Bobby searching his room instead of answering him. When Bobby pointed at Mario's dresser, he turned in that direction, seeing them at the same time that Bobby walked to the dresser.

"Wait!" Mario jumped across his room, pushing Bobby away from the dresser before he could pick up the small case of flash drives. "Why are they there?"

"I don't know, Boss. Maybe you left them there." Bobby dropped his hand and stepped away from the dresser, shrugging at the same time as if it weren't a big deal where the flash drives were.

"Maybe I left them there?" Mario hissed, turning an evil glare on the blond American. "And maybe I just lost my fucking mind, too, eh?" he roared, with the urge to wipe that smug look off the face of the man who simply stared at him, looking mildly tolerant at best. "Do you think I'm a damned moron?"

Mario grabbed the flash drive case, mumbling in Italian that some people had a lot of nerve questioning the hand that fed them, clothed them, and kept a roof over their heads. Either Bobby understood Italian better than he let on or he just had the good sense to start behaving. His expression turned humble as he followed Mario back to his desk.

"I'll check the security cameras to see who was in here, Boss. Whoever moved them will be reporting to you before the hour is out."

"Good." Mario opened the case but then simply gawked at the empty container. "They're gone." His head started spinning. The board game was on backup on one of the flash drives. His personal financial information was on another. No one ever entered his home, not without him present. Only the few house servants, of whom all were family and too damned ignorant to understand how to use a computer, were ever in his house. Bobby was the only man with free reign of Mario's house who had any computer knowledge at all.

Mario hurled the empty case at his bedroom wall. It made a loud racket and shattered in several pieces as it crashed to the floor. As satisfying as that was, it wasn't enough. He picked up his gun, wrapping his fingers around the hard metal, and wished it were colder. A fever ignited inside him, and it climbed in a mad rush as he took in the contents of his room, looking for anything else that might be out of place.

"Where are the flash drives?" he asked, keeping his voice low, cool, collected.

Bobby stood there like a fucking moron, with that relaxed expression on his face mocking Mario. "I don't know, Boss. I told you—"

"You were here. Are you going to stand there and tell me you don't know without looking at the fucking security tapes if someone was in my bedroom or not?"

"I would say no one was in here."

"Which obviously isn't the truth now, is it?" Mario turned

his attention on the man, staring him in the eye and searching for the deception that would peg the man as guilty.

Bobby had the good sense to back up toward the doorway. "I'll go look right now."

"You don't have to look, do you? No. I think you don't have to look." There was no way Bobby wouldn't know what had happened in this house. He'd been with Mario all this time and always knew everything that went on around the place. At first it had unnerved Mario, but then he grew to rely on the man's intuitive nature. Mario grabbed the gun and released the safety. He stared down at Bobby's surprised reaction. "Where are my fucking flash drives?" he demanded.

"I don't know." Bobby walked backward, reaching the doorway and moving into the hallway. "You aren't thinking right and I'm not going to die for you." Bobby took off down the hallway.

Mario raced into the hallway, pulled the trigger, and put a hole in his wall at the end of the hall. God damn, Bobby was quick.

"Find another scapegoat!" Bobby yelled, his voice coming from the bottom of the stairs.

Mario staggered, the realization hitting him as to the extent of the damage if his personal files landed in the wrong hands. Every file on those flash drives, along with the ones on his computer, was password protected. It would take the best of computer hackers a lot of time to access any of his files.

Now he had to figure out who took his goddamned flash drives and figure out how to rebuild his army with the feds watching him. There was no way he'd forfeit the game. Once he won, not even the feds would be able to touch him. Instead they would answer to him. The whole goddamned world would answer to him. Mario turned around in his room slowly, snapping his fingers as he did.

"That's it," he whispered to himself. "One of them tipped off the law." It was the only explanation. His two opponents in the game both knew they hadn't stood a chance against him. But if his army disappeared, Mario couldn't continue with the game. It was one of two people. And it wouldn't take him long to figure out which one.

Mario walked over to his bedroom door, closed and locked it. Then moving to his closet, he pushed the large closet doors, causing them to roll sideways and open his large, organized closet. Mario stared at the five rows of clothes, all of his suits and formal wear hanging in orderly fashion on each bar. There was plenty of space between each row to step into the closet, choose what he wanted, and try it on while standing, facing the row. Mirrors and proper lighting were the finishing touches for what Mario would have to say was the perfect closet.

He stepped between two rows and moved to the back of his closet where shelves held pair after pair of shoes, and casual attire he had folded on the opposite wall. Ignoring his clothes, Mario knelt in front of the large cage pushed back in the corner.

"Hello, *puttana*. Would you like to come out and play?"

The beautiful young woman lifted her head, her long, thick black hair streaming over her shoulder and her bare back. She didn't answer but stared at him, her dark eyes round and blank. Mario wondered what she'd be like if he took her off the slave juice. She was young, very young by the looks of her body. He'd had a piss-poor night, though, and wasn't feeling as scrupulous as he usually did. Maybe she was old enough to fuck.

"How old are you, my precious *puttana*?"

She continued staring, her mouth opening to answer, but she closed it. Mario was patient. "Come here," he ordered, softening his voice as if he were talking to a small child.

Mario opened the cage door and reached inside to help the woman when she began crawling toward him. She stumbled when she tried to stand, which was probably a result of his leaving her in there too long.

"Lean on me, sweet *puttana*," he instructed, offering his arm gallantly.

She wrapped her cool, slender fingers around his arm but remained hunched over, walking like an old hag as she took baby steps toward his closet door. They made it into his room as far as his bed before Mario picked her up by her waist and tossed her on his bed. She crumpled, appearing deflated, and didn't move from the position in which she'd fallen.

Mario scratched his head. She didn't look like she'd be much fun to play with right now. Maybe if he fed her something. Under different circumstances, Mario would order food sent to his room. His *puttana* was his secret, though. No one knew he'd pulled her out of his army, except Bobby. Mario had instructed him to personally see to moving the young *puttana* to his bedroom closet.

"Don't move," he instructed, and fought off the urge to laugh at his own joke as he made sure he had the key to his bedroom, let himself out, then locked the door again. He would feed his *puttana,* wash her, and dress her.

Putting something slutty on her would lift her spirits. Mario remembered how she'd walked with pride, wearing practically nothing, the evening she'd ordered those two morons to drive into the side of the nightclub wall in Los Angeles. She liked wearing clothes that showed off how much she wanted a man to play with her body.

Mario rummaged through the kitchen, made a meat and cheese sandwich, and grabbed a beer. No one was around as he hauled his food back to his room.

"Be my good little *puttana* and I'll feed you some of my sandwich," Mario offered after locking his bedroom door behind him and placing the sandwich and beer on the table by his bed.

The woman hadn't moved, not an inch. If only his men would follow his orders as well. Maybe he'd be smart to put all of the assholes on slave juice. Mario stared at the woman. Her hair fell down her back, draped over her arm, and successfully covered almost half of her naked body.

"*Puttana,* sit," he ordered, still keeping his voice calm and peaceful.

Her arms moved and she pushed against the bed, making the effort to push herself into a sitting position. Mario couldn't remember what Evelyn had said about feeding his people while they were on the slave juice. He'd been busy most of this week and hadn't had time for his *puttana*. Maybe he had left her in her cage for too long without food and water.

If he was going to feed her, she was going to get a bath first. "All right, *puttana*. Let's go. We'll get the stench off of you and then have some fun." He took her by the arm, lifting her as a child might lift a favorite doll, and dragged her into the bathroom.

Chapter Seventeen

Angela's heart pounded so loud it created a rushing sound in her brain. She couldn't steady the laptop in her hands.

Jake backed out of the closet. "Shut that thing down," he whispered in her ear, grabbing her arms and pulling her out with him.

"Okay." She shot a furtive look at her bedroom window.

It was the worst sensation in the world, being the one who was hunted. Jake kept arguing neither of them had done anything wrong. It was true. They hadn't. The FBI had asked her to come with them to answer questions, and she'd snuck out and fled. That was her only crime. Angela hated being accused of anything, though, and despised even worse actually being guilty.

Jake walked over to her bedroom window and stared outside. "Looks like several cars. It's hard to say how many are out there, though."

"I guess I'll go let them in before they wake the neighbors." Angela shut down her computer, closed it, and left it on her bed.

"Don't let them intimidate you," Jake said, glancing back at her laptop before following her out of her bedroom. "We're going to have to work with them, though," he mumbled, gripping her shoulders and massaging them as he and Angela headed toward the stairs.

"If they'll let us work with them," she whispered.

"Don't worry." Jake followed her down the stairs, then managed to step around her and reach her front door first. He gripped her door handle and touched her chin with his other hand. "There is a lot to do with this case," he said, still whispering. "They want our information or wouldn't be here. But we're all on the same side."

"Yes, we are." She straightened, sucked in a deep breath, and smoothed her hair with her fingers before nodding at the door. "Better let them in," she said.

Another hard pounding vibrated the living room wall and made the picture she had hanging next to her door vibrate. Jake ignored it, his stare hard on her, when he took her arm and yanked her up against his virile body.

"Whether they take us off this case or not, we're still going to work together." His eyes had never burrowed deeper into her soul than they did just now as he held her arm, almost lifted her off her feet, and held her close for another moment before releasing her.

Angela barely managed not to stumble to the side when Jake turned his back on her, unlocked the door, then opened it. Of all times for Jake to tell her he had feelings for her.

"Gentlemen," Angela said, nodding and staring at a tall blond man. There were two men behind him, both in white collared shirts with thin black ties.

"What took you so long to answer the door?" the blond man asked. He didn't look like FBI.

Angela wouldn't let him, or any of these men, unnerve her. "We were busy." She kept a straight face and didn't blush. Let them form their own conclusions over her statement. She and Jake really had been busy. "You might as well come in before you wake my neighbors."

"Why are you in the dark?" The blond was full of questions.

"Because we didn't want anyone knowing we were here." Jake spoke before she could.

Angela closed the door and caught Jake giving the blond an appraising stare. "Bobby," he grunted.

Angela shot her attention to the blond. "The Bobby who works for Mario?" she gasped, instinctively taking a step toward Jake. She'd assumed the other two men were FBI. They looked like FBI. Had Mario sent them over here?

"I've been living in Mandela's home, working undercover, for a year now," Bobby said, giving Angela a punishing stare. "Mandela isn't an easy man to build trust with and I pulled it off, but it took months of enduring his rants and pretending to be humble and assuring him he was right about everything. It wasn't a job many men could have pulled off."

Angela stared at the badge he produced, then forced her insides to calm down. If this Bobby character wanted to blame her or Jake somehow for busting his operation wide open, he would just have to get through his tantrum. She wasn't about to take the fallout because his life might have just been made into more of a living hell.

"You've been working this case almost as long as I have," Angela informed him. "I was in Mexico when the FBI took out Marty Byrd's mansion. I had spoken with an agent while in Tijuana."

"When you were in Mexico you used the name Angela Huxtable."

She nodded. "My mother's last name is now Torres. I borrowed it from her." She wasn't about to feel sorry for an FBI agent if he couldn't figure out she was the same person.

"When Mandela's uncle stumbled upon an old picture on the Internet showing private investigator Huxtable and his daughter, I became suspicious of you using a cover to get close to Mario. Obviously blowing your cover would have been as advantageous as you blowing mine."

"Neither one of us has blown your cover," Jake informed him.

"And it's going to stay that way," Bobby told them, his voice rough and demanding.

Angela hit the light switch on the wall, savoring a moment

of pleasure when Bobby and the others squinted until their eyes adjusted to the light. "Have a seat, gentlemen," she said, walking between all of them to the couch. "There isn't anything in the house, since I haven't been here for a while, but we can at least be comfortable. I'm dying to hear your findings after the bust Jake set up for you."

"We aren't here to share information with you." Bobby didn't sit, and although the two other agents looked as if they might have taken her up on her offer, they held their ground when Bobby didn't budge.

"That's a shame." Angela got comfortable at the corner of her couch.

Jake walked past the men, moving to stand at the edge of the couch behind her. If any of the FBI men had wondered if there was something going on between her and Jake, he removed all doubt. He rested his hand on her shoulder, then brushed his thumb up and down the side of her neck. All three agents dropped their attention to the small action before shifting their gazes elsewhere.

"You've interfered with our investigation," Bobby began, "as I'm sure you're both aware by now. You're both professionals." Bobby's eyes were an almost transparent shade of blue, the light color unique and at the same time almost disturbing. "I'm sure you would react the same way if someone tried stepping on your toes during one of your cases. Not to mention, King, bounty hunting isn't legal in the state of Illinois. You here just for moral support?" he sneered, his eyes darkening.

"Hardly," Jake growled.

Angela reached for his hand and gave it a tight squeeze as she stood. The others weren't sitting, and the charge of adrenaline that suddenly filled the room was as fierce as if she'd just been seriously shocked by electricity. She managed a smile at Bobby, getting the oddest impression he was a bad guy instead of a good guy.

"Why are you here?" Bobby demanded, looking as if he'd love to start trouble.

Jake pulled his hand from Angela's and appeared to grow

in size as he faced all three agents. "You're more than welcome to check the validity of my PI license."

"I take it, since you're ordering us off this case, that you have all the information you need off Mario's computer?" she asked, softening her tone. "The game board, the names of the other players, the locations of the next attack?"

"I have everything I need except the flash drives," Bobby stated, then held his hand out to Angela. "Hand them over."

She had no idea what he was talking about. "Flash drives?" She shook her head. "What flash drives?"

"Don't play stupid with me," he snarled. "You took Mandela's backup flash drives off his desk in his bedroom. You were the only one in there. Mandela is certifiably insane and paranoid. There are hidden cameras in every room of his house. And I went through the security tapes. You took something next to his computer the other night when you were there, and, darling, that is exactly where the flash drives were. If you don't hand them over I'll have you arrested for interfering with a serious FBI investigation."

Bobby stared past Angela at Jake, who in turn watched Bobby. There was a calm, almost eerie expression on Jake's face when Angela shifted to see both men. One thing about being a private investigator, as well as self-employed, was that it was imperative to know every law out there. Angela didn't doubt Bobby was equally versed in what he could and couldn't do right now. Angela and Jake weren't criminals, they hadn't broken any laws, and implying they had infringed on an investigation would be pushing it. They sure as hell hadn't stolen anything off Mario's property.

"Neither one of us took any flash drives," Jake informed Bobby.

Bobby ignored Jake and stared at Angela. "The gig is up," he said, his voice too smooth and soft-spoken. "Any evidence you have now isn't going to do you any good. And I'm sure you don't want our jobs hindered and the game to be allowed to carry on a minute longer than it has to. Give me Mandela's backup flash drives."

Angela shook her head. "Jake is right. I don't know anything about flash drives. You're right also. Neither of us would do anything to allow the game to carry on. I would be thrilled if it ended right now, no matter who ended it."

"I'm sure that isn't the case." Bobby turned toward the door, and the agents behind him stepped out of the way, then also started to leave. "If I find you've lied to me just now, Miss Huxtable, you will go to jail. If you suddenly remember where those backup flash drives might be, turn them over to the police. I might then let this moment of insubordination go unnoticed."

Once again Jake managed to move around her easier than she'd expect a man his size to be able to move in a living room full of people. He had his hand on the doorknob before any of the agents reached for it.

"Satisfy our curiosity," he suggested, leaning against the handle. No one was going to be able to leave until he moved. "Is Mandela arrested right now? You've got his army, right?"

When no one said anything after a few moments Jake glanced her way. She had remained behind all three agents and frowned at the curious look he gave her.

"You've got to understand why we would want to know. Both of us have been dealing with the game, on our own as well as with each other, for quite a while now." Jake let go of the door handle, gesturing, but stood blocking the front door so the three agents faced him. "The kidnapped victims were all in the outbuilding, right?"

Bobby sighed and the two other agents looked at him, appearing indifferent to what information he did or didn't give Jake and Angela. "Yes," Bobby said, sounding exasperated. "They were in the outbuilding and moved the day you showed up to follow them to the airport. And since we're shedding light on matters, how did you know they were going to be moved?"

Jake didn't hesitate. "You probably found it, since you're FBI, but Angela had the outbuilding wired. Of course, she hasn't had a chance to listen to all of it yet, but we did catch the discussion of the hostages being moved."

Bobby looked down, giving Jake's words some thought

and probably trying to remember all conversations that had occurred around and in the outbuilding, since Jake hadn't specified where the bugs were. At the same time, Angela suddenly understood Jake's method of attack. Bobby had suggested, and it had been caught on tape, that he had sex with one of the hostages. He hadn't been forced to, since he had come out of the building and joined Mario when the conversation started. Angela met Jake's serious stare, grinning at him to let him know she understood where he was going with this. None of the agents saw her face, since they were all staring at Jake.

"You'll turn all recordings over to the FBI." Bobby held his ground when he looked at Jake.

"Mandela isn't a stable man." Jake ignored Bobby's order. "How is he handling his favorite female prisoner missing?" Jake asked, shifting his attention to Bobby slowly as he cocked an eyebrow. "Angela told me there was one he was rather infatuated with."

Jake was fishing to see if Mario might have Marianna. He hadn't seen her in the truck, but it was dark and he had said the crates were stacked on top of one another. Angela's heart started pounding ruthlessly in her chest. If Marianna was here in Chicago, the entire FBI and police department wouldn't be able to stop Angela from going after her.

"Mario knows his army is gone," Bobby said, ignoring Jake's comment and instead turning a cold stare on Angela. "He thinks you're responsible."

"Why would he think that?" she asked, understanding now why he hadn't tried calling her after she left him at the restaurant. Although in the past when she'd disappeared, he'd come on even stronger.

"Probably because of how you left him at dinner."

"That was the FBI's fault, not mine," she pointed out.

"True." Bobby tapped his lip. "Mandela formed his own conclusions. I didn't correct him."

"Is it true you only brought in nine of the hostages after the raid?" Angela didn't shift her attention but watched Bobby's reaction to her question.

"You have quite a bit of information, young lady." Bobby narrowed his gaze on her, but his pompous attitude was too annoying for her to feel threatened by him. "Apparently Mandela didn't tell you one of the hostages died last week. I wasn't able to prevent it. Mandela intended on replacing him, which he has been able to do too easily. It's terrifying. After he had one of his women order two men Mandela dubbed as idiots to drive into a brick wall out in L.A., which killed both of them, he replaced both men the next day."

Bobby turned from Angela, pulling a business card out of his pocket, and handed it to Jake as he approached. "Give us a call when you leave town," he informed Jake.

Jake didn't hesitate but opened the door for all three men. Angela stood there, remaining quiet as she watched the agents disappear out her front door, then Jake close and lock it behind her. It took her a moment to catch Jake's cold grin when she finally looked up at him.

"What?"

His grin widened as he closed in on her. "I do believe I know where your sister is."

Chapter Eighteen

"We're headed back to Mandela's place." Jake took her hands in his, lifting them, then holding them as he squeezed. "Your sister is there somewhere."

"It's a crime scene. No way are we going to get in there." His enthusiasm was contagious, and she searched his face, wanting to understand everything he was thinking at the moment. "What makes you think Marianna is there?"

"It might not be marked as a crime scene. Mandela hasn't been arrested and there are two more members of the game who will disappear and never be found if they get wind that the FBI is crawling around Mandela." Jake rubbed his thumb over the back of her hand, his calloused thumb igniting sparks as he caressed her flesh. "And you played him very well, my dear. It's an old trick but never fails. Make them believe you know more than they do and they always give out more information."

"What did he say that makes you think she's at Mandela's house?"

"The day before we met with your father, there was a news clip about two men driving into the wall of a popular night-club. It grabbed our attention because it referred to slave juice. Natasha, who is my cousin and our office manager," he added quickly, as if he suspected mentioning another woman's name would upset Angela, "watched the news clip with me. When did you say your sister arrived in L.A.?"

"On Sunday," she said, frowning.

Jake released one of her hands but guided her to her couch. When he sat, he pulled her in next to him but adjusted both of them so they faced each other. "Bobby just told us Mandela was responsible for that terrible accident. He made two members of his army that he didn't think were good enough for whatever reasons drive into that wall and kill themselves."

"Seems a bit dramatic." She shook her head, doubting she'd ever get accustomed to the level of evil that existed inside Mario. "If they weren't performing the way he wanted them to, why didn't he just kill them instead of making such a public scene over their deaths?"

Jake's smile was absolutely wicked. His eyes glowed as if he'd just solved everything. "Maybe because he was testing out a new member of his army he'd just picked up."

Angela stared at Jake a moment before understanding kicked in. "You think he kidnapped Marianna from the airport and made her kill those two men?" Angela almost jumped off the couch suddenly incredibly sick to her stomach.

"It's a running theory. Bobby was lying to us and feeding us half-truths. I'm anxious to find out why."

"What is your plan?" Angela's heart was pounding so hard she could barely catch her breath. "And why are you looking at me like that?"

"Like what?" he asked, with an innocent purr that sounded dangerous as hell. He intentionally gave her a slow once-over before staring into her eyes. "Darling, I'm sure every man with a heartbeat would look at you like is," he added.

"What is your plan?" she asked, trying to look stern.

"Anyone ever tell you how adorable you are when you're dying to dive into a hunt?"

Oddly enough, her father had told her that more than once over the years to get under her skin. He hadn't used the word "hunt," but the meaning had been the same.

"Is there a reason you aren't telling me this plan?" she said, giving Jake a cool look although her insides were starting to boil.

"Maybe I like teasing and torturing you." His grin turned roguish and he flicked his finger at her nipple.

An electric current zapped from her breast straight through her until it swelled between her legs. Angela grabbed his wrist, damn near growling at him. He'd told her regardless of how this case ended, they were going to keep working together. She didn't know if he meant in her town or his. Would she be able to handle going out to L.A., where so many women obviously sniffed after him like bitches in heat? It seemed a lot more logical to her for him to remain here. That wasn't something they were going to discuss right now, though. All that mattered now was finding her sister and ending the game.

When she'd remained quiet another moment, Jake began explaining: "Let's lock this place up and head over to Mandela's. I'm not convinced your cover has been blown with him, but we'll find out."

"I'd hate to find out the hard way," she said, moving to stand.

Jake grabbed her and yanked her up against his muscular chest. "You've got the best backup in the world, sweetheart," he growled, wrapping his arms around her and pressing his mouth against hers. The kiss added to the torture already ransacking her body and ended too soon. "I will never let anything happen to you."

"I've got your back, too." She initiated the next kiss.

Jake was possessive, aggressive, demanding—traits she'd always believed she would find annoying in a man. Fantasies of men in shining armor dragging a lady into their lair and demanding her submission were hot but only if they remained fantasies. In real life Angela wanted more control.

At the moment, though, she could barely move. Muscles as solid as steel and stronger than she was trapped her against the most virile body she'd ever known. Hell, that she'd ever fantasized about. Jake went beyond commanding submission. He took her where he wanted her faster than her brain had time to react.

Every inch of her sizzled in response. If she could have moved her hands, raised her arms, and wrapped them around him, Angela probably would have tried pulling him closer. As it was, the kiss was hot, sensual, and filled with heated promises that made her insides swell and pulse with need.

Jake sighed when he ended the kiss. Angela blinked, opening her eyes in time to see his heavily hooded gaze. His actions had been rough but ended with a soft sigh that sounded so gentle. He was a man of extremes, offering everything from hot, aggressive, feverish moments to gentle, soothing, and sensual gestures. This was a man who walked into her life with a stream of women chasing after him. He came across as rough and larger than life, with his incredibly muscular weight lifter's body and a stature so much taller than most men. Yet he was capable of slinking through yards and dark shadows and spying on others without being seen. Jake was well-rounded, intelligent, with a craving for the hunt and solving a mystery.

She sucked in a deep breath, tasting him on her lips and inhaling his unique smell, one of soap and that all-man aroma that turned her on as much as the rest of him did. Looking away before he could make eye contact, Angela feared she was falling hard for him. It scared her to death and she wasn't sure she'd be able to handle it if she learned that it was just the hunt that turned Jake on. Once he caught what he chased down, though, would he still be interested?

"Better get going," she said, whispering, since his face was still mere inches from hers. "What are we doing once we get there?"

Jake moved his hand and rubbed his thumb along her jawline. "We're going on a hunt. You've got your gun?"

Half an hour later the sun shone brightly on the horizon, giving promises of another hot and muggy day. She was grateful to be able to wear her hair up again, which was how she usually wore it while staking out a property. Wearing it down to impress Mario had damn near driven her crazy, although not as bad as Mario had. Jake slowed in Angela's small midnight blue Probe, which she'd been impressed he was able to drive considering his size. It had been parked at her home while she'd been undercover at the Drake. Jake's rental car had probably already been acknowledged as his. No one would know her Probe, though, unless they ran the tags.

Jake slowed as he and Angela rounded the corner by Mario's mansion. He parked on the edge of the blacktop road a couple houses down from Mario's. Angela got out on her side before Jake was around the front of the car.

"Let's go." He pulled her toward the house directly across the street.

"Why are we going this way?"

"To confuse anyone who might be watching."

Angela was continually impressed by how easily and fluidly Jake moved for a man well over six foot. They remained alongside each other, moving between Mario's rod iron fence and a tight row of spruce trees that lined the neighbor's property. Angela had to break into a pretty good sprint to keep up with Jake and didn't slow until he did after reaching the back side of Mario's home.

Jake pulled her to the ground when one of three garage doors began opening.

"I think it's Marco," she whispered, lying flat in the grass next to Jake, propped up on her elbows and with her chin resting in her hands.

Jake had assumed the same position. "If he leaves, how many would still be in the house?"

"Well," she began, giving it some thought. "If Bobby isn't in there and Marco leaves it might very well just be Mario inside."

"Perfect." Jake kept his attention narrowly focused on the back of the house as he spoke. "And even more perfect if Marco leaves the garage door up when he leaves."

"If there are FBI watching I bet they aren't back here."
Angela glanced around her and Jake, taking in the tall trees
between the homes and the large yards that separated each
property. "They would be watching the garage, though."

"Let's go!" Jake hissed, leaping off the ground and grabbing her as he sprang to his feet.

"What?" Angela stumbled, trying to keep up and maintain her footing when Jake hurried toward the open garage
door. Marco wasn't even halfway down the driveway, although the way the drive curved around and headed to the
front of the house and the street, he wouldn't see them by
now. "That was a bit of a close call," she hissed under her
breath when they slid into the garage.

"I wanted to hurry in case the door was on an automatic
timer." Jake moved to the sidewall of the garage.

As if to prove him right, a humming kicked on, then the
garage door began closing. Angela would be damned if
she'd let Jake see how on edge her nerves were. She hadn't
spent a lot of the four years she'd been a private investigator
breaking into people's homes. The urge to leap toward Jake,
ensure her safety, was a hard one to stifle. Angela moved
quickly but then stepped in front of him, looking at the closed
door that would lead into the house.

She'd never seen or heard of anyone else being in the
house other than the few men Mario had waiting on him.
Things could have changed since his army had been busted.
In spite of her heart pounding in her chest, Angela had to
show Jake she didn't cower when things got scary. Not to
mention, if Marianna was somewhere in this house she'd
endured a lot more terror than anything Angela was about to
experience sneaking through Mario's home.

When she gripped the doorknob to the door leading into
the house, Jake put his hand on her shoulder. "Which way
are you headed?"

"I've never been in the kitchen. Most garage doors open
into a kitchen or utility room. I won't know until I'm inside."

"We head inside, but I'm going first. No offense, sweetheart, but if we have company on the other side of the door,

I can take them down easier than you can." He was still whispering, but the gentle way he spoke to her made her think he'd guessed her determination to show him she could handle this kind of situation as well as he could.

Angela realized he probably did a lot more sneaking around as a bounty hunter than she did investigating. And he had a point: Jake *could* take someone down a lot easier than she could. She nodded once, stepped to the side, and stuck close to his backside when he opened the door and entered the house.

It was quiet, almost too quiet. The times she'd been here with Mario he had spent a lot of time yelling at his hired help. Her nerves had always been frazzled, and she'd focused most of her attention on making sure his hands weren't on her any more than she could tolerate. But now, as she and Jake walked through a very large kitchen, complete with two stoves and ovens and large, deep sinks on both sides of the room, she would have sworn there wasn't a soul around.

Jake glanced over his shoulder, nodding at her. It was time for her to take the lead. She knew the layout of the house, and he didn't. Angela stepped lightly, although the house was well built and floorboards didn't squeak under the soft, thick carpet when they moved down a hallway. Although she'd had a tour, she wasn't sure where they were until they entered the large room with the sliding glass doors. She paused a moment to stare at the outbuilding, which looked as it always did, visible through the doors.

Angela looked away first. "Mario's room is upstairs," she whispered,

"Is that where you want to start?"

For some reason, she hadn't thought of starting anywhere else. Angela wasn't sure what drew her to his room, but she nodded and turned to the stairs. They were halfway up them when someone opened a door downstairs.

Angela's heart exploded in her chest, and she froze, suddenly incapable of lifting her foot to continue climbing the stairs. Jake grabbed her, almost lifting her up the remaining steps, then pressed her flat against the wall at the top of the stairs next to him.

"God damn, it's hot out there." A male's voice boomed through the downstairs, and heavy footsteps sounded against bare wood floors. It was Bobby.

Angela's nerves twisted into painful knots inside her as a moist sheen of perspiration broke out over her flesh. She swore she heard someone else say something, but if she did that person was whispering. When Bobby responded with a sharper, hissing whisper, she tried to keep her legs from trembling.

"Mario? You here?" Again Bobby yelled into the house, his voice creating an echo as it boomed off walls.

No one answered and the whispering resumed. They were getting closer.

"Check his room first." Bobby was at the bottom of the stairs.

She looked wide-eyed up at Jake when he turned his head and stared down at her. He didn't speak but instead mouthed the words, *Don't move.*

Angela wouldn't have guessed his next move. She also didn't understand why he didn't want her moving, especially when a couple sets of footsteps began ascending the stairs. She was trembling so hard it would have been impossible to move. Her tongue was stuck to the top of her mouth as her heart throbbed in her head, her chest, and throughout the rest of her body. Her eyes burned from staring wide-eyed in Jake's direction, not daring to move.

The footsteps neared the top of the stairs, and Jake leapt out in front of the two men, not making a sound as he lifted his leg and kicked both of them back down the stairs. It made a terrible crashing sound, accompanied by howling and cursing as they tumbled backward, head over feet, until they crashed at the bottom of the steps. Jake remained at the top of the steps, staring down at them, his hardened expression terrifying, making Angela damn glad he was on her side.

Jake remained where he was, not moving, or looking in her direction but watching, staring down the stairs, until finally, slowly, he walked to where she stood, her backside stuck to the wall.

"They aren't moving. At least one of them is dead. It's apparent by the way he's laying." Jake didn't look remorseful over killing a man.

Angela had shot both men and women before but knew without a doubt she'd never killed anyone. "I wonder why they were here. If Bobby was whispering it seems as if he didn't want anyone knowing he was here. I wonder why."

"That thought crossed my mind, too." They were still whispering, and Jake put his hand in the middle of her back when she stepped away from the wall. "I have a feeling it has to do with flash drives."

"I think there was a plastic case next to Mario's computer in his bedroom," she said, staring in Jake's face as she continued whispering. "I never gave it much thought, but there wasn't much on the desk other than the computer and the case next to it. I'm not sure if those were the backup files or not."

Angela needed to lead the way to Mario's room, which required crossing the top of the flight of stairs. She could point to the closed door at the other end of the hall. Jake would willingly shield her and lead the way. She sucked in a breath, looking past Jake. She was strong, capable of handling terrifying situations to learn the truth and solve a case. Just because she had a man the size of Hercules next to her, Angela wouldn't grow weak and allow him to protect her.

"Do you want to tell me why you knocked two FBI agents down a flight of stairs" she added.

Jake wasn't watching her but staring at the floor, his head tilted, as if he was listening.

"What?" she whispered.

He held his hand up, waited a heartbeat, then shook his head. "Nothing. Trying to tell if Mario is in his room. I'm not hearing anything."

If Mario had been in his room, he would have come racing out the moment he heard the two men falling down the stairs. If anyone were anywhere in the house, they would have heard it and acted. Jake and Angela very well could be alone in the house; in which case where was Mario?

Angela's heart pounded hard enough she doubted she'd hear any small sounds around her. She started down the hall, moving past Jake and stepping into the open so she could see down the flight of stairs. Maybe she shouldn't have looked down, but human curiosity was sometimes stronger than fear.

Her heart swelled into her throat, and in spite of her determination to remain strong and handle any blow this case threw her way, she gripped her throat with her hand, fighting to keep the bile down. Bobby and a man she didn't recognize lay at the bottom of the stairs. Bobby was sprawled out on top of the other man, motionless. The man underneath Bobby was twisted in an unnatural position, which gave her the sensation of fingernails scratching a chalkboard. She shuddered, her insides lurching up her esophagus.

"Keep walking." Jake's strong hands were warm when he gripped her shoulders from behind and guided her past the stairwell.

Angela's body still pumped with adrenaline, and she hated her legs being wobbly. Especially when she felt Jake's strength through his fingers as he continued gripping her shoulders as she led them to the end of the hall.

There wasn't much time to give herself a convincing pep talk, but she tried anyway. It was too important, especially in the heat of the moment, that Jake knew she was strong enough to run the show. If he grew suspicious at all that she might have a weakness or get squirmish when it was most important she remain clearheaded and observant, he would start acting too protective and demanding around her. She'd already decided she liked this guy, liked him a lot, maybe more than a lot, and if he turned into a macho he-man he would turn her off.

Not to mention, she ran the show. She could handle situations like this. Even if the sight of broken bodies lying twisted in impossible positions made her sick to her stomach, it sure as hell didn't mean she needed to be protected from every ugly part of life.

Angela walked without making a sound, moving in on Mario's closed bedroom door. Her pep talk to herself helped a bit, and she reached for Mario's bedroom door.

Jake's grip on her shoulder tightened.

"Stop that," she whispered, looking over her shoulder at him. "Keep your head clear and let's do this."

The look on his face didn't help her stomach settle. She turned, letting go of the door. He looked the way he had before, when he'd been listening to the silent house. Instead of questioning him, Angela listened as well, trying to hear past the blood rushing in her veins from her heart pounding so hard in her chest. There were house sounds, the hum of air-conditioning, but nothing that came across as odd.

She snapped her attention to Jake's when he looked at her. "I'm hearing things," he whispered.

"Quit it," she snapped, trying to give him a stern look, but found new sensations whipping around the tension and nerves already ransacked inside her.

"I'll go in first." Jake stroked her cheek, his gaze warming as he stared at her.

She gave a firm shake of her head. "You're backup, remember?" she whispered, and spun around, gripped the doorknob, and turned it.

Angela wasn't ready for a naked woman to scream and race into her. It took Angela aback, shocked, so she didn't dodge when the woman swung a baseball bat.

"Angela!" Jake howled behind her.

At the same time, a cracking sounded so loud it ruptured her eardrum. Pain erupted in her head, and she staggered, her knees burning against the carpet when she fell. She gripped her head, but the naked woman was trampling her, still screaming.

"Angela!" Jake yelled again.

She wanted to snap at him to shut up. Every time he yelled, it pierced her brain, and she already had the worst headache of her life. In spite of some crazy woman stomping on top of her and Jake ready to fall on top of her, crawling out of their way seemed impossible.

Angela reached for her head and pulled her fingers away, confused as to why they were sticky. Everything was growing darker, but she swore when she looked up she saw Mario standing in his bedroom, grinning cruelly at her.

Chapter Nineteen

Jake grabbed the naked woman, who was still screaming. She had thick, long hair that was damp. He breathed in an array of aromas, shampoo and perfumes, as if she'd just bathed and hadn't bothered dressing when she decided to attack.

"Stop it," he snarled, wrapping his arm around her bare waist and grabbing the baseball bat out of her hand. He almost dropped her when she went limp in his arms.

"They are a pair of feisty bitches, aren't they?" Mario's smooth accent matched the fresh khaki pants and pullover shirt he wore. He looked as if he were getting ready to spend the day on a yacht.

Jake held the woman with her backside pressed against his chest and her feet dangling as he maintained his grip and stared over her at the gun Mario held aimed at him.

"Are you the doting boyfriend?" Mario snarled, moving closer until he stood dangerously close to Angela.

She lay crumpled on the floor in the doorway to Mario's bedroom with her hand touching her head. Whether she was unconscious or not Jake couldn't tell. He prayed if she was just enduring one hell of a headache that she remained still. It would be easier handling this situation without having to deal with two hurt women. If he guessed right, the woman he held against him was drugged on slave juice.

"Is this Marianna?" he asked, staring over the woman's mop of long, black hair at Mario.

"She is *puttana*," Mario spit. "Any other identity no longer matters."

"*Puttana*?" Jake kept his attention on the gun Mario continued pointing at him as he compared Spanish to Italian. "Slut? That is hardly a name for a lady."

"She is a *puttana*, just as this one is." Mario raised his gun, pointing it at Jake's head, and squatted and grabbed Angela's arm.

She moaned slightly when he began dragging her into his bedroom.

"Don't even try it," Jake snarled, lunging forward. He adjusted his grip on the naked woman, prepared to drag her and Angela out of there if necessary.

"Have that one for a while. I would say from what I know of both of them it's a fair trade." Mario's grin was pure evil as he tugged on Angela, yanking her across the floor and dropping her at his feet inside his room. He straightened, aiming his gun lower, so if he fired he would hit the woman and Jake. "*Puttana,* kick! Attack that bastard holding you."

The woman in Jake's arms came to life, flipping against him, swinging her arms and legs while her hair flew madly around her.

"Hold still," Jake hissed, almost dropping her as Mario's bedroom door slammed in Jake's face.

The woman fell, her feet landing on the floor, but not too surprisingly, she didn't try to run. Jake stared past her at the closed door, not liking the idea of Angela being alone in that room with Mario for even a minute.

The naked woman stood, not moving or even bothering to move her thick strands of hair from her face. She looked like a wild woman, crazed and drugged from years of institutionalization. Jake knew his opinion derived from too many movies but didn't have time to learn the woman's story, other than knowing he couldn't leave her standing there naked. Jake knew enough about slave juice to know the woman, drugged or not, could think rationally deep inside her mind, but she was unable to take over her own actions. If she was drugged, she would do whatever she was told to do until the drug wore off.

He ripped off his shirt and pulled it over her head. "Put this on," he instructed, not having time to dress her. "And straighten your hair."

Jake didn't bother watching to see if she'd comply. Already the woman had done as she was told. Jake grabbed the doorknob, giving it a ruthless shake when he discovered the door was locked.

"Open the goddamn door, Mandela!" Jake bellowed, shaking the door harder. "You know I could break it down with little effort."

"Please do. It would make my day knowing you would hold the memory of your girlfriend getting her head blown off for the rest of your life."

"You lay one hand on Angela and you will suffer a long time before you beg for your death to come swiftly," Jake roared, shaking the door hard enough he heard the door frame around it creak under the pressure.

There wasn't time to play games with an insane Mafia lord. Jake stepped back, sizing up the door before lunging at it with his shoulder. Mario actually screamed worse than a hysterical woman when Jake and the door went flying into the bedroom.

"You aren't going to take what's mine!" Mandela bellowed, grabbing Angela's shirt and dragging her like a limp rag doll around the side of his bed. He pointed his gun at Jake, pulling the trigger. There wasn't a silencer on the gun, and the explosion in the bedroom was excruciating. "Mess with a Mandela and you die! It happens every time!" he screamed.

Jake felt as if he did an impressive roll when he hit the ground and tumbled around the desk to the other side of the bed. The bullet went into the wall alongside him, missing Jake by a fair distance. Either Mandela wasn't that good of a shot or he'd cracked under the pressure of knowing he was destroyed. That the man had remained quiet in his room

with the naked woman, not responding to the men tumbling
down the flight of stairs, proved he wasn't reacting to things
around him normally. More than likely he knew he was
going down, but his ego couldn't handle the knowledge.
Jake had seen men, and women, crack under that awareness
before.

"Put down the gun." Jake remained on the floor as he
reached into his pant pocket for his phone. "You aren't getting
out of this one, Mandela. Think about it. You'd do better not
to go down with more murder charges against you."

"Fucking prick!" Mandela snarled. "I'm not going down."

"You've already fallen," Jake said, flipping his phone
open and dialing 911. An operator answered immediately,
asking what his emergency was. Jake rattled off Mandela's
address.

"What the fuck are you doing?" Mandela screamed, his
accent thickening.

When Mandela leapt onto his bed, Jake rolled to the end of
the bed and began crawling toward Angela. "Send a squad
over here immediately," Jake hissed into the phone, ignoring
the excited questions the operator had begun asking him.
"I'm being shot at and we have two women down. Hurry!"

The operator insisted he remain on the line until officers
showed up. Mandela fired again, missed again, and helped
encourage the 911 operator to assure Jake there were officers
within a few blocks and they would be on the scene in minutes. He pulled his Glock from the back of his pants, gripping
it as he scurried across the floor. Jake hadn't seen them but he
felt safe to say the FBI was watching the house. The second
they got wind of a 911 call, they would be inside the place in
droves.

"Angela," Jake whispered, keeping the line open as he
held the phone in one hand and the gun in the other and hurried toward her crumpled body.

"Stay away from her! She's mine!" Mario leapt around
the bed, standing over Jake.

Jake hurried to his feet, standing in front of Angela, who
was rolled into a ball on the floor near the end of the bed. He

faced the end of the gun, wishing to hell local PD, or the FBI, would show up soon.

Jake raised his gun, not surprised when Mario didn't look at it but continued glaring at Jake with eyes so cold and dark it looked as if the man might never have had a soul.

"Better shoot now," Jake said, deciding for a calm, soft tone. He swore Angela groaned from the floor behind him. Even damn near knocked out, she still tried getting her two cents in. Jake hoped he would live to have the chance to laugh over that fact. "You heard me call 911. Cops are going to be here within the next couple minutes. And trust me, Mandela, they hurry to get to a home in this neighborhood."

Jake didn't have a clue whether that was true or not. But they were in a very wealthy part of town. Mandela was renting this home and probably hadn't lived here long enough to know whether Jake spoke the truth or not.

Mandela sneered at Jake, not looking away from his face when he shifted his aim so fast Jake didn't catch him do it. In the next moment, Jake's Glock flew out of his hand as a fierce sting shot up his fingers. He looked long enough to see blood stream down his hand.

"Did you really think I was a bad shot?" Mandela hissed, his accent even thicker. "Move away from Angela. Do it now!" Mandela fired again, this time aiming at Jake's feet.

Jake did a quick dance, leaping backward over Angela. Mandela dove at her, grabbing her hair and tugging her toward him. She groaned louder, moving her hand, although not fast enough to show she was okay and faking it, but Mandela pulled harder.

"Police!" a man bellowed downstairs.

Mandela pulled Angela to him, aiming his gun at Jake. "It's all over, my friend," Mandela snarled, and moved the gun so that he aimed it at Angela's head.

Jake didn't think for a moment Mandela wouldn't pull that trigger. "Upstairs!" he screamed, and leapt at Mandela.

The two men rolled backward, Mandela proving to be rather strong for being a man at least half a foot shorter than Jake. Mandela's gun fired, but Jake didn't feel any intense pain and had to believe the wall had been shot again. Although he swore he heard feet pounding the floor as they raced up the stairs, he wouldn't wait for the police to save the day.

"Give it up," he growled, fighting for Mandela's gun.

The man's face was contorted with fury, and he managed to keep his gun in his hand.

"Police!" a man yelled from behind them.

Several hands grabbed Jake, managing to lift and pull him backward. Jake stared down at Mandela, who lay flat on his back, and didn't look away in time to miss seeing the man shoot his brains out.

Angela sat on her couch, grinning at her half sister. Marianna had a melodic laugh. She sat at the opposite end of the couch, cross-legged, her pretty face glowing as she stared at Angela.

"So the game is over?" Marianna asked, glancing from Angela to Jake when he entered the room carrying three bottles of beer.

"I just got off the phone with Dad." Angela curled her legs, shifting so she could see Jake, who sat in the oversized chair facing her couch. "The FBI took out the other two players in the game. Over thirty kidnapped victims are returning home, or have already returned home."

"I wasn't sure if my life got better, or worse, when Bobby started telling Mario he was giving me my dose of slave juice but didn't really give it to me." Marianna stared at her bottle after accepting it from Jake. "I had to pretend I was under the influence, which was so hard to do when I was terrified I would be found out."

"I'm so sorry you had to go through all of this," Angela said, her voice cracking as she leaned forward and took her sister's hand. "Apparently Bobby was keeping the doses of slave juice you were supposed to get. He was going to argue he was confiscating them, but apparently he confessed while in the hospital he thought he could sell the doses on the black market. It seems he decided somewhere along the line while living with Mario for a year that he wasn't getting paid enough by the Bureau to endure the undercover work he was doing."

"The creep," Marianna muttered.

Jake fought not to look too sympathetic. He'd learned over the past week that Marianna and her sister were a lot alike in spite of having different fathers and spending years growing up as only daughters. Marianna didn't want pity for what she'd endured. She'd shared quite a bit of the nightmares she'd been through during the time she was under the influence of slave juice. All of them agreed the worst part of the drug was remembering everything once the drug wore off. It would take Marianna a while to come to terms with having ordered two men to their deaths.

"There won't be any slave juice showing up anywhere for quite a long time, if ever," Jake said, keeping his expression serious when both women looked at him as he sat in the La-Z-Boy and stretched his legs out in front of him. Both were so incredibly beautiful in their own way. Where Angela glowed with intelligence and determination, her younger sister held on to an aura of innocence and wonder, in spite of the hell she was recovering from. "Evelyn Van Cooper will be going away for quite a few years and apparently was responsible for distributing the drug to dealers around the country. Hopefully none of them tried breaking it down and learning its recipe. Authorities still haven't able to get out of her how she created the drug."

"May that knowledge rot in hell along with her," Angela said, raising her beer bottle in a toast.

"Here, here," Jake and Marianna said in unison.

"You know you're going to have to keep him in the family." Marianna spoke with a soft, fluent sound that added to her beauty.

"Makes me sound like I'm a pet," Jake grumbled with his beer bottle to his lips.

He already knew he wasn't going anywhere. If he ever did, Angela was going with him.

"I do believe my little sister has a crush on you," Angela suggested.

There wasn't a hint of jealousy on her face. Jake noticed any woman who gave him a second look faced the wrath of Angela, whether she knew it or not. Angela saw no wrong in her little sister and adored her with open and unadulterated love.

"I meant that you'd have to keep in the family any man who meets your sister naked," Marianna explained.

"And swinging a baseball bat," he reminded her, then sipped at his beer, enjoying the glowing happiness on both ladies' faces.

"Lord, yes!" Marianna giggled, shaking her head. "Swinging a baseball bat and knocking out her older sister."

"Don't remind me." Angela gingerly brushed her fingers over the side of her head. She had one hell of a lump that was still detectable, although she wasn't complaining of headaches as much as she had the first few days after they'd returned to her home.

"So you're saying a man who meets my little sister naked and swinging a bat, causing bodily harm to her sister, shouldn't be allowed to get away?" Angela asked, staring at Marianna, although she grinned broadly.

"Yes. Exactly." Marianna brushed her thick hair behind her shoulder and sipped her beer. Even when she made a face she was as adorable as they came. "How can you two drink this stuff?" she complained. "Beer in my country is so much better."

Angela and Jake laughed, grinning at each other. Jake watched Angela's eyes darken as she held on to his gaze. He hadn't pressed her since they'd returned home, but the way she'd been looking at him all day he was wondering if her head injury had healed enough she might want to make love later that night.

"And if he has an available brother he should be sent to me immediately," Marianna continued.

"I'm afraid I'm the last of the King sons who is still available."

Angela stood, her expression shifting from a broad grin to a hard glare as she moved in on Jake. He wasn't sure if choosing her overstuffed La-Z-Boy chair to sit in was such a wise idea when she stalked toward him, bending over as she grabbed the hair on the side of his head.

"Excuse me, mister," Angela whispered, her pretty eyes flashing as she stared at him. "You're not available."

Jake grinned, grabbing her and enjoying her squeal as he pulled her into his lap. "Are you asking for a commitment, sweetheart?"

Angela stilled and he adjusted her, cradling her against his chest as he placed his beer on the side table next to his chair. He took her beer from her, too, then brushed her hair from her face, watching her expression sober.

"Don't either of you dare ask me to leave the room," Marianna announced, remaining cuddled in the corner of the couch, grinning at both of them. "After what I've been through I am entitled to witness happiness and love at its best."

"Love?" Jake whispered, focusing on Angela.

She didn't try getting out of his lap and, in fact, relaxed further as she stared up at him, displaying the emotion he'd just suggested.

"Is that what we're feeling, sweetheart?" he asked, still murmuring, although he didn't care whether Angela's younger sister heard him or not.

"I think so, maybe," Angela said, her voice cracking. "I've never felt this before."

"Me, either," he told her, positive of his answer. But he knew what he felt for Angela was real. "I love you."

The way her face lit up, he thought for a moment she might leap at him and braced himself for the attack.

"Jake," she muttered, her voice cracking. "You live in California."

"I'm going to live wherever you live, lady," he said, not hesitating.

She let out a squeal so loud he actually missed the moment when she leapt at him, banging his nose when she wrapped her arms around him, laughing and crying at the same time.

"I love you, Jake King. I swear I've loved you since I first saw you."

"Same here, darling," he said, wrapping his arms around her as her hair fluttered over her face, barely allowing him to see Marianna clasp her hands and laugh behind them. He closed his eyes, holding the woman he loved. Jake finally knew what it felt like to believe there was only one woman on the planet, and it was the best damned feeling he'd ever felt in his life.

RUN WILD

"Cold-hearted city girl," Matilda muttered as she bustled down the stairs and returned to the kitchen. "Oh, Trent, there you are. Well, she's here. Can't say much about her, but she's checked in."

Trent Oakley helped himself to Matilda's coffee, then blew on the hot brew. "You can't say much about her?" He knew Matilda well enough to know the woman would have a lot to say about anyone, even if they'd just met.

Matilda pursed her lips, wiping her hands on her apron as her chin puckered into tiny dimples. "You know what the first thing is she says to me?"

"What's that?" Trent leaned against the wooden counter-top on the large island in the middle of Matilda's large kitchen, getting comfortable.

"She informs me she isn't here for a week. She tells me as smooth as can be she's got an appointment tomorrow and will be leaving right after that. Heartless woman," Matilda muttered, turning her back on Trent as she began clattering pots in her large lower kitchen drawer until she found one large enough to boil a bag of potatoes. Hefting it to her kitchen sink, she turned on the water. "I showed her to the Emerald Room."

He wouldn't get her started. Matilda would offer good

insight on Natasha King once the woman was settled. All Matilda would need was time spent with her, possibly over dinner, and Trent would have all the details on her that he couldn't find online. Matilda was a pro at getting people to talk, then forming strong opinions about them. With Matilda it was love or hate, no middle ground.

Trent didn't know enough about Natasha, yet. He'd done a background check on her. Natasha King lived in Los Angeles, had attended a two-year community college, lived in an apartment that was priced way too high, and had worked for her uncle, the renowned bounty hunter, Greg King, for three years now. Trent guessed Natasha's father was Greg's brother, which would undoubtedly make things a bit trickier. It wouldn't take him long, once he sat and visited with Natasha, to learn how well she, and possibly the rest of her family, upheld the law.

Trent knew a good-looking woman when he saw one, and Natasha blew any notions he had on beauty out of the water. From just her driver's license picture, it was obvious she was hot as hell. There weren't any other photographs of her online anywhere. Trent knew she was twenty-six years old, five feet, seven inches tall, and one hundred fifty pounds, although no one stated their true weight for their license. She had a sultry smile and smooth-looking tan skin that definitely wasn't the same shade as her eyes.

Of course, Matilda wouldn't see her with the same eyes Trent would, which was why he valued the older woman's opinion and knew it would take little to get it out of her. Trent sipped his coffee, then took a bigger gulp and enjoyed its rich, smooth texture. It was already too cold in the mornings and not warming up much by afternoon, a sign of an early and hard winter around the corner. He put his cup on her counter as he watched Matilda move methodically in her kitchen.

"Good coffee," he muttered.

"Thank you." She started running a very sharp knife through potatoes.

Trent hadn't been able to stop the gossip from flowing

once the newspaper reported the murder at Trinity Ranch. He knew almost everyone in Weaverville, having been born on his family's ranch north of town, but reporters flew in, camped out, and didn't give a rat's ass about his investigation, other than to question why he hadn't caught the murderer yet. Trent had his methods. This wasn't his first case and it wasn't the first time he'd dealt with snooping reporters.

When his father passed, no one had questioned Trent filling his shoes. He was elected as sheriff almost unanimously and learned, as his father had, to use gossip to his advantage instead of trying to keep a lid on it. There wasn't any reason to add to speculation, though, when he'd told Matilda to reserve a room for Natasha King. Matilda made her own assumptions when she believed Natasha would know any details about what had transpired over the past month.

There was a crunch of gravel alongside the house, and Matilda left her task of peeling and slicing potatoes as she scuttled through the doorway leading into the dining room. Long narrow windows lined the far wall and allowed her to see whoever might be driving to her back parking lot.

"Jerry Packard," she mumbled, immediately fussing with her hair. "You fill your Thermos with hot coffee before you leave, Sheriff," she said, waving her hand over her shoulder as she hurried into her outer office.

Trent didn't bother saying anything. Matilda and Jerry, the mailman, would stand out there at the counter and gossip a good thirty minutes. Natasha King couldn't have timed her arrival better.

Trent topped off his coffee and walked through the large, old house. Matilda did a wonderful job of keeping the place authentic-looking. The long, narrow windows in the dining and living room had thin, veneer curtains hanging, which allowed natural light to flood over shiny hardwood floors and antique furniture in both rooms.

An older couple, probably in their sixties, glanced up from the loveseat, where they sat glancing over brochures. Trent nodded, wondering how many guests Matilda had at the moment. He made a note to find out as he turned into the formal entryway and headed for the stairs.

Pearl's was a three-story house built in the late 1800s and on the National Registry of historic houses, as were many in Weaverville. The community was proud of their history and did a good job of preserving it. They also relied heavily on revenue from tourists who came here to escape fast-paced city life and stressful jobs.

More than once, Trent considered kicking the dust from the place off his boots and heading out for some of that big-city life. He wasn't sure what kept him here. He'd been sheriff for six years and, as far as anyone in town was concerned, would be until he retired, just like his father had been. Maybe it was his mother's blood. She had always yearned for big-city lights and fast-moving cars. Trent's father, Bill Oakley, had done his best to oblige Sharon Oakley. When Trent was ten, Sharon asked for a divorce. Bill never denied her anything, and he didn't fight the divorce. The only thing Sharon didn't get as she left town without turning back was custody of Trent.

There were times when Trent wondered how different his life would have been if he'd taken off when his father retired, after his third heart attack. He could have gone to college, seen the country, hit the road, and enjoyed his youth. But the town pressured him to fill the role of the new sheriff. Trent might have been able to ignore their persuasion, but it was hard as hell telling his father no when he pressured Trent as well. Three months after he was sworn in, his mother died of cancer. It had hit so hard and fast there was no saving her. His father passed away less than a year later.

After burying his father on their property next to his mother, Trent thought he'd remain sheriff a year or so, then take off for those big-city lights his mother had always talked about. Six years later he was still here, the longing to see the world not quite as strong. It was the same thing that had happened to his father. The land and mountains were part of him. It was more than just a job protecting them. When something like this went down, a murder on a ranch and a drifter disappearing at the same time, Trent had to set things back to right.

He climbed to the third floor where the Emerald Room was, breathing in the thick smell of flowers from bowls of dried petals Matilda had on practically every table in the house. Taking a sip of his coffee, he stared down the dust-free hallway. It was time to meet Miss Natasha King.

Did she agree to meet him because curiosity bested her? Was she sincerely concerned about her father? Or was it that she did know his whereabouts and felt a need to drive up here and do damage control?

She might be from L.A. and work for a prestigious bounty hunter, but she wouldn't be any better than he was. Trent knew how to play the simple, small-town lawman, though. He didn't have a problem with keeping it low key until he knew this woman's nature.

Trent knocked firmly on the door and waited, relaxing and holding his cup in one hand as he stared down the hallway. He focused on sounds on the other side of the door, though, and heard none. Not until the lock clicked. This house was sturdy enough to stand another hundred years. It didn't surprise him he wouldn't be able to hear anything going on behind a closed door. He glanced at the doorknob, watching it turn, then lifted his gaze as the door opened.

"Natasha King," he said and stared into eyes so bright and vibrant they reminded him of sunshine reflecting off a clear mountain lake. He wasn't sure who had decided to call them tan, but they were definitely wrong. Natasha's eyes were how he'd picture natural, raw gems, straight from the ground might look. Not the shiny, flashy color of gold worn in jewelry, but a more primitive, basic shade.

Her dark skin suggested a mixed background although he wouldn't begin to speculate on what nationalities. George King was definitely American so whatever mixed heritage was in her came from her mother. Long black hair tumbled over her shoulders and matched the color of her thick lashes, which currently hooded her gaze as she took him in as well.

"I'm Sheriff Trent Oakley," he offered. He noticed her grip on the door, and the wary look she gave him. He wasn't sure whether he'd compare her to a trapped animal, ready to run, or something more dangerous on the verge of attacking. "Call me Trent. Welcome to Weaverville."

"Thank you." She didn't have a problem taking in every inch of him, as if putting him to memory from his boots to the top of his head.

One thing was very clear. Natasha was more than distractingly beautiful. He noticed she wasn't wearing makeup, which in itself was refreshing to see. She didn't have on any jewelry he could see. She wore blue jeans that hugged her incredible figure and a plain T-shirt that ended at her waist. She might be trying, but Natasha King would never be able to pull off nondescript.

"Do you have a minute to talk?"

"I thought our meeting was tomorrow." Her voice was smooth, soft and alluring. There wasn't any hesitation, though, and, although she didn't open the door far enough for him to see beyond her into her room, there was no fear or wariness in her eyes.

"Just trying to be neighborly." Trent offered her a grin he'd been told more than once added to his bad-boy good looks. Not that he'd bought into much of what ladies he'd went to high school with suggested when he knew they either wanted to get laid, or had ideas of becoming a sheriff's wife. "You're a stranger in our town and we do our best to make anyone welcome," he added, though that was until they did someone, or something, wrong.

The smile didn't change Natasha's expression. "I think you're here to check me out."

"You're blunt." He liked that.

"I'm honest."

He'd be the judge of that.

Natasha returned outside the same way she'd been led upstairs. When she came to the door leading to the closed-in back porch where the high counter was and where Matilda had checked her in, she hesitated when she heard voices.

"It's got to be the only reason he brought her here, Mat," a man said.

"Well, you know it wasn't just for her good looks. The sheriff could have his pick of the county."

Matilda and the man laughed at her comment. Natasha froze, her hand on the door, wondering if they would say more. They had to be talking about her. He was the sheriff and how many other people had he brought here? She scowled, looking down, listening for something more revealing to be said.

"Do you think she knows about the murder?" the man asked.

"Of course she does. The sheriff said she didn't hesitate in coming here. He'll use her to flush out George King. You mark my words."

"Are you a private dick now?"

Matilda found that question very funny and broke out into a deep, gut-clenching laugh.

Natasha pushed the door open, knowing if she stood there a moment longer she'd hear something that would really piss her off, or she'd get busted. The sheriff was still here, waiting for her outside. If she took too long, he'd come looking for her. She didn't doubt he was a man on a mission and for some reason believed she could help him achieve his goal. She also didn't doubt what she'd just overheard was true, that he could have any woman in the area. Well, she wasn't from this area and men as good-looking as the sheriff, or at least close, had tried seducing her before. Natasha knew how to stay on her toes, remain alert, and see when someone acting friendly was doing just that—acting.

Matilda and a mailman held coffee cups and looked as if they could be posing for a postcard. They stopped talking, and the mailman held his cup poised in front of him, as if he were bringing it to his lips and seeing her made him forget what he was about to do.

"Hello," she said, nodding, then heading past them out the back door. She swore she heard her name whispered as she headed outside. Her skin crawled on the back of her neck and down her spine.

She'd overheard murder and her father's name, a subtle reminder no one here was her friend. As soon as possible, she needed to find out what the hell was going on. If that meant doing some acting as well, so be it. There was one person who would have all the facts, or at least more than anyone else in Weaverville, and he was watching her with brooding eyes when she stepped outside.

The crisp air was dropping in temperature quickly as the sun began setting. Natasha pushed the button on her key chain to unlock the Avalanche but focused on Trent Oakley. He leaned against the back of his black Suburban but pushed away and approached as she neared her uncle's truck.

Trent wore a button-down, plaid shirt with the sleeves rolled up to his elbows. Natasha immediately noticed roped muscle stretching under skin that was sprinkled with coarse-looking, black hair. He wore a T-shirt under the flannel shirt, but she didn't miss how broad his shoulders were, or how he appeared not to have an ounce of fat on him. The mountain-man sheriff kept in shape. If she had to guess, she'd put him in his thirties somewhere, which begged the next question, why was he single?

He moved silently across the parking lot, which was impressive in his black boots and the gravel. Her own shoes crunched over the fine, white pebbles but she didn't care. Anymore than she cared how Sheriff Oakley reminded her of a deadly predator, approaching with skills so fine tuned- and a body so vital she imagined every inch of him was hard-packed under his rugged exterior. His faded jeans looked comfortable and hugged long, muscular legs. He was tall, and his black wavy hair was as dark as a starless sky.

He had a lazy stroll, moving as everyone else here seemed to do. She doubted there was anything lazy about Trent Oakley, though. The way he watched her gave her the impression he didn't miss a thing that went on around him.

She was also acutely aware of how carefully he watched her, as if trying to understand something about her that he didn't want to ask. He was studying her, making mental inventory, and it made her want to scream.

Just ask what you want to know and I'll tell you, if it's any of your business. His scrutinizing stare was about business, but Natasha didn't miss the sizzling sexual undertones surrounding him as well.

Something in his eyes made her wary. They were a simple green, although the way they pierced through her made them seem anything other than ordinary. His thick, black hair helped set off his sharp facial features: his straight nose, broad cheekbones, and his mouth, which was currently pressed into a thin line. The man was beyond gorgeous, and as he moved closer, he seemed to set the air around them into a charged state of anticipation. This was a guy who made things happen, took the bull by the horns, possibly literally, and controlled even the air she breathed when he paused next to her. She inhaled the sexual energy charged around her and told herself it came completely from him.

"Need help carrying anything to your room?" he asked, his slow drawl sounding as dangerous as the rest of him appeared.

"No, but thanks." She'd decided on impulse, as a way to avoid allowing the sheriff into her room, that she'd come downstairs and pull the GPS system her uncle had installed in each truck out of the dash. She was able to do the same with the CD player. Better safe than sorry and she didn't want it stolen. "The room is nice by the way. Thanks for recommending this place."

"Matilda will be thrilled to hear that." Trent followed her around to her driver's side and paused, resting his hand on the roof of the midnight-blue Avalanche. "This your truck?"

Natasha looked at him, but he was focused on the truck's interior. "Why do I think you already know the answer to that question?" she asked. If it had been her, she would have already run the tags. The way he watched her like a hawk she wouldn't be surprised if he ran as thorough a background check on her as she had on him.

He didn't answer her question, nor did his expression change when she slid into the driver's seat and snapped the GPS out of the dash. She did the same with the CD player.

Trent glanced at both items in her hands when she slid out of the truck and the corner of his mouth curved. "Is that what you came down here to get?"

"There's no reason to invite someone to break into my truck," she informed him, watching when those alert eyes of his lifted to her face.

"Nope. I agree." He still looked amused.

"What?" she demanded. It was so incredibly tempting to flirt with him, or spar a bit. She was only here for a day, and he was one hell of a sexy man. A bit of exchange would help him show off his true nature.

"Nothing." He dropped his attention to the GPS system and CD player, or maybe it was her breasts.

"Do you find it amusing when people lock everything and remove valuables from their cars?" she demanded. "Let me guess, no one around here locks anything."

"Not until recently," he said, his voice lowering a notch and his facial features turning harder than they were a moment before.

"And why is that?" she asked, lowering her voice as well and turning to face him. She hugged the two items against her as she squared off with the sheriff.

"Because up until recently, crime wasn't the main focus for folks around here."

"What's changed that?"

The sheriff didn't answer right away. He searched her face, possibly looking for signs of deception. Natasha wasn't sure why he believed she would know anything about what was going on in this small town when she lived in LA and worked for a very successful company. She had her own crimes and criminals to keep her busy. She didn't break eye contact, but she wasn't going to remain under his compelling gaze for long.

Natasha let another moment pass, then shrugged. "Tomorrow at 2 PM," she said, shut the truck door, and started around the front of the truck, once again pushing the button on her key chain and making the truck beep as it locked.

Trent grabbed her arm.

Natasha froze, glancing down at where strong, long fingers wrapped around her bicep.

"If you're hiding anything, Miss King, I will find out." He barely whispered and his fingers tightened around her arm. "Don't judge someone's abilities because they come from a small town."

"And I'm sure you aren't judging someone's abilities based on their gender," she shot back at him. "Let go of my arm now, Sheriff," she said, matching his low, dangerous tone.

Trent studied her, really studied her, holding her firmly and taking his time as his gaze traveled from her head to her feet, and back up again. Natasha hated the fire that ignited inside her the longer he kept her pinned in front of him.

"Why did you agree to come up here?" he asked when he looked at her face once again.

There wasn't any reason to lie. "If there is something wrong with my dad, I'm going to help him," she said flatly.

"I see."

"Wouldn't you do the same?"

"Yup."

"You're still holding my arm."

Trent lazily studied his fingers, moving them easily over her shirt sleeve, but not letting go. Natasha breathed in a cleansing breath, fighting to keep her cool when she ached to show this chauvinistic brute exactly what she thought of being manhandled.

"Let go of me, Sheriff. Unless you'd rather I make you let go of me."

Trent's gaze shot to hers. A fire ignited in his eyes that hadn't been there a second ago.

"Is that a threat?"

"It's a promise."